A Girl Named Striker

Call of the Wilderness

A novel by

Peggy Poe Stern

Moody Valley
Boone, North Carolina

Published by
Moody Valley
475 Church Hollow Road
Boone, N C 28607
moodyvalley@skybest.com

Cover painting by Peggy Poe Stern
Cover design by David Kenneth Stern
Edited December 20, 2018 by Pamela Baldwin
Published December 30, 2018
Edited January 1, 2019
ISBN: 978-1-59513-069-3

Dedicated to

All who have served for our country

Chapter 1

~~~~

"Broken ribs, lots of 'em. My insides are crushed." her dad managed to tell her when Striker found him in the water. "Careless. Tree twisted."

Striker knew exactly what had happened. Her dad had been cutting down the tree for firewood. It wasn't a big tree, but it was big enough to do this kind of hurt to a man weighing over two hundred pounds.

When her dad hadn't returned home, Striker had gone to hunt for him. What she found was worse than she feared. The tree had pinned him in the water. It took great determination along with all his strength to hold his face out of the water until she had found him.

"If not for leaving my girl, I'd drown to stop the pain," he managed to confess as Striker pried out rocks with her hands until her fingers bled. She found a strong stick for a lever and continued prying until she'd dug out enough rocks and sand to pull him from underneath the tree. Once she managed to drag him onto the bank of the creek, he sent her home for the sled. For him to crawl even one foot caused too much pain to his broken body. Striker was too small to carry him. Dragging him would have caused worse pain. Getting him out of the water and up the bank had been torture.

Striker didn't want to leave him alone. An injured man was easy prey for animals, but she had no choice. She ran all the way to their cabin, found the sled her dad had made to haul wood, and ran back pulling it behind her. Twice she tripped and fell, skinning her knees, but she felt little pain. Getting back to her dad overcame any pain she might feel.

Color had left his face by the time she got back with the sled. He gritted his teeth and did his best to help move his body but couldn't stop himself from crying out with pain. He tried to stifle his screams as she leaned the sled sideways to roll his injured body onto the flat surface. He moaned with every bump and dip she hit as she struggled to pull him through the woods. Pulling her two-hundred-pound dad was almost more than a sixty-five-pound girl could manage. It wasn't easy getting the sled through the cabin doors, but she managed. He screamed out in pain when she rolled him off the sled onto the low bed her dad had built inches off the floor.

Once he was safely on the bed, she didn't know what to do next. There was no one and no place she could go for help. Her dad and she were completely alone, just the way her dad had always wanted.

"Striker," he whispered so low she had to put her ear to his lips to hear what he was saying. "I'm a goner for certain," he shuddered and then heaved for air. Bloody froth foamed pink at the corners of his mouth.

Striker felt his chest rise beneath her arm as she leaned over him. He was still shivering so hard he shook the roughly constructed bed.

"You're freezing. I'll warm you up," she said and rushed to heat rocks on the wood stove where she had a supper fire burning. When the rocks were hot, she wrapped them in what few clothes they possessed, and put them in the bed with Dad. She hoped if he warmed up from the chilling cold of the water, he would be alright. He'd been in the water a long time before she found him and got him back to the house. The heated rocks didn't provide the miracle she'd hoped for. He was still shaking with chills and chattering teeth.

"There's nothing like the miracle of warmth to cure what ails you," her dad always told her when she was sick or injured. Many a time he'd warmed rocks to put in her bed, especially during cold winter nights.

"I've made bad mistakes," he managed to tell her. "Done wrong by bringing you here," he admitted, causing the pink foam to increase and darken to red. "You've got relatives. Go find 'em. You can't survive in a place like this without me. You're too little," he told her. His face contorted with the pain caused by talking.

Being little was nothing new to Striker – being told she had relatives was.

Her dad always claimed all they had was each other. "It's like we're the only two people alive," he'd tell her often.

She knew there were people beyond the rugged National Forest, but she'd never seen them. All her knowledge about people came from the books her dad brought home for her to read. Her dad had moved them into the rugged mountains before her memory began. She only had strange dream-like images of their first coming to the deep wooded area. She wasn't sure if she remembered having a mother or if it was only wishful thinking.

Surviving without her dad was something she didn't know if she could do or not, but she had a sickening feeling she was about to find out. She'd been able to survive for days at time without him. Thing was, she always knew he would be coming back, bringing her books and supplies. Sometimes he even brought her back a toy of sorts.

As she looked down at her dad's broken body, she didn't bother saying anything or bursting into tears. She knew her dad was beyond listening to her fears and pleadings. If she cried and went to pieces, it would only make his dying regrets worse. He was using every ounce of his strength to tell her what she was supposed to do after he was gone.

"You hear me, Striker?" he wheezed out. "You hear me?"

"I hear you," she assured him as she watched red blood trickling through what was once pink foam. Each word he said brought more blood up with it.

"Be careful. There're mean devils out there. Trust nobody," he repeated what he'd told her often. "Trust nobody. They're all out to get you," he heaved out in a coarse whisper. "I know it for a fact," he managed to add in a breathless plea.

Her dad had always been protective. He made sure no one could find the little cabin he had built. He'd chosen the place, made sure it was hidden miles back in the rugged National Forest.

"I won't trust anybody," she assured him. His words of warning had sunk in long before now. She believed there was pure evil beyond the mountains surrounding their cabin.

"N-nev-er thought I'd leave you like this. D-did-n't see it comin'," he managed to get out in a shaky voice that was even more pain-ridden.

She never thought he would leave her either, at least not for more than a few days at a time.

Her dad was a big, strong man with broad shoulders and rippling muscles. His hands were rough and callused by the hard, physical labor he had done.

Her dad was proud they got along just fine with what little they had. He claimed they had everything they could want: rain when the weather was dry, sun that rose every morning to remind them it was time to get up, darkness when they needed to bed-down and rest for the night.

Her dad let her to do a lot of the work by herself. He said the best way for a person to learn things was the hands-on way

"A job worth doing is a job worth doing well," he'd say. "The most important thing in life is to learn from experience – both your own and other people's."

That's why he ventured off the mountain at times to learn things and bring home all the books he could carry. He wanted his daughter to learn things also, but she was never once allowed to go off the mountain with him, no matter how much she begged.

"Don't want the men to know I've got a beautiful daughter. If they see you, they'll come hunting for you sooner or later, and I'd rather not have to kill another human being. I had enough of killing in war. I was a sniper, a crack shot."

She didn't know what war was. When she asked about it, her dad refused to go into details. "It was time spent in hell," was all he would say.

She believed her dad was strong enough to kill just about anything if it came down to it. He'd hunt deer and wild hogs with a crossbow and arrows. He made a crossbow for her when she was ten years old. The pull of her crossbow had less power than the ones he made for himself, but she could take down a deer if her aim was just right. Didn't take her long to develop enough strength in her arms, chest, and shoulders to shoot his weapons almost as good as he could. *Almost* was bragging a bit, but then she was certain no man could shoot a bow and arrow as good as her dad.

"You need to use red oak or hickory for making bows," her dad explained. "That's the kind of hardwood that has both strength and bend." The arrows had to be straight, slender, and deadly. "You can use a softer wood for making arrows. Creek willows and bamboo are usable for arrows."

She had allowed her mind to wander while giving her dad some needed time. She understood there were a lot of things he wanted to tell her, but they both realized there was little time left.

"I've always done what I thought was best for you," he whispered, and seemed to grow a bit stronger, although there was a wheezing, gurgling sound coming from inside his chest.

Her dad started talking again, and she bent closer to be able to hear him.

"Your . . Aunt . . Nellie's who you're to . . live with. Other folks . . are no accounts. Don't . . trust nobody," he repeated the no trust thing again.

What got her attention was the mention that she had an aunt named Nellie. Exactly where was this aunt located? And more important, how was she to go about finding her?

He grasped her hand and held on with more strength than she thought he possessed. "Promise you'll . . find her. Promise!"

"I promise," she squeezed his hand to assure him she understood and would do as he said. "I'll find her," she added, and she would, but she didn't know where or when she'd be able to do such a thing.

"More . . I need . . to tell you," he put all his strength into whispering the words, but instead of telling her more, he gasped and went silent as a stream of blood ran from his mouth washing the froth down his neck to pool on his chest.

His grip on her hand loosened. His eyes did something strange as they gazed off into space, his struggle to keep his chest rising and falling ended. His entire body went limp and settled into the bed as though it was already trying to return to the earth.

Striker kneeled beside her dad, staring without seeing a thing. Her world had gone blank. She didn't know what to do next, other than sit there waiting for something to happen.

~~~~

Odd how people and animals changed once life ran out of their bodies. No matter how hard someone tried, life couldn't be made to go back inside. She'd never understood why life couldn't return after it ran out. She'd held many animals in her hands while the warmth of the body was still there, but life had left. The heart, the lungs, the brain, everything was there, so why did the breath of life vanish as though it had never existed?

She'd once asked her dad if he could make an animal live after the breath of life left.

"No, Striker. Only God can do that, but He seldom does."

Her dad went on to tell her the story of how God brought his only begotten son back to life after being dead for three days. The spirit clings nearby for three days. If the spirit can't reunite with its body during that time, it leaves for good. "The day God's son, Jesus, died is called Good Friday, and the day he came back to life is called Easter."

Okay, but she puzzled on how the Friday Jesus died could be called good? Seemed to her it was a bad Friday.

"Where did Jesus' life go for those three days?" she'd asked with a child's curiosity.

"It depends, Striker."

"On what?"

"On many things."

"What kind of things?" she persisted. Her dad never was able to explain all things to her satisfaction. When he was stumped for an answer, he usually hunted through the stack of books until he picked one and told her to read the book in order to find answers to her questions.

"Don't exactly know what kind of things. To the best of my thinking it depends on what kind of spirit was inside the person. If the spirit chose to be kind and helpful, the spirit is granted a peaceful existence. If the spirit was mean and hurtful, it's required to spend time being punished."

"When the spirit leaves the body, why can't it go back?" she'd asked again, not satisfied with the answer he'd given.

"There are many reasons for the spirit not to return, such as the body is too injured to sustain the spirit, or the body's parts have stopped working. Sometimes the body simply gets too old to continue functioning. And then there are times when the greatest spirit of all, the one that created heaven and earth, recalls a certain spirit because it is needed elsewhere."

Her dad believed there was a great spirit who watched over the earth, and the name God was as good a name to call the great spirit as anything else.

"If God is such a great and powerful spirit, why does He let things die?" she'd persisted.

"Some things die so other things can live."

"I don't understand," she told him, feeling irritated with his answer and with God.

"The earth would be too overcrowded if nothing died. There would never be room for new animals, plants, or people."

She frowned at such an idea and had to think on what her dad said for a long time. She supposed it was true, but she still didn't like the idea of things dying. There was a whole lot of room for everything on the mountain where they lived. Enough room for everything to live for a very long time without overcrowding.

She stopped using the past as a distraction and looked at her dad's face, grabbed him by the shoulders and shook him as hard as she could, hoping the jarring would cause him to draw in breath again. If he would just make an effort to take a breath, she was sure she could help trap life inside his body. She blamed herself for not concentrating hard enough on the present. She was sure she could have made him keep breathing if only she'd tried harder.

There was no response, no gasping, no intake of breath from her dad. She yelled at him, shook him harder, trying to force him to come back, but he didn't. Finally, she eased him back onto the pillow and started to cry in soul-aching tears. She had to accept he was a goner for certain this time, and there was nothing she could do to change things.

"Learn to accept what you can't change," she thought she heard her dad telling her from a long way off. She sat there with silent tears running down her cheeks, watching for breath to enter her dad's chest again. It didn't.

She reminded herself what her dad had told her about God and Easter. It gave her hope. Surely, God wouldn't be so cruel as to leave her completely alone in what seemed like never-ending forested mountains without her dad for protection and guidance. He'd bring him back to life in three days' time. All she had to do was wait

~~~~

Spring time was almost always cool on their mountain, but it was warm enough to spoil meat. Her dad was meat – human meat. Odor rose from his bed the second day life had left his body. By the third day she feared God might not perform a miracle, but she still had hope. The fourth day she forced herself to get the shovel and dig a deep grave right in the middle of the soft garden dirt. Her dad had worked for as long as she could remember to build up garden soil. He gathered sack after sack of leaves each fall and winter to dig into the dirt. Any animal he found dead that was unfit for them to eat, he buried in the garden.

"Organic fertilizer. It's too precious to waste. When I die, bury me in the center of the garden," he always said jokingly. She now took his words as truth. She could imagine her dad using his own body to make food grow so she wouldn't go hungry during the bitter cold winter that was surely to come. In all the years they had lived on the mountain winters became extremely cold early and lasted long.

Their garden was a distance from the cabin in a natural clearing. If her dad had cleared a section of ground near the cabin, it could have been spotted from overhead, not to mention by some hunter. There were times when they heard the barking of dogs along with the sound of gun fire several mountains over. "Hunters," her dad would tell her. He kept his eyes and his ears open for anything that might alert him to danger. "Most likely they won't come this far into these high mountains," he would say, trying to assure her and himself. So far, they hadn't.

Once she'd dug the hole deep enough that the shovels of dirt fell back in her face when she tried to throw them out, she braced her shovel against the side, stepped on the handle and sprung out of the freshly dug grave. She lay on her belly, grabbed the shovel handle and pulled it out. Her dad taught her the importance of taking care of what little they had because they might never have the chance of getting it again. "It's not like tools drop out of the sky," her dad would say.

She carried the shovel back to the cabin, praying with every step she took that God had seen fit to resurrect her dad the same way He had done to His only begotten son. The smell that was still coming from inside the cabin was enough to let her know God didn't consider giving her dad equal treatment He had given His only begotten son.

Tears of disappointment added to her tears of bereavement as she tied the rag used as a kitchen towel around her mouth and nose. She hoped her dad would forgive her and understand why she waited this long to do what had to be done. She should have known miracles didn't happen just because she wanted them to happen. They never had. "Don't trust anybody," sounded in her head again. She wondered if she should apply that warning to God. Somewhere, perhaps in her own head, she heard the words, "No, child. Trust him."

She threw the cover off her dad and grabbed hold of his bare feet to roll him out of bed onto the sled. Much to her horror some skin slid off into her dirty hand. She whimpered out loud, gagged, and ran outside shaking her hand to rid her dad's skin from it. She shivered and shook while trying to get herself under control and stiffen her backbone, as her dad was always telling her to do when there was work to be done that she feared to undertake.

"There's always more than one way to skin a cat." She could hear her dad's voice telling her. "Figure it out Striker. You'll have to be a big girl now."

She poked holes with a knife in both edges of the deer hide her dad always slept on and tied them together with thin strips of leather made from groundhog hide. She rolled her dad's badly decaying body out of bed without rupturing any part of his flesh. Grabbing hold of his feet had taught her a lesson she didn't want to repeat.

She couldn't believe how heavy he was to roll. she climbed over the top of him and got behind him. She closed her eyes and tried to pretend it wasn't her dad she was trying to get onto the sled. Every time she pushed on the deer hide a stronger stink arose from his decaying body.

She finally held her breath, put both feet against the deer hide and gave a huge shove. Her dad's body landed rather haphazardly on the sled, but at least he was on it. She used another hide-rope to tie him on, so she could get him through the door when she turned the sled sideways again. She did everything she could to keep from gagging as she harnessed herself to the sled.

By the time she got him to the garden, she was soaked in sweat, heaving for each lung full of air, and crying so hard the whole garden was nothing but a blur. It took every bit of her determination to roll him from the sled into the hole. Striker squeezed her eyes closed at the sight of her dad lying there with dirt falling in on him. She sank down on her knees in the fresh-dug dirt and screamed to the top of her lungs. She didn't care if her anguished cries echoed from the mountains tops down into the valleys. A time of mourning had taken its hold.

The sun had gone down, and the gloaming of night was setting in before she forced herself to rise up and start shoveling the dirt on top of her dad. Every shovel full was a reminder her dad was gone. Every shovelful left her more alone.

Maybe that was the reason she'd waited so long to bury her dad. It hadn't felt as much like he was gone while his body was in bed. Once he was in the grave and covered in dirt, she could no longer pretend the breath of life would return.

By the time she finished shoveling, the sun was rising over the eastern mountain range causing the sky to turn from rosy pink to blood red. She cringed. The color reminded her of the foam coming from her dad's mouth. Clouds were settling low, warning that a storm was brewing not too far off. Somehow, it seemed fitting that a storm should arrive once her dad was in his grave.

"No good ever comes from being sad," her dad used to tell her. "Even the weather responds to our feelings and vice versa. So, smile, Striker, make the sun shine."

If that were true, then she'd best prepare for sky-ripping lightning strikes and earth-trembling thunder along with torrential rains. The sky would surely open up and flood the heavens and earth. The entire world would come to an end because her world, as she'd always know it had come to an end.

Her dad said she should find an Aunt Nellie, but she and Aunt Nellie might as well be on two separate planets. Finding her would be just as likely as finding diamonds and gold sparkling in the creek bed. No such things existed, as her dad had proven many times over.

"Diamonds and gold equals money. If we had enough money, our life might be different, then again, it might not," her dad would lament when he was feeling down.

Striker didn't even know what Aunt Nellie looked like. The only people she'd ever seen other than her dad, had been in the books her dad carried up the mountain in a sack.

"We might not be able to live in our own world forever," he had warned her ever since she was old enough to remember. "Therefore, it's my duty to teach you what the world inhabited by cruel, selfish people is like."

And that was what he did.

He brought home an entire set of Britannica encyclopedias and taught her about people and everything else contained within the many pages. Her dad made a point of telling her that he didn't like people, and neither should she, even the ones who were said to be kind were only one step away from being evil. Her dad didn't exactly tell her the people she read about in the books were evil, but she knew it had to be true – otherwise, she and her dad would not be living this far away from everyone.

Striker liked learning from books okay, but they weren't nearly as good as having her dad teach her how to survive in their mountains. They had spent almost every minute of every day together except during extremely rare occasions when he left the mountains to sell his furs and herbs. Sometimes he returned with a worried, fearful expression on his face. Once he saw her, his fear left him. "You did good," he would tell her. "You knew how to stay safe."

This praise meant everything to her. She would laugh and be happy for days.

"You're the most important thing in this world to me, Striker," he often told her." I want you to grow up living the good life, safe from all the horrible things that go on in the land of so-called civilization."

How could she possibly live the good life now that her dad was dead? He'd taught her well, but she had enough sense to realize she was only a small child. She was strong, and she was capable, but she wasn't her dad. He hadn't finished her training yet. She realized she had a lot to learn and couldn't possibly do the hard work and heavy lifting her dad had done. She couldn't cut down trees and repair their cabin, or grow, kill, and skin food the same way her dad did, but what choice did she have? Improvise. Her dad often told her. When you can't produce what you need, improvise.

Chapter 2

~~~~

Griff knew instincts in people, as well as in animals, cannot be taught or learned. Instincts are the one thing you are born with – or you're not. Instincts are the ruler of your unconscious self. They are the silent force that protects you when you need protecting. Instincts make you run or ready yourself to fight when you feel threatened. Instincts and survival go hand in hand. Without instincts you are subjected to whatever comes at you.

Kang, a Kangal pup, had been born from parents with supreme intelligence along with strong guardian instincts. Both parents were independent and yet calm, sensitive, alert and extremely protective over what they considered belonged to them. Kang was born with an unusual amount of intelligence and an abundance of fierceness, even for a Kangal dog. Both came together from the pairing of his parents to maximize these traits and work amazingly well in this one offspring. The rest of his ten siblings were average. They would sell as livestock guardians. It was a guess as to what Kang would grow up to become.

There was something about Kang's independent nature that could keep potential buyers for choosing him – or make them determined to own him. He was the exception that came along rarely regardless of how many litters a dog produced.

Griff had always known a Kangal's survival instincts would be popular in an illegal dog fighting ring. They were the only dogs claimed to be able to kill a mountain lion, which Griff questioned. The big cats' best defense was to roll on their backs and use their hind legs to rip the guts out of a dog. The biggest drawback in making a Kangal into a fighting dog was the long length of a Kangal's legs. If a short-legged Pitbull was trained to charge low and break an opponent's front leg, it would put a long-legged dog at a greater disadvantage. A Kangal had strong leg bones, but they were breakable.

Griff worked for Lady Biswell as a kennel manager.

"That pup has the Devil shining out of both eyes," Griff told Lady Biswell. "It'll take one strong and determined master to control that one."

"Umm," she mumbled. "Reminds me of my second husband."

Griff grinned. He wasn't altogether sure if Lady Biswell had trouble controlling each of her four now departed husbands or if they had trouble controlling her. If he was a betting man, he'd put his money on no one being able to control such a stubborn, hard-headed woman. She had married older and more difficult husbands than most women chose to take on. Folks claimed that was how she became wealthy, but he suspected marrying her was how her husbands became wealthy. As far as marrying went, she chose wisely with her head instead of her heart, at least with the last three. Griff also knew she had loved only one of the four – her first husband, a policeman who had died early in the line of duty.

The pain of losing her dearly beloved first husband had surely forced her insides to callus over with scar tissue. She became a hard-shelled nut, impossible to crack. From then on, she chose older, wealthy men who could assist in giving her what she wanted.

The only thing that seemed to touch a soft spot in her hardened heart were her dogs. She cherished every one of her Kangal dogs. Griff knew it was because they were proclaimed to be one of the strongest, most capable, and

loyal dogs in existence. Lady Biswell put great value on such
as that.

"They're a lot like me," Griff overheard her say one time
when she thought no one was listening. "We're both loyal in
our own way."

Griff never let on that he ever eavesdropped when she
talked to herself. It was the only way he could find out what
really went on inside that woman's head.

"A dog that can kill mountain lions has to be exceptional
in both mental and physical abilities," she told Griff. "Their
instincts have to be superb. I suppose you realize that
instincts cannot be taught. Even the greatest dog trainer in
the world cannot teach a hunting dog to hunt, or a treeing dog
to tree, or a Kangal dog how to keep a mountain lion from
ripping its guts out."

Yes, Griff knew that, but he didn't tell Lady Biswell. She
enjoyed talking about dogs and their instincts too much for
him to curb her pleasure of lecturing him on their abilities.

"That's not to say instincts cannot be strengthened or
weakened for they certainly can. The instincts, or devil as
you call it, in this pup can either go for bad or good. That's
why I've decided to keep him and train him myself. He's too
much dog for an ordinary person to handle."

"You're keeping him as a breeding male?" Griff asked.

"As a hunting dog. As for a breeding male, we'll see how
he matures."

"I know little about training a hunting dog," Griff did not
hesitate to inform her. "What do you want him to hunt?" He
thought Lady Biswell gave herself far more credit than she
deserved where dogs were concerned.

Lady Biswell ignored his question as to what she was to
train him to hunt.

"When buyers show up, keep him hidden. If someone
happens to see him, say he's already sold and paid for. Again,
make sure the other pups are only sold for livestock guardian
purposes on farms." She had heard rumors about illegal dog

fighting going on in the county. The law should do something about that, but they seemed to turn a blind eye.

"He'll be a hard one to handle," Griff couldn't stop himself from telling her.

"Not for me," she assured him as she turned and walked away.

Griff liked working for Lady Biswell. She was a fair woman and a fair employer. She did not tolerate foolishness from her dogs, husbands, or from people. At the same time, he also felt a kind of sympathy for her. There was something inside the woman that kept her from being completely happy. He suspected it was a longing that could never be fulfilled. Perhaps the tragic loss of her true love had done greater damage than even he knew about. His soft spot ached for her, but he certainly wasn't going to be the next old man who was foolish enough to give her a try in wedlock or in her bed. Besides, he wasn't and never would be rich enough to draw her attention. He was only good enough to care for her dogs.

Which was okay by him.

He got to watch her from a safe distance. She wasn't a beauty, but she was attractive enough to cause him to dream about her at night – and yes, especially during dog breeding times. He called it male instinct.

Chapter 3

~~~~

The next morning Striker found wolf tracks leading to her dad's grave. She carried his powerful crossbow with her. Carrying his instead of hers made her feel a little closer to him, plus it was more powerful than her smaller one. There were some animals her dad liked and some he hated. Wolves were one he hated.

"Wolves are mean and selfish," her dad always told her. "They care only for numero uno. There is no equality in the members of their pack. One male and one female rule the others. Plus, they are the only two allowed to breed and reproduce." He considered it a good thing since the members of the pack were usually the offspring of the alpha male and female.

"Survival of the fittest is a good thing to have in animals and people. Unfortunately, humans have gotten to the point where they cater to the unfit instead of the fit. The unfit humans have special privileges because they're considered a minority. They are even encouraged to breed and reproduce more of the unfit because of their presumed rights. A dictator by the name of Hitler took it upon himself to eliminate what he considered the unfit and only allow what he considered the fittest to reproduce. I've brought home books on him for you to read should you become interested. I've always found his cruelty mind-boggling, but I do understand the concept and somewhat agree with it. The question is how to go back to the survival of the fittest in humans?"

Striker was glad she'd taken the time to dig her dad's grave deep. The wolves had been trying to dig him up during the night. She'd left too much of his decaying smell on the ground. According to the tracks, the wolves had given up and left after digging down about two feet, which was odd. Something must have scared them off, but they would be back. To them the smell of decomposing flesh was irresistible.

"I'm sorry I waited so long to bury you, Dad. I was hoping - - -" she didn't finish. There was no need. Hope was just that. It had no validity – no power. Hope certainly wouldn't bring people back to life – not even after three days.

She went back to the cabin and returned with the shovel to refill the grave. She wasn't too much afraid of wolves during daylight hours if she had the crossbow handy.

"You'll need to be fast to kill a wolf with a crossbow," her dad had warned her. "They are sneak attackers where humans are concerned. They stalk you and give no warning before attacking. You have to see a wolf coming at you before you can shoot it. And there's always more than one wolf. You'll have to reload an arrow before you can take out the second one. That's why you need to make sure you always have a knife in your scabbard on your belt. Not that you'll be able to kill a wolf with a knife, but you'll at least have a fighting chance."

He told her the wolves in this area were red wolves or even crosses between wolves and coyotes. Sometimes even a dog would cross with wolves. Gray wolves and timber wolves were much bigger than the red wolf. A dog wolf cross was even more dangerous because dogs had little fear of people. "Wildlife experts claim there are no longer wolves in the national forests, but we know better, don't we Striker."

Yes, they knew better.

"Why do they lie?" she'd asked.

"The way I see it, there are several reasons. The government doesn't want folks to know how they cater to lobbyists who work for the rich. Plus, the crazy wildlife organizations don't want people to hunt the animals down and kill them," her dad told her. "The government is always funding things that will torment folks. The government is like a flood. Once it gets started there's no way to control the damage it does. Laws," he snorted in disgust. "They're made to control the people who don't need laws for them to do what is right. No criminal will ever abide by a law."

She understood. They were living in these mountains for the same reason. To get away from people along with the stupid government and stupid laws. "To live free," Dad often made a point of saying. "That's what we're after, Striker. To live free."

When she finished filling in her dad's grave, she carried rocks and stacked them over and around it. She knew her dad would not approve because the rocks made it too obvious there was a grave, but it was better than having his bones dragged all over the mountains. Besides, who would be on the mountain to find her dad's grave other than animals?

As she carried the rocks, she thought about the trips her dad made off the mountain. Returning from one of his trading trips took him a full day and night to climb back up the mountain – and that was going at a consistent trot. Her dad was a long-legged man.

"I'm not one of those fast Kentucky Derby sprinters. I'm more like a workhorse. I hit my speed and keep on going until I get where I'm headed," he told her

She went back to the cabin and stored the shovel in her dad's bedroom. Most all his tools were kept in his bedroom. Replacing them would be too difficult if one ever went missing or got ruined. Now that he was gone, replacement would be impossible. The only thing she could reproduce, besides food, were arrows, and her dad had made sure she had become good at it. He taught her how to scrape the bark and heat the wood to get crooks out. A straight arrow was an accurate arrow. A crooked arrow curved when shot. She was even better than her dad when it came to chipping flint rocks to make arrowheads. He had claimed it was because her hands were small and her vision precise.

She dreaded going to the traps without her dad, but they had to be checked. "Don't leave a caught animal in pain." He always insisted on being considerate of animals. He didn't like anything suffering needlessly because they required food and supplies. She was thankful it was no longer winter, and they were not running traplines to get hides. In the spring they set only a few traps for food. Now that her dad was gone, there would be no hides carried off the mountain to trade for supplies. She would be trapping mostly rabbits, which were good eating when roasted with wild onions, potatoes and herbs. She often made a watery gravy to go with it. They had no milk-gravy and seldom had what her dad called coffee.

He had told her when they first moved there, he had a milk-goat for her to have milk to drink. With no billy-goat near, the old nanny goat stopped producing milk and eventually ended up in her dad's stew pot. "Waste not, want not," was another of his sayings.

She took her crossbow and deer hide sack her dad used to carry game in and headed out to check what remained of their trapline.

She walked through the woods where the trees grew tall and straight, thinking it didn't seem right for her to enjoy the fresh spring air when her dad no longer could. Ferns were starting to lift their heads above the black soil giving off their pungent aroma. Tiny blue violets bloomed in areas where the sun filtered down through the trees. Speckled trout lilies grew in shaded areas. Even the birds were singing as they flitted from tree to tree. How could all this happen like normal when her dad was rotting in his grave? It wasn't right. It simply wasn't right.

"All things die. Death is as normal as birth." Her dad's words came to her, but she didn't want to acknowledge death. She wanted life, wanted everything to live, even the rabbit that was caught in the first steel trap. Had its hind legs not been butchered up so badly, she would have set it free – declare today a day when nothing would die. Unfortunately for her and the poor rabbit, she loaded the worst arrow she'd made and put the rabbit out of its misery. She cried as she watched it die, something her dad would have disapproved of. She put the rabbit in the sack and continued checking the traps, relieved that nothing else had been caught. Death was too real and too hurtful for the time being.

When she got back to the cabin, she skinned the rabbit, careful not to damage its hide. She used rabbit skins to make mittens and moccasins. Rabbit hide didn't make the best moccasins, but they were suitable for spring and summer when her feet needed only a little protection. Most of the time she ran barefoot until the bottoms of her feet hardened like leather. But there were times when walking on sharp rocks or running through vicious thorny growth required some protection. She found that out it was never good to run on rocks and getting what her dad called stone bruises on the bottom of her feet.

~~~~

That night she laid in bed thinking about her dad and how she was left all alone. He'd told her to find Aunt Nellie. *Her Aunt Nellie*, a relative she never knew existed. If she knew how, she might try to find her. Why hadn't her dad ever mentioned an Aunt Nellie? If such a person existed, hadn't she deserved to know? Thinking about an aunt brought another question. Was she her mother's sister or her father's? Did she have other relatives he'd neglected to tell her about? If so, did any of them know she existed?

When she read about families in books, a deep longing rose inside her until tears ran down her cheeks. She wanted a mother and a father. She wanted brothers and sisters and a dog named spot. She'd never wanted an Aunt Nellie.

It took a long time to finally fall asleep only to be awakened by the sound of barking dogs. At first, she thought she'd imagined the barking. When she sat up and listened carefully, she realized the barking was real. She got out of bed and went to the door. She gripped her father's hunting knife while easing the door open a crack in order to hear better.

After listening carefully, she decided the barking was coming from down in the valley. The wind was blowing just right to carry sound up the mountain. It had happened before when her dad was alive.

"It's okay," he would assure her. "The hunters are on the prowl again, but we're safe. They won't find us. We're safe."

Even though her dad assured her they were safe, such hunting parties would put him on edge. He made sure they both stayed well-hidden during times hunters were on the prowl. Not once had hunters or dogs come to their mountain.

Her dad had taken the extra precaution of digging an underground cellar in one of the caves he'd found to make sure they could stay hidden and protected. His efforts resulted in a combination storage area and hiding place.

The cave hadn't been easy for her dad to find or easy to get to, but it certainly served its purpose. They stored their winter supply of vegetables in the underground cellar. It consisted mostly of potatoes, both Irish and sweet, cabbage, winter squash, and turnips. Sometimes they'd even cure the hams from wild hogs and store them in the underground cellar. The thought of that hog meat frying made her mouth water. She feared she would never know the taste of such meat again.

Chapter 4

~~~~

Kang had the power and strength Lady Biswell always hoped to find in one of her pups. At the same time, this pup gave off signs he would not be mastered or controlled. He would respect only the ones he thought deserving. Without establishing a mutual respect, a Kangal dog could become uncontrollable. She planned on being the one who earned Kang's respect. She willingly became Kang's companion instead of him hers. She intruded into his space, fed him, caressed him, and at times even fell asleep lying beside him in the softness of green grass and the warmth of the sunshine. She became attached to her pup in a type of bliss that allowed her imagination to run wild as to the kind of dog Kang would become.

He had already accepted her as a friend, but the devil still shined out of his eyes, especially when he looked at Griff. Neither she or Griff understood Kang's dislike of Griff. The kindly caretaker always made sure he did nothing to offend the pup.

"He has a natural hatred of men," Lady Biswell told Griff. "Instinct," she added. "Cell memory that comes from his ancestors. During his previous existence he must have been abused by a man or men. Such a sad thought isn't it, what animals and humans carry over from their previous lives? But then, I've always suspected atonement was required for sins committed in our past lives."

Griff did his best not to roll his eyes or contradict her. He did not believe in pre-existence or reincarnation. Things lived, things died, and that was it. As for cell memory and instinct, he might go with those even if he didn't understand exactly how they worked. What he knew for a fact was animals and people did carry traits of their ancestors.

~~~~

Kang was growing fast. He was lean and ravenous. Lady Biswell took it upon herself to feed and care for him but did not eliminate Griff from taking his usual care of Kang and the other dogs. Kang needed to accept Griff. Kang never developed any kind of attachment to Griff, but he came to tolerate him.

"That devil dog would come closer to gutting me than liking me," Griff told Lady Biswell as they both looked down on the half-grown pup. "He's a danger, I tell you. He's not predictable."

Lady Biswell laughed at Griff's concern. "You're reading him wrong, Griff. He's really a loving dog with a lot of caution. He knows not to trust blindly. Distrust is bred into a Kangal's heredity. That's what makes them good guard dogs. Their trust has to be earned, not blindly accepted."

"To your way of thinking, maybe, but I wouldn't go so far as to use the word loving where he's concerned. My advice is not to put too much trust in him. Always, be leery of the wild devil inside this dog. I'm telling you, his wild ancestry comes to the forefront."

She almost smiled. Griff telling her to be leery? Surely, he realized by now that she was always leery. Not only was leery in her nature, it was a lesson she had learned many times over. "He's a fantastic dog. I can't understand why you don't see it."

"I'm not blinded by what I want the dog to become. I see what he is."

"So do I, Griff. If you read up on Kangal dogs, you'll find they are and always will be a one-person dog." And she was determined to be that one-person.

By the time Kang was twelve weeks old, all his litter mates had been sold as livestock guardians. Lady Biswell was extremely picky who got her dogs. She made a point of telling potential buyers that Kangal dogs were working dogs. Becoming a companion to a child was not what they were best suited for, although they would most likely become devoted to a child and think it their job to protect the child. She explained that it would be impossible for the child and dog to be together every minute of every day and that was what a Kangal dog expected.

Kangals need a farm with lots of animals to protect on a twenty-four-seven basis. Lady Biswell wasn't even sure she was the person who could meet the demands of such a dog. She already had Kang training as a farm dog alongside his mother. She also raised registered black angus cattle on her farm to sell as breeding stock. There were times when wolves, coyotes, and even bears came down out of the mountains in search of food, especially during the winter months. She'd even heard other farmers claim there were mountain lions living high up in the mountains, but she'd never seen one. Still, it was wise to have dogs guarding her herd.

It was time to train Kang as a hunting dog, one who could survive on his own without a constant caretaker. She hoped she could accomplish the task.

Lady Biswell purchased raw buffalo meat as a treat for Kang. She hand fed him a small portion every day in addition to his regular meals. She was pleased to see that her extra care was working wonders with her dog. He was growing extremely fast and large. His tan coat of fur took on glistening signs of health, and the ripple of corded muscles were showing beneath his puppy skin.

She was pleased with what she imagined as her dog's future.

~~~~

Lady Biswell Lived off the beaten path and expected no visitors to show up unannounced. She opened the wrought iron gate to her farm and left it open for her return. She was getting Kang used to the lead and by taking him for a short run on the paved road. She believed Kang should be subjected to everything including hardtop traffic. She wanted nothing to be ignored in his training of her special dog.

Ronald Buckworth heard of Lady Biswell's dogs and decided to take it upon himself to check them out.

Buckworth's black Suburban passed the woman and the half-grown dog. His attention was drawn instantly to the pup. The pup could prove to be the kind of dog he was searching for, but he didn't stop or slow down. Instead, he drove a little way farther and turned into the open gate, knowing the woman and dog would do the same. He had learned never to appear too interested in a dog.

He'd heard a lot of gossip about her and the criteria she had for purchasing her dogs. A man could adopt a kid easier than he could get one of her dogs. However, he wasn't interested in adopting a kid or purchasing a dog. He only wanted to inspect the dog's fighting ability and stamina. He wanted dogs that had a drive to fight to the death without holding back.

A man with a garden rake and large plastic bucket looked up in surprise as Buckworth drove through the gates. The man frowned, stopped raking, and stared at the intruder.

~~~~

Griff knew Lady Biswell was not expecting a visitor. She would not be pleased, but at least she was the one who had left the gates open – something he disapproved of doing. An open gate was a welcome sign, and strangers weren't welcome on Lady Biswell's farm. If anything, Griff was more of a recluse than his boss. He cherished privacy along with an uneventful existence. To put it mildly, he yearned for invisibility.

Seeing the black Surburban made his skin crawl even before the vehicle came to a stop. There was something about tinted car windows and dark sunglasses that screamed *watch out*. Having a vehicle with tinted windows show up unexpectedly was not good. He stiffened his backbone, gritted his teeth, and waited for the driver to present himself. He had no intention of taking a step away from where he stood. Moving forward indicated welcome; moving backward indicated fear; staying put was a sign of holding one's own.

The driver's door opened, and a man stepped out. He was taller than average, nearing six feet. His weight was too much. His belly was overlapping his belt. A middle-aged man going to seed fast, Griff noted. This stranger was either unhealthy, lazy, or perhaps a combination of both.

The man lumbered toward Griff with a welcoming smile on his thin lips and extended a handshake to Griff. When Griff looked down at his own gloved hands with traces of the fresh fecal droppings from the dogs, the man withdrew his hand.

"Good day to you. Hope I'm not interrupting something important," he said to Griff in a soft-spoken, honey-toned voice.

Griff instinctively summed him up as someone who shouldn't be there – someone not to be trusted. "Are you lost or merely in the wrong place?" Griff asked.

"Neither. I've heard about the fantastic guard dogs you raise here. I have a farm adjacent to government land where I run goats and cattle. Wolves and other wild predators are cutting into my flock. I'm searching for a good guard dog, maybe two."

"How many acres of land?" Griff asked to find out more about this stranger. Griff had been around long enough to smell out an imposter.

"A couple of hundred," the man answered.

"How many head of stock are you talking about?"

"Fifty goats and forty head of cattle."

"Takes a lot of grass land to graze that many animals. Goats always eat a massive amount of grass. They're worse to eat the grass down to its roots than sheep," Griff said, knowing goats were browsers instead of grazers.

"That's a fact," the man agreed.

"Take cattle, now. They're more of the browser kind," Griff added an untruth to see how the stranger would answer.

"Right," the man smiled and nodded in agreement with Griff as though his statement was true.

"What breed of goats and cattle do you have?" Griff continued.

"Does it matter?"

"It does. Some types of cattle don't get along with dogs. Try to kill 'em, they do."

"Actually, both my goats and cattle are mixed breeds. I'm a firm believer that mixing breeds results in hardier stock."

"Run 'em on the same pasture, do you?" Griff wanted to know.

"That's right."

Griff nodded. "Saves a lot of fencing when you do that, right?"

"Right. I'd like to look at what dogs you have available."

"Pups or adults?"

"I'd prefer adults. The tougher the better. You know, those ready to go right to work killing wolves and the occasional mountain lion."

"Got mountain lions on your farm?"

"Some. They come down out of the government land during birthing season."

Griff nodded. "Drawn to the sound of bleating."

"Most likely."

"I reckon they show up only in the spring of the year?"

"That's right. Like I said, predators are most active during birthing season."

At least the man got that right. "We don't have a thing, puppy or adult available at this time."

"What about the dogs I see near the barn. You'll find I'm willing to pay a fair price for 'em."

"They're breeders. It's too late to make farm dogs out of them."

"Could I take a closer look? I'm willing to put in an order for a pup if the parents are to my satisfaction."

"Nope. Lady Biswell doesn't show her breeders. She already has a long waiting list for pups. She'll be glad to put your name, address, and phone number down on her list if you'll provide me with your driver's license and phone number."

"Don't want to be put on a waiting list without being allowed to see the parents," he had suddenly transformed to be pushy. Sign of a man who would forcefully take what he wanted.

"That be as it may," Griff told him. "Hope you have a good day. I'd best get back to work."

The man tried to hide his surge of irritation by appearing even more smiling and friendly, but the look in his eyes told Griff all he needed to know.

Griff understood a fury burned inside the stranger, but the fancy-assed man didn't want the filth-covered, red-neck worker to see his fury. Griff also knew the man had seen enough of the breeder dogs to judge the size and strength of Kangal dogs. Griff could sense what this man was thinking. He'd come across such men before in his line of work. They thought dogs needed to be crossed with the fierce, short-legged fighting Pit Bull dogs. This man had evidently heard about Lady Biswell's dogs, but he'd seen no proof of their ability. The man wanted a pup such as Kang to find out what fighting ability Kangal dogs had.

There was something about these men that set them apart from decent men. Griff despised people who ran dog fighting rings. Unless he missed his guess, Buckworth could easily be such a man.

Griff watched Buckworth get in his SUV and drive away. A bad feeling came to him.

"Who was that?" Lady Biswell asked after the man had left and Griff had hurriedly locked the gate behind him.

"Don't know, but I didn't like him. Don't think he was a farmer. Most farmers don't run goats and cattle together, plus he didn't know a thing about how much land it took to graze an animal on. Reckon he thought I was stupid."

"Did he give you his name?"

"Nope."

"Did you get his tag number?"

"No," Griff admitted, feeling stupid. "I should have got it."

"Don't worry. I'll keep the gate closed from now on. Didn't expect anyone to show up," Lady Biswell said.

"Wise of you to bring Kang in the back way. Wouldn't want him to set his eyes on such a dog as Kang."

"Why not?" she found herself asking.

"In my judgement, he's the kind to want a devil dog."

Lady Biswell wasn't sure if Griff was being complimentary to Kang or not. He still claimed Kang had more of the devil in him every time he talked about him. At the same time, Griff also exhibited a growing fondness for the headstrong pup, but Kang still didn't show fondness for Griff. He was a woman's dog.

Lady Biswell didn't tell Griff the man had passed her and Kang on the road. The fact that the man had shown up brought an uneasy feeling.

Chapter 5

~~~~

During the times her dad was away, Striker had been frightened, but it was nothing compared to how she was feeling now. Knowing he would never return was difficult for her to accept. Being totally by herself was beyond anything she had ever known. How could she possibly stay alive?

If the spirit God saw fit to let her dad have an accident that took him away, then why didn't that same God see fit to take her too? She had a right to be with her dad. He was all she had ever known, all she had. They had a right to live together and die together, but she hadn't died. She wasn't even with him when he had the accident. She concluded if she died, it was meant to be, for she would be where she belonged. This conclusion consoled her but did nothing to ease her fear.

Hard work not only helped her sleep at night, it kept her from being driven crazy with loneliness. Her dad had always been there for her to talk to and listen. He told her things he thought she should know about life in the wilderness. He was even good at telling her fables and fairy tales, making a point of doing what he called dissecting those fables and fairy tales until they formed lessons for her to learn. Sometimes she didn't like or agree with the lessons, but she always tried to learn from them.

There was little she could do about her fear other than face the fact that she was afraid, and for a good reason.

Striker realized her survival would depend on a miracle. Her dad had also realized the same thing when he told her to find Aunt Nellie. Saying those words was much easier than accomplishing the task. In her memory Striker had never met an Aunt Nellie or even a woman. All she had ever done was study women and men in books. She knew more about squirrels than she did about people.

"Did I have a mother?" she'd asked him repeatedly.

"Every living creature has a mother," he'd answered.

"Including me?"

"Including you."

"Where is she?" she asked, daring to feel some stirring inside her that she recognized as hope.

"She's dead."

Those two words, softly spoken, ripped hope right out of her. She ached with the pain. Yet, there remained the need to know more.

"Why did she die?" Striker continued to question.

"It was the will of God," he said with a great sadness. "The good die young," he added. "Your mother was a good one in a world filled with bad people."

Her dad had patted her on the head with a gentle hand, turned and walked away, but not before she saw the longing on his face. He wanted her mother as much as she did, maybe more, for he had known her love for a while. She hadn't – at least not that she could remember.

"A body doesn't miss what they've never had, be it good or bad," her dad assured her. "Striker, girl, I do believe we are two of the luckiest people in the world. Look around at what we have. People are fools to live in cramped little holes called apartments when all this is available. If they had enough backbone, they could move to a place such as this."

Striker looked at the vastness of the never-ending forests. The tall mountains rose up until they touched the sky. She longed to climb to the highest mountain, her dad called the bald, just to see if it really did touch the blue sky, but her dad insisted her endurance wasn't strong enough to make the long trip. For the time being, it was best to stay on their mountain.

"What kind of cramped holes are apartments?" She wanted to know.

"Apartments, even houses are nothing but holes where people hide from other people. Some are willing to steal from other people instead of earning for themselves. Such people are known as criminals. The criminals want to take things from the people who leave their holes of a morning to go to their jobs in order to afford their holes. They are basically chained to their holes and their jobs. You and I have our freedom, Striker. We're chained to nothing. We can do as we please, and that, my girl, is the essence of being alive."

"Why don't the people leave their holes to live as we do," she asked, as she tried to figure out why anyone would remain in a hole.

"They are afraid, Striker, afraid of change and the unknown. They become set in their ways and feel more secure with the devil they know, than the devil they don't know."

At first, Striker was puzzled with the things her dad told her, but as time passed, and she read more books, she began to understand what he was talking about even though she had no experience with people. She longed to observe them but couldn't stop herself from fearing people and the unknown.

Striker took the shovel from her dad's room and went to the garden. It was time for her to turn over the soil and get ready to plant the vegetables She needed to survive.

By the time the sun was high in the sky, she had only dug up a tiny space of ground. She feared the job was far bigger than her ability, far more difficult than she had expected. Her dad had made it look so effortless, but it was taking all her power to sink the shovel, bring up the dirt, dump it, and start all over again. By the time the sun was going down, she dragged herself to the cabin with blistered hands and aching back. She drank a glass of water and ate a raw potato and instantly fell in bed. Pain from the shoveling made her wake up several times during the night to hear the wind howling in the trees that surrounded the cabin. It whined and cried like something that was lost, much like she was crying.

"Big girls Don't cry," her dad used to tell her, but she wasn't a big girl. She was little, and she cried.

Striker's spirit was a little more optimistic with the arrival of dawn, but her entire body still ached something fierce. The pain she was feeling surprised her. She had convinced herself she was made of tougher stuff, but she was being taught different. It wasn't like she sat on her bottom and did nothing. She was going from daylight to dark following in her dad's footsteps. What he did, she did, or at least tried to do what he did. Her dad always bragged on her, saying how capable she was. He claimed she could do what no other child her age could – then why couldn't she shovel up a garden without hurting this much?

~~~~

Striker had the garden only half way shoveled up when a cold snap hit. The air turned crackling cold by the time the moon came out. She opened the cabin door and looked outside to see if there was any wind stirring. There wasn't. Without the wind blowing, she knew by morning there would be a bone-chilling freeze. She was glad the shoveling had made her late getting anything planted. Seeds were too precious to lose. She had to keep a constant watch on their garden from the time the seeds were planted until every vegetable was harvested. Birds, rats, ground squirrels, gray squirrels, boomers, groundhogs, bears, and everything in between wanted to feast on their garden.

Her dad had been deadly with a slingshot. She was also good with a slingshot and throwing rocks, and she intended to get better.

"Learn to use what you have at hand for a weapon, Striker. That way you'll never be left unarmed," her dad made a point of instructing her.

Any type of squirrel became meat for her stew pot. Without her dad the stew pot remained mostly empty. She'd never realized how much food her dad contributed compared to how little she contributed.

The potatoes were still safely stored in the potato hole. If she'd planted them earlier, they would have chilled and turned blackish gray on the inside. Even if she had them in the cabin, they might also have chilled. She hadn't bothered to keep a fire in the little stove. Without her dad to chop wood, keeping enough deadfall was becoming difficult. She would have to start now to gather enough firewood for the winter that always came hard and cold to the mountains. There was no question she would have to learn how to saw down large trees with a hand saw and then saw them to fit in the stove. The small stuff her dad allowed her to cut would never be enough to keep her from freezing to death come winter.

Striker drew in a breath of freezing air that burned her lungs. She tried to take away her uneasy feeling by looking at the beauty of the cold night. Everything the moonlight touched shimmered silver. The sudden cold snap had silenced every woods creature. Every insect, bird and critter had hunkered down to suffer the cold in silence. She closed the cabin door and leaned her back against it. She would crawl under her blankets and do the same.

On top of her ragged blankets she placed the bear hide her dad had tanned for keeping warm. She cried herself to sleep again.

Striker awoke frightened by the dream she'd been having only to discover it wasn't a dream. She was alone and cold. She got out of bed with the bear hide still wrapped around her and tried to find something to eat in hopes food would ease the pain in her stomach. Her fire had gone out, but there was little to cook even if it had been burning hot. Food in early spring was almost as difficult to find as during the winter months. What her dad and she had stored was gone and nature wasn't providing much food this early. She knew better than to eat any of the potatoes or garden seeds. Knowing she'd have to go outside in the cold to reach the cave where the potatoes were buried helped to save them.

She clutched the bear skin tighter about her once she'd opened the door and gone outside. The frost her bare feet walked on was so thick it could pass as a light snow. She made her way through the woods to a sheltered cove in hope the young hemlocks that had germinated there had put out new growth. Luck was with her, a few of them had pale yellow, half-inch of new growth. She picked every single one of the tender shoots and ate them, letting the frost melt in her mouth. It gave her morning hunger some ease.

She made her way back to the cabin, relunctly put the bear skin back on the bed, and gathered her slingshot along with her bow and arrows. She put on the deer-skin vest Dad had made and headed out to check the trap line in hopes she could get a rabbit. "Protein keeps us warm," her dad often told her. She needed to get warm, as well as ease the rumbling in her stomach.

The traps were empty. She had forgotten to reset them. She made a point of setting them and went to the creek to lift rocks in hopes of finding a few crawdads for the stew pot. She found two small ones. "Eat one, leave one," her dad had always warned her. "Don't get greedy or you will eliminate your food supply."

She put one in her leather pouch and made her way down stream to where cattails grew. She dug up one root with her hands. Cattails tasted similar to potatoes. She carried her breakfast back to the cabin and set to getting a fire started with a flint and striker. She longed for the matches her dad had brought home. She remembered striking two just to see how they worked. She now condemned herself for being wasteful. She never knew how important a match was until she no longer had any.

By the time she had a fire started in the little stove and boiled the cattail root and crawdad to make a watery stew, the sun was melting off the frost. She got the shovel from under the bed to continue digging up the garden. At least hard physical work would get her warm.

Chapter 6

~~~~

Days were filled with new learning experiences for both Kang and Lady Biswell. Kang loved nothing better than to be out of his lot regardless of the type of training Lady Biswell had in mind for him. He was no longer allowed to run free in the fields while his mother watched over the cattle.

Lady Biswell had undertaken his training with the same determination as with everything she set her mind to. Her dog and his training had become the most important thing in her day. The one thing Kang hated was the leash. He didn't want to be controlled or have his body limited by someone. He craved freedom. Lady Biswell understood. She didn't like being controlled either, but a huge dog with too much exuberance, along with a head-strong nature, had to learn the meaning of control. She used a body harness because she didn't like to use collars. She claimed collars choked dogs when they were clipped to a leash. A body halter gave more control over the dogs without them being able to pull backward.

Kang tolerated her controlling him. If he hadn't become devoted to her, he'd show her what he was made of, which was eighty pounds of exuberant pup struggling to become an independent adult dog. Lady Biswell knew she had to establish control before he reached his full growth. Judging from her other dogs, she estimated his grown weight would be at least 185 pounds or maybe more. He was already big for his age. His size and his intelligence were two of the reasons she had chosen to keep him. A dog such as Kang was rare.

Lady Biswell was sure he would make a fantastic stud dog that could also track and hunt game. Hunting and tracking were not the typical use for a Kangal, but Kang was special. He was always lifting his nose in the air to scent the wind. He continuously cocked his ears to listen to far-away sounds. Sometimes he would look toward the rugged National Forest land and whine as though he was longing to rush into their wilderness. She realized it was his wild instincts calling him – the same wild instincts his undomesticated ancestors had possessed.

Often, even she felt the call of nature urging her to take off into the wilderness. That call was what made the blood run hot in the spring and the wild geese fly before the snows set in. It was fiery, wild yearnings that could never be satisfied – not completely. She felt it struggling in herself and raging in Kang.

Soon, they would both venture into those wilds in search of soothing the wild beast within them. Maybe, just maybe, she might be able to find peace – acceptance of what life had dealt her. She still had hope but didn't expect miracles. Not once in her life had she received a miracle, but she did have a dogged determination to keep on keeping-on regardless of what life threw at her.

She understood it was not the devil shining out of her dog's eyes, as Griff claimed. It was the equivalent of pure intelligence. She was certain he could understand the words she said to him. All she had to do was repeat a command several times, and Kang would know exactly what she expected of him from then on. If he was unsure what she wanted, he would cock his head to the side and look directly into her eyes. Sometimes he would let out a small whine as if questioning her.

She knew Griff watched when she worked with Kang and did his best to remain silent, but temptation always got the best of him. He thought he knew best and considered her a hard-headed woman working with a hard-headed dog. Still, he couldn't keep his advice to himself.

"Don't count over much on that dog becoming what you imagine," Griff warned her as she clipped the training leash on the dog.

"Kang will easily surpass every hope I've ever had for him," Lady Biswell said, as she bent down and gave the dog a fierce hug. "Griff, has anyone ever told you that you have a fear of things that aren't mundane?"

"You," he answered.

"And yet, never once have you believed me."

"No reason to," he added with more than a touch of stubbornness in his ruddy face.

"Don't want to is more like it, but that is neither here or there. This dog, the one, I've got my arms around, is something special. You may not know it yet, but he and I do. Don't we boy?" she said, as she gave the dog an extra pat and received an extra spurt of exuberance from Kang. She started to add that they were the only two whose opinion counted, but she didn't want to insult Griff.

Chapter 7

~~~~

Ronald Buckworth hadn't told a complete lie to Griff. There was one element of truth to his story. He owned a parcel of land, with a tiny house on it, backed up against thousands of acres of National Forest. He had no cattle, goats, or anything related to farming. What he did have, hidden miles back into the deep woods, was a roughly constructed wooden building with low ceilings and shingle roof. Both the roof and side of the building were covered in large squares of Poplar bark singles in order to camouflage the building. There were no windows and only one narrow door reinforced with steel along with a large chain and locks.

Most of the time the building was silent and empty. At other times, there was such commotion the timbers themselves trembled. Men were loaded into enclosed vans, hauled along fire service roads into the National Forest, and then escorted in a roundabout way to the wooden building. These men had a thorough background check done on them before they became part of the group. Secrecy was priority. Ronald Buckworth and the men he trusted went out of their way to make sure the groups they brought in had no idea where the building was located. Great care had to be taken to make sure no undercover law enforcements found their way into the select group of men. And it was a select group of men, except for one. She was a woman named Alice Danbert.

People hardly ever noticed she wasn't a man. She had a man's build and a man's face, minus the beard, although there were several long hairs scattered about her chin and upper lip, which she didn't seem to mind. She had a mass of straw-colored hair that stood on end all the time, causing her to keep it cut close to her scalp. She had been a veterinarian until she lost her license on a bogus charge. She hadn't forgotten those who set her up, or the crooked lawmen who were on the dole of the good-ole-boys who decided she was competition for their cronies.

Alice was the one who patched up the dogs and saved their lives. Unfortunately, in most cases her care resulted in them being able to fight another day. No dog owner wanted to have his expensive dog die during a fight, but it happened. It would happen more often if it wasn't for her. When a dog was almost to the point where it couldn't be saved, some of the men gave her permission to step in and call the fight. This saved the men's pride by stopping the fighting because their dog was losing.

She despised dog fighting, but fights would continue regardless if she were there or not. At least she could be there to attempt to save the dogs' lives.

Ronald Buckworth trusted her because he knew her hatred of law enforcement was greater than her hatred of the dog fighting ring. She would never give anything away to the law regardless of what happened. Besides, she considered it her mission to save the injured dogs. She dreamed of the day when no dogs would fight or die.

The fact that she was as ugly as a mud fence assured that men ignored her for all other reasons and purposes. Plus, she was big-boned and stronger than any man. Her hands were callused and rough. She'd been known to pick up a fighting Pit Bull without gloves on and toss it out of the pit like it was rooster.

Occasionally, Buckworth held chicken fights, but it didn't bring in enough money to offset the effort and expense put into it. Alice didn't have the same degree of compassion for the roosters as she had for the dogs. Roosters had tiny pea brains that could never learn. It was pure instinct that make the male game fowl want to fight. Not to mention the men would always harass the roosters to make them mad enough to fight. They also cut all the red comb off their heads and fed the combs back to them. A rooster's most vulnerable place was its comb. In her opinion, dogs were almost people. She felt for certain the sorriest of dog was far better than the best human she'd ever come across.

Buckworth demanded half of her vet bill earnings. He also stood as her collector to make sure the men paid whatever she charged for saving their dogs. If they didn't pay up, they didn't come back. He had yet to discover she overcharged any man. However, there were a few men she added all the extras to their bill, and a few she didn't. Ronald had never complained about either. He knew his was a win-win situation.

The man she hated even more than Ronald Buckworth was Phillip Godard, the man who made Buckworth's dogs vicious enough to fight. He was an overweight, pompous-ass of a man with nothing but cruelty inside of him. He not only enjoyed the fighting, he craved the bloody gore of it. He would quiver with excitement, unable to contain himself, as he leaped into the air and shouted with delight when a fang slit a jugular, pumping blood over the ring. He was especially happy when Alice could not stop the flow to save a dog, yet he was one of the men Ronald used to train his dog.

Alice cringed when she saw the black SUV pull up to the front door of her little house. It meant another dog fight was in the making. Her footsteps were slow and plodding as she went to the front door to let him in. She'd learned long ago not to ever leave a door, or a window unlocked, not that it made much difference. A lock, or window could not keep anyone out, but it did give the person inside a few seconds longer to prepare a defense. A few seconds could make all the difference in outcome.

The door opened as Ronald lifted his fist to knock. "What?" Alice asked.

"Come to let you know to get in extra supplies."

Alice's eyes narrowed. Only when he had set up a big night of fighting did he tell her to get extra supplies. "Why?" she ventured to ask.

"Coming up from Atlanta," he bragged. "Big boys. Big money."

Alice looked him in the eyes but said nothing about his decision. They both knew it was not a good idea to bring in the so-called *Big Boys*. They ate the *Little Boys* up and squirted them out. Ronald Buckworth ought to have enough sense to stay away from them, but he evidently didn't. Buckworth went after the *big money* no matter how much it cost him.

Alice only nodded. "When?" she asked.

"Monday week," he grinned as though he had accomplished a special feat.

"How many?"

"Ought to be a crowd. I'm guessing full to overflowing."

She longed to point out a crowd of people would leave a lot of tracks. A lot of tracks would leave a trail that would be easily followed. There were times when Ronald Buckworth proved to be more stupid than she thought possible.

~~~~

Buckorth liked that Alice never argued with him. Showed she had a degree of intelligence. As far as he could tell, she never argued with anyone about anything. The only things she cared about were the animals she tried to keep alive, and that was okay. It was what she was supposed to do. She did what he hired her to do and did it well. Alice Danbert never complained, never asked for favors. If it wasn't for that crazed look in her pale blue eyes, she would be just about perfect for the purpose she served. That crazed look was there all the time, and it caused a chill to creep over him more times than he cared to admit. Although she always did the right and expected thing, she also made him wonder when the crazy part would extend beyond her eyes. If such as that happened, it shouldn't make much of a difference. Ronald was confident he controlled everything within his realm, including her. He was a powerful man with plenty of paid backup. His people were loyal to him. They knew all too well what would happen if he detected any form of disloyalty.

A grin twisted his mouth. One thing was for certain, if he ever decided to sponsor a ring of fighting women, he was already in possession of a winner.

Chapter 8

~~~~

Striker lay on the bed trying to remember being somewhere other than on this mountain. To the best of her memory, she was around three or four years old when her dad moved them here. Time was difficult for her to keep track of. Yet, she knew there were good times and bad times that flowed into each other. It was the bad times that vaguely troubled her memory. Thankfully, there weren't many of those memories. Her dad had always been her protector from all that was bad.

Striker wasn't sure if she actually remembered being around people and living in a house, or if her memory came from the books her dad brought her to read. Her dad tried his best not to tell her about the life he and her mother once lived – even when she asked him specific questions. She did know that her mother died right before they left so-called civilization behind. What she didn't know was exactly why they had left. Her dad telling her it was to enable them to live the 'good life' was a suitable answer when she was little, but it didn't suffice as she grew older and wiser and developed her own ability to think and question.

She did remember living in a tent while Dad cut trees to build the cabin. He cut them a long distance from the spot he chose to build the cabin, making sure he didn't take more than one or two from the same area. He didn't want planes or helicopters to notice timber being cut or a cleared spot in the forest in case they flew over their location. Fortunately, the forest was over-populated with trees the perfect size her dad could manage to drag. A lot of the older trees were far too big to saw down with a hand saw. He pointed out that a chainsaw would make too much noise, as would chopping with an ax. Hammering was also a no-no. Silence was always what he wanted. Sound carried on the wind. They even talked in a whispered tone of voice when they were in a location where noise would carry. Never, ever, was she allowed to holler for her dad no matter the reason. There was also a lot of deadfall that Dad could use for building as well as for burning. Her dad always insisted their meat had to be cooked to the point of near-burning.

"Parasites," he said. "You always have to be on the lookout for parasites and know how to kill them. Wild animals along with everything else have parasites. They're in every place and everything. People are parasites too. Human parasites are cannibals. They might not actually eat the flesh of their own kind, but they live off other people in more ways than one."

"People eat people?" she had questioned, feeling repulsion and shock at what her dad had just said.

"In a way – and also in reality." He went on to explain about ancient tribes of cannibals that actually did eat human flesh. He then taught her about metaphors and similes. Her dad explained although they were living a remote hermit's life, there was no excuse not to become educated as best possible. "My daughter will not grow up being illiterate or uneducated. Your mother would never forgive me if I allowed that to happen to our beloved daughter."

Striker felt her eyes grow wide as she became afraid. Was that why her dad ran away from people? Was he afraid of cannibals? "Did an ancient tribe eat my mother?" she dared ask her dad. Was that why she didn't have a mother?

"Ah, Striker, I've scared you when I didn't intend to. No, cannibals did not eat your mother. Life, well, life can be cruel, but it's important to never become afraid of things.

Learn what can harm you, and then learn how to defeat it, or at the very least avoid it. That's what I did after your mother died. I took you into my arms and moved us both to the most beautiful place on earth. These mountains, Striker, are truly heaven on earth."

"How do I not be afraid?" she whispered.

"Knowledge, Striker. I'll teach you everything I know, along with everything we can learn together," he told her in the reassuring way he had of making her feel safe. "Knowledge is the key that opens all doors and conquers all fears. Fortunately, we have plenty of time for learning, and I promise I'll get you books with information about everything. Encyclopedias are almost free for the taking. I'll get you an entire set, plus many more books. I want my girl to have a way of finding answers to all her questions."

He was wrong. They didn't have plenty of time for learning. His time had run out – and most likely, so had hers. With her dad gone, she feared her learning had come to an end. She would surely die on this mountain without him. But she wouldn't die without putting up a good fight.

One of the worst things was the loneliness that descended on her when she least expected it. She would turn to say something to her dad only to find he wasn't there and never would be.

For the first few days after she had buried her dad, she had tried to sooth herself by pretending he had only left the mountains to bring back something special for her to enjoy, but her pretense only lasted until the darkness overcame the light of day, and she had to climb into bed with the night sounds calling out hauntingly. All the fears she'd ever experienced gathered during the long and lonely nights to torture her. In her restless dreams, she saw her mother being eaten by cannibals that looked like huge maggots – just as her father's flesh beneath the ground was being eaten away by those same cannibals.

She would wake up screaming for her dad, but he never came. All she had for protection were the ragged blankets she pulled over her head. She was always surprised to find she was still alive when mornings came.

Striker longed to find Aunt Nellie, but all her knowledge came from the books. How could she possibly find someone when she had no idea which direction she was supposed to start walking in?

Her dad made sure he never left a path leading off their mountain or back on it. He always made a point of backtracking many times in order to confuse a human tracker or dogs. His behavior didn't seem odd to Striker. It was simply the way her dad did things.

"You have to be smart like a fox," he'd say. "You have to learn how to double back and lay a false trail. Can't be too careful, Striker. You never know what might happen to make you wish you had."

Striker took a day to climb to the top of the highest mountaintop above the tree line. There were no trees growing on the very top. Her dad had told her it was called a natural bald. From here, she looked in all directions, but she had to be careful. If she could see far off, then she could also be seen from far off.

"Always take cover, Striker. Never leave yourself in the open," her dad instructed. "You mustn't ever become easily seen."

From on top of the bald, she still could not see any sign of human life. There were no dwellings, no smoke rising from a fire, no signs of cut timber, or even a trail leading out of the forest. she didn't even know the name of the mountain range she was on. Dad never told her the name of anything that would allow her to know where they were located. The only direction her dad went when he left the mountain was down, so how was she to find Aunt Nellie in a world she knew nothing about? Books taught her there were three hundred and sixty degrees of directions in which to go down the mountain.

Still, she'd promised her dad she would find Aunt Nellie, and she would do her best to keep that promise, but it would have to wait. Right now, her major objective was to remain alive.

She stood on the bald until the sun disappeared behind a far mountain. A glimmer of sun light remained in the sky for a few minutes giving off a purple glow until the glimmer disappeared. A cold wind stirred the sparse growth on the bald making her realize she had to hurry back to the security of the cabin before darkness made it more dangerous to be outside. Predators came out to hunt and feed once darkness concealed them. The darkness would also make it more difficult for her to find her way through the thick growth of forest and underbrush. She wasn't afraid, she assured herself. But she was intelligent enough to remember her dad's teachings. "Lack of fear has a way of tempting fate, Striker. Don't ever forget that," he'd warned. "When you allow yourself to start feeling secure enough to ignore caution, the unthinkable happens."

Her dad had proved that statement to be true. She was certain he had cut down hundreds of trees without so much as one injury in all these years. The one time her dad let his guard down, the tree twisted unexpectedly. And that was when the unthinkable happened.

The bald still had daylight, while the forest was becoming saturated with the gloom of nighttime shadows. Realizing she had stayed too long disturbed her greatly. She knew better than to be caught in the wooded areas when the night predators were feeding. She put an arrow in her bow and held it at ready as she ran. Not that it would have provided much protection in her blind run for the cabin, but it helped her feel a little bit safer. She was at least somewhat prepared to fight the hidden demons that could attack her.

By the time she had reached the cabin, her lungs were burning in her chest as she heaved for air. She had run as hard and fast as her legs would go, jumping over rocks and tree roots, trying to ignore the sting of undergrowth slapping her in the face. Her race for the cabin did her little good. Her dad wasn't there. All that awaited in the cabin was the silence broken only by her sobs. Striker used her dirty hands to wipe at her damp cheeks, closed the cabin door behind her, and fastened the bar across the door in an attempt to shut out all the fears that had chased her home.

"I'm safe, Dad," she whispered into the darkened cabin. "I won't forget about fear and caution ever again. I promise.

Chapter 9

~~~~

It was easy to tell Kang believed himself to be the ruler of his world, which consisted of the confines of her farm and kennels. He loved nothing more than to strut by her side with his head lifted in arrogant majesty. He longed to be let off his leash to run wild and free over the sweet-smelling grass into the fields of dark colored cattle. The aroma the cattle gave off was intoxicating, their droppings left a tangy drawing power in the air. He instincts were to romp and roll in that tanginess, to chase a cow with friendly delight. He also knew that Lady Biswell would not approve of such puppy actions.

One thing utmost in his entire training was to please his mistress. He became more devoted to her with every day that passed. To feel her hand pat him on the head and hear her say "Good boy!" seemed to make his spirit soar with delight. He had become attached to her as only a faithful dog becomes attached to a beloved master. Lady Biswell knew he loved her smell, her touch, the very appearance of her body and face. In Kang's mind she belonged to him and in her mind Kang belonged to her.

Never had it occurred to either of them that he might become separated from his beloved mistress. They were like sunshine and warmth, like happiness and laughter. They were where they belonged – together.

Lady Biswell was positive she would grow old with Kang being the top stud dog as well as her very own personal companion. Although she had always loved dogs, she had no idea she could possibly become attached to a dog the way she had become attached to Kang. He almost made up for all the things she had secretly longed for in life and had never gotten. Not that she ever made public her longings. How could she possibly express any kind of complaints when she outwardly appeared to have everything others dreamed of having? But these were only outward appearances. She let no one see her heart, certainly not her last three husbands.

"The world has been good to me," she would say – and then ended the sentence by whispering, "Except in the things that really matter."

~~~~

"It's not natural," Griff would mumble to himself as he watched dog and woman together. "They talk and understand each other, they do. It not good for animal and human to be that close. What if something happened to one or the other. Not good. No, sireee, not a good thing."

Griff had long ago learned not to criticize Kang, although he still thought the dog to be unsafe, if not plum crazy. But then in her own kind of way, Lady Biswell could very possibly be just as crazy as Kang. Who was he to judge? So, he remained silent, but still opinionated.

Kang was maturing into a hard-muscled, fiercely protective male dog that far surpassed Griff's expectations during his puppyhood. He was even allowed to father a litter of pups, which did wonders to his already keenly developed ego.

"Watch him strut his stuff," Griff had laughingly pointed out to Lady Biswell. "He thinks he's in the land of Heaven for sure and certain."

Lady Biswell had also grinned at the pride Kang was showing in himself. She barely managed to hold her tongue in reminding Griff of what a fantastic dog she'd told him Kang would become – the father of champions.

~~~~

It wasn't only Lady Biswell and Griff who realized Kang was special. Ronald Buckworth also had Norman James keep a watch on the dog. He had gotten Norman James to steal all the good fighting dogs he could get his hands on. Buckworth had even given in and bought a few. Trouble with having good fighting dogs was that someone else always had a better fighting dog. One that was able to lock onto the throat and kill his dog before Alice could pry them loose.

"Kill or be killed is the name of the game," he had told Alice. But inside he was raging furious at his losses. He had to find better fighting dogs or go busted. He was already in financial trouble because he couldn't pay all the bets he'd lost. He was hanging on by nothing more than the skin of his own teeth. "Is there anything you can give our dogs before they go into the ring to fight that'll make them win," he asked Alice.

"Nothing the judges wouldn't pick up in the blood samples," she told him in no uncertain terms. "Trying something like that would be foolish. It would ruin you faster than cutting your own dogs' throats."

There were always two impartial judges who oversaw the blood samples she took just before the dogs went into the ring to fight and the moment the fight ended. Otherwise, some crook would be sure to drug the dogs. If one, or both, of the judges proved to be dishonest, he or they suffered a fate worse than the dog who lost.

As for the man who tried to cheat, it was best not to go into those kinds of details. The National Forest land was pockmarked by unmarked graves.

Ronald had no choice other than to find better dogs – dogs he could steal since he couldn't afford to buy a spot to spit on – not that he had anything against stealing. Chances were the dogs wouldn't last long enough to be traced back to him.

Alice was wise enough to keep her opinions to herself. She had known bringing the big-boys up from Atlanta was bad in the worst sort of way, but Ronald kept them coming – and he kept losing.

Ronald Buckworth had spent years knowing where every dog in several counties were located that had good fight potential. He had no use for a dog who would belly-up and die in the first minutes of being attacked. The Biswell woman's male Kangal dog was one of his picks. The only things he didn't like about the dog was that he was short haired and long legged. A short haired dog was easier to have his flesh lashed open. A long-legged dog had an exposed belly. Take a Chow and Saint Bernard crossed with a Pit Bull, and that was the best kind of dog to put in the fighting ring. Trouble was, it took a lot of time and training to cross-breed and train what he considered to be the perfect dog. Even dogs from the same litter ended up being different. Not many had the ability to become fierce fighters.

Alice might have the knowledge to combine the right crosses to make the kind of dog he'd always dreamed of having. He'd check with her on that. Trouble was, at this time, he didn't have the money to buy the breeding dogs she would need. He wondered if it might be possible to steal them without getting caught.

Chapter 10

~~~~

Once again, the cold of winter left the mountains in what seemed to Striker as being overnight. The winds of March returned with a taste of spring. Along with the winds, March brought glorious promise of warmth and flowers. Soon, existing on the mountain would become easier.

The valleys down below filled up with morning mists rising slowly as it waited to be burned off as soon as the sun squeezed out a little more warmth. Dews were so heavy it felt like rain was clinging to every living thing, encouraging the return of life.

The previous winters had been milder than she had expected. She feared the next winter would be different. All the signs her dad had taught her to look for pointed to the possibility that the next winter would be a bad one. Plus, all the stock pile of supplies her dad had stored were gone. Even her supply of seeds for the garden had shrunk.

Striker found herself working like she had never worked before. Every minute of every daylight hour was spent in an effort to assure her survival. Much too often her nights were filled with worrying about what needed to be done instead of getting the sleep she needed. Knowing her supplies were gone, a new kind of fear developed and grew in proportion to the fear of starving to death. How could she possibly grow enough food to last her all year long. Yet, she had no choice in the matter. There was no one other than her to accomplish the tasks that had to be done, and no place for her to go – no

Aunt Nellie to be found, and no way of knowing where such a person lived. Aunt Nellie was only a name in a world Striker had never known and most likely would never know. Striker knew if she ever left her familiar surroundings, her safety would be greatly lessened. It would be easy to get lost or injured. Both perils would make her prey for wild animals.

She also feared the men her father always warned her about, even though she had never encountered any and did not want to do so. She knew they were out there somewhere. She had no mirror to look at herself, but the past years of extra hard work had aided in giving her a strong, hard body – a woman's body. She had not expected to transform into the beginning of womanhood instead of remaining a child. She understood being a child. All she had ever known of a woman was what she read in books.

Not for one minute had she allowed her mind to wander from the need of working to assure her survival.

"It takes an idiot to let their mind wander," she again remembered what her dad often told her.

She wondered why his mind had wandered when he miscalculated the way the killing tree would fall. One thing was for sure, losing her dad taught her not to allow her mind to wander from the task at hand – and yet there were times.

Right now, she was buck-naked as she stood in the middle of the stream, near where her dad had been killed, washing the stink from what few clothes she had left. She could no longer stand the sweaty stink of them or the odor of herself. All the soap had been used up. She had to rely on sand to scrub everything including her head of long hair. She had done her best to keep the tangles combed out. Finding she could no longer let its massive length hang loose, she now wore it a bun at the back of her head and secured it with sticks whittled smooth. She had gathered a bunch of mint to rub in her hair, on her body and clothes once she had everything as clean as possible.

Mint helped keep the insects away. The past spring and summer had proven to be a prolific time for insects. The previously mild winter-weather had allowed them to become a constant aggravation. Her dad always told her a brutally cold winter served a purpose. It thinned out insects and sickly things that had become of little benefit. "Sickly things actually do have a purpose," her dad would add. "They feed the strong."

She never wanted to become sickly.

Another of her concerns were clothes. She was outgrowing the few clothes her dad had brought back for her to wear several years before. Not only that, they had also become threadbare. There was no cloth - nothing to patch the holes with. At least she had her dad's extra shirt and bibbed overalls, but she was saving them, along with his warm underwear, for the winter months. There was little chance she'd outgrow them, but in time they would wear out. She had no idea how long she would have to stay on the mountain before she grew brave enough to leave. The big question haunting her courage was once she left, then what?

Again, she was thankful for the previously mild winters. Had they been the bitter, frozen winters they had most often experienced, she might not have survived. Her fire was always going out, and she wasn't as good as her dad at striking a flint to get it started again. She had spent most of the winters huddled in bed wearing every article of clothing along with every blanket and fur cocooned around her.

She was now older, stronger, bigger, and wiser on what preparations she'd need to do for the coming winters. Spring, summer, and fall living wasn't exactly easy, but it was a sweet breeze compared to high-mountain winters. No wonder animals hibernated.

She finished washing her clothes, twisted them as dry as possible, climbed out of the water and hung them on tree limbs to dry in the breeze and beams of the sun. She climbed on a sun-warmed rock and stretched out. The sun tanned her skin and made it tougher. The darker her skin became the less bug bites and briar scratches bothered her.

When her dad was alive, she would never have stripped off naked. He had not approved of exposing one's flesh. Never had she seen her dad so much as take off his shirt, even in hot weather. To her way of thinking, there was no longer a chance of anyone seeing her, so what did it matter? Once her meager supply of clothing wore out, she wouldn't have much choice during the warm months other than going naked. Winters were different. She'd best start making clothes out of animal hides right now. She cringed at the thought of how many small hides it would take.

While lying there thinking, she noticed a crow in a tree several hundred feet from where she lay. There was a nest in the top of the tree that hadn't been there several days before. A freshly built nest meant freshly laid eggs. Always hungry, her stomach rumbled at the thought of eggs. It had been a long while since she'd eaten eggs. Wild turkey eggs were her favorite, but they were as difficult to find as turkey's teeth. Crow's eggs would be small, but there just might be several depending on when they were laid. She didn't want them if they had been set on long enough to start a chick developing. She jumped up and made for the tree.

Her dad always told her she could climb like a squirrel, which was true, but she had gotten heavier through the years. She now had to be more careful of the trees she climbed, making sure the top limbs were strong enough to hold her weight. Top limbs in white pines were always small and brittle, but hunger for eggs drove her onward. At least the day's heat made the limbs more pliable and less likely to snap as they tended to do in cold weather. The heat also brought out the pine rosin to stick all over her body and in her hair. She'd be rubbing sand and dirt on the sticky places for days.

Finally, she reached the nest, causing a flutter of black wings to flap in her face as her head rose enough to see into the nest. She paid no attention to the squawking crow flying about as she eyed the three eggs in the nest. She knew crows laid from two to six eggs. As there were only three, she figured the crow had not finished laying her clutch. She took one egg, broke it open and dumped the contents in the palm of her hand. It was still fresh without so much as a blood speck. Lifting her hand to her mouth, she swallowed the slimy bit of protein. she took one more egg leaving one for the crow. Most likely the crow would lay more eggs to go with it. If not, she wouldn't be harming the crow population. According to the book she read, crows had a life span of seventeen years.

Like a screaming black streak two crows zoomed at her face with flapping wings and sharp, striking beaks causing her to lean backward a little too far as she flailed at the attacking crows. She felt the limb she was standing on give and then snap. She was falling downward from a fifty-foot white pine tree. Frantically, she grabbed for limbs to stop her fall. Each limb her hands grabbed broke. Other limbs were scraping her body as she spiraled downward. Images of Dad laying injured trapped underneath the tree flashed through her mind, and she knew she would join him in death any moment now. Like her dad, she had ignored caution for only a moment?

Limbs on the lower portion of the tree were larger and stronger. she hit one with a jarring thud. Her bruised and skinned hands clutched at the limb for dear life. Finally, her hands managed to get a life-saving hold on one of the branches. Stunned, it took her a few moments to realize she was no longer bouncing from limb to limb.

She heaved in a breath, said a reverent prayer of thanks, and slowly eased herself the rest of the way down. Once she reached the ground, her shaky legs gave out. She sunk to the ground, breathing hard, and trembling from head to toe. She had escaped death or fatal injury, but she hadn't come out of the fall unscathed. Her entire body was stinging with pain and covered in pine sap and debris. Pine bark had scrubbed itself into her raw flesh. Blood oozed and even dripped in a few places. Still, she said another prayer of thanks knowing she could have been in much worse condition, with no one to haul her back to the cabin on a sled.

Chapter 11

~~~~

Griff fed and watered all the dogs, making sure their runs were clean before seeking out Lady Biswell. Kang had watched him with distrustful eyes. Griff could feel the dog's gaze following him with every move he made, which was rather unusual. The dog watched what was going on more closely than any dog he'd encountered, but today the dog's watchfulness had a different feeling. There was something more than wariness in those eyes. It was more like a restless anger, but that wasn't Griff's problem. It was the dog's problem as well as Lady Biswell's. He'd washed his hands of giving her good advice where Kang was concerned.

Griff cleaned up from his work, put on clean clothes and boots that didn't smell like dog and the kennels, dumped a dab of hair tonic on his hands and rubbed his hands through his hair. Once he combed his hair, he went to find Lady Biswell.

"I'm headin' into town to fetch the supplies you ordered," he told her as she came out the back door.

Lady Biswell only glanced at him, ignoring the fact that he had taken extra time in grooming himself.

"Sounds good. Did Kang eat all his food?" she asked.

Griff nodded. All she cared about was that dog. In his opinion she'd let the dog replace all her dead husbands, along with the children she'd never had. He didn't think her obsession with that dog was a good thing, but who was he to advise her? It wasn't like he had a happy family. He was more alone than she was.

"Since when has that dog not eaten all his food?" Griff made a point of asking. "He eats three times what the other dogs do."

"He seemed a little off last night. Kind of nervous and ill at ease, but I couldn't detect anything wrong with him. Did you?" Lady Biswell continued to question him about her beloved dog.

As usual, Griff thought she sounded overly concerned.

"Don't think there's anything wrong with him far as I can tell. I've been watching him extra close just like you told me to. He seems as healthy as ever. Only thing I noticed was he's been sticking his nose in the air and scenting the wind more than normal. Must be a racoon or some other kind of animal maundering about out there in the deep woods. Spring's that time of year, you know. Animals seeking each other."

"You're probably right. Upsets him terrible when something strange comes around. I probably shouldn't turn him loose to run free today."

"Up to you," Griff told her. He wouldn't be turning that dog loose according to the restless way he was behaving, but Lady Biswell never listened to him where her favorite dog was concerned, or much of anything else. She was one woman who did what she wanted when she wanted.

It was just her everlasting hardheaded stubbornness that was always at the forefront of everything. If she was determined the sun was shining, it didn't matter how many times you told her it was raining, she wouldn't believe it until she proved it to herself.

At the same time, Griff respected that kind of attitude. Wimpy women who couldn't do a thing for themselves weren't his type. Lady Biswell was still a firm-bodied woman with callused hands and steady step. He often wondered what type of man her next husband would be? He didn't believe she was the kind of woman who needed a man. He did believe she was the kind of woman who would be willing to marry in order to better her situation, not that her situation wasn't just fine the way it was. In Griff's opinion Lady Biswell was always looking for opportunities that would make life better for her and, admittedly, some lonely rich man willing to trade his worldly assets after his death for a good life while he was still alive on earth.

Griff didn't know if it was fortunate or unfortunate that he had no worldly assets.

Chapter 12

~~~~

Striker was as sore as all get out after falling from the pine tree, but she'd determined nothing was broken.

"I'm alright Dad. Won't be so careless the next time," she told him as though her dad was still beside her.

The intense silence of the thick forests made her crave someone to talk to. Her dad was the logical person. She was certain his spirit was with her, listening to every word she said. She even believed, in his own way, he talked back to her.

"I reckon I've got to learn the hard way," she added as she limped her way back to the cabin. "Not sure if those little eggs were worth it."

The sound of her own voice seemed to help when she was feeling down, but there was no way to get the sound of her dad's voice talking back other than in her mind. At least the birds and animals called back at her when she mimicked them. She'd become good at making animal sounds, almost better than making human sounds.

She went to bed that night certain all would be healed by the next morning. It wasn't the first time she'd been bruised up and sore. She had not expected to wake up with a terrible stomach ache. She tried to think of what she had eaten that might have given her the trots but nothing came to mind. She'd eaten a few berries, one potato, branch lettuce leaves, and the crow eggs. Yep, it must have been the crow eggs.

"The crow's revenge," she said out-loud as she went outside to find a place to squat where she hadn't gone before. Her dad had always said it was best to pick a different place every time they had to relieve themselves. That way they were less likely to leave a smell that would draw animals. He had one exception to that rule. They were always to relieve themselves in the perimeter around the garden when the crops were in the ground hoping their human smell would keep deer away.

She walked a good way from the cabin and squatted down. What she expected to be loose and runny was as normal as could be. She picked a handful of leaves from the bush she squatted near and wiped herself. What she saw caused her suck in her breath. There was the red of fresh blood on the leaves.

"Oh, no, dad," she mumbled as fear gripped her. "I've done gone and hurt myself bad."

She was certain she would pay the same price for being careless as her dad had paid. Death. The thought of death shocked her. She hadn't realized until now, how much she wanted to live.

There would be nobody to bury her the way she'd buried her dad. Crows would pick her eyeballs out. Flies would blow her flesh until maggots filled her mouth and other openings. The stink of her rotting flesh would draw wolves and vultures to rip at her body and carry off her bones.

She stood and made her way back to the cabin, silent tears rolling down her cheeks as her stomach cramped harder. She sat down on her bed and cried until she realized a small amount of blood was seeping into her bed. She stood, used her fingers to detect a wound on her bottom side where she couldn't see. She bent down and tried to look. She saw no wound, felt no wound. She finally determined the blood was coming from inside her. She had surely ruptured something in her stomach when she fell through the tree limbs.

What was she to do? What could she do? She cried some more and thought about what would surely happen to her. After a while, she took the shovel from under her dad's bed and went to the garden to dig her own grave beside her dad's. If she was going to die, perhaps she'd be able to fall into her grave all by herself – but how would she be able to cover herself up with dirt?

It took her three days of digging her own grave to get it deep enough to fall into. She still hadn't figured out exactly how she could manage to cover herself up with dirt once she was in her grave. She had cut tree limbs with the leaves still on, laid them on the edge of the grave with the wooden ends sticking out over the edge of the grave with dirt on the leaves and smaller twigs. Perhaps when she lowered herself into the grave, she'd be able to grab hold of the branches and pull hard enough to make the dirt fall on her. Most likely she wouldn't be alive long enough to know if it worked or not.

The bleeding slowed down on the fourth day, and by the fifth day the bleeding stopped completely. She awoke with no stomach cramps, feeling normal and thankful her body had healed itself instead of dying.

She went about her work for three weeks, completely forgetting about her injury and near death, until her stomach cramping started again followed by bleeding. Something strange was going on with her, and she had no idea what, or even how to find out about her injury. Her only solution was to pull all the books her dad had brought home on plants, herbs, natural medicines, healings and start reading in hopes she could find an answer.

"Don't matter what happens to you out here in God's country. He has provided a cure for everything if we just know what it is," her dad had assured her. "Hopefully we can find answers in these books if we should ever need to. That's one of the reasons I've made sure you have plenty of reading materials, Striker. There're answers in those books I can't tell you and don't even know myself. Sometime other folks have figured out the answers to our questions and wrote them down in books. When you're seeking answers to things, read."

Chapter 13

~~~~

Ronald Buckworth fought to keep down the gut-gnawing fear growing inside him. He was doing everything in his power to turn the queasy feeling of doom into vengeful anger. Those crooks from Atlanta were robbing him blind along with killing his best fighting dogs. Things couldn't keep going the way they were going. Some changes would have to be made in a hurry.

He concluded those Atlanta crooks were giving their dogs some type of hard to trace illegal drugs before the fights, but then what was legal about dog fighting? It wasn't exactly a sport based on honor. His only solution was having Alice draw more blood from the dogs to test for different kinds of drugs before and after each fight.

There were two problems with that. One was the cost of buying the equipment to test the blood samples and the other was the objections from the dog owners. He'd rather not have the Atlanta boys if they were going to cheat. It occurred to him that only the crooked dog owners would complain.

His regulars would pay for the testing if it meant they had a fair chance of their dogs winning. His regulars were already dropping out. Why put your dog in a fight when you knew it would lose or be killed? The regulars would quickly take their dogs and their money somewhere else. Soon there would only be the Atlanta boys fighting each other, and that wouldn't go over well.

"What does it matter if the Atlanta boys only have each other to fight?" Alice said as he talked to her about doing the extra blood testing. "What's the worst that could happen?"

Buckworth frowned as he considered the worst. He already knew the answer.

"They won't bring their dogs." Which meant he wouldn't be getting their entry fees – nor would he be paying out more than was brought in. All bets were being placed on the Atlanta dogs. Even his regulars sneaked around to bet against their own dogs.

"What's so bad about that?" Alice asked in her no-nonsense way.

"They'll put me out of business."

"If you ask me, that would be a good thing."

Buckworth gave her an angry glare, but she continued.

"If you try to get rid of the Atlanta boys, they'll have it in for you, but if they think they put you out of business, it'll make them happy enough to forget about you."

"What about my regulars?"

"You're already out of business with the regulars, and there's no wonder. We both know they're not going to bring in their dogs to be killed. It's only your own dogs that are getting ripped to pieces."

That was true. He was going under fast.

"If it was me, I'd close down."

"But - - -."

"For a short time, while you change locations," she added, it made good business sense.

"It would take too long," he objected at not having regular dog fights.

"While you're finding a better place to set up, you can use the time to train more dogs."

The thought of having Phillip Godard around training dogs made her cringed. Why she was giving good advice to a man such as Ronald Buckworth, she didn't know. If she ever got the time and money together, she just might decide to have her head examined.

"Besides you need down time to get your injured dogs back into fighting condition. Those Atlanta boys put some kind of suffering on your dogs. It'll take another month to get them healthy."

"I'll think on it," he told her.

He needed time to make her ideas his ideas. Just because she had some good suggestions didn't mean he liked her getting credit for a good idea.

Chapter 14

~~~~

Norman James wasn't exactly pleased about having to spend the night in the chilly, damp woods, but it was his job to stay hidden and undetected until both the kennel keeper and the woman were both away long enough for him to do *his thing*. He took pride in being good at stealing.

In his line of work, night time was the best time for him to do his thing. He believed in observation. It allowed a man to understand what was going one. No surprises was the name of the game as far as he was concerned.

Last night the woman proved to be restless. She was outside roaming about several times during the night. Many times, he felt the urge to make her disappear. He could do it as easily as he could make her dog disappear, but Buckworth had put his foot down on anything that would cause an investigation, or even too much interest. A missing dog was simply a missing dog. It could have escaped its enclosure with no criminal investigation involved. A missing woman would be an entirely different matter.

His only mission was to steal the dog, and when the opportunity arrived for him to do so, he was to move quickly the same as he'd done many times before. Ole, Ronald Buckworth didn't pay the best, but at least he paid enough to keep Norman doing *his thing* – stealing. Not only did Norman James steal the dogs Buckworth wanted, he always found a few things to steal for himself. Since Buckworth was so stingy, it was only fitting to sweeten his own pot with a few prime items. Not many folks cared about, or even noticed, what he took? They were always more concerned about their missing dogs.

It didn't make sense to him how people could become attached to dogs. They were nothing but animals and ought to be treated as such. Their lives didn't matter a flip. Dogs were easily replaced. Ronald Buckworth was a prime example of a man who showed how easy it was to replace dogs. Every week or two a dozen or more dogs were taken off to some undisclosed location. Most of those dogs never returned, which was a good thing where he was concerned. A dead dog was hard to trace, plus he got paid for stealing more replacement dogs.

His attention perked up when he saw the kennel worker come out of the barn all cleaned up and strutting his stuff. It was safe to say a cleaned-up worker with slicked back hair was probably taking some time off – or maybe thinking of having a little divergence with the woman of the house. James kept his binoculars focused on the worker who was headed for the fancy house. Okay, divergence it was.

Oops. He might have concluded wrong, for Biswell herself came into his range of view before the worker got to the porch. They talked for a minute or two before the worker walked off and the woman went to the kennel.

Again, he allowed his thoughts to run slightly amuck. His hand caressed his tranquilizer gun as he watched the lone woman. He had used his gun a few times when he'd had a beautiful woman in his sights. Sometimes having his way with an unconscious woman was just as much fun as having his way with a conscious one, plus an unconscious woman could never testify to what he looked like. The only problem was in today's fancy DNA shit. It allowed a man to be traced.

All things considered, he changed his mind. This Biswell woman wouldn't be worth his time. She wasn't young enough or pretty enough to take a chance on. Besides, spending the night being cold and damp had taken away most of what little want-to he still had.

He stifled a regretful grunt. He was no longer a young buck with an unquenchable want-to. Time had already had its way with him long before he realized what was happening. It had turned his thinning hair and long beard into a dirty gray. His muscles had gone slack and his belly hung over his belt buckle. Not to mention the only thing that could get stiff on him were his arthritic joints. It was a fact that father time did unseemly things to a man, things he didn't want to acknowledge or even think about.

Such thoughts made him want to aim his gun at the woman and let fly just because he was angry with life – and rich folks such as the Biswell woman. She'd had an easy life, gotten all the good out of life without so much as lifting a finger. Unlike him, she'd never had to steal to keep from starving. He was certain a woman such as her was handed everything she'd ever wanted on a silver platter. He hated women like her. Hell, he hated men like her even more. They deserved to have everything taken from them.

He gritted his teeth, hunkered up in a tighter squat, and continued to watch as the woman went into the lot to pet and pamper the long-legged dog.

Why in the world Buckworth was foolish enough to pay good money for him to steal such a gangly, overgrown dog was beyond him. There were actually some dogs out there that would be a much better choice, but Buckworth never asked his opinion on anything.

Oh, well, the dog would make a good dog to train a Pit Bull how to go for the belly, but was this dog worth the price Buckworth would pay for stealing it? Rich women had the money to offer rewards. Oh, well, not his problem – only his job.

Doing his job had caused him to endure a miserable night and he had no intention of enduring another. He was going to get that dog one way or other. Today. The Kennel keeper was gone and hadn't come back, which was a good thing. He had no idea how often the keeper left the place, nor did he care. All he needed was one chance at the dog. With the keeper gone he was sure he could handle the woman, and would have loved doing so, but he reminded himself again that Buckworth was always a stickler for having a dog disappear without a trace or suspicion. If he wanted future jobs from Buckworth, he'd better do as he was told – pretty much, anyway.

He made a point of checking his tranquilizer gun to make sure everything was ready. He lifted his binoculars and studied the kennel and house again. The woman had come outside again. This time she was dressed in short britches, white shirt, and what appeared to be running shoes.

"Shit," he mumbled, as the woman went over to the dog lots. If she was taking that big male dog for a run, he'd have to wait longer to have at him – unless he somehow got loose from her and ran away.

The dog reared up on the chain link fence and stuck his head over the wire for the woman to pet him. No doubt about it, Buckworth was crazy to want this type of dog. The man didn't have the brains of a duck, but Buckworth had enough viciousness in him to make up for intelligence.

James chuckled silently as he thought about the men and dogs Buckworth was bringing in from down Atlanta way. Everybody knew what happened when those mob guys came in. Blood got shed that wasn't always dog blood, but as long as Buckworth paid him, nothing was his concern.

The woman was talking to the dog as she patted him on his huge head. He wasn't close enough to hear what the woman was saying, not that it mattered one iota. All that mattered was that she left without the dog. He almost held his breath – almost said a prayer to the powers that be for the woman to go away without the dog, but he wasn't the prayer-saying kind. Never had been, never would be. What happened, happened. Nothing more, nothing less.

The woman walked halfway to the gate leading to the main road, hesitated, turned around and came back, walked past the dog lots to the barn. She came back out with a long dog leash.

"Shit," James mumbled again. The woman wasn't leaving without the dog.

A sudden plan ran through his mind how he just might get the big dog to break loose from the hold the woman had on his leash. Dogs and men alike have instincts that drive them stronger than hunger and loyalty. It was the need to reproduce. He'd noticed that old man Sutton had a bitch dog in full heat when he'd driven by his place a day or so ago. There had been several male dogs hanging out around her lot while Sutton was at work. The male dogs couldn't get to her by climbing or digging. The lot had a tin roof and a concrete floor. All he had to do was open the gate and take her out. Sutton would think she had escaped.

The Sutton place was only a few miles away from where he was hiding. He could go through the woods back to his vehicle, drive to the Sutton place, get the bitch, and hopefully be back before the woman returned from her jaunt with the dog. If it took him longer, he'd still have the bitch as a lure for later.

Chapter 15

~~~~

It was late, almost dark when Griff got back home from his afternoon off. He'd gotten with a few of his barroom acquaintances and had a few more drinks than he usually did. Not that he was drunk, or anything like that. He was simply feeling more content and a lot sleepier than usual. A lay-down or even a short nap was what he craved.

He wasn't about to neglect his job, even if it was his day off. He checked the dog runs; their food and water were good. He frowned slightly when he came to Kang's run. It was empty, plus his food and water hadn't been touched. Why had Lady Biswell taken such a long outing with the dog? It wasn't like her, unless she decided to let Kang run free. Surely, she hadn't considering how restless the dog had been during the night and morning hours.

He didn't have time to think about it. Lady Biswell came running through the gate and headed straight for Griff. Her normally neat clothes were hanging out, dirty and ripped in several places. Her well-coiffured hair was a tangled mess sticking out in all directions. Her face was streaked with dirt and crisscrossed with bloody scratches. He knew instantly something had gone bad wrong.

"Thank the Lord you're back," she huffed as she ran up to him desperately grabbing his arms. "It's Kang. He got loose from me, and I can't find him."

"How did he get loose?" he asked.

"He became excited and lunged forward causing me to lose my balance. I fell down and dropped his lead. He took off toward the wooded area near the mountains. I went after him, called for him to come back, but I never caught sight of him again."

That was unusual. That dog minded her every command. "Was he chasing after something? Did he growl or bark?"

"No," she shook her head and gripped his arms tighter in desperation. "He seemed to know where he was going and was in a hurry to get there."

"He wasn't angry, whetting up for a fight then?"

"No, I don't think so."

Griff had never seen the dog wanting to fight. He was unusually well behaved for a stud dog his size.

"We've got to find him," she pleaded.

"He'll probably come back here," Griff was trying to be logical. "That dog would never leave your side for long."

"That's what I thought, but he has. I searched for hours and called until I'm hoarse. He simply disappeared."

"First, you need to call animal control and the sheriff's department to report him as missing. Then we'll take the four-wheeler and head out in the direction he ran. Maybe we can find some clues."

Chapter 16

~~~~

Norman James chuckled as he watched the woman and dog through his binoculars. The woman had such a loose hold on the leash, the dog had easily broken free from her. He hadn't expected the bitch dog to be sending out such a powerful scent from such a long distance. She certainly was ready for the male, and the male dog was more than willing to accommodate her.

James watched the big male run at full speed straight through the heavy undergrowth and into the wooded area where he waited with the bitch dog. When the male was within a hundred feet of the female, he laid down his binoculars and lifted the tranquilizer gun. The dart hit the dog in the hip with the first shot. The male was wobbling from the fast-acting shot when he reached the female. She whined happily as she twisted around turning her back in invitation to the male. He reared up on unstable legs a moment before he fell sideways onto the ground.

"Works every time," he chuckled as though the sight struck him as funny. "Nothing like a bitch in heat."

The female whined and pawed at the downed male. He unsnapped her leash and turned her loose to run in whichever direction she wanted. Much to his irritation, she bounced and twirled around the unconscious male. He kicked at the bitch and grabbed the male's hind legs and dragged him toward the four-wheeler. He needed to be long gone before the woman got close enough to hear the sound of the engine when he drove away.

"Damned heavy dog," he complained. He hadn't expected that long-legged, stringy-bodied dog to weigh as much as he did. Must be all muscle. The dog had to weigh a hundred fifty or sixty pounds – and it was all limber limbs and dead weight.

He tried to lift the front end of the dog onto the rack of the four-wheeler but found that the dog's back end dragged the front end off. He then tried to lift the backend in first. The dog slid off even faster. Finally, he got the dog centered on the rack and tied with the lead still around his neck. Sweating and irritated, he started the four-wheeler and headed through the woods. He hadn't gotten far when he stopped suddenly.

"Shit," he had almost forgotten about the tracks he had left behind. A good tracker might be able to read what happened. He broke off a handful of tall weeds, went back and brushed the ground with them from where the dog had fallen to where he'd stopped the four-wheeler. He wished he could brush out all the tire tracks through the woods, but it would take too long and end up being impossible. His best bet was to get his van he'd parked a mile away as fast as he could. He could already hear the woman calling for her dog.

Much to his irritation, the bitch dog followed behind him. He reached for his tranquilizer gun but changed his mind. He didn't want to leave an unconscious dog for someone to find. Let the bitch follow. Once he reached the van and drove the four-wheeler, he'd be able to leave the bitch far behind. She would eventually find another willing male before she found her way back home.

Norman James was feeling both pleased and irritated with himself. The miserable night he'd spent in the woods had his bones stiff and his head aching. He didn't want to admit it, but he just might be getting too old to enjoy doing such work. It was much easier to steal outright than to capture dogs. If Buckworth wanted bait dogs, he could go to the pound. It wouldn't be the best scenario for Buckworth's operation. The number of dogs required would cause a red flag, unless he used a variety of people to adopt dogs, and that wasn't an option. The more people who were involved, the greater the risk.

Yep, he was a much-needed asset to Buckworth's operation. The man ought to pay him extra for delivering this dog, especially since he didn't get to pilfer anything. Regretfully, there would be no chance of getting extra money out of Ronald Buckworth. Rumors had it Buckworth was in financial trouble. He was being screwed to the wall by the Atlanta mafia. Just to be on the safe side, he wouldn't turn over the dog until he got paid in cash.

Norman James pulled up to the shack where Buckworth kept dogs being trained along with ripped up dogs the butch woman was trying to keep alive. James neither liked nor disliked the woman. She was kind of a nonentity necessity for Buckworth.

The woman stood at the corner of the shack with her arms crossed as she waited for him to get out of the van.

"Got the dog. You got my money?" He didn't feel like wasting words or time with her.

"Buckworth wants the dog inspected before you're paid."

"He can have at it," James gritted his teeth. Buckworth always wanted to inspect the dogs as a stalling tactic in hopes he could browbeat him down on the price. It wasn't going to work this time.

"Bring the dog out," Alice ordered.

James said nothing more as he opened the back of the van, let the tailgate down, got in and drove the four-wheeler out. The dog hadn't come around, but he was twitching and making sounds.

"Looks half dead," Alice frown.

"Big dog. Gave him a strong dose. You can give him an antidote shot if you want him to wake up faster."

"Put him in the back enclosure while I get the antidote," The woman told him as she went inside the building.

James mumbled a slew of curse words as he drove the four-wheeler behind the building to the enclosure where he always left the stolen dogs. He considered letting the antidote take effect before he got the dog off the four-wheeler. Nope, best drag the heavy dog into the enclosure while he was still out cold. A dog that size could put a hurting on a man if he so chose. He could see the length of the gleaming white teeth sticking out of a drooling mouth. He unsnapped the fancy leash and stowed it in the van. He could get a few bucks by selling the fancy leash at a flea market.

Selling stolen goods at flea markets and yard sales were his way of bringing in extra cash. He preferred using yard sales to get rid of his stolen merchandise. He could set up anonymously and then disappear without a trace.

The woman returned with a syringe and a cell phone. She took a picture of the dog lying on the concrete before administering the shot. Cautiously, she backed out of the enclosed lot and closed the gate behind her.

James grinned. The woman wasn't taking careless chances.

"He's coming around," Alice needlessly said as the dog's muscles started twitching harder as he tried to lift his head, slobber drooling from his big mouth. "Once he's standing, I'll send these pictures to Buckworth, for him to approve your payment."

It was the same protocol Buckworth always put him through. This time he found it more irritating than normal. It would be easy enough to slug the woman out as cold as the dog and take all the cash along with everything of value. He could cover his deed by tossing the woman in with one of the aggressive pit bulls making it look like a dog kill. Buckworth would never report the woman's death. She would be buried the same way he buried the dead dogs. Good idea, thought of too late. She'd already let Buckworth know he was here, plus he was sure there were hidden cameras everywhere. Best to remain a legit business man for a while longer.

Chapter 17

~~~~

Kang opened his eyes in confusion. He had no idea where he was or what put him in such a place. He knew it wasn't his usual dog run. He tried to regain his senses, but his memory seemed dim and distant. The last things he remembered were the scent and sight of the bitch tied to a tree as he made for her. He'd bred before and he knew exactly what his mind and body longed for. Instead of accomplishing his desires, there had been a stab of pain in his hip, and now he was here on a slab of horrible concrete containing many fearful scents. The strange odors of urine, feces, blood and fear were surrounding him. He smelled his own scent of urine unwillingly leaking from his body.

A growl started deep in his chest and rose to his throat as he lifted his head and made an attempt to sit up. He was shaky, disoriented, and extremely angry. A strange sense of fear gripped his guts.

Instincts tugged at ancestral heredity bred into his DNA. His heredity was of fighting dogs. A Turkish breed of dog used to protect the flock, while strong enough to stand their ground as they fought to kill their enemies.

Kang looked about and saw no visible enemy other than his surroundings. Still, he sensed he was in great danger. A danger he could not understand or fight against at the moment.

"He's on his feet. Get another picture so I can get paid."

Kang instantly recognized the smell of the man and the sound of his voice. Both had reached him moments before everything went black. He still had the smell of the man on his body.

"You're deliberately wasting my time," Norman James told Alice with his usual impatience. "I've got better things to do than stand around here catering to the demands of a man like Buckworth. One of these days he'll get what's coming to him and so will you."

"Is that a threat?" the woman asked as her eyes narrowed to slits.

"No threat. Only stating a matter of fact. If you were smart, you'd get out while the getting is good. There's a lot of talk going around you know. According to rumor, this dog fighting ring is gonna get busted. Those Atlanta boys have set him up." His words of warning puzzled him. He didn't like the woman. Why should he give her advice?

"And you know this how?" she demanded.

"Rumor, gossip, having my ears close to the ground, call it whatever you want."

"And yet you stole this dog for him? Stealing dogs is a federal offence, you know."

"Way I see it, if worse comes to worse, you and I both can pull a plea bargain if we're caught, and we're willing to testify against Buckworth."

The woman remained silent as she snapped a picture of Kang through a crack in the gate, fastened the gate firmly, and hit send.

"How's the dog?" Buckworth texted back.

"Growling and angry."

"Good. What's your opinion of him? Did James bring in the right dog?"

"Affirmative on both counts."

"Pay him the agreed amount – no more, no less."

Once the man and woman left, Kang lay back down on the cold concrete in the corner of the enclosure. He eyed every inch of his surroundings in hopes of seeing a way to escape, but there was none. He couldn't dig through concrete. Even the overhead was enclosed. He started licking himself in an attempt to get the hated smell of the man off him. The hackles on his back raised. It was the smell of an enemy he would never forget.

He found himself longing for his mistress along with the familiar security of his home. Not having his body and brain able to work as they should was new to him. It was something he didn't understand and was eager to fight against, if only he knew what it was he needed to fight.

"He's not aggressive," The woman said.

He had been laying on the cold concrete for two days. He'd been given water to drink and stinking raw meat, which he hadn't been able to eat much of.

His stomach was rumbling. A new kind of angry desperation was building in him. It was called pure hatred.

"That will change soon enough," Ronald Buckworth told her. "He'll become as aggressive as the rest of the dogs. I know how to make 'em mean and so does Phillip, but first I've got to move my operation somewhere else. I got word those Atlanta crooks have set me up."

Alice wasn't the least bit surprised. Even Norman James knew it was coming.

"Before the crack of dawn tomorrow, several of my regular buddies will show up with equipment to take this place down to the ground. Last week they built a place better than this way back in the wilds on a piece of god-forsaken no man's land. Tranquilize all the dogs just as dark sets in. We'll be moving the dogs out at midnight."

"You should have warned me ahead of time. It won't be easy to have everything packed and all the dogs ready to move, even if they are tranquilized," she sounded accusing and irritated.

"I'm letting you know now," he said none to pleasantly.

"It takes time to prepare everything for such a move."

"You've got until midnight."

"I can't perform miracles."

"I know that, but I do expect you to get your ass in high gear. Pack everything up. You can sort everything out at the new place."

The woman gave an angry grunt but said no more. The man stopped looking at him through the crack in the enclosure gate. Anger and fear mixed together as Kang heard them both walking away.

Chapter 18

~~~~

Ronald Buckworth didn't have the money to buy a place for his operation and wouldn't have done so even if he had the money. He didn't want his name linked to anything. He'd been foolish to have the fighting ring on land he owned. Moving was the right thing to do. Those Atlanta boys had done him a favor without them ever knowing it.

Luckily, he found exactly what he wanted, almost. It was an old barn hidden in an overgrowth of virgin timber – along with laurel hells and kudzu vines. The land and barn were covered with the aggressive vines until the barn was almost impossible to spot from the air or on foot. The land backed up to the National Forest, which was even better.

The land and barn had belonged to a man named Otis Brown seventy years in the past. Thirty years before, Otis died, leaving behind a will. Everything went to his only son, Otis Brown, Jr. No one had seen hide or hair of Otis Jr. in thirty-five years. Junior got fed up with breaking his back working from sun up to sun down on a rocky, useless piece of dirt and headed west to seek his fortune and found himself a Texas wife instead. He obviously knew he had inherited his father's derelict, fallen-down house and still standing barn because he paid the taxes on it every year. According to Phillip Godard, Buckworth's go-fer and all-around piece of shit, the cashier's checks Brown sent were all postmarked from Texas.

If Phillip Godard ever had a full load in the brains department, that load had been shifted so many time things had been scrambled together in one big unpredictable mess. Ronald Buckworth didn't mind. Phillip was mean enough and crazy enough to do exactly what Buckworth told him to do.

"The man's dangerous," Alice had warned Buckworth. He has no soul, no sense of what's wrong and what's right."

Phillip Godard was a short, squatty man with a powerful looking build and a bald head. His face was pock marked from acne and a variety of other scars. It appeared that coal dust had become embedded in every crack and crevice of his face, neck and hands. She refused to imagine what the rest of his body looked like. He always had a greasy look about him that made Alice wonder if he ever bathed with a bar of soap. She made a point of never getting close enough to find out if he smelled rancid.

"Exactly what I need," Buckworth told her. "His looks alone scares folks."

"He's what you need until he doesn't do what you tell him to do," Alice pointed out. "Then he'll turn on you as brutally as he handles your dogs.

"That day will never come," Buckworth bragged. "He's devoted to me."

Sure, Alice thought, just like she, along with every dog in this place, was devoted to him. The only reason she was there was because of her love for the dogs and her hatred for the law. She was the only hope – the only salvation the dogs had. As for the law, in that area they were as corrupt as Buckworth and those crooks from Atlanta. At least after relocating in this hell hole, there was a chance Buckworth might avoid both the law and the Atlanta boys for a short period of time.

Alice gave him one of her silent looks. If Buckworth believed Phillip Godard would never go against him, then his load had shifted worse than Godard's had. Considering what Buckworth did for his living, that was already a given.

"This place isn't fit for a dog," Alice informed him.

"It'll do. You can turn the hog pens out back into your very own hospital after you get paid for saving other men's dogs."

"And until then?" she questioned.

"Use one of the back stalls in the barn. I'll have Godard take the two front stalls out and use the extra room and lumber to build a fighting ring."

Chapter 19

~~~~

Years had come and gone since the death of Striker's dad – years of learning to live regardless of how difficult her struggles became, and there were times when they had become extremely difficult. She remembered the time when she thought she was dying from an injury, only to search in book after book to find out every girl bled when she turned into a woman. It was another lesson in life she had learned the hard way. Thank goodness her dad had brought her books. She hadn't seen bleeding from animals, but then most of the animals she observed were birds and insects. Neither birds or insects bled when they came into season although some had interesting behavior. Take the praying mantis for instance. The female ate the male while he was mating with her. It was after his death that his seed released itself into the female. Bees were another species she found interesting. It was only one female called the queen that laid all the eggs to keep the species going. The queen came about by the worker bees feeding her, and only her, royal jelly. It made her grow big and strong and fertile. When she was ready, a drone bee mated with her.

If the worker bees happened to mess up and feed another larva bee the royal jelly, two queens were accomplished. Two queens would not live together. Therefore, they formed a swarm where one queen and her followers had to leave to form another hive of their own. This was Strikers simple conclusions after reading about bees.

She had learned from reading books that she would never reproduce as long as there was no male human to dump his seed into her, which, in a way, was a relief. Yet, in another way, there were times when she longed for another human being – a baby she could hold in her arms and mother. She wouldn't be nearly as lonely if she had a baby. She and her dad weren't as lonely when they had each other. However, her loneliness wasn't nearly as important as her daily need to survive. If she had been able to reproduce, she wasn't sure she'd be able to provide for herself and a baby – but she and her dad has survived better.

Her expertise with the bow and arrow resulted in thinning out the animal population. She didn't understand how living there for years with her dad had not wiped out the animal population, but she seemed to have done so. She had to travel farther and farther away in search of game. Even the turkeys had left the mountain, leaving her with no hope of finding eggs.

Food was the thing she sought every daylight hour. Her small garden was the one stable thing that kept her alive. Unfortunately, it took a tremendous amount of time. If she left the garden unguarded, the few remaining animals, birds and crows were certain to devour it. If she stayed in the garden guarding it, she couldn't set traps or hunt for game.

The only way she could secure her crop was to kill the animals that devoured them and hang their bodies in the garden. It worked well with crows. Not so good with some of the other animals such as rabbits and squirrels. Setting traps in and around her garden helped save her vegetables. At the same time, it helped to provide her with a little meat protein for her meager meals. She was surprised by how little food her body required to live on.

Good and bad always had tradeoffs with each other. Unfortunately, the bad seemed to overpower the good.

Back when her dad was alive, she hadn't realized how important it was having two people to watch after things.

There were far too many things for one person to attend to. She also realized how much his trips off the mountain contributed to their survival. Animal skins, ginseng, and other herbs paid for the necessities they needed that could not be gleaned from nature. There was no getting such necessities now that he was gone.

She now used animal skins to make clothing and herbs for medicine. There was no longer a need for her to gather ginseng and herbs for anything other than her personal use. She did not know where to take them to trade even if she had wanted. In time she had become little more than a wild animal struggling for her own survival. Animals were a danger, but not nearly the danger of surviving a long cold winter. There was an equal chance of starving to death versus freezing to death. Keeping enough deadfall wood to keep her stove giving off a little warmth was a full-time job. Fortunately, at least she sometimes considered it fortunate, the fierce winds, heavy snows, and ice storms brought down limbs and sometime trees. On occasions she would resort to cutting down a tree, but not often. The image of her dad lying beneath the tree haunted her.

Winter was arriving fast. The winds held a stinging chill, and the timber seemed to have changed color overnight. She had to spend extra time gathering acorns, hickory nuts, and late season apples for drying if she was to survive winter. She had already picked wild blackberries and raspberries and dried them on flat rocks. She had also gathered all the raspberry and blackberry leaves she could find to dry for medicine. Just as important as the fruit and herbs were to her survival, she had to kill animals for winter meat as well as for hides to make winter clothing.

To accomplish this, she would have to travel a longer distance from her mountain. Thankfully, the government forest land covered thousands of uninhabited acres. Yet, she never felt safe going into an unfamiliar area, but she had no other choice if she wanted to survive.

Preparing meat for winter had been much easier when her dad had gone off the mountain to bring home salt. Their supply of salt had run out last fall when she salted down a deer. The time it took to slice the thin meat strips to dry in the sun was tremendous, but it had to be done. She also put thin slices of meat on top of the little heating stove with a warm fire in the grate to dry meat. If she killed a deer during winter months, she could always keep the meat frozen, but it was risky. Raw, frozen meat drew animals almost as fast as rotting meat.

She'd read stories in her books about how bears would hibernate during the winter, but she had discovered it wasn't true – at least for the most part. Sow bears tended to go into a longer sleep pattern than boar bears, especially if they were to have cubs.

Boar bears left their dens to search for food regardless of how cold the winter weather. Boar bears were large, dangerous and hard to kill. Most dangerous were sow bears in the spring when they had cubs and were searching for enough food to produce milk. The mother bear's protective instinct toward her babies was something Striker admired. Often a longing grew in her chest for a mother to protect her.

The lack of small animals and birds near her cabin was a blessing and a curse. The blessing was more berries for her to gather. The curse was more berries to attract bears.

She would love to have a nice fat bear for its hide, grease and meat, but she had never killed one on her own. She remembered the time her dad killed one when he was robbing a bee tree. The sweet taste of honey was a treasured treat she and her dad seldom had. Trouble was bears loved its taste as much as they did.

She had been with her dad carrying a basket that was tightly woven out of reeds and sealed with pine rosin to carry the honey home in. She'd had her little bow, while her dad carried his big bow and a smoldering torch to smoke the bees with. He must have had a premonition about what would happen because he told her if a bear showed up, she wasn't to run. She was to hide behind a large tree and not move.

"Bears have excellent vision," he told her. "They see in color the same as people do. They're also quick to detect any movement. That's why you need to hide and not move. Remember animals can always run faster than you."

Her dad positioned her in thick undergrowth to keep from getting bee stung while he climbed the tree. "Once I get 'em smoked calm, come out of the undergrowth. I'll toss down the torch and you toss up the basket. Grab the torch quick to make sure it catches nothing on fire."

He'd swung his bow and arrows over his shoulder to hang on his back while climbing with one hand and holding the lit torch with the other. She had no concern about her dad falling. He never had.

Once her dad was near the hollow in the tree where the bees had their stash of honey, he gathered green leaves and wrapped them around the slowly burning torch. The leaves sizzled and put out a plume of smoke. The bees swarmed around him and she knew he was being stung even though he'd worn all the clothes he had. He didn't seem to mind. After a lot of smoke and a few bad words, her dad called for her to come out and toss up the basket. He dropped the torch while she tossed up the basket and grabbed the smoking torch.

She held the torch in front of her as she watched her dad use his hands to shovel out honey comb dripping with honey. She heard a noise and looked behind her as a huge black bear stood up on its hind feet sniffing the air. It was no more than eight feet from where she stood. Her first thought was to run. Her second thought was to get behind a tree, but she'd have to run.

"Dad!" she yelled, causing the bear to turn toward her with a vicious growl focused straight at her. Fear, and her dad's warning not to run, had her frozen to the spot.

A loud whistle pierced the air. She and the bear both looked up the tree where her dad was. At the same time an arrow whizzed inches over her head into the bear's chest.

"Run! Hide!" her dad yelled as a maddened roar came from the bear. Its paws flailed at the few inches of shaft sticking out of its chest. Her dad had put enough power behind the arrow to all but bury the shaft in the thick hide.

She ran behind the bee tree as another arrow hit the bear in the side of the neck. Instead of killing the bear, it became even more enraged with the pain. Her dad whistled again as another arrow hit the bear in the shoulder. The bear ignored the arrow in the shoulder as it headed for the bee tree. Striker shrunk up as small as she could make herself, but the bear wasn't after her. All four paws dug into the tree bark as it started its climb toward her dad.

She hadn't intended to move – hadn't realized she had until she jabbed the burning torch to the back end of the bear. The bear paid the torch no attention. The pain from the arrows were greater than the smoldering torch singing its fur.

Her dad was doing his best to shoot arrows into the bear's face and head, but the tree branches were hindering his aim and blocking the arrows. She stepped into the clearing, dropped the torch and shot an arrow at the bear. The arrowhead punctured the hide but went no further. The bear was still climbing when the smoldering flames drew wind and caught the bear's fur on fire.

Flames covered the bear's hindquarters. It let out a roar as its head turned toward the flames. Its front paws flailed, trying to rip its fur off. Its hind paws lost grip on the bark and it tumbled down the trunk hitting the ground with a thud.

"Hide!" her dad yelled. She wasted no time taking cover behind another tree, but she didn't stop shooting her arrows and neither did her dad until the bear disappeared through the underbrush.

"Stay here!" her dad yelled as his feet hit the ground. "Grab that torch and put the fire out."

She picked up the torch and kicked dirt on the charred ground. It was pure luck the ground was wet, and no leaves or bramble had caught fire. She didn't stay there. She ran after her dad, trying to stay in sight of him. Following offered no problem. The bear and her dad were leaving a trail of torn up ground and broken limbs.

Her legs were aching, and breath was coming hard when she finally caught up with her dad. He was standing near a mud wallow watching the bear roll and kick.

"I told you to stay put," her dad said.

"Couldn't," she managed to get out.

"Why not?"

"Thought you might need the torch."

Her dad nodded in a thoughtful sort of way. "The bear's dying," he said. "We're lucky it didn't leave a fire trail through the woods instead of a blood trail."

And that was all her dad had to say about her setting the bear's fur on fire.

They went back after the basket of honey. It took all that evening and into the night to cut up the bear meat and haul it home in their sled. Her dad dragged the muddy hide to the creek and anchored it with rocks, so the water would wash it clean. Once the hide was clean, he'd use the bear's brains to tan the hide.

Chapter 20

~~~~

Ronald Buckworth watched Phillip Godard worked with Kang. Phillip had a special knack for cruelty. He knew how to push a dog to its limit, how to make an animal hate, how to push Kang until he was willing to fight. Death was the only thing that would make the dog stop fighting – or Alice and her break rod.

"He's a fast learner," Phillip told Buckworth as the roar of dogs fighting filled the air. "He's put on pounds and gained muscle. Most important, he's learned how to fight. See how quickly he ripped into the bait dog?" Phillip shook his head in amazement. "Have to admit, you know your dogs for a fact. When I first laid eyes on that scrawny dog, I wouldn't have given a plug nickel for his fighting ability. Legs too long, temperament too reserved. He changed."

"You changed him," Ronald said. "Same as you change all the dogs."

"Fight or die is what I teach 'em," Phillip bragged. "Want me to let him finish the bait dog off or stop the fight?"

"Finish him off. No need to spend time doctorin' a wounded bait dog. Easy enough to pick up bait dogs."

Alice listened to them talk from a different room. She gritted her teeth in a mixture of anger and disgust. She didn't know which she hated worse, Ronald Buckworth or Phillip Godard. Both were the scum of the earth, bottom feeders, evil to their very core. How she'd love to see them put in a ring to fight each other until death. If that ever occurred, they might be glad if someone called to stop the fight. They might then be glad for someone like her to patch up their wounds in an effort to keep them alive. In other words, they might appreciate her instead of looking down on her as nothing more than a necessity.

"Is he ready for the upcoming fight against Harris Markson's dog, Brutus? You know how tough that dog is. He's killed every dog he's gone up against before Alice could break his hold."

"He's also suffered some mighty bad wounds. Sometimes the pain and suffering does something to a dog's brain. Sometimes it puts a kind of fear in them that makes them hesitate."

"Or makes them meaner than a sack full of devils," Buckworth pointed out.

"That's a fact. It can go either way. A man never knows."

"This Kangal dog has gotten meaner than I expected," Buckworth needlessly pointed out.

"And smarter," Phillip added. "You can see it in his eyes. Pure hatred shines out of 'em. I know better than to turn my back to him. He'd rather attack me than another dog."

Alice was listening from another room. She knew better than to turn her back on either of them.

~~~~

Two armed men stood at the gate, a heavy chain stretched between two posts, stopping vehicles, so they could inspect and search. The men they knew and approved were let through the gate and told to park in the woods where their vehicles couldn't be seen. The vehicles containing crated dogs were sent up the narrow dirt pathway to the barn. The men whom the guards didn't know were told to go back the way they had come with a warning they'd best not return. The guns the men carried were deterrents for arguments. No one was allowed in unless they were vouched for by a reliable regular. Buckworth knew better than to take chances on strangers – along with some of the men he knew all too well.

At the old barn, security was even tighter. Several of the toughest looking regulars were scattered about, armed to the teeth with rifles and shotguns. Buckworth wasn't taking any chances. He figured he wouldn't be able to keep his operation at this place too long since traffic left tracks and tracks into a deserted place eventually got checked out. Being able to pick up and leave in a hurry was the beauty of a place such as this. No money involved – no loss. One never knew what might come about. It was best to always be prepared.

Ten competitors had paid to enter their dogs to fight. Buckworth's dog, King's Ransom, was signed up to go against Brutus, Markson's dog. Most were standard fighting bulldogs, but occasionally dogs of different breeds were brought in to fight each other. Buckworth called them oddball fighters. Such fights drew a lot of interest and higher bets as one never knew for sure how the dogs would fight. Odds were against King's Ransom as he was twenty pounds lighter than the heaver Brutus, but weight wasn't a consideration in such fights. Sometimes the smaller dog could be faster and more vicious than the larger dog.

Buckworth had little confidence in King Ransom's winning the fight. He had one of his trusted buddies place a thousand dollar bet on Brutus. He had a rule about the owners of a dog betting against their own dogs. Men were too willing to sacrifice their dogs for cash, which was exactly what Buckworth was doing tonight. A man in desperate need of money was willing to resort to desperate measures.

When bets were getting ready to be made, the first two dogs were brought into the ring on stout leads and taken to their corners so bettors could take a closer look at them. The first two dogs were standard-sized bulldogs, weighing between fifty-five and sixty pounds each. They were short-legged bulldogs standing no more than eighteen inches at the shoulders. Smaller dogs were considered bantam weight dogs. Larger dogs were heavyweights. Then there were the oddball fights that King and Brutus were participating in. These fights drew a lot of interest and entertainment. Sometimes for these special events a bobcat or even a mountain lion was brought in to go against dogs.

Once the bets were placed, the dogs were readied for the fight to begin. Each dog's handler approached the rival dog with a bucket of soapy water, wash cloth and towel. The dogs were thoroughly washed to remove any poison or capsicum that could get into the opponent's mouth or blinding agent that might hinder another dog's fighting ability. After the washing, Alice entered the ring and drew a vial of blood from a vein in each dog's front leg. Some of the dog owners didn't approve of such and made a point of standing over the handlers and Alice to inspect everything they did. The owners and handlers relunctly allowed Alice to test the dogs to lessen the likelihood of a dog being pumped full of drugs that would enhance their fighting ability. Some even demanded she draw two vials, so they could double check Alice's blood samples to make sure she didn't cheat. She never did, but dog fights weren't based on trust and goodwill.

Once all the other dogs had fought, and fresh sawdust applied, the oddballs were brought in to fight. The roar of the battle was fierce. Flesh from each dog was ripped open. Blood turned the sawdust a soggy red.

King's Ransom went down. Brutus, the big mix breed Saint Bernard-Mastiff-Pitbull had him by the throat. His fangs had sunk mere centimeters from his jugular and windpipe. Still, Buckworth didn't call the fight. Brutus had to win. Had too. He needed money more than he need the dog.

Alice was crossing the dirt floor to Buckworth when she saw how badly King's Ransom was faring. "Call it," she demanded of Buckworth.

He didn't say a word, didn't even acknowledge her presence. No way was he going to call the fight. He'd let his best dog's throat be ripped out before he'd call it. It was Alice who grabbed the breaking rod, squatted slightly for leverage and sprang her powerful body over the four-foot wall of the fighting pit.

"I'm calling it!" she shouted as she rammed the rod in the side jaw of Brutus's mouth and twisted. It loosened Brutus' bite, but the big mix breed held on while roaring his killing rage.

"Get in here," Alice yelled to Brutus' owner, Harris Markson, or I'll break out every tooth in his mouth."

"Don't you harm my dog," Harris Markson yelled a warning at Alice, but he was too much of a coward to go into a fighting ring especially when his own dog was winning the kill. Dogs that are fighting mad turn on people more often than not. How that woman hadn't been ripped apart long before now, he didn't know.

"I'll break 'em!" Alice shouted as she twisted the rod hard. Brutus loosened his grip a little more, but not enough. Alice knew if she jerked the pry rod, she'd be taking a chance of also causing the dog's powerful fangs to rip the juggler.

A man Alice only knew as Blackburn jumped the enclosure, ran to the fighting dogs and clamped his huge hands around Brutus' neck. His hands became a vice squeezing breath from Brutus. The dog loosened his hold on King Ransom's neck, opened his jaws wide enough to jerk away from the pry rod in an effort to sink his teeth into Blackburn.

"Go for his back legs. I can't turn him lose," Blackburn told Alice.

She grabbed the dog by the hind legs, the muscles in her arms, chest and back burning as she heaved up the weight of the big, heavy dog. "Now!" she yelled to Blackburn as she began the half circle swing of the dog. She let go of the hind legs letting the dog fly over the enclosure into the crowd of bystanders. The crowd parted at a run, in case Brutus was still wanting to fight, but fight was no longer raging in the big dog. He appeared stunned and confused by what had just happened.

Seeing that Brutus was no longer in a fighting mood, Harris Markson rushed to his dog, snapping a collar and lead around his neck. He didn't care if the opponent-dog was alive or dead. He had won. Brutus would live to fight another time.

Alice called for the plywood slab used to carry dead and injured dogs out of the pit. One of the men threw it over the wooden barrier. Blackburn got it and helped Alice lift the injured dog on it. He then helped her carry the dog to an adjacent shack of a building where she had rigged up to be her surgery.

Chapter 21

~~~~

Ronald Buckworth and Phillip Godard had spent hours, days, and months baiting and tormenting Kang until his fury was at its peak. This dog was Buckworth's chance to win the fight against Harris Markson's dog, Brutus. It had been months since the fight between King's Ramson and Brutus. Alice had managed to save King's Ramson'slife, but he no longer had the will to fight. Buckworth wasn't sure if that vicious fighting rage would ever return to King's Ramson. If not, he'd only be fit to use as a bait dog.

All his time and effort had gone into getting Kang in top fighting condition. The dog had spirit and guts. Kang wasn't a quitter. His continuous torture had brought out his wolf instincts full force, yet Buckworth wasn't entirely sure the long-legged dog would be a killer dog in the pit. Not only would Kang have to be willing to fight like hell was on fire, he'd have to be smart enough and quick enough to counter Brutus' fighting technique of going for the throat or belly. Long legs and a non-hairy throat meant payday for Brutus. However, Kang appeared to be ready to fight anything and everything as Phillip Godard led the dog to the fighting ring on a choke chain. It was obvious the dog longed to turn on his handler or anyone else who got close him. Kang's eyes were burning with rage as slobber dripped from his mouth. His entire body was quivering with the need to avenge his anger.

"That dog's rabid," one man called out. "Look how he's slobbering."

"He's a crazy devil," another added. "Look at him. He wants to kill his handler."

"Two crazy devils," the man named Blackburn added to stir up the crowd even more. Blackburn had placed a small amount of bet-money on Kang even though he feared the dog had a better than average chance of losing the fight. He'd watched Brutus fight several times and knew what a neck-ripper he was. He'd never seen Kang fight. Buckworth had kept Kang and his fighting abilities hidden from the public. Bets had already been placed before Phillip Godard brought Kang into view.

Everybody there knew Brutus' reputation. They had also heard rumors to how desperately Buckworth was in need of a big win. The man had to try almost anything to stay afloat – even putting a long-legged, short-haired, stringy-built dog into the fighting ring against a killer dog such as Brutus.

The crowd became excited. Not only did they place bets, they reveled in seeing the blood, gore and the desperation of a dying dog. The longer the fight, the more ripping and tearing of flesh, the better.

Markson's handler led Brutus into the center of the ring to the cheers of the crowd. The crowd could tell by looking that the dog was back in top condition and eager to fight. This was the dog most of them placed their bets on. Even Buckworth had secretly placed a bet on Brutus. He was hedging his losses in case Kang didn't perform.

Alice did something she had never done before. She also placed a bet – on Kang. She had seen something in the dog Buckworth hadn't seen. Not only did she see intelligence and cunning, she saw his determination to never give up.

Buckworth had not gained enough courage to lead Kang into the center of the ring. He had Alice do it instead. If the muzzle ever came off Kang when Phillip Godard was near, he would have torn the man to shreds. Alice led Kang into the center of the pit, although she was glowering at Buckworth and Godard as viciously as the dog she led.

It was obvious Kang was readying himself to fight man or beast. Brutus was more than ready as he strained against the lead wanting to get at Kang. His lips were curled back showing inch long fangs and roared his challenge sounding like an angry bull. Kang wasn't showing his fangs or pulling on the lead. He knew what was to come and wasn't about to waste one ounce of fighting energy before it was time. Godard heard the deep rumbling growl coming from deep inside Kang chest and was thankful he was now focused on Brutus and not on him.

"Ready your dogs," the ref called out. "Unleash your dogs."

Each owner unsnapped their dogs choke collars and made a run for the gates of the enclosure. The ref was out of the ring first. No one wanted to be in the ring when two crazed, dogs were fighting.

Alice leaned against the enclosure with her prybar in her hand. She had no intention of allowing Kang to be killed. If Kang went down, she'd call it – even if Buckworth raised holy-hell and docked her meager pay.

Kang did not check himself or go straight in to meet the charge coming from Brutus. He leaped sideways, dodging Brutus' attack. The big mix breed was too sure of himself. He'd fought many fights in which he'd depended on brute strength and intimidation.

Kang's wild instincts were to dodge the attack and then go in. Kang whirled and went for Brutus' back leg, but the Brutus was quick. He whirled, and Kang's fangs only ripped a gash in Brutus' hip, which enraged Brutus to the point of blind daring. Kang met Brutus' next charge shoulder to shoulder. The impact was so great it caused both dogs to miss their strike at each other's throat. Brutus' fangs sliced Kang's shoulder. Kang's fangs caught Brutus' face, ripping a gash from his eye toward his nose. Both dogs had drawn blood flow.

Renewed rage hit Brutus making him careless with his next charge. Both dogs met head on, missing the throat with mouth locking onto mouth. Lips gashed open with more blood flowing into the sawdust of the dirt pit floor. Brutus dropped in an attempt to break the mouth grips in hopes he would have success in going under the long-legged dog to rip out his guts.

Kang dropped and rolled with him. Kangal dogs were bred to fight the big cats whose main ability was dropping to the ground and using their hind claws to rip a dog's guts out. Natural instinct served Kang well. He rolled away from Brutus and went into a snarling crouch. He waited on Brutus' charge which happened in the blink of an eye. Kang got hold of what he was after, Brutus' front leg. His powerful jaws locked down until the bone crunched, breaking Brutus' front leg. It was a near victory hold for Kang, but it hadn't come without a price. Brutus' fangs sunk into the back of Kang's neck ripping flesh and muscles from the neck down his front shoulder.

Bitter rage filled both dogs. Never had Brutus had his legs attacked much less broken. Rage was also in Kang, but not a blind rage such as was in Brutus. Kang never forgot that his enemy was also in like passion to rend and destroy. Kang wanted to destroy Brutus, but he knew not to rush. A broken leg was a near death toll, but it might not stop the big dog from locking onto Kang's throat. He backed off and waited to receive Brutus' next rush of attack. It came delivered on three legs.

Kang had learned one lesson very well. He either mastered or was mastered. Showing mercy had become a weakness. Such a thing as mercy could no longer exist in Kang's world. Mercy and weakness were also a sign of fear. To show fear was an open invitation to be killed. In the world

Kang now existed, it was kill or be killed, eat or be eaten, fight to survive or die.

Kang dropped and rolled to the side dodging a frontal attack. Brutus ripped a gash along Kang's backbone, but Kang's jaws latched onto what he went after. The other front leg. He held on until he felt the bone crush. As the big mixed breed went down, Kang got hold of what every dog's instinct went after. The throat. Kang's fangs were a fraction of an inch longer than the mix breed's. They hit the juggler. Blood squirted over Kang's face and into his eyes, but he held on for dear life. Brutus kept struggling, fighting with ever fiber in him to break Kang's hold. He couldn't.

Alice gripped the prybar. She was ready to jump the enclosure wall and pry Kang's jaws loose, but Harris Markson didn't call it. He and everyone else knew there was no need. It was better to let Brutus die now than to have his life prolonged. If Alice made an attempt to clamp the juggler, all she could possibly accomplish was causing Brutus to live a few minutes longer.

Once Brutus twitched his last, Alice still had to go in and break Kang's hold on Brutus' neck. A vicious growl was still rumbling deep in Kang's chest.

"That's one brave woman," someone in the crowd said.

"One foolish woman if you ask me," another said.

"I'd hate to fight her," another chimed in. "She could whip all of us put together."

Blackburn grinned. He admired what was inside Alice. He wasn't sure if it was strength, kindness, or plain determination. Whatever it was, she had an abundance of it.

"Bring the slab," Alice called out when she saw how badly Kang was injured.

Blackburn brought her the slab and helped her move Kang onto it.

"Easy boy," Alice crooned soothingly as she checked Kang's massive injuries. "I've got you. I'll have you sewn up in no time. You'll make it, boy. You'll make it," she added as though trying to convince herself more than she was trying to convenience the dog.

Blackburn watched her handle the dog with approval. He carried one end of the slab wanting to help this woman in any way he could.

Chapter 22

~~~~

Kang knew the woman was trying to help him. He felt the gentleness in her hands and understood the meaning of her softly spoken whispers. He welcomed the numbing shots she injected near his wounds. Without as much pain, he attempted to get to his feet, but lacked the strength to do more than raise his head.

"Easy boy," the woman whispered. "You're weak from blood loss. I've got to get you sewn up and pump some more blood into you"

Blood for a transfusion was the only good thing about having bait dogs. Their blood could save the life of another dog. She mumbled under her breath exactly what she'd like to do to Buckworth and the men like him.

Kang closed his eyes and didn't move. In his mind he was reliving the days of his puppyhood, reliving the time he had known nothing but love from Lady Biswell.

"How's that damned dog?" Buckworth yelled as he came into the small room Alice used as a surgery.

Speak of the devil and he shows up, Alice thought when she heard his voice. "Weak," she told him. She hated dog fighting and the men who profited from its cruel practice. Most of all, she hated Phillip Godard and Buckworth.

"Can you save him?" Buckworth demanded. "Make him fit to fight again?"

"It's questionable."

"If he can't fight, let him die. Don't waste time and effort for no reason."

Alice gritted her teeth for a moment before she spoke. "His injuries were far more than the other dog's, and yet he killed his opponent. That says a lot in favor of this dog getting well. One thing is for sure, he surprised everybody. Even you'll have to admit he's one hell of a fighter."

"He did earn enough money to get me out of a damned hole. Reckon he just might be worth the time and effort to get him well and then see if he can do it again."

The sound of Buckworth's voice penetrated Kang's peaceful stupor. A hate-filled growl sounded in his chest. His instinct was to come up off the table and leap for the man's jugular, but the weakness inside him held him down.

"Easy," Alice tried to sooth the angry dog. "Easy boy."

"What's the matter with that damned dog?" Buckworth asked.

"He still wants to fight," Alice told him. "He's the kind that will fight until his last breath."

Alice gently caressed one of the few uninjured spots on Kang's back. The feel of her gentle hand reminded him again of his much-loved Lady Biswell. He settled down slightly, but his greatest desire was to attack the man who had helped make his life a living hell.

~~~~

Striker had her dad's bow slung over her shoulder and his knife strapped to her side. Her clothes consisted of a strip of deer skin with her head stuck through the center. She'd cut away the part that would impede her arms. The skin reached her mid-thigh although she wished it had been longer. The more the skin covered, the less likely another deer would pick up her scent.

She found a spot the deer used beneath an oak tree. She could see deer tracks and several newly fallen acorns. She found a concealed spot in the undergrowth where she would be downwind of the deer.

The lesson of patience was something her dad had taught her. Hunger and time had driven the lesson home. She no longer expected anything to happen fast. If she wanted something, she had to work hard and then wait.

She didn't like being out in the wooded mountain range after darkness arrived. She judged how long she had been hiding in the undergrowth against the amount of light in the woods. It was late evening, she decided. After the sun had gone down and the shadows were darkening was the perfect time for deer to find food before they bedded down for the night. Thing was, she was on another mountain range over from her cabin. If she killed a deer, she would be dragging it home during the darkness of night, but it was the price she'd have to pay.

She was getting ready to stand up and go home when she heard the faintest sound followed by a snort. She didn't move, didn't even breathe. A minute later two deer appeared beneath the oak tree. A doe and her spring fawn. The doe was a big old gal. Her size said she'd been around for several years. She had snorted as an act of caution instead of picking up Striker's scent. If Striker got her, it would be a long, heavy haul to drag her home. The fawn was a male with small horn buds showing on his head. His weight was more than Striker's weight, and that meant he was big enough.

She had the arrow fitted in the crossbow and pointing toward the oak tree. Deer had poor eyesight, but they were good at picking up movement, even better at smelling danger. That was why she stayed downwind and kept her crossbow ready to fire. There was only a slight wheezing sound an instant before the young buck crumpled to his knees. The doe disappeared before Striker could let out the breath she'd been holding.

She placed another arrow in the crossbow and fired it behind the deer's front leg into the heart, inches from where the first arrow has struck.

"Best to kill 'em with the first shot," her dad always told her. "If you're not sure they're dead, put the second arrow through the heart. A wounded animal will kill you, but almost as important is never allow them to suffer. It's the least you can grant them in return for taking their life."

Striker took the knife from the scabbard and swiftly slit the deer's throat to bleed it before the heart's pulsing stopped. Otherwise, there would be blood throughout the meat. She then slit open its belly and took out the guts, making it weigh less and be easier for her to drag it home. She knew the smell of blood and guts would draw wild animals, but it could also provide them food long enough while she got herself and her kill safely home.

~~~~

Kang's survival instinct became equal to those of his wild ancestors. A strong will to survive his many injuries was surging through his veins. The woman's care and administrations had garnered him a surge of renewed strength. He no longer wanted to attack the woman who treated him, but not for a moment, did he consider staying near the woman or allowing her to feed and care for him any longer than he was forced to do so. She had the same smell about her as the men and fighting dogs. She was one of them. Even though she had saved his life, she was his enemy.

Kang was determined to get out of that place the first chance he got. He was intelligent enough to remain docile and bide his time until the right opportunity presented itself.

When the woman came near him, his only attempt at standing on his own four legs was to eat and drink. At such times he wobbled unsteadily, which, at first, wasn't always faked weakness. He had lost a lot of blood and knew he needed rest and lots of good food to bring recovery.

This time he not only smelled the woman's scent coming toward him, he smelled the fresh raw meat she was carrying. He wanted the meat, needed it. A gush of saliva rushed to his mouth causing him to slobber hungrily. His instinct was to stand and lunge for the meat as soon as the woman opened the door, but he knew better than to stand, much less lunge. Something almost human in the dog's reasoning told him once he was strong again, the woman would hand him over.

Much to his anger, the meat was not brought to him. Instead, he got wind of his two hated enemies, Buckworth and Godard.

Two other injured dogs the woman had been treating from injuries, were now being handed over when they were barely recovered. Both of the dogs started whining in fear as soon as the men's scent reached them. The dogs whining had turned into whimpering when the two men entered the room with the woman.

"How are they doing?" Buckworth had asked the woman as he stepped into the room to look at the four dogs lying down in their separate cages. Godard remained silent.

"The Pit Bull might be good enough to leave. The Rottweiler is definitely ready to go. He's been here for almost two weeks. He's one mean sucker, I can verify that for a fact," she said. "He tries to attack me every time I feed him."

"And the other two?" Buckworth asked impatiently.

"The Saint Bernard is coming along. He'll be ready to go next week."

"What about the Kangal," Buckworth asked with an uncaring impatience.

"He didn't have the long hair to protect him the way two of the dogs did. His wounds were deeper and more severe. It will take another week if not two before he's ready to go back into training, much less into the fighting pit."

"Are you sure about that?" Buckworth demanded with his usual flare of impatience.

"He's still wobbling when he stands, and he's not eating his food the way he should."

"If you ask me, you seem rather partial to that dog."

"Humph," she let out a disgusted grunt. "I'm not partial to anything, living or dead. I do my job and that's it."

Godard let out a derogatory laugh. "You told the truth that time," he said. "Keep the damned dog as long as it takes. I'm not going to pussy-foot around with a weakling dog. Weaklings are only good as sacrifices to train the killers on. If he doesn't heal properly, he'll become a bait dog."

Buckworth nodded in agreement.

Both Kang and Alice had seen what happened to the bait dogs. They did their best to put up a good fight, but always lost. Their bodies were ripped to pieces, flesh shredded from their bones, while Godard shouted encouragements to the killer dog.

What they did turned Alice's stomach, as did Godard and Buckworth, but she always held her tongue, along with doing everything in her power not to witness such an abomination.

Kang wasn't so lucky. He was forced to watch and participate in the fights. In a matter between fighting or dying. He had chosen to fight.

Godard had done a mighty fine job of teaching him how to hate along with how to fight. Those were two lessons he learned well and would never forget. Yet, so far, he had been the tougher, stronger dog, but he was also intelligent enough to know such wouldn't always be the case. His last fight had proven that much to him. His choice was between gaining his freedom or certain death.

After Buckworth and Godard left, the woman brought him ground up raw meat instead of the soupy slurry that passed as food. She watched as Kang slowly inched his way on his belly toward the raw meat. He longed to guzzle it down in one fast gulp but knew better. He ate a small bite, laid his head down and whined as though he was in pain.

"Humph," the woman mumbled to herself. "This bottle of vitamins is empty. I'll have to go back to the storage room for another bottle."

She closed his cage door, but the latching click didn't sound to Kang's sensitive hearing. Thinking the cage door had latched, she left the outside door to the room cracked. Kang had a view of the outside world – and freedom. He did not hesitate. He gulped the hunk of raw meat in his mouth the same instant he made a run for the crack in the door. He almost knocked the woman over as she saw what he was doing and made a pitiful attempt to stop him. His powerful lunge for freedom had caught her off guard and she fell flat.

"Hell fire," she mumbled as she got to her feet and watched him streak across the outside enclosure, his body bunched and his hind legs served to spring him upward. He scaled the fence of the enclosure as easily as an overgrown house cat could have done. All she saw was a tan streak disappear into the woods.

"If that don't beat all," she shook her head in bewilderment. "What am I to tell Buckworth? Most likely he'll try to take the cost of the dog out of my measly pay. For a brief moment, she considered telling Buckworth the dog had died, but a lie would never do. She always told the truth, regardless.

The call of Kang's long-ago ancestors was pumping hot and fast through his veins. He had gained his precious freedom, and he was in flight or fight mode. Flight was what would save him. What he sought as strongly as he sought life was his freedom, and freedom came from the deep dark forest that enclosed the rough, high mountains. Instinct told him to go, up and higher up. The farther away from humans and their hated smell the better.

His sudden burst of speed was soon to take its toll forcing his race for freedom to turn into a slow, determined trot. He came upon what might have been an old deer trail and slowed down enough to make sure he didn't overtax the strength he had left. His flight had expended strength. Scaling a six-foot fence would be a challenge if he was in prime condition. Yet, he knew he had to keep going if he didn't want to be chased down and caught.

He had been traveling a long time when he suddenly turned away from the old trail and headed in a different direction. He was heading straight up into the high mountains as the undergrowth became thick and challenging. Rhododendron hells were everywhere. In damp places dog hobble grew in a tangle, but he continued onward.

After miles of slow trotting, the mountains narrowed to fold in around him on all sides. This was what he desperately sought, protection, security, freedom only those high mountains offered.

Right now, he needed rest.

He finally came upon a large outcropping of rocks where a deep, two-foot-high and five feet deep crevice opened into a small cave. Winds from the past fall and winter had blown the crevice full of dried leaves making a perfect hide-away bed for a big dog to take shelter. He slunk inside the crevice, sniffed the air for dangerous scents, found none, turned in a circle several times and eased himself down to rest, sleep, and heal.

As he lay in his bed of leaves a new set of instincts began to develop in Kang. He became much older than the days he had been alive. An eternity of his ancient ancestors' knowledge seeped from the heavens and earth to throb though his injured body and mind. He unwittingly was being drawn back in time when to be wild and free was the essence of life. All the survival instincts his ancestors knew were returning to his body and brain. Freedom meant becoming wild again.

Although he had spent his years of existence with humans, he now feared and hated them and their intentional cruelty. It was the forested mountains dense with underbrush that was calling him. It filled him with anticipation and the strangest of desires.

He became aware of wild yearnings he knew not of what or why, and yet he knew he had to pursue those strange awakenings, just as soon as he got the rest he needed. A deep rumble rose from his chest as he lifted his nose into the air to catch scents from the high mountain ranges that loomed far above him.

Finally, peacefulness replaced blind fury and hatred. He closed his eyes and slept a much-needed kind of sleep.

He awoke to the pangs of hunger. His stomach rumbled for food in the worst sort of way. Never in his entire life had he been required to seek out his own food. Food had been placed in his bowl without him ever knowing from where it came.

He rose to his feet and stretched his sore muscles. His wounds had been aggravated greatly, but they would heal in their own time. No longer would he be tortured by men and forced to fight other dogs to stay alive.

He made his way out of the crevice, lifted his nose in the air to scent the wind again. Nothing smelled like food, but he did scent water. He found a little stream running down the hill making a small pool. He drank his fill. For one moment, he considered going back down the mountain in search of food at the shack where the woman had fed him, but only for an instant. He headed farther up into the high mountains ignoring his hunger and sore body the best he could.

A sudden need to travel faster took hold of him. He picked up his pace to a trot as the sun traveled across the sky. Before long, the sun would sink behind another tall mountain and darkness would arrive. He scented something that smelled like the decaying meat he'd been fed back at the shed and increased his speed as best he could.

Vultures, crows, and a variety of other animals were gorging on the remains of deer guts left beneath a huge oak tree. He made a rush toward the pile, scattering flapping black wings. He surveyed his surroundings making sure it was safe before he lay down to consume what was left of a deer's guts.

Once the remains were all gone, he licked himself clean, and then sniffed the ground where he picked up a faint human scent. He wanted nothing to do with any human and headed away from the smell to find a safe place to lie down and rest.

Chapter 23

~~~~

"Where could he have gotten? What can we do next?" Lady Biswell rung her hands as she asked Griff for something neither he, nor any of the searchers she'd hired, had an answer to. No one had seen hide nor hair of her beloved dog during the time he'd been missing. Lady Biswell wasn't about to give up or let up on her insistent search.

"After all this time there's not much that can be done," Griff told her gently, but he knew she would never give up on finding her dog regardless of how much time passed.

She had put up posters everywhere, even bought ads in newspapers offering a two-thousand-dollar reward for the return or information leading to the return of her dog. No one collected the reward, although she'd had a number of crazy phone calls.

One man called to see if she'd go ten thousand dollars if he returned her dog. She'd asked for his name, which he'd refused to give her.

"Will you?" he'd demanded.

"I'd have to see the dog before I'd agree to anything," she'd told him.

"Would you go the ten if I show you his picture?"

"I'll give you a thousand for his picture," she told him. "If there's some way you can prove it was taken after he went missing. Once I'm sure it's my dog, we can discuss increasing the reward for his return."

"You leave the thousand inside that rusty old car in the woods on the Dosh farm, and I'll leave you a picture along with the proof you need."

She had no idea where the Dosh farm was much less a rusty car in the woods. "No deal. You meet me at the bank in town with the picture of him wearing a purple bandana around his neck, and I'll give you the money."

"I'm not that big of a fool," he told her.

"You think I am?" she'd returned.

"Don't want your dog back, do you?" he said, and hung up the phone.

She'd immediately called the sheriff's department and tried to get a trace on the phone call but was unable to do so. It seemed a missing dog wasn't top priority to law enforcement, especially one that had run away instead of being stolen.

"Had to be a crank call in an attempt to scam money from you," Griff told her. "Besides, you haven't had a call in over a year."

"I think you're right," she admitted, but she wasn't entirely sure. She didn't trust the man, however there was something about his tone of voice that had her puzzled. That something had made her almost believe he was for real.

Greed, she decided. The caller was after a lot of money, more than a thousand dollars or two, but was he telling the truth? Did he have information about her dog after all this time, if so, why hadn't he called before now? Who was he? How could she find out?

~~~~

Norman James figured he deserved more money than the paltry amount Ronald Buckworth had paid him for stealing the dog. Stealing a dog was a federal offence. If he got caught, he'd claim he'd found the dog roaming loose, and Buckworth claimed the dog belonged to him. Buckworth had raked in a small fortune in winnings from fighting the dog. Right now, the dog was still alive. Most likely he wouldn't be any good in the fighting ring ever again, so why not get what he could out of the woman? If that was the case, Buckworth would have him bury the dead dog after he was ripped apart. Instead of burying a dead dog, he planned on raking in the reward money and the old broad could have her dog back.

He needed to set the old broad up for more reward money first. She'd balked at his first contact, but he knew how to work women like her. He'd done it many times before. All it would take was a little more time and a few more phone calls.

James' phone rang. He pulled it out of his pocket to see Buckworth's private number displayed on the screen.

"Yeah?" he answered.

"James?" Buckworth questioned.

"Who the hell else did you call?"

Buckworth ignored James' mouth, as James knew he would. Buckworth obviously had a job needing to be done and Norman James had always been the one to do it.

"Got a job for you."

"Why don't that come as a surprise," James smarted off.

Buckworth knew several unpleasant ways of shutting a mouth permanently, but he needed James to find that dog before it made its way back to the woman. It wouldn't take a brain surgeon to figure out the dog had been used for fighting once the dog's injuries were seen. Once there was proof of dog fighting going on, the law would be out in force searching every crook and cranny from there to hell and back.

"Want the job or not?" Buckworth asked.

"What is the job?"

"Finding that Kangal dog you stole from the Biswell woman."

"What does it pay?"

"Two hundred."

"To do what?"

"Tracking down that damned Kangal dog before somebody finds him."

"Thought Alice had him shut up recuperating."

"The damned hussy let him get loose," Buckworth accused through gritted teeth.

James let out a laugh. "Two thousand," he countered, hoping Buckworth realized it was the amount of reward money offered for information about the dog's whereabout.

"Hell no."

"Since the old broad is willing to pay that amount to get her dog back – thought you might be willing to pay the same amount."

"You know what happens to those who cross me," Buckworth said.

"We both know what'll happen if that dog is found by a good Samaritan. By the way, are you wanting to hire me or scare me? You ought to know I don't scare. Plus. I keep a few insurance policies in case I don't show up again. Pays when you're in my kind of business."

Buckworth was silent for a few heartbeats. "Wasn't talking about you," Buckworth was quick to tell him. "I was talking about so called good Samaritans."

Buckworth couldn't be sure what a dregs-of-life, no-account man such as Norman James would do. James would willingly turn on him in an instant. They both realized if they weren't good at doing their jobs, they'd both have disappeared a long time ago.

"Want the two-grand up front" James said. He could hear Buckworth gritting his teeth over the phone.

"A thousand up front and a thousand when the dog's delivered back to me."

"Dead or alive?"

"Alive."

"Hell no. He's gonna be hard to catch. Most likely I'll have to shoot him."

"He's been injured. Hain't got enough strength to be hard to catch."

"Had enough strength to escape. Should have enough strength to get back to the old broad. It's up to you."

"Fifteen hundred dead. Five hundred more if he's brought back alive and that's it. I've got another tracker in mind, but thought you already had a stake in this dog."

"I'll be there to pick up the thousand," James told him, not believing there was another tracker unless he intended to force Alice to do it, which he doubted. She was too valuable at keeping the injured dogs alive.

He gathered food and supplies in a backpack, along with a goose-down sleeping bag and a fifth of whiskey. A man needed a little comfort.

Norman James arrived at the shack an hour later. Alice met him before he'd gotten ten feet from his truck. She handed him an envelope.

"All there?" he questioned.

"Ten hundred-dollar bills," she said none too friendly as she turned to leave.

"Wait a minute. I want to know how, when and where the dog escaped."

"This morning," she said as she walked behind the shack to the dog cages. "The dog was in his cage He had never stood up without trembling, still had to crawl about. I was feeding him. Didn't realize his cage door hadn't latched when I went for a new bottle of vitamins. He hit the cage door and was into the run before I knew he'd moved."

"The runs are enclosed," James said.

"Right. The dog went over the fence like he was a deer."

"Those long legs," James said. "Which direction did he head?"

"Don't know. Couldn't tell."

James suspected she did know. She was the kind to have inspected his tracks and read them almost as good as he could. One thing was sure, she wasn't the kind to tell anything of importance to make capturing the dog easier.

"Where do you want me to park my truck?" he asked her.

"You're going after him now?"

"Know of a better time?"

"Thought you might go to the woman's place and search backward."

Norman James shook his greasy head of unwashed hair. "It's been years. Godard beat the brains outta that dog to make him mean enough to fight. He won't go back to the old broad. He'll get as far away from people as he can."

"What makes you think that?"

"Read up on his kind. Come from a foreign place called Turkey. You know how life goes, uncivilized people, uncivilized dogs."

Alice shrugged her broad shoulders not willing to converse, much less argue, with a stupid man. Let him think what he would. Dogs weren't dumb.

"Park it down in the lower woods where it can't be seen." She didn't want James or his truck anywhere near her.

She watched out the window as James drove off only to walk back a short time later. He went to the spot where the dog had jumped the fence. She knew he'd easily find the bent down weeds where the dog had landed. The dog still dragged one leg from the hip injury Brutus had given him, enough to leave a trail. James would also find faint tracks where he'd headed straight for the mountains, but then he just might lose the trail, or he might not. She'd followed the dog's tracks for a good way herself just to make sure he hadn't collapsed. Jumping over the enclosure fence and landing hard had to make his injuries worse. Too bad it hadn't rained since the dog escaped. Part of her hoped the dog would find its way back to the old woman, while another part of her hoped he continued heading toward the high mountains where he'd become as wild as a coyote and twice as vicious as a panther. The only problem was how would he find food? Never once in his life had he killed for food. But then, the dog did know how to fight and how to kill. He'd done both often enough.

~~~~

The phone call from the man had opened up old sorrows for Lady Biswell. Losing her beloved dog went deeper than she would ever admit to anyone, perhaps even deeper than she could admit to herself. She left Griff to do the feeding and finish up anything else that needed doing. He'd been there to pick up her slack for years and, thankfully, was still doing so.

Sometimes she saw the sadness in Griff's eyes when he looked at her. She suspected he saw her unhappiness even though she was trying to keep it hidden. Never had she wanted anyone to know her life story, not even her last husband. Her first husband – well, that was another story entirely. One she tried not to think about too often. The hurt of losing him went too deep, hurt too much.

She had been weak and stupid, had allowed herself to become so crazed by the loss of her beloved husband, she'd lost everything. It had taken her a long time to recover. But recover she did. Well, almost, if she was truthful with herself. There were still old wounds that festered up when least expected.

Like right now.

She made her way to the house and climbed into the attic. She dragged the old trunk from its hiding place, took the key from the chain she still wore around her neck, and unlocked the chest. The first thing she took out was the picture of her last husband, Lord Arthur Biswell. He was as old as the hills when she married him. His hair was gray, his beard was gray, unkept and tobacco stained, but he had something she wanted. He had land, money, and a house in need of repairs.

It was his land she first fell in love with. His house and money tied for second place.

He had fallen in love with nothing, not even her, not even himself. Everything he owned had come from the hard work of his father and grandfather. He and his mother were nothing more than hot house flowers who had been petted and pampered into uselessness. When the father died, everything went into the hands of his mother, a woman who had no idea if her own head was meant to go up or down. Her only son took after her.

"Idiots," Lady Biswell considered her husband and mother-in-law. How they had survived this long was beyond her.

Lady Biswell thought marrying the man and saddling herself with caring for him and his mother a meager price to pay for owning the land she craved. Neither romance nor sex had come into play. She realized early on that Arthur was not capable of such intimacy. She doubted he'd ever been, even in his younger years. As for his mother, her presence alone would have castrated the balls off a brass monkey. How Arthur's father ever managed to get his mother pregnant was surely a mystery as well as a feat.

Mother Biswell went into fits of hysteria if so much as a speck of dirt happened to touch her hand or her shoes. Even the slightest smell of something she thought unpleasant also sent her into fits. The woman had fainting spells at least three times a day. Each spell required her to rest in bed for hours in order to get over each and every one.

Her son was almost as bad. He carried a scented hankie up his shirt sleeve and tried his best to never need it.

Lady Biswell couldn't stop herself from grinning every time she thought of Mother Biswell being pregnant much less enduring the pain of childbirth. One thing was for certain, she never did it more than once. Having to live with Mother Biswell and her son convinced Lady Biswell the woman should not have done it the first time.

In Lady Biswell's opinion the arrangement she had with the Biswells was well worth it. She was now the only living

Biswell in existence and owned this wonderful land along with everything else that had belonged to the Biswell estate. Her life wasn't the life she had dreamed about having, but it was the life she had.

Chapter 24

~~~~

Darkness was coming on fast by the time Striker had the deer dragged up to the next mountain from where she had killed the deer. Her arms and back ached to the extreme. The deer had to be twice her weight. Even her legs had started to tremble as she struggled onward. She considered heading downhill with her load. It would put her closer home and also give her body some rest. But pulling the weight up the last mountain would be worse than continuing along the ridges.

She longed to stop and rest if only for a few minutes, but she knew better. Once she stopped her body would stiffen up making it more difficult for her to start again. Not only that, but a far-away yipping sound was carried upwind. She knew the sound only too well. She hoped the wolves hadn't scented her kill. They had multiplied greatly in the last few years, probably another reason why game was getting scarce. Hopefully, the amounts of blood and guts she'd left behind would give off more scent than the carcass she was dragging.

"I can do this, dad. I can do this," she repeated over and over as she forged onward. "It's just a little deer. I can do this, dad. You know I can." Even with determination, each step was almost more than she could manage.

The sound of her own voice in the chilling darkness was strange to her ears, if not frightening. She had learned the value of silence and seldom spoke, but her words helped drive her onward when she might have otherwise hesitated or stopped. If only the tree roots and underbrush would thin out enough not to snag the deer and impede her slow progress. Equally as bad were the rocks that tripped her and stubbed her toes. For a fleeting moment, she considered making an attempt to drag the carcass into a tree and leaving it until morning, but that was taking a chance on it not being there when daylight came. If she stayed in the tree with her kill, she would be risking her own life.

She had seen strange tracks at the edge of a far mountain stream bed that concerned her more than the yipping wolves. She searched in the books her dad had provided to find out what kind of animal those tracks belonged to. Just as she feared, they belonged to a large cat. Unlike on a large dog, the toenails were retracted into the pads of the foot, plus the book stated the hind edge of the foot pad had three lobes where dogs only had two.

She found several different names attributed to the cat tracks, puma, mountain lion, and panther were three. She had continued to read about how they stalked their prey, and how their woman-like screams could rip through a dark night. She had also read how they were more afraid of men than women. There was something about a woman's smell that attracted the big cats.

"It's always the darkest right before the dawning," her dad would say, and she discovered that to be true. Not only was she having trouble putting one foot before the other, she couldn't see in front of her. The darkness was so complete she was afraid to move and at the same time afraid not to.

Suddenly, the thick blackness surrounding her lessened. A shade of gray lightened the sky until she was able to see the outline of trees. She was on her mountain now, almost within sight of her little cabin. Her arms stretched out behind her and both deer's hind legs in her hands. She was still pulling the deer toward her cabin. She didn't meander or try to leave a false trail leading away from her cabin as her dad always insisted. All she could think about was getting safely

to her cabin with the meat her aching body had paid dearly
to drag home.

"I made it, dad," she heaved out as she pushed open the
cabin door and dragged the deer inside. "I told you I could
do it."

Finally, after a long painful night, she and her deer were
home.   Her fingers slowly unclutched the deer's legs
allowing it to drop to the floor. She left it laying and made
her way to her bed.

Striker awoke hours later. Her body ached from head to
toe, but she welcomed the ache. She had proved she could
provide for herself. She got her dad's skinning knife and
started to work on the deer. As usual, insects had already
gathered to take in a meal of her kill. Insects were a
consistent bother during the warm times. The only thing that
got rid of the insects were the freezing cold winters, but some
always survived. Sometimes she thought of herself as being
like an insect. So far, regardless of the freezing winters,
regardless of what bad things happened, she had survived.

She wished she could take the meat outside to cut it up,
but she knew better. During the early morning hours, she had
heard something big scratching at the cabin door. She feared
an animal had followed the blood and meat trail she'd left by
dragging the deer. She had no idea what it was but suspected
a wolf. She wasn't taking any chances on cutting the deer up
outside when her only weapon was a knife in her hand.

Yet, there were times when a knife could be better than a
bow and arrow if she was jumped unexpectedly. A bow and
arrow required enough space and time to insert an arrow, pull
back and let go. A knife was for closeup fighting. All summer
and fall she had tied together bundles of weeds and hung
them from tree limbs. She'd pretended they were animals
attacking her suddenly as she bumped against them. She'd
practiced pulling her father's knife out of the scabbard,
slashing at the throat and stomach. She'd jabbed the knife in
the imagined eye sockets and through the ribcage into the

heart, until she could do it quickly and smoothly without having to think about what she was doing.

She'd also practiced with the bow and arrow until she could hit her target without needing time to aim. That wasn't all she'd worked on. She fine-tuned using the slingshot her dad had made until she was accurate and powerful. She also practiced throwing rocks just in case she found herself without any other weapon.

Her dad had told her the story of David and Goliath, ending with it wasn't always the biggest and strongest who won.

Her confidence grew, but not to the point of cockiness. No matter what kind of weapon she had, an animal would always be superior in its fighting ability.

As for the men her dad had warned her about, she hadn't seen one of those in the flesh. The only man she could remember ever seeing was her dad, unless she counted the few pictures she found in books. The first book she remembered reading was about Dick and Jane, and a dog named Spot. She had never seen a dog before, but her dad told her people used them to hunt with or just to have as pets They were a lot like wolves. She certainly knew what wolves looked like. They raided her traps and got into the cave where she stored food. She had been forced to use her dad's bedroom to store food in.

One trip he brought back a book on the different breeds of dogs. The variety and sizes puzzled her. How could they all be dogs when they were so different? Wolves, foxes, and ground hogs were kind of similar, but they were different species. Why weren't different looking dogs different species? Her dad had tried to explain how people bred dogs to look different. When she asked how people bred dogs, her father became silent and went off to do something extremely important.

She was familiar with her dad's tactics when he didn't want to talk about something. His silent treatment made her even more curious and thoughtful. Trouble was she had no way of finding answers to her questions if it wasn't in books.

She couldn't stop herself from wondering about people – about her own kind. What were they like? How did their voices sound? What kind of words did they use to communicate with each other? How did they look outside of books? Were people bred to look different, the same as dogs? Were all men to be afraid of? Would they all want to harm or kill her? If so, why?

Since her dad's death, there was no one, and no new books to give her answers. What she had to rely on now, were the behaviors of animals along with the musings of her own mind.

Chapter 25

~~~~

Norman James bent down in the weeds where the dog had landed after jumping over the fence. A section of weeds had been mashed over, but what was more impressive was the long distance the dog had landed from the fence. No injured dog should have been able to jump that far. Never in his life had he known of a dog in prime condition being able to clear a six feet high fence. Climb it maybe, but not jump it like a deer.

He didn't distrust Alice's story of the jump. What he questioned was Alice's story of how injured the dog still was. Had she willingly faked the dog's disabled state, or had the dog forced himself to give one last act of determination. Either way, the dog had gained his freedom, which gave James a good deal of amusement, along with one thousand dollars in his pocket plus another five hundred, when he dragged the dead dog in.

Maybe, just maybe, he'd be able to tranquilize the dog long enough to get the other five hundred, but he wasn't counting on it. According to the powerful length of the dog's running stride, he was moving fast.

The Kangal dog left a fairly easy trail to follow in the loamy soil of the woods. It was when he came to a stream that James lost the dog's trail. As he squatted near the creek bank where the dog entered the water, he wondered if the dog was cunning enough to go to water like a fox in order to hide his trail, or was the water only a way to soothe his aching feet and legs? James had always suspected this dog had stronger instincts, along with a bigger brain than most dogs he came into contact with, which, in his opinion, was nothing to brag about. Regardless of the dog's smarts or lack thereof, he had either walked upstream or downstream in the water. Which meant he had to search on both sides of the stream to find the place where the dog came out.

He searched both banks downstream without finding one single dog track in the soft mud. James finally decided to take a chance on the dog heading back toward the Biswell woman's place instead of upward into the higher mountain ranges.

It took him until late afternoon to make his way through the woods to the old woman's place without so much as seeing a single dog track. He pulled out his binoculars and watched the place until the sun went down. The caretaker fed and watered all the dogs, but the dog he was looking for was not in sight. He cursed some more as he realized he'd made a wrong call. No tracks. No dog. A waste of time and of daylight.

He'd have to follow the stream back toward the mountains in hopes of finding where the dog came out of the water, but not tonight. He couldn't track worth a flip in the dark. No man could. He bedded down in a sheltered place to wait for morning. It didn't take long for him to decide he was getting too old to spend nights on the hard, damp ground. There was a lot more pleasure in comfort than in roughing it. At least he had brought a bedroll with him, food, and a fifth of his favorite whiskey. All of which made lonely nights in the woods more bearable.

It was just his luck for this job to be more difficult than he imagined. Looked as though he would have to put in some time and work for the fifteen hunderd dollars. As for the other five hundred, it would be more difficult to drag a tranquilized dog out of the mountains than a dead one, but he would see what happened. He carried his tranquilizer gun and a Glock pistol – not to mention the vile of deadly poison in his backpack. This dog just might have enough smarts to get wind of him and keep out of range of the tranquilizer gun and pistol. In that case, a little poison on a dead rabbit would do the trick.

Chapter 26

~~~~

The sky was becoming lighter in color. Minutes later the woods turned into a paler shade of darkness instead of the deep, dark blackness that had told Kang it was time for rest. Several hours of sleep had eased the worst pains of his wounds. What rest hadn't eased were his hunger pains.

Kang got up from his bed of leaves and lifted his nose in the air. The scent of deer was still strong. He lowered his nose to the ground and followed the scent-trail of the dead deer, while winding another scent. It was a human scent and yet it was entirely different from human scents he'd smelled before. There was no smell of soap or artificial flowers. No odor of smoke, or the hateful, burning smell of liquor and sweat the men in the fighting ring had about them. It was a more natural smell, almost an animal smell, and yet it definitely belonged to a female human. There was a strong difference in the smell of a human female and a male. The remembrance of hated man-smell caused him to growl deep and low in his throat.

To Kang smells answered all questions. This human also gave of the scent of fresh-killed meat. He had faintly scented her on the guts he had feasted on, but at the time, he had been too hungry and exhausted to rationalize what had left that faintly familiar scent.

He felt no fear of the woman's scent as he neared the cabin. He was familiar with enclosures and had no fear of them if he was free on the outside. It was being enclosed that he'd learned to hate. He lifted his foot and scratched at the thick door hoping to get at the deer meat. The only sound from inside the place was the sound of breathing. His instincts told him the female was asleep. It also told him there was fresh deer meat waiting for him if he could get to it. His hunger made him scratch even harder, which seemed to cause the female to stir. His hunger was greater than his fear of the female human. Never in his existence had a female human offered to hurt him, but he no longer wanted to come into contact with humans of any kind.

When he heard the female gain her feet, he eased away from the door to blend into the shadows and lie down in underbrush where he could watch the log cabin while remaining undetected. The human came outside and moved a good distance away from the log cabin, squatted down and relieved herself. Unfortunately, for him and his hunger, she'd closed the door behind her.

The hot odor of her refuse hit him full force. It wasn't the hated smell he was familiar with coming from humans. It smelled of things that grew in nature, of leaves, and berries, and bark. There was very little odor of meat in what he smelled. Neither did it contain the familiar scent of the food when he was a pup, and yet the female human caused him to remember the woman who had tenderly cared for him during his growing time. This remembered smell drew him to the female human.

His previous brutality from the hands of men caused him to remain hidden. Trusting a human was something he was not willing to do again, and yet he could not stop himself from lying there in silence, waiting, and watching her.

Chapter 27

~~~~

Morning brought Norman James awake to a beautiful sunny morning along with a bitch of a headache. He silently cursed the bright sunshine for hurting his eyes and causing him to need to squint out the painful light. As the night wore on, the fifth of whiskey had become less and less. He hadn't intentionally drunk so much. The liquor had simply slipped down his throat as easy as pie when a man had nothing better to do with his time. Thoughts of the Biswell woman, or any woman, didn't have enough appeal to keep him interested or even awake. Much as he hated to admit it, his *want to* was slipping away faster than the hair on his head. Even a pretty, young woman took a greater deal of time and determination to get his *want to* up and going.

He'd always known older women went through what was called *the change of life*, but he never once suspected men would also go through something similar. If someone had told him five years ago such a thing would happen to him, he'd have called them a liar. This morning he tried not to think about it. Even the thought of such a thing happening to him was damaging to his pride.

He took out his binoculars and had a good look around the place just in case the dog had snuck in during the night. There was nothing to see. Even the caretaker wasn't up this early. He rolled his sleeping bag tight, tied it to his pack, took out a summer sausage and started eating and walking in an attempt to ignore his headache. It wasn't like he wasn't

140

familiar with hangover headaches, it was the confounded waste of time that troubled him most. Just because he wasn't able to travel in the woods at night didn't mean that Kangal dog couldn't.

Maybe if the dog really was in poor condition, the lack of food would play doubly hard on him, making him even weaker. A weak dog wouldn't be able to travel fast for long. He would use up his stamina in his burst of speed and then have to lay up for a long while.

It took several hours for Norman James to reach the place the dog went into the creek. He spent another two hours following the creek higher into the mountains before he found tracks where the dog came out. Again, James wondered if the dog was intelligent enough to know he was being followed. In his opinion all animals were dumb creatures without any sort of human feelings.

The dog was making no effort to hide his tracks any longer, neither was he roaming about aimlessly. He was traveling in a straight line almost like he knew where he was going, which couldn't be. Most likely the dog had winded something and was making a beeline toward it. Hunger was what James figured had taken over. He'd seen no sign where the dog had eaten since his escape. The dog was no longer running, but he wasn't limping along either, which meant he wasn't in as bad condition as Alice had claimed.

James let out a few curse words as the trail headed up a steep mountain incline. That crazy dog really was headed for the high mountains instead of circling back to the Biswell woman. How odd. As far as James knew, that dog had never been anywhere near those high mountains. Why would he go there now instead of heading to more familiar ground? It didn't make good sense to James.

Only the toughest, wildest animals could survive in such an inhospitable terrain. Even the most determined hikers and campers stayed away from those mountains, and for good reason. It would be all too easy to get lost, break a leg, get bitten by a timber rattler, attacked by wild animals, or fall down a rock cliff. He didn't want to spend the night in this place, and he had certainly not planned on spending a lengthy time or getting such a workout by going after the dog, but money was money. He assured himself he wasn't in the least afraid of the mountains regardless of how remote and inaccessible they were. He'd spent most of his life maneuvering through uninhabitable places either going after something or running away from something.

He cursed some more before deciding he would continue after the dog as long the tracks were easy to follow. James was the kind of man who got what he went after regardless of the opposition.

James was sweating profusely by the time he found where the dog had bedded down in a rhododendron hell for a night. Unfortunately, there was no blood trace on the leaves, which meant the dog hadn't torn any of his wounds loose.

The sun was setting, and shadows were darkening the deep woods, making tracking harder, but the dog was still leaving a trail. He wouldn't be able to follow the tracks much longer. Might as well keep going until he could no longer see signs before he laid out his sleeping bag for another miserable night in the woods.

James stopped, mopped his forehead with a musty handkerchief, stuck it back in his hind pocket, and reached in his knapsack for a bottle of water. He drank only half the bottle, realizing it was the last bottle he'd brought. He hadn't thought he would need more than two bottles. He emptied one before midday. He'd be able to find a stream somewhere on the mountain, but there was no assurance a fresh running stream didn't have giardia in it. Racoons and other animals were a known carrier of those microscopic spirochetes, and racoons delighted in crapping in water. He'd learned that the hard way. He hated to admit it, but it was Alice who clued him in to what his problem was a year or so back.

One of the dogs he'd stolen as a bait dog for Buckworth was squirting liquid stools streaked with blood.

"Why the hell did you bring a sick dog in here?" Alice demanded of him.

"Didn't know anything was wrong with it," James told her in a huff. "Buckworth said to bring in six big dogs and I did. Didn't exactly have time to check what came out of every dog's hind end."

"Looks to me like he's got either coccidia or giardia. Hopefully, you've not brought parvo in here. If you have, I'll personally beat your ass six ways to sundown."

"Ah, stop your bitchin'. Folks give their dogs shots," he'd told her.

"You know that for a fact?" she'd spat her anger at him. It was people's beloved pets that were stolen to be killed as bait dogs that enraged her more than anything else. "I suppose you always steal a dog's shot record along with a dog."

"Stop bitchin' and give me my money for bringin' these dogs in," he watched as she opened a cabinet and took out a bottle marked Albon and a bottle marked Flagel.

"Hold this dog while I poke this medicine down it. I'll have to keep him in quarantine. If he dies, Buckworth will take his price out of your hide."

Once Norman James got a chance, he looked up both coccidia and giardia on the computer, and he had a good idea why he had the running squirts. He made a point of sneaking back to Alice's medicine shelves while she and Buckworth were at the fighting ring to steal half of both bottles of Albon and Flagel.

One thing was for certain. He didn't want what he had twice.

Chapter 28

~~~~

It wasn't easy or pleasant to skin and cut up a deer, especially inside the small cabin. A chill had crawled up her spine warning her to be extra cautious. She had the strangest feeling of being watched. She feared wolves had picked up the deer trail and were lying in wait for a chance to get at the meat and her. She'd heard wolves howling most every night lately, but they had been on a distant mountain. But distance meant little to a hungry pack of wolves.

For her own safety, it was best to get the meat cured as fast as possible. She thinly sliced the meat to dry on her wood stove. If she had salt to make a brine, preserving the meat would be a lot easier. All she had was wild onion and garlic plus a few other herbs she didn't know the name of, but her dad had used them in preserving meat. It would take several days of drying before she had the job done.

As soon as she got through with the deer, she'd have to clean the cabin as well as herself to get rid of the blood scent. Her dad always warned her to never leave the scent of blood on her body or on her clothes.

"Blood is one of the most powerful elements in existence," he'd add as his eyes took on a faraway look.

Striker knew he was haunted by the war and memories of what happened to him and others.

"I walked in puddles of blood during the war. Slept in it. Couldn't get the smell of it off me," he'd say, as he remembered the horrors of war.

Her dad would go silent, and then he'd stalk off to be alone for a long while.

Cleaning the cabin would not be an easy job, but it was necessary. She would have to carry sand and water from the creek to clean the cabin. At least she could dip herself in the creek, which wasn't exactly pleasant this time of year. Heating water on the stove would be a luxury, one she didn't want to spend the time doing. If she waited until the sun was starting to go down slightly, the temperature would be warmer, and she wouldn't get nearly as chilled while bathing. Oh, well, she had a lot of work to do before the cleaning up began.

"Jerky." Her dad had called the dried meat. "Gives your jaws a workout when you eat it."

Striker smiled at the truth in what her dad had said. When she got tired of exercising her jaws, she'd put the jerky in water and boil it until it softened. She would also put potatoes, carrot, and turnips in with the liquid to make stew.

It seemed to her everything gave her too much of a workout. Staying alive was a workout in itself, but what choice did she have? At least what little garden she'd managed to grow was harvested and stored in the cave or in the cabin. Her potatoes had done exceptionally well, especially over the spot where she buried her dad.

"Dead things and manure," her dad claimed. "The worst stinking stuff there is will always grow the best plants. If you put dirt on the stove and cooked it, killing the good rotting stuff, plants wouldn't grow nearly as good as in the uncooked dirt."

She still had the hole beside her dad's grave where she'd dug a grave for herself some time back. Thankfully, she wasn't going to need it, at least not yet, and not for the reason she had feared. She'd read everything she could find on how a woman's body functioned. She'd learned that bleeding was a woman thing, but she despised it. Why a woman had to endure such as that was beyond her.

As for as her grave was concerned, she wasn't sure why she hadn't filled it in. In a way it made her feel slightly closer to her dad. In another way it was superstition. As long as she had a grave waiting for her, fate might keep her from needing it.

Chapter 29

~~~~

Norman James sat down near where the dog had bedded down, drank a small portion of his bottled water and ate a handful of trail mix. Nuts, raisins, oats, and chocolate were a good snack, but there was no way he could eat enough to fill him up. Had he known he'd be chasing after the dog for this long, he'd have brought something more substantial to keep up his strength. If he got much hungrier, he'd try to find a rabbit to shoot. Thing was, he hadn't seen one rabbit or even a squirrel since he'd been in the woods, which was odd.

It had been years since he had ventured far into the high mountains, but according to his memory, there had been an abundance of wild game, including pheasant and quail in about every thick growth of underbrush.

"Wolves," he decided. He hadn't come into contact with any, but he'd heard other men talking about how abundant they were becoming, and how much game they were killing. Since he didn't spend much time hunting any more, the lack of game didn't bother him – unless he got a lot hungrier than he was right now. It did mean the dog wouldn't be finding much food, which would make him weaker and easier to catch.

Before he realized how late it was, the last of the daylight faded and darkness set in like a deep blue shadow had been cast over everything. Even if he could still track the dog, it would be too dangerous to keep going in this mountainous terrain. A man could walk off a cliff without knowing it was there. Stepping on a slippery rock or log and breaking a leg would be an easy thing to do. He hadn't thought to bring along an emergency medical kit or even antivenom in case he was snake bitten. These mountains had timber rattlers as long as he was tall along with bodies as thick as his arms. One bite from those big snakes contained enough venom to kill a dozen men. His best bet would be to pull out his sleeping bag and sleep the darkness away. Hopefully, the dog would also bed down for the night the same as last night.

He picked up a long stick and checked for snakes near where the dog had bedded down before he spread his sleeping bag. There were a lot of leaves to rake through, but he found nothing harmful, not even a lizard. The crisp night wind was already freezing cold this high up in the mountains, which helped keep the insects to a minimum but did nothing for his disposition. At least that dog had been smart enough to pick a place where the wind didn't hit too badly.

A sudden flare of anger hit him as he crawled between the folds of his sleeping bag. The discomfort of being out in the middle of nowhere on a night that threatened to be colder than a witches' tit was far more than he bargained for. All this misery for a chewed up, good for nothing dog. There was no guarantee he would ever be able to fight again even if he was brought in alive.

Odd that the dog wasn't headed back toward civilization where nosy people would see him and know he'd been used for fighting. That dog was heading higher and higher into no man's land.

When James awoke early the next morning, his sleeping bag crackled as he stuck his head out. What little warmth the sleeping bag provided had not kept him warm. He'd been shaking and shivering for hours as he waited for enough daylight to see his surrounds. Rime frost had settled on everything until it looked like a thin layer of white ice had covered everything during the night. He'd slept in his clothes and shoes, but it hadn't been enough to keep him warm.

The first thing he did was reach for his whiskey bottle. He'd drunk another third during the night and only had a third left. He'd wanted to drink the entire bottle last night, but he'd saved some for today. Whisky gave him determination and kept him doing what he might not otherwise do.

"Hair of the dog," he said out loud as he turned the bottle up.

The mention of the dog made him feel mean. The instant he saw that dog he was going to empty his gun into it. Forget about bringing it in alive. Spending another night in this high mountain range wasn't worth five hundred bucks. He could steal more than that in one night, and then sleep warm in a comfortable bed. Again, he regretted taking on this job, but the money in his pocket kept him going.

Another couple of deep swallows, and he felt insulated enough to crawl all the way out of the sleeping bag. He picked up the sleeping bag and beat it against the ground trying to knock as much of the icy frost off as possible. Most likely the weather would heat up enough during mid-afternoon to melt what little frost was left on his sleeping bag making it damp and less likely to keep him warm. But then, he hoped he wouldn't be spending another night on the mountain. Once he'd killed the dog, he wouldn't have to track it. He could make good time dragging it straight down the mountain.

He ate a few handfuls of the trail mix followed by more of the whiskey until he felt capable and confident. He might as well scout the area until he picked up the dog's tracks again. The trouble with such a heavy frost was that it covered up the dog's tracks, but the sun would soon melt the frost.

At first Norman James thought he'd found a place where the dog had made a kill, but when he looked closer, he saw a drag line leading away from the stained, scuffed up ground. He picked up a handful of dirt where the ground had been disturbed the most and held it to his nose. Just as he thought, he was smelling fresh blood along with a trace of manure. Something had been killed here. On closer inspection, he picked up the dog's tracks again. He was certain the tracks came from the same dog he'd been following. These tracks were far too large to belong to wolves, although he'd seen a few wolf tracks further down the mountain. The lack of bear or mountain lion tracks near the kill surprised him. Nothing drew wild animals like the smell of fresh guts.

He left the place where he found the guts and followed the drag line. Not only had the ground been smoothed and vegetation bent over, there was actual inch-long tan and white deer hair lingering in places where rocks and bramble had yanked the hair from the hide. What little hair remained on his own head stood on end when he considered the possibility a mountain lion had dragged the deer carcass through the woods. No telling where a mountain lion would hole up with its kill. He'd known them to climb trees with their kill in their mouths and lodge the carcass high in a forked limb.

"Nope," he mumbled as reason came to him. Mountain lions dragged their kill in their mouths with the carcass dangling mostly between their front legs. There would be tracks from the cat's hind feet along with varied drag line where mountain lions would drop and then readjust their hold on the carcass. But this drag line continued in the same smooth pattern with no tracks at all, which meant something was pulling the deer carcass behind them wiping out the tracks.

"Humph," he grunted. Could there possibly be a hunter this far up in the mountains? The kill site appeared to be fresh. Why hadn't he heard a gunshot? A few dozen feet further and he picked up the dog tracks again. It was obvious the dog was hungry and hoping for another meal as he followed the scent of the deer.

He stopped, took out his bottle and drunk another long swallow or two of whiskey. Something wasn't making good sense to him. He walked back to where the deer had been gutted and started walking in circles looking for something – anything that might give him a better idea of what happened.

Much to his amazement he saw the shaft of a broken arrow sticking out of the ground. He pulled it out of the dirt and examined it carefully in the early morning light.

"I'll be damned," he mumbled. "Never seen nothing like this." It wasn't the kind of commercial arrow the bow hunters used. The fletching, which was used to create wind drag and help the arrow to spin enough to give the arrow stability and accuracy as it sped along in flight, was made from real crow feathers. This fletching looked more like it had been added onto a handmade arrow with black crow feathers – similar to the kind he imagined Indians made years before.

Was some Indian want-a-be going back to nature? If so, he did a mighty fine job of making an arrow and killing a deer. He looked about for signs of a four-wheeler but found none. It wasn't likely a four-wheeler would be able to maneuver in such a thick wooded area and over rough rocky ground. Maybe it was parked down in a valley, and the hunter was dragging the deer to it. The hunter was dragging the deer in a strange direction. It seemed the hunter wasn't trying to drag it into the valley but was heading toward another mountain range.

One thing was for sure, the Kangal dog was following the trail of the deer being dragged, which made tracking a lot easier. James picked up his walking speed just in case the hunter might get a good look at the dog. That crazy Biswell woman was still posting pictures and offering reward money for information leading to the return of her dog.

If that crazy broad had upped the price like he'd wanted, she'd have her dog back by now, but she didn't. That meant he had no choice other than taking what money he could get out of Buckworth. Besides, it was a lot safer to kill the dog than take a chance on Buckworth finding out he squealed on him.

The trail continued along the ridge, around a huge rock formation that formed a rocky ledge above a steep drop into a ravine. Shit, it was just his luck to be a man who got rubber knees when confronted with heights. He'd been afraid of heights ever since he could remember. To add to the height, the ledge was barely wide enough to drag a deer on. He was glad he hadn't continued on during the night. There would have been a real possibility he would have stepped off the ledge in the dark. One misstep and that would be it. If a man wasn't killed instantly, he would have suffered some mighty bad injuries. Here on this mountain, it was a sure thing that a man would be long dead by the time someone found him.

Not that it was likely someone would run across a body way up here, unless it was hunters. Most likely a dead man would become food for wolves and vultures.

Relief flooded him as the rock ledge ended and his feet were on solid ground again. He heaved in a few good breaths, took out his whiskey bottle and downed another slug of the much-loved liquid. Both the whiskey and the water were running low. The whiskey seemed to hit him harder than usual. It was probably because he'd drunk it on a near empty stomach.

He hurried his walking speed again, not wanting to spend another night freezing his hind end off on this desolate mountain. It appeared he was traveling faster than the deer had been dragged, but he couldn't be sure. He wondered how far in front of him, and how far behind the hunter the dog was? He had no doubt the dog could catch up with the deer and hunter if he wanted.

He knew for a fact that dog's long legs could run as fast as any deer. He'd watched him run when he broke free of the Biswell woman to get to the bitch dog.

He squatted down and touched some of the vegetation. There was still the dampness of the frost, which meant the drag line was made before the frost had fallen.

James reached the ridge on the third mountain range when the sun appeared to be directly overhead. He looked at his watch, it was past one o'clock, not mid-day as he'd thought. He looked at the sun again. Hell, it wasn't staying in the same place. It was weaving about. He let out a little laugh. It wasn't only the sun that was weaving. Some of the trees were weaving as well. He turned up his bottle again to find he'd drunk it all.

"Shit!" he mumbled as he threw the empty bottle against a tree. It hit with a thud and rolled to the ground unbroken.

He'd drunk the entire bottle of whiskey when he'd hoped to save some in case he had to spend another night on the mountain. At least he was no longer feeling tired. Actually, he was feeling pretty damned good.

He felt like singing a rowdy song or two, but he feared the wind might carry his voice to the hunter or the dog. The drag line and dog tracks looked to be a lot fresher every time he could get the tracks stop wobbling long enough for him to get a good look at them.

~~~~

Striker was covered in blood and gore by the time she had the deer sliced, skewered on sticks and hung all around the cabin and above the little stove to dry. She'd take turns switching the sticks over the stove to make the drying go quicker. She didn't want to chance the meat rotting instead of drying. She would need to gather more deadfall to keep the stove burning hot, but at the moment, she felt like a sticky mess of bait she and her dad put in their traps to serve as lure for wild animals to gorge on before the trap sprung.

She decided it was time to wash up in the creek. Even the weather had taken a warm turn, which was good for scrubbing down in the cold mountain water. It would probably be the last time the weather would be warm enough to wash in the creek. From now on she would spot wash herself in water heated on her little stove.

"Washing don't matter much one way or another," she mumbled as she looked down at herself. She was the only person who would be smelling her stink. Still, she did like being clean. It gave her a feeling of satisfaction.

She figured such a feeling was natural. She'd spend hours watching birds wash in shallow pools of water, especially after a rain. It seemed to make them happy and carefree, the same as it did her. She might as well enjoy what little pleasure she could get before the really cold weather set in.

She left the cabin, closing the door firmly behind her. She drew in a breath of the pungent, crisp air. There was something about fall of the year that made her feel sad and restless. She figured it was the same kind of instinct that made the birds gather to fly south, and the squirrels rush about to gather nuts for the winter.

It was the worst time of the entire year for loneliness to get a hold on her. Every animal and fowl had their own kind gathered together, but she didn't. If it wasn't for the words she spoke, she wouldn't know the sound of a human voice.

She thought a lot about her dad and her Aunt Nellie, but thought was a useless thing.

She tried to assure herself of how lucky she was to be living in such beauty as she made her way through the woods to the creek near where her father had been killed. She made a point of staying away from that exact spot. It held too many bad memories for her.

That spot in the creek was a reminder of how much her life changed in one day's time – how things would never be the same again. She made a point of doing all her washing and water gathering in a sheltered place below where her dad was killed.

The water pooled to her waist and was open enough for the sun to warm the water slightly, but she still turned kind of blue if she stayed in the water for long. The sun also warmed a large flat rock she usually lay on to dry off and warm up from the cold water.

For a brief moment, she thought again of a person named Aunt Nellie. That mysterious woman came to mind rather often lately, but the passing of time also convinced Striker she'd never be able to find the woman. There were some promises impossible to keep.

Her dad might as well have asked her to catch the moon and hang it around her neck on a piece of leather.

Staying alive was still her biggest challenge.

~~~~

Kang lay hidden in the thick underbrush. His mouth watering at the smell of fresh deer meat oozing out the cracks in the cabin. The odor of meat cooking brought back fond memories of another woman who was gentle and kind. Most of all, he remembered cruel men and being forced to fight to stay alive. He remembered pain, and anger, and fear. He remembered the call of his distant ancestors urging him to seek the freedom surviving in the wilderness provided.

He longed to break through the door and eat his fill, but he knew that would be impossible. He'd realized the impenetrable strength of the door and log cabin when he'd scratched on the door during the early morning hours. He'd been penned up enough to sense any weak spot in an enclosure. This cabin had none. His best bet was to wait until the door was left open and make a rush for it.

He stood up as he heard the door being opened, but the girl closed it too fast for him to make a mad rush for the opening. Again, the smell coming from the girl intrigued and confused him. She smelled familiar, while at the same time smelling of deer and the earth. Even the aroma of cooked meat hovered around her. He didn't move an inch as she moved past his hiding place. Once she was out of sight, he went to the cabin, circled it in hopes he'd overlooked an entrance during the night, but he hadn't. He considered climbing onto the top of the rock above the roof but decided against it. His instinct was telling him to follow behind the girl like an invisible shadow. He left the cabin to follow her using the undergrowth to remain unseen.

~~~~

Striker was feeling good about herself. She'd killed, dragged home, and was drying the deer without her father's help. This winter would not be nearly as difficult as the previous winters had been. After her dad died it was all she could do to keep body and soul together. During those years she'd barely harvested enough fruit and vegetables to get herself through the winter months without starving. This year she'd calculated the amount it would take each day to keep her from going hungry.

This harvest season had been a good one. She'd grown more and learned more about survival. She'd watched nature and animals more closely, learning from both about how to survive.

Had her dad been alive, he would have told her she was learning the ways of the wild, learning how to survive with mother nature. She'd also learned to travel farther into the other mountains and valleys to harvest berries and apples. Apples grew in the valleys, along with spring and summer berries. In the late summer blue berries grew high up on the mountain. The problem with gathering the fruit was that she had to always be on the lookout for wild animals such as bears. She had never tried to gather wild honey after the experience she and her dad had with the bear.

She'd grown confident enough to set her traps on a different mountain to catch rabbits and small game. She'd also been dragging in deadfall from the woods and storing it near her cabin until she could saw it into sections that would fit into her little wood stove. Life wasn't nearly as worrisome as it had once been, and she was thankful.

She ran her fingers through her hair after she'd unbraided it. She held a little fat in her hand and rubbed it in her hair as she walked. Once she reached the creek, she jumped into the pool of water clothes and all. No need to ease into the cold water a little at a time, so she could get used to the chill. There was no getting used to it. Best to get it over with fast by holding her breath and taking a leap.

She gasped, squatted down and lay back her head to get her hair wet. She reached for the bottom of the creek, grasping hands full of sand and rubbing it on her hair, trying not to tangle it any more than it was already tangled. When she killed something with fat on it, she'd rub the fat into her hair and scalp to help take out the tangles.

She'd only found a tiny amount of fat on the deer. She felt a little guilty about using it on her hair instead of saving it for cooking but consoled herself by thinking fat didn't dry into jerky. Besides, she needed to unplait the long braid of dark brown hair that hung down her back to her hips. Her dad had always told her to never cut her hair, and she hadn't. It would have made her life much easier if she had whacked her hair off as short as possible, but she wanted to live by her dad's wishes. Every request and word he'd told her had become a precious memory.

Memories were all she had left.

When she'd finished washing her hair, she gathered more handfuls of sand to scrub the clothes she still wore. Once she had the clothes scrubbed, she took them off to rinse them free of dirt and sand. Next, she took care in rubbing sand over her body and legs, arms and face, making sure not to scrub too hard. Sand had a way of taking off skin.

Satisfied she was clean enough, and turning a shade of blue, she hurriedly wrung out her clothes, got out of the water and hung her clothes on bushes to dry. She wasted no time lying down on the sun warmed rock to stop her body from shivering. As her body warmed, sleepiness overcame her. She had spent most of the night dragging the deer home. She might as well get in as much sleep as possible while her clothes dried. She had an hour or so before she'd have to put wood in her little stove to continue drying the meat.

~~~~

Norman James was following the drag line when he heard the sound of splashing water and with the faint sound of mumbled words as he neared a creek. He left the drag line and headed toward the sound. There was no doubt that he had finally caught up with the deer hunter. Best to remain unseen until he discovered what was going on. He wasn't exactly worried. He had guns compared to a bow and arrow, at least he hoped that was the case.

He silently crept behind trees and brush for cover, making as little noise as possible, which wasn't exactly an easy task since he'd drunk too much whiskey. To be honest with himself, his senses were not as sharp as he'd like right now, but he assured himself he was well used to the effects of alcohol, He could drink most men under the table and all it did was make him kind of feel-good crazy. It also gave him courage he didn't normally have, not that he was a coward, he assured himself.

He'd never been a coward, but alcohol gave him a reckless kind of bravado he might not have had otherwise. He'd always made a point of doing what he wanted.

He remained hidden as he listened for more sound. When he heard none, he eased from tree trunk to tree trunk trying not to step on twigs that would snap and give his presence away. When he reached a spot where he had a clear view of the creek, he stopped in his tracks. He wasn't seeing the deer hunter as he expected. What he saw was a man's dream come true.

There in the middle of the creek stood a sight for sore eyes. The prettiest girl he'd ever seen in his life was stark naked in a pool of water. His heart rate sped up. His breathing became faster. He felt a surge between his legs like he hadn't felt since he was a teenage boy.

It hit him like a slap in the face. He wanted sex with that girl worse than he'd ever wanted sex in his entire life, but what was the chance a young girl would go for such a thing with him?

"Little to none," he told himself silently. Besides, she might belong to that deer hunter. He leaned against the tree trunk and remained silent, watching as she left the water, hung her wet clothes on bushes, and then went to a big rock and laid down.

"Hell, all mighty," he barely kept himself from groaning out loud. His eyes narrowed as he looked all around to see if there was another man around. He sure didn't want an arrow skewering him to the tree he was hiding behind.

He waited and watched for what seemed forever. He saw no sign of another person, while the girl appeared to have fallen asleep in the warmth of the sun. His wanting of her increased until his blood was throbbing in his ears so loud, he was all but going crazy. At the same time, he knew a young girl with her looks would have nothing to do with a man such as him. He was old, ugly, drunk, and as horny as a billy-goat.

A plan formed in his mind with blinding speed. He knew how to creep though the woods without making a sound. She hadn't heard him approach when she was awake.

He could close the distance between them without waking her. He gripped his rifle in both hands as he moved, holding his breath without ever taking his eyes off the girl. He wanted that girl bad enough to shoot the deer hunter if he showed up.

He was within two feet of the girl when she must have sensed his presence and raised up. Before he realized what he was doing, he swung the rifle at her, hitting her just above her temple. She tottered for a moment before she collapsed backward.

"Ah, hell," he mumbled, surprised at what he'd done. Suddenly, he was chuckling. It didn't matter to him if she was out cold. His pleasure would be the same.

He laid his rifle down and jerked the galluses to his bib overalls down exposing the bottom half of his naked body. He took great pleasure at seeing his manhood ready and willing to do the job. He was on top of her in a flash, prying her legs apart with his hands and knees. Her body was firm, muscled, and tight. His hands sought her small breasts as his mouth tried to bend down far enough to suck on one. He was humped up and pumping when the girl moaned, and her eyes fluttered open.

In an instant the girl was screaming, kicking, and clawing at his face as she tried to buck him off her. Her knee came up to hit him in the hind end barely missing his balls. He tried to grip her arms, press her down with his heavy body, and pin her legs with his. She kept on scratching, kicking and screaming like a caught wildcat.

The next thing he knew a weight hit his back full force as unbelievable pain shot through the back of his neck. He managed to twist his head enough to see the belly and legs of the Kangal dog he'd been tracking.

"Get off," he squalled as he rolled away from the girl, but the dog rolled with him without loosening the hold on the back of his neck. He felt the powerful jaws pull his head backward. His head was being shaken back and forth as a rumbling growl of raging fury sounded deep in the dog's chest.

"No! No! Stop it!" Norman James managed to yell out, but it did no good. The dog was trained to fight and kill and that was exactly what he was doing to the man he hated.

James did his best to grab hold of the dog's front legs. His hand clasped onto one leg and he yanked with all the strength he had left in him. All his struggling accomplished was that he and the dog were flung on top of the girl, causing her head to hit the rock again. The big powerful dog had been trained not to loosen his hold until the enemy was dead.

Chapter 30

~~~~

Striker opened her eyes to see that something was fighting over the top of her. The raging fight going on scared her enough to make her try to sit up, but the raging fight was knocking her against the big rock. Her head hit the rock hard as pain shot through her head. The trees limbs started twirling around and around against the blue sky. There was a buzzing sound between her ears a moment before everything went dark.

The next thing she knew she was being licked in the face by a damp tongue. She lifted both hands to push on warm fur. The licking stopped followed by a whine. Her eyes slowly cracked open to see some sort of animal standing over her. Fear gripped her. Was that what had attacked her? She didn't think so. This thing was the color of a mountain lion, but the face hovering above hers looked more like a wolf, but not exactly.

She didn't know if she should fight it, or pretend she was dead. She suddenly realized she was being licked in the face not bitten. She rolled her eyes to see that she was still on the rock only inches from water. In one quick movement, she rolled her body sideways into the water and crawled on the creek bed with her head in the water until she had to come up for air. She gulped in oxygen as she looked back toward the rock.

The animal was standing there watching her. She wasn't sure what kind of animal it was. She was certain she had seen similar pictures in books. Her eyes widened when she realized the tan fur was covered in blood. She looked down into the water fearing it would be stained red. The water was running clear. She was not bleeding, and she could not detect any bite or claw marks on her skin. Her body did ache, and she felt sore and bruised, but it couldn't possibly be her blood on the animal. There was simply too much of it.

She took a closer look at the animal.

"Dog," she whispered.

That thing looked like a dog – a mighty big dog. It was almost as big as the young bear she and her dad had killed years before. A shiver crept over her as she recalled the raging fight between the man and the dog. while she lay on the rock.

Exactly what had happened? Her head felt strange and she was still somewhat confused and aching all over.

Slowly, as the water chilled her body, her mind began to clear. She remembered falling asleep on the warm rock after she had washed all traces of the deer from her clothes and body, remembered sensing something wasn't right and raised up to see what it was.

A man!

The horrible thing her dad had always warned her about. She really had seen a man an instant before she was hit in the head with something hard. There had been pain accompanied by a flash of light then darkness. When she'd come to herself again, the man was on top of her, hurting her. She'd fought with every ounce of her strength, but the man was terribly heavy, and he was fighting her right back.

Get off. No! No! Stop it! She'd heard the man squall out as a dog appeared and grabbed hold of him.

That same dog was now standing on the rock covered in blood looking at her and whining. Where was the man? Where did all that blood come from?

The dog turned his head to look into the weeds a few feet away from the rock. She saw what looked like bloody cloth sticking out of wallowed down weeds and undergrowth. The dog turned his head back, looked at her, whined, and then leaped off the rock and disappeared into the woods.

Striker huddled in the water until the clouds covered the sun and the cold water had her teeth chattering. The dog was obviously gone, but the bloody cloth was still there. She eased out of the water and ran for her clothes. She grasped her knife and jerked it out of the scabbard. Shaking with cold and caution, she eased her way toward the bloody cloth.

Her breath caught in her throat with a gasp. What she saw was almost beyond belief. There was a man lying there – or more correctly what remained of one. He looked to be a large man with nearly all of his clothes ripped off. His boots were still on his feet. The ragged remains of his britches were down and gathered against his boots. His legs, hips, and back had deep, gaping gashes still oozing a bloody liquid. His neck and head made her feel a little sick. She had skinned and gutted animals since she could remember, but she had never seen anything like this.

She turned away from the man and tried to think. Where had he come from? What was he doing here? Was the dog his? Why had it killed him? Even more terrifying was the possibility there were more men in the woods waiting to attack her?

She hurriedly pulled on her clothes, thankful for their warmth even though they weren't completely dry. She found her bow and arrows and ran to the cabin as fast as her trembling legs would take her. She barred the door and put more wood in the stove. Her deer meat had to dry, and she had to be prepared to fight off more men when they came after her. She was thankful her dad had built the cabin strong. If a man broke her door down, she'd put an arrow through his heart.

She'd tried to stay awake all night, feeding wood in the stove, listening for sounds. There was nothing but silence along with a slight popping of the wood burning in the stove.

She busied herself by moving her skewers of meat around, but nothing took away her fear, or the sight of the man ripped to pieces by the dog.

Sometime before dawn, she heard wolves howling. They had evidently smelled the blood and gore from the dead man. She hoped by morning they would have every single trace of him eaten up and his bones dragged away.

It wasn't long after the howling until she heard the familiar roaring sound of fighting going on. Had another man arrived, or was the dog and wolves fighting? After listening for a few minutes, she decided it was the dog and wolves.

Striker stayed inside the cabin until the last stick of her firewood was gone. If she wanted to continue drying the meat, she'd have to go outside for more wood. She took a deep breath to build up her determination. She'd heard no sounds of anything other the wolves and fighting, and that had been hours before. She didn't want her fire to go out and all her hard-earned meat ruined. She touched her knife in the scabbard fastened to her waist, picked up her bow and arrow and opened the door. She left the door open so she could get back inside quicker if need be. She made a mad rush for the pile of wood, picked up three sticks and ran back inside, slamming the door shut. Her heart caught in her throat at what she saw. The big dog was huddled in the corner eating the deer meat off one of her skewers.

He wagged his tail when she looked at him.

She held her breath as she opened the door. "Get out," she ordered, trying to keep her voice from shaking.

The big dog got to his feet with the skewer of meat still in his mouth and walked out the door. She closed the door and dared to take a normal breath again.

The next time she went outside for wood, she closed the door behind her, looked around, but didn't see the dog. Thoughts of the man's body down by the creek was haunting her. As much as she wanted him to be gone, she feared he was still there. Slowly, with her bow and arrow at the ready, she eased toward the creek while keeping a lookout for men or other wild creatures that might do her harm.

She smelled the man before she reached him. Unfortunately, he was still laying exactly as she'd left him. If the wolves had gotten a single bite of him, she couldn't tell it. What she could tell was that his body was bloating, and the color of his skin was changing.

She recalled leaving her dad's body for three days hoping he would be resurrected by God. One thing was for sure, she didn't want this man resurrected. She didn't want him lying there stinking up the place either. Her only choice was to bury him.

"Sorry, Dad," she whispered as she recalled the grave she'd dug for herself and hadn't filled in. "Maybe if his grave is close yours, you can torture him for attacking me."

She lifted her hand and touched the side of her head where he'd hit her. There was a knot half the size of her fist. It was so sore she could barely stand to touch it. Not only that, but her entire body ached from that knot to the bottom of her feet. Even her insides ached, especially when she thought about what happened. There were even a few scratches on her body where she figured the dog's toe nails had scratched her while he was fighting the man. She relived the feel of being stomped and knocked about while the fight went on.

She forced herself to look at the man again. He was wearing boots and clothes. She thought about stripping them off and saving them for her own use. All she wore now were animal skins and the ragged remains of the clothes her dad had left behind. Her own clothes had grown too small, been patched together, and worn to threads long before now.

"No," she shook her head firmly. She wanted to save nothing the man was wearing. She forced herself to reach down and grab hold of his boots. She dragged him a few feet when she heard something ding against a rock. She dropped his feet and took a closer look.

It was a pistol that had bumped a rock when she'd pulled him. She recognized the pistol from pictures in books. She picked up the pistol and looked toward the rock. Her first thought was to toss it into the creek. Her second thought was that she could kill bears as well as deer easier with a gun than a bow and arrow.

She went to the big rock to lay the pistol down, while she dragged the man to the grave. There on the ground next to the rock was another gun. It was much bigger with wood and a long barrel. She'd also seen a picture of it in books, but she didn't remember what it was called. She got both guns and hid them in the undergrowth, went back to the man, picked up his feet again, and started pulling. He was heavier and much harder to drag than the gutted deer had been. Half way to the grave his clothes caught on rocks and tore. A leather square she recognized as a billfold fell out. She picked it up to find a picture of him and words that read, driver's license.

There were also several one hundred-dollar bills. Her dad had taught her about money, and some of the things money could buy. He had used animal hides to get money. He'd used the money to buy the things he brought back home. She took the billfold and money back to the cabin and hid it under her dad's bed before she went back after the man.

It seemed to take forever to pull the man to the garden, roll him into the grave, and cover him up with dirt, but she kept at it until the job was done.

The accomplishment did not give her the least amount of pleasure. Instead, a strange kind of fear started growing inside her, a fear she didn't know a name for.

Chapter 31

~~~~

The girl hadn't reached the creek when Kang got wind of the man he hated. His first instinct was to run away before the man caught him. His second instinct was to stay hidden and watch the girl. There was something about her that brought out his natural guarding instincts bred into his ancestors.

When he was first captured, he'd been terrified of the cruel man he was now scenting. For the past two years, Kang had cowered and shook every time he got wind of the men who had beat him and sicced other dogs on him. There had also been other men who had hurt him and forced him to fight for his life. After a time, a change took place within him until he no longer feared the men. Instead, he hated them with every fiber of his body. Given the chance, he would rip these men limb from limb. These men had become his enemy the same as the dogs he was thrown into the pit with were his enemies. It was kill or be killed.

Oddly enough, the girl wasn't his enemy. Instead, his protective instincts had focused on her. He saw her as being weak and in need of him. She was also the one who had provided him deer guts when he was hungry. Her scent had mingled with deer for him to follow. The girl allowed his mind to conjure images of good things he had experienced such as food, Alice, and Lady Biswell. The things that had been his life before he had awakened to find himself surrounded by cruel men he'd come to hate.

When the girl had gone into the water, he had laid down in the undergrowth to watch her and wait for his enemy to arrive.

Kang remained on his belly, silently stalking the man, His keen sense of smell scented the guns the man carried and warned him to be cautious. He had witnessed what happened when those guns were lifted and fired, they killed things. He'd smelled their scent, seen their flame, heard their roar when they were turned on severely wounded dogs. He'd learned to fear and avoid men and their guns. As long as the man held the gun in his hands, Kang knew to remain hidden and silent.

Kang patiently watched as the girl washed herself, hung her clothes on brush, and then lay down on the rock. He knew when her breathing became deep and peaceful as she fell asleep.

Hackles raised on his back when he saw the man sneaking up on the sleeping girl, but he didn't move, for the man carried the gun in his hand. His body tensed when the man hit the girl, laid the gun down, dropped his britches and attacked the girl.

When the girl started screaming and fighting, something came alive inside of him. His ancestral instincts slammed into action. He did what he and all his kind before him were bred to do. He became the protector.

A good protector did not stop fighting until the enemy no longer drew breath. Kang didn't stop even then. He wanted to destroy flesh, bone, blood, even the very scent of his enemy. All of which was impossible, but he did his utmost best until he grew tired of the thing he hated, who no longer offered fight or threat.

His attention focused on the girl. Her chest was rising and falling, but her eyes were closed. She had gone back to sleep when she needed to wake up, see what he had done, and praise him. He went to her, trying to wake her by licking her in the face.

It worked. She woke up and rolled into the water.

Satisfied he'd done his job, he disappeared into the woods to lie down and rest.

Later on that night, he was awakened by an unknown scent. In the woods a good distance from him slinked a furry form he was not familiar with. In a moment's time, two more furry forms appeared from behind two other trees, almost surrounding him. The first one lifted its nose into the air and let out a piercing howl. The other two joined in.

A warning rumble sounded deep in Kang's chest. He'd seen hate filled eyes before. Every dog that entered a fighting ring had that same hatred, that same desire to kill in their eyes. These three had both the hatred and the need to kill in abundance, probably more so than any of the dogs he'd been pitted against. Never before had he fought three enemies at the same time, but he was willing if they persisted.

The first animal ended the howl and lowered his head until he was gazing fiercely into Kang's eyes. His upper lip snarled backward showing sharp fangs. The other two stopped howling to flank Kang from different sides. Kang stood his ground, challenge rumbling deep in his chest.

He was much larger than the adolescent wolves but the odds of three to one gave them courage. In the blink of an eye all three charged at the same time. The first one went for Kang's throat, which was a deadly mistake. Kang's jaws clamped onto the back of his neck, much like he'd clamped onto Norman James' neck. One wolf sank his teeth into Kang's hip as Kang whirled around to dislodge the hold with the first wolf still in his jaws but failed to loosen the wolf's hold. He shook and slung the first wolf as though he was a weapon hitting the third wolf as he grabbed for Kang's hind leg. The third wolf hit the ground and rolled over several times from the force of the impact.

Kang dropped the first wolf knowing his neck was broken. He grabbed for the head and ears of the second wolf that was still latched onto his hip. His huge mouth closed over the head and ears and crunched down. Bones crunched as the wolf struggled to get lose, but his struggle turned into death kicks. When Kang turned to meet the third wolf's attack he was not there. The third had turned tail and ran away after he'd stopped tumbling and regained his footing.

Kang left the two wolves laying where they'd died and went to the creek to wash himself off and lick his hip wound. He scented the hated man, growled his disdain, and trotted near the cabin where the girl had enclosed herself. He laid down, so he would be near if anything else threatened her.

When morning came, the girl opened the door and left it open a crack. He'd learned to be quick if he was to get what he wanted, and he wanted some of the wonderful meat he'd been smelling all night long.

He streaked inside the cabin and grabbed the first stick of meat he came too. His hunger was too great for him to run with the meat. Instead, he laid down and was chomping on the meat with gusto when the girl returned. "Get out," she demanded. He clutched the stick of meat in his teeth and did as she ordered.

When the girl left the cabin again, she made sure she closed the door to keep him from getting at the wonderful smelling meat again. He whined slightly but followed in the shadows as she went back to the creek where the hated man lay dead. He watched as she took a booted foot in each hand and slowly dragged him through the wooded area. She left him for a few minutes before she returned to drag him to a soft patch of dirt where a hole was already dug. She rolled him into the hole, went back to the cabin and got a shovel. He continued to silently watch her as filled the hole with dirt.

The smell of the hated man was no longer as strong.

~~~~

Striker woke up hungry. She eased out of bed feeling surprised at how sore she was. The big rock, as well as the man, had bruised her as she fought. Pulling the heavy man and burying him hadn't helped her soreness any, but she didn't think it added to it much.

She even felt the soreness and pain as she squatted to relieve herself, but it wasn't as hurtful as it was the day before. Again, she reprimanded herself for falling asleep when she should have remained watchful. She had made the mistake of becoming complacent, which was a deadly mistake. She wouldn't make the same mistake twice.

"You were right, Dad. You feared a man would come for me, and one did. Did you also know a dog would kill him when I couldn't? I wasn't watchful enough, Dad. I hadn't kept my weapons close at hand. I wrongly believed I was safe.

"The dog puzzles me, Dad. I don't know what to make of him."

She'd read in one of the books that a dog was man's best friend. This dog sure wasn't that man's best friend. Would the dog rip her to shreds if he ever got the chance?

She filled the stove with firewood, placed a skewer of the rawest meat on top of the stove to cook for her breakfast. She thought of the dog that had killed the man. She was thankful for him and at the same time she was afraid of him. She had no idea what the man would have done to her if it hadn't been for the dog. She was grateful to the dog. She took a second skewer of meat and went outside.

"Dog," she called out cautiously, but nothing moved. Perhaps the dog had gone back where he'd come from. Just in case he was still around, she laid the skewer of meat a foot or so from her door and went back inside. Maybe, if the dog was well fed, it wouldn't be as inclined to attack. She waited a few minutes before she opened the door and looked out. The skewer of meat was gone. Part of her was glad the dog was still there. The big tan dog could kill her as easily as he killed the man – but he hadn't.

She stayed inside the cabin and ate the meat. It gave her jaws the workout she expected. Later on today, she would treat herself by slicing a potato on top of the stove until it turned golden brown. That was how she and her dad used to eat them during the winter when they wanted a snack. The only difference was that she didn't have salt to sprinkle on the potato slices. She didn't have her dad either.

Gathering her courage along with her bow and quiver of arrows, she opened the door and went outside into the crisp fall air. She looked about for the dog but did not see him. She remembered the guns she'd left near the rock and decided she should get them to hide under the bed with the billfold. She looked about and listened carefully to detect anything unusual. She had failed to do so before the man slipped up on her. She should have known something wasn't right as she remembered how silent the birds and squirrels had become before she'd laid down on the rock.

They weren't silent now. She could hear the chirping and quarreling sounds of squirrels where they were fighting over acorns and hickory nuts. She'd tried to gather as many hickory nuts as she could, but the squirrels were faster than she was, which was okay. If she found herself starving during the winter months, she could always use the slingshot to pick off a squirrel. That was one of the reasons she'd started hunting farther away from the cabin. As for the acorns, she also gathered them. They were so bitter she could hardly stand the taste, but they would keep her alive if there was nothing else to eat.

Most of the birds had flown away, but there were still a few remaining. As soon as the bitter snows started to cover everything, the birds would be gone too. She shuttered as she thought of the long, hard winter that was ahead of her, but she'd learned to take what came and endure what she couldn't change.

The decay smell of the man was still there, along with the dried blood stains on the rock. It would be a long time before she'd be able to sun herself on that rock, if she ever did again. She found both guns were still where she'd left them. That probably meant the man came alone. She couldn't stop herself from wondering in what direction he'd come from. Perhaps, if she followed his tracks, she would discover the way out of these mountains, not that she would be willing to leave. She was willing to know how to get to Aunt Nellie, if and when, she ever decided to honor the promise she made to her dad – but she didn't think she'd ever be able to accomplish such a feat. Each time she stood on the bald, she realized how small she was in a world that was so large.

She hadn't gone fifty feet when she discovered the backpack the man had obviously laid down. It contained a warm sleeping bag, what she thought were shells for the guns, half a bottle of water, and a plastic bag containing seeds and stuff she decided was food that he'd brought with him. He had surely been one of the hunters she had heard in the far distance that always made her father desperate with worry. The tan dog must have come with him, but if it was his dog, why had it attacked him and not her?

She placed the guns on top of the backpack to pick up on her way back to the cabin and followed his trail farther into the woods. Much to her surprise, she came upon the bodies of two half grown wolves. The dog had surely killed them sometime during the night when she had heard the howling and then the fighting. He had to be a mighty fighter to kill both wolves.

She had never eaten wolf meat before and didn't know if it would be any good. But then good didn't matter if a body was starving. Food was food, and hide was shoes, mittens, or clothing. She grabbed a hind leg of each wolf and dragged them toward the cabin. Together they weighed as much as the gutted deer. Once she had the wolves inside the cabin, she went back for the guns and backpack.

If she skinned, gutted, and cut up the wolves, she wouldn't have time today to backtrack the man, but she didn't care. She would do it later if it didn't rain during the night and wipe out his tracks.

She skinned the wolves and tossed their guts outside a good distance from the cabin. If the dog was still there, it could have at them. If not, then crows and vultures would have a feast. She cut up a few squares of meat and put it in a kettle of water to boil. She'd find out soon enough how wolf meat tasted.

As her dad used to tell her, "When you're living in the wild, you eat what doesn't kill you."

Chapter 32

~~~~

"**W**here the hell is that man?" Buckworth yelled at Alice when a week had passed without Norman James showing up. "I want that dog back alive."

"How would I know?" Alice shot back. "You and I both know it's not likely he'll find that dog much less bring him back alive."

"Since, you claim to know every damned thing else, thought you might know where James is at too."

"All I know is his truck is still parked down there in the woods where he left it."

"You're sure about that?"

"Go look for yourself." She was sick and tired of listening to him, especially when he questioned every word she told him. He was obviously in an extra foul mood today, and so was she.

"What direction did you say that dog took off in?"

"As far as I could tell, he ran up hill a way before he vanished in the underbrush."

"What direction did James go in?"

"He went up hill a way before he vanished in the undergrowth," she smarted off. "I assume he was following the dog's tracks, and that's all I know."

"Do you think that dog would head back to the old woman?"

"Don't have any idea."

"If James took off with my thousand dollars, I'll throw him in the pit with all three of my pit bulls."

The three pit bulls Buckworth owned weren't in good enough shape to fight a big rat. He was lucky she had been able to save them after he insisted on putting them in the ring before they were completely healed. If the Kangal dog hadn't escaped, he would have been put back in the ring too soon as well. Good sense and greed didn't mix well.

"He wouldn't take off with your money without taking his truck. It's worth more than a thousand dollars."

"Good. If he doesn't show up soon, I'll sell his truck."

"If he doesn't show up soon, he's dead or lost. If he got lost in those mountains, he might as well be dead."

She'd overheard some wild stories about those mountains when she went to the farm store to get supplies. The stories were that no one ever ventured into those mountains and came out again. A few years back, two hikers had decided to climb to the bald only to be found at the bottom of the first rock cliff two weeks later. Their death had been declared accidental, although some questioned that conclusion.

"Then I'll get to bid good riddance to that ugly son of a baboon."

Buckworth's words brought Alice back to the present. Buckworth had no room to call anybody ugly, neither did she. Unfortunately, no one got to determine the outcome of their genetics. She'd often thought it was too bad people weren't being bred for a certain outcome, the way animals were. People's happenstance breeding was producing a world filled with inferior human beings and no one seemed to care. The fittest were being overrun by the unfit. How long could the human race survive after the fit were overrun by the unfit? She had to admit that she, Buckworth, and Phillip Godard were prime examples of poor genetic breeding.

"I've heard Norman James was a right nice-looking man in his younger days," Alice said. For some reason, she thought she ought to defend him, which went to show how stupid she was. In her opinion it was Phillip Godard who took the prize for ugliness. He was uglier than the rear end of a baboon with a case of the running scours.

"I've got a fight coming up in two days," Buckworth said as though James' absence would keep it from happening.

"Norman James' disappearance won't hinder that fight one way or another."

"I might need all the workers I can get if those Atlanta boys show up."

"They won't. If they do, you'll need to move to a different location again, and get Norman James to steal you another batch of dogs to turn into killers. Those Atlanta boys have just about wiped out every fighting dog in three counties. The law ought to send them a thank you card."

"Been thinking about that some. There're not many good fighting dogs left around here. I've figured out a way to get rich. I'm going to take my best bitch and breed her to the meanest, son of a bitch male dog I can find."

"So?" She'd heard all kinds of bragging talk coming from him, and bragging was as far as anything went.

"So, you're the one who is going to raise me some fighting dogs."

"That would take at least three years if not four." She didn't mention the fact that he didn't have a *best bitch* dog or even the *best male* dog.

"Hell, don't complain. You're not too old to live that long."

Alice did her best to ignore his intended insult regarding her age. If she had her way, he'd be somewhere with Norman James right now. It would be a blessing if Buckworth and his entire crowd of cronies disappeared off the face of the earth.

"I need James to show up to steal me a bitch and male dog from those boys down in Atlanta," Buckworth finally admitted.

Alice almost laughed. Not even Norman James could pull off a feat such as that. Those Atlanta boys were as dangerous as they came. They were rumored to have mob connections. Fortunately for Buckworth, his operation proved to be so pennyante it was not worth those big boys' time.

Buckworth's brow furrowed as if he was in deep thought. "You know that dark brown red-nose bitch pit dog ole Bentley Doss has signed up to fight?"

"No, I don't know it."

What she did know was that the red-nosed strain of dogs was known to be particularly aggressive and determined. They were known to continue fighting until the last drop of blood and the last breath of air left their bodies.

"Doss has put his dog up against Harris Markson's dog. Markson's bitch is not the fighter Brutus was, but she's good. If either one of those dogs go down, I want you to declare her dead, haul her off to be buried, and then bring her back to life."

Alice let out a laugh at that. "I'm not that good," she told him. "I've read that God is the only one who has resurrected the dead."

"Hell, I'm not expecting you to resurrect anything. I just want you to keep either one of those dogs alive while making the owner think she's dead."

Alice shook her head. "Mission impossible, I'm afraid. Men like to bury their own dead dogs."

"Not if they get too drunk to know what's going on around them."

"Neither Doss nor Markson has ever gotten that drunk," she pointed out.

"Doss might if he was given a shot of free liquor."

"It would take a lot more than one free drink. Have to admit he wouldn't be nearly as hard to handle as Markson would be."

"Might not take but one drink if you slipped some of your dog tranquilizer in it."

Alice's eyes widened. "No way. I won't stoop that low, even for you." She didn't add especially for the likes of a man such as him.

"Sure, you will."

"No, I won't," she told him firmly. "I'll leave here before I'll drug a man or a dog."

Buckworth knew she meant it. If he persisted, there was a chance she'd stub up on him. He'd noticed her unrest lately and marked it up to her going through the change of life. He knew for a fact that women turned meaner than any fighting bitch dog when they were going through that period of time. "All right then. Show me what kind of tranquilizer to use and I'll put it in his drink. You're not going to object to keeping a near dead dog alive, are you?"

"Wouldn't it be a lot cheaper and easier on you to buy yourself two good breeding dogs?" she asked, although she already knew the answer. He didn't have enough money to buy jack shit, much less good breeding dogs.

"If James shows up, I might have him steal another one of those Kangal dogs from that woman. If I breed Doss' pit to one of those big Kangal's, they might just throw the kind of fighting dogs I'm after. That male dog James has gone after proved their fighting ability."

"Might, or might not be what you need," Alice was quick to tell him.

Buckworth gave her one of his hateful looks, which she found amusing. She knew there were times when Buckworth would like to smack her up the side of her head for being so damned right. Instead of making her mad, it gave her great pleasure to know she disturbed him.

There had been a time or two when Alice could muster up a tiny grain of sympathy for Buckworth. Right now wasn't one of those times. She took pleasure in thinking one of these days he would show up at the crummy shack she had to live in and find that every single dog had gone missing, along with her.

~~~~

Bentley Doss and his handler carried his crated dog into the old barn and set the bitch's wooden crate against the barn wall. Seven other dogs in wooden crates were already there. Doss always liked to bring his dog in last when he could. His handler stayed with the dog, like the rest of the handlers did. Not a one of them trusted the others not to sneak something to their dogs that would keep them from winning a fight. Oddly enough both the owners and handlers kind of trusted Alice to be honest and fair – as long as they remained vigilant. They didn't trust Buckworth as far as they could lift and throw a full-grown jack mule.

Buckworth had been watching for Doss to enter the barn. As Doss strode up to pay his entry fee and place his bet, Buckworth poured himself a drink from a bottle and took a big swallow.

"Your dog ready to go up against Markson's?"

"She's ready," Doss said with an attitude.

"Markson's dog is good. Have to admit that handler of his knows how to train a dog."

"So does mine," Doss replied, feeling slightly insulted.

"Right. Didn't mean to insinuate he didn't, or nothing like that. I was only stating a fact. Remember how my dog whipped his dog? I'm figuring your dog will do the same with this dog of his."

"I'm bettin' on it," Doss was quick to reply.

Buckworth took another drink from his plastic cup. "Damn, this is good whiskey. The best I've ever tasted. Here," he said as he took another plastic cup from behind the counter. "Try a little of this. First drink is on the house considering how both our dogs can whip Markson's dogs."

Buckworth filled the cup half way full and handed it to Doss. He poured a little more from the bottle into his own cup and took another long swallow. Doss did the same.

"Never thought I'd see the day you'd give a man a free drink," Doss told him.

"Don't get used to it," Buckworth said with a grin. "This here is mighty fine whiskey, I tell you."

"Don't taste exactly like the rotgut you usually sell to folks."

"Hain't. It's my own private stuff. Carries a kick like a mule. Most men can't handle whiskey this high proof. Makes their heads spin Here, hand me your cup and I'll give you one more shot. Don't tell nobody I'm giving away whiskey, though. Probably won't never happen again."

"That's a fact," Doss was quick to say.

Buckworth drained his own cup and tossed it toward the trash can. He took Doss's cup, picked up the bottle and poured another small shot before he put the bottle back in the inside pocket of his jacket. He watched as Doss downed the shot and tossed his cup in the trash can.

"Good luck to you," Buckworth said as Doss walked away. Doss hadn't noticed the watch Buckworth wore. All Buckworth had to do was push on a section of the thick watch band and dump the dog tranquilizer into the cup without an unobservant person being the wiser. He'd had the watch specially made years before. It had earned the price he paid for it many times over.

Tonight's fights consisted of standard sized bulldogs, each weighing about fifty pound each and standing no more than eighteen inches high at the shoulders. There were no heavyweight dogs fighting tonight, and not even a single fight with mixed breed dogs. Nor did they have bait dogs to sacrifice in order to get the spectators blood and gore excitement at a high pitch.

The number of Doss and Markson's female dogs had drawn out of the hat for the first fight. Even though bitch dogs were as vicious fighters as the male dogs, the crowd always got more excited when the male dogs fought.

When it was time for paired dogs to fight, their handlers brought their dogs from the crates onto the floor where they were taken into the pit and to their corners where the spectators could see them. Watching how the dogs behaved before the fight started was a good way to increase the betting.

Alice provided a bucket of soapy water and a towel. The water was divided into two buckets and the towel torn in half. The number 1 and 2 was placed on the buckets. Alice held the same numbers in each hand. A coin was flipped to see who chose her hand first.

Markson won the coin toss and picked her left hand. She opened her hand to show the piece of paper with 2 on it. She opened her other hand to show the paper with 1 on it.

The handlers got the buckets and towels and started washing the opponent's dog as was the standard procedure. When they were finished washing, Alice drew blood and let the dog owners watch as she tested both vials for drugs. By the time she was finished, bets were all made, and the fight was ready to begin.

Each handler held their dogs in their corners stroking their bodies with encouraging hands as their words incited the dogs to be ready to fight. The bitch dogs quivered with excitement as they dug and scratched their feet in the dirt of the barn floor. Their eyes glaring pure hatred at their opponent.

"Are your dogs ready?" A man in the center ring called out. This fight was going to be by the rules instead of throwing two dogs in the ring and let them have at it. "All right then, pit 'em."

Chapter 33

~~~~

Wolf meat was stringy and tough. It reminded her of the bobcat her father had killed and cooked for them to eat. The secret to eating tough meat was cutting it cross-grain into tiny pieces and boiling it on the stove for hours. Since she had to keep a fire in the stove to dry deer jerky, boiling the wolf meat was no problem. Even the tan dog was willing to eat the boiled meat and crunched down on the bones after she had boiled them to make bone broth for her to drink.

Striker didn't begrudge giving the wolf meat and bones to the dog. He was the one who had killed them. He deserved more of them than she did.

She had been afraid of the dog after seeing what he had done to the man. Slowly, the dog was gaining her trust. When she left the cabin, she could see the dog watching her from a short distance away. When she carried wolf meat outside for him to eat, he waited until she laid the meat down and went back inside the cabin before he ate it.

She searched through books her dad had brought her in an effort to find out what kind of dog this was. Dogs of such a size and color were referred to as livestock guardian dogs. It did seem to watch her, but she wasn't sure if it was protecting her or protecting its next meal, which could be her if she stopped feeding it.

One of the things she despised doing was tanning the hides of the deer and wolves. Her dad had taught her to use the brains in the tanning process. She spent days of scraping and rubbing brains into the hides. Finally, she declared she'd prepared them enough and fastened the hides to the insides of her dad's bedroom walls to cure. She had fastened a makeshift door of strapped-together saplings to the bedroom. It stayed almost as cold in there as it did outside, making a safe place to store meat for the winter. She had worked too hard to risk fastening the hides on the outside walls of the cabin where the dog or other wild animals could get at them. Winter time was a desperate time when food was scarce and survival difficult.

Past winters of near starvation had taught her a lot. She spent months gathering everything that was editable and storing it in her dad's bedroom, except for her potatoes and cabbage. She stored them in the bury-hole of the cave. She'd not been able to grow all the vegetables her dad had grown. He had gone off the mountain to bring back carrot, turnip and other seeds. It took her a while to figure out how to harvest seed from cabbage and turnips.

She had stored her cabbage much the same as she had stored her potatoes, except she'd stored the entire cabbage head with its roots still attached. Cut off cabbage heads tended to rot. When spring arrived, she replanted the roots still attached to the heads. Much to her amazement a shoot grew out of the head and tiny blooms appeared. When the blooms turned into seeds, she gathered and planted the seeds.

Turnips had been much easier to grow. They readily produced seeds in the fall. She also grew tomatoes and saved those seeds. She learned how to dry tomatoes by slicing them as thin as possible and placing them on rocks in the sun. She did the same with apples and other fruits. Sometimes she would string vegetables and fruits on dried Greenbriars and hang them from the cabin's ceiling. By the time the first snow fell she couldn't walk through the cabin without brushing her head on all the foodstuff hanging down.

Her biggest problem was keeping predators out of her garden. Her slingshot, along with bow and arrows helped with that problem, while providing her with meat.

What she hadn't counted on, ever, had been a man showing up. Her dad had often warned her it could happen, but when it hadn't happened in her fifteen years of life, it no longer seemed a possibility. How was she to prepare against it happening again? Could she set traps to catch them? Did she use her bow and arrow to kill them?

The Bible read "Thou shalt not kill." Yet she and her dad killed animals, insects, and other pests. The Bible said it was okay to kill split-hooved animals for food. Wolves, bears, rabbits and squirrels didn't have split hooves, but they had splits between their toes. Did that mean they could also be killed for food?

People had splits between their toes too. The big tan dog hadn't eaten the man he'd killed. Neither had she considered doing so. She knew other animals ate humans. Her dad had told her about cannibals – people who ate other people. Had she wasted a food supply when she buried the man?

She tried to stop her mind for asking questions about such things. Life and death were already too difficult for her to figure out.

Chapter 34

~~~~

Just as Buckworth hoped it would happen, Bentley Doss' bitch dog took a beating and Doss was too out of it to call the fight off. The spectators were yelling and stomping their feet in excitement. The two fighting dogs were almost equally matched and willing to fight to their death. A fight such a this was why the spectators came, and why bets were placed on both dogs.

Doss's bitch had made a miss judgement in her attack, which gave the opening to Markson's bitch.

"Hay, Doss," one man yelled. "Call it now or your bitch is a dead dog."

Doss wasn't even looking toward the pit. His face was overly red, with a huge grin on his face. He was doing his best to sing some sort of country song while slurring the words.

"Is he ever plastered," another man said. "He doesn't know what's going on." The man sitting beside Doss gave him a hard shove on the shoulder causing him to tumble over and start laughing.

"Hey, now," Doss mumbled as his laughter grew louder.

"He called it," the man who gave Doss a shove yelled. "He called the fight. Break 'em"

"Break 'em," the referee shouted. "Doss has called it.

Both handlers' ran into the ring with their breaking sticks. Markson's dog handler put the stick in the mouth of Markson's dog, but it didn't take much force to pry the dog's mouth open. The bitch was showing signs of exhaustion, but she had more life in her than Doss' bitch. Markson's dog was declared the winner.

Alice hat gotten to Doss' dog before the handler did. She was shaking her head, showing little emotion other than compassion for the injured dogs. She had gotten good at not letting her anger show at what went on in the pit. If she had her way, there would never be another dog fight – never another man who enjoyed watching brutality in action. Alice concluded she would never see the day when that happened. All she could do was try to keep the dogs alive. Sometimes she berated herself for doing such a fine job. Keeping a dog alive meant they would live to fight again, or if injured too bad to go back into the pit, they would become bait dogs.

Markson's and his handler carried their bitch out of the pit. Blackburn appeared out of the crowd with a board to help Alice carry out Doss's bitch.

"She's done for," the handler admitted as he looked at the dog.

"Will you take her home to bury her or had you rather we toss her in our bury hole?" Alice asked the handler.

"Toss her," the handler said. "Doss is in no shape to do anything. Most likely he'll not be able to find his own way home until he sobers up tomorrow"

Alice and Blackburn carried the dog from the barn to Alice's shack where she lived and doctored the animals.

"Why are you always willing to help?" Alice asked him.

"I like dogs," he answered.

"A man who likes dogs doesn't attend brutal fights." Alice pointed out.

"Do you like dogs?" he countered with a question of his own.

"What I don't like is seeing dogs die. I'm here to do what I can to save each dog's life. You're only a spectator." Plus, he did a lot of betting on dogs that usually won.

"I don't like seeing dogs die, either. That's why I'm willing to help you," he told her. "Anything I can do now? Like help you carry the bitch to the bury hole?"

"No. I'll stay with her until she breathes her last before I take her outside," Alice told him with a frown. All he'd done to save dogs lives was to help her carry them out of the pit to her little place.

"Good luck," Blackburn said, and left the room.

Alice did what she always did with wounded dogs. She put the dog on oxygen, stopped the bleeding, hooked up an IV to administer blood transfusions, fluids and medicine, stitched up the wounds, and did a lot of praying that she could keep the dog's heart beating and its lungs drawing breath.

Less than an hour later another dog was brought in by Blackburn and the dog's handler. This dog was a male pit with more gashes than body parts.

"He's bleeding out," Blackburn told her.

"Bury him," the handler told her. "No need to waste more expense on trying to doctor a no-account dog. I warned Reeves the dog couldn't hold out in the pit. Never did have a fighting heart, but Reeves wouldn't listen." The handler turned his back on the dog and stalked off.

"Who is doing the blood testing?" Alice suddenly asked after realizing the fights were going on without her being there. Usually, she had a little time between fights to do the doctoring while the handlers were showing off dogs, the usual preparations taking place, and bets were being made.

"I am," Blackburn told her.

Alice was surprised that the handlers and dog owners put any trust in him. "No complaints?" she questioned.

"Not really. They wanted to continue the fighting and didn't want to wait for your return. You were taking longer than normal." He didn't ask why she was late. He understood she was trying to save the bitch even when there was little hope.

"Since when do you know how to draw and test blood?" Alice asked with raised brows.

"I was a doctor – once," he told her and then hurriedly turned away and left the room.

"A people doctor or a veterinarian" she questioned as she looked at his disappearing back but got no answer.

Buckworth was all but laughing in glee once the fighting was over and he searched out Alice in what she referred to as her surgery.

"I came out ahead for once," he bragged. "This fight brought in more cash than any fight so far."

Alice had warned him it would be a mistake trying to go big – and then wondered why she was giving him good advice. As much as she hated dog fighting, why wouldn't she want him to go broke and out of business? Staying little and inconspicuous was the best rule of the game. Going with the locals brought him in a profit, if a small profit. Trying to feed his ego by gaining a reputation as a big man in dog fighting was betting on disaster – as well as being busted by the feds. Buckworth let his ego rule instead of using his brain.

"Did the bitch live?" Buckworth wanted to know.

"I've still got her on life support," Alice told him. "I stopped her bleeding and gave her blood transfusion from those bait dogs you've got in the pens. I've done the same with the male pit I was told to toss into the bury hole."

"Reese's pit? The one that lost the fight?"

"He's the one."

"I thought he was declared dead in the pit."

"Same as Doss' bitch dog," Alice pointed out.

"Are they worth saving?" Buckworth asked.

"All dogs are worth saving," she answered.

"I mean as potential breeders?"

"Who knows? Sometimes sorry dogs produce the best offspring. Other times the best dogs produce sorry off-springs. It all goes back to genetics and what's in the dog's pedigrees. Dogs usually throwback to distant ancestors,"

Alice told him. She would much rather talk about genetics than the cruelty of pitting dogs to rip each other apart for the entertainment and profit of those she considered deranged.

Buckworth nodded, but he didn't give a rat's ass about genetics. What he wanted was ill tempered fighting dogs. "Who's that guy called Blackburn?"

"You know as much about him as I do."

"He's always helping you carry out dogs. He rakes in a lot of cash betting on winners," Buckworth told her.

"Reckon he knows good dog flesh when he sees it," she told him.

"Why is he willing to help you?"

"Might be he's a rare man with a kind heart," she said, although she knew all too well that a kind-hearted man didn't frequent dog fighting rings.

Chapter 35

~~~~

Lady Biswell had come to hate winters. Her hatred surely increased with age. When she was young, she loved to see the snow fall as she ran about trying to catch snowflakes on her tongue. The cold hadn't even bothered her all those years ago. It had been a treat to wake up of a morning to find her world covered in a pristine white. Her mother would have a fire going in the cookstove. Her father had kept a fire going all night long in the heating stove.

The smell of coal and cook wood mixed with sausage, biscuits baking, along with gravy being stirred in a cast iron pan would fill the house. She'd lay awake in her warm bed for a few minutes longer before jumping up to brave the chilly bedroom as she hurriedly pulled on her warm clothes.

"Good morning," her mother would always greet her. "Breakfast is almost ready."

She'd rush to the window and look out. There would be her father's foot prints leading away from the house toward the barn. No matter how cold it got, or how deep the snow, her father always took care of the animals first thing before breakfast of a morning and the last thing before he ate supper of an evening.

"It's my job to see that they're fed before I am," he'd tell her.

Her father had hogs to slop, chickens to shell corn for, cows to grain and milk. He also kept a mule named ole Dan.

He loved that mule like it was a son. He talked to him all the time and swore the mule would communicate right back.

It had been a good childhood, a safe one. Everything had been familiar and everlasting. Nothing could possibly go wrong in her world back then, and it hadn't. It was later on in life when all the good disappeared. Even now, there was still a big empty hole in her soul that would never be filled. She tried not to admit it, but her precious dogs couldn't fill that hole no matter how hard she tried to make them. She realized long ago there were some hurts that could never be healed, regardless of all the remedies that were applied.

Lady Biswell looked out her kitchen window at the heavy snowfall. Griff was wading through snow doing his early morning feeding, leaving tracks much the same as her father had done all those years ago, but she couldn't pull up the same feelings she had when she watched her father.

If she was smart, if she was feeling whole, she would be out there helping Griff, or at least overseeing the morning feeding and checking on the conditions of her dogs. She believed she always knew what was best for them even though she knew Griff was both capable and observant. He realized when something wasn't right, and usually knew what should be done to correct the problem.

She also knew Griff had tender feelings for her. He'd had those feeling since she'd first hired him right after she'd married Lord Arthur Biswell. In a way Griff's feelings flattered her, being they were only feelings and not the thing called real love. Griff's feelings might also contain a little bit of lust, but no such thing was possible on her part. Lust had only come alive where her first husband was concerned. Her lust had died the day Sam Braden had died and had never resurrected itself. She didn't miss it – didn't want it. She supposed it made her an odd ball, but she didn't mind.

"I still miss you, Sam Braden, and will to the day I die," she said as she lifted her hand and touched the cold window glass. Thinking back to her beloved husband was like looking through the glass window at a world she was only observing. The glass separated her from the life beyond it. No matter how hard she tried, no matter if she did somehow manage to break the glass, those long-ago memories would never become reality again.

She turned away from the window and made her way up to the attic. She took the chain with the little key on it from around her neck and opened the trunk. The last time she had opened it, she'd only taken out the picture of her late husband, Arthur Biswell. She had looked at the picture for only a short time before replacing it and relocked the trunk. This time she took out the picture of her third husband.

Reg McFarland was his name. He, too, had been dead old when she married him, and that was one of the reasons she had married him. He was too old to be physical with her in any kind of way. Neither of them considered what they had together as an actual marriage. It was more of a convenience for both of them.

Reg had been what she needed at the time, and she had been what he needed. Reg was an attorney who was known to be the top of his field during his younger days. She had sought him out to help her get free of her second husband, Joe Whitson.

Reg had been known as an attorney who would do anything under the sun to win a case for his client. It didn't matter if his client was guilty or innocent. He did what he had to do to win regardless if it was legal or not. He had a reputation of being determined and headstrong. Folks claimed he would beat his opponent in the courtroom or preferably, before they ever reached the courtroom.

Reg McFarland had not gone to court on her behalf. Joe died of a heart attack three days before their court date. Everyone thought the upcoming divorce proceedings had put too much stress on Joe's heart, but Lady Biswell thought different. She suspected Joe's heart attack had a lot more to do with Reg McFarland than it did with the condition of Joe's heart.

She took the wedding picture of her and Joe Whitson from the trunk and laid it beside Reg and Arthur's pictures. Wedding pictures had been taken of her and her first two husbands, but not the last two. In her opinion, there were no real marriages to remember by having pictures taken. They were man and wife only where the law was concerned

She remembered the day she walked into Reg McFarland's office, before Joe Whitson's death.

"I need the best attorney I can get. I've been told you are him."

She'd been wearing a thick coat of concealing makeup on her face, especially around her left eye. Reg noticed it right off.

"Why do you need an attorney, abuse?" he didn't hesitate to come to the obvious conclusion, or even make an attempt to soften his approach.

"I have a husband who beat the shit out of me," she decided to be as direct in what happened as he was.

"And you want to divorce him?"

"I not only want to divorce him, I want revenge. Plus, I want compensation for everything he took away from me, along with every dollar he has or will make for the rest of his life."

Reg grinned. "You sound like my kind of woman. What's business profession is this wife beater in?"

"He calls himself an attorney, but he's actually the biggest scam artist in the business."

"What's his name?" Reg asked as though he wasn't much interested.

"Joe Whitson."

Reg laughed right out loud until tears were running down his cheeks. He finally took his handkerchief from his suit pocket and wiped his eyes.

"Care to explain your humor. I've found nothing funny whatsoever while being his wife."

"I can believe it," Reg managed to say through new bouts of laughter.

"Well?" She questioned.

"I laughed because one of my greatest desires has been answered. I've wanted a chance to go after Joe Whitson for years, but never had a reason to do so. You're right, he's a crooked attorney. Even more crooked than I am, and I'll admit I don't like taking second place in anything."

"Will you represent me, or will you run away scared?"

"How do you plan on paying me? Do you have a job?"

"I have a small trust fund set up by my parents. I can only draw out so much each month. Joe hasn't been able to take that away from me, yet. He's taken everything else, and I do mean everything."

"Such as?"

"The insurance money from my first husband's death. What little savings I had in my personal account when we were married. The land my parent's left me. It all went into my husband's greedy hands."

"If he's such a bad person, why did you marry him?" Reg shot the question at her.

She didn't even wince. "I'd come straight out of a mental asylum and was still as crazy as a bedbug."

Those words got his attention. "For real?" he questioned.

"For real," she answered back.

"Why were you in a mental asylum?"

"My parents died in a farming accident, which devastated me. I hadn't gotten over the horrible way they died when my husband was killed in the line of duty. My mind refused to function after the second traumatic shock. I felt like I was in some horrible coma I wasn't able to wake up from."

"Was your first husband a . . ."

"Police officer," she supplied the word before he could finish asking the question. The day we were married, he took out a half million-dollar life insurance policy on himself. When he discovered I was pregnant, he doubled the amount."

"You have a child."

"Yes. I have a daughter somewhere."

"Somewhere?"

"She was born while I was in the mental asylum. They – by *they* I mean whoever was in charge – claimed I was mentally unfit to have a child much less raise it. Joe told me the state took over my baby's welfare and arranged for her adoption. I haven't been able to get her back."

"You know where she is?"

"No. I'm afraid I don't. That's the reason I agreed to marry Joe Whitson. He said if I married him, he'd help me find my daughter. He was involved in her so-called adoption."

"How was he involved?"

"He referred the so-called adoptive couple to the asylum and then handled all the legalities. I later discovered he often did this for other babies born at the asylum."

"How did that work?"

"I wasn't informed of the events that took place. I was put to sleep during my labor and when I woke up, I was alone and without my baby. I didn't get to see her – didn't even get to hear her cry."

"Are you incompetent now?"

"Crazy, yes, but incompetent, no. I assure you my mental capacity is equal to yours, if not better. When they took my daughter from me, I realized I had to start fighting for myself and my daughter instead of not caring what happened to me."

"How?" he asked bluntly.

"The first step was to stop taking the medication they were giving me three times a day."

"How did you manage that."

"Easy. Once they watched me swallow the medicine, I went to the bathroom a few minutes after they went on to other patients and stuck my finger down my throat until I puked it up."

He lifted his brows at that. "They didn't figure out what you were doing?

"Their job was to see the medication was swallowed. What happened afterwards wasn't their job."

"Did you seek Whitson out?"

"No, he sought me out."

"An attorney sought you out? Why?" Reg questioned?

"He discovered how much money was in my trust fund when he helped take my baby away from me."

"Now I understand," Reg told her. "Like I told you, I've never dealt with Joe Whitson, but I have heard a lot about him. I've actually had clients who were familiar with the man. Did you know his first wife died of a drug overdose?"

"I learned of that after I'd married him."

"How long have you two been married?"

"Two years. I'm twenty-three years old. I don't get the full benefit of my parent's trust fund until I reach the age of twenty-five. After which time I'm sure I'll die of an overdose of some type or perhaps a well disguised accident."

"Either that or you'll be sent back to the mental asylum with him having power of attorney over you."

"Now you've getting the picture."

"What happens if you are deceased before your twenty-fifth birthday?"

"Everything goes to Mother and Dad's favorite charity."

"What about the fact that you have a daughter?"

"It would go to her, I think."

"You don't know for certain?"

"Joe is a very secretive man. He's told me nothing about my daughter or my finances. Actually, he's trying to use her whereabouts to control me."

"I see. What happens to you and your daughter after you divorce your husband?"

"I'll hire you to protect me from him plus find my daughter and get her back."

"How old is she now?"

"She's five years old."

"You were eighteen when she was born?"

"Yes."

"I see," he said. And she thought he just might.

"Are you going to take my case?"

"I'll be delighted to take your case," the tough, old, attorney told her with a sly grin.

Chapter 36

~~~~

Winter set in with a vengeance like Striker had never experienced before. Cold temperatures came in wave after colder wave before all the leaves had fallen from the timber. When she went outside the cabin to the rock, she could see thick fog containing ice crystals rolling in. All things, trees, rocks, ground, were covered in hoar frost that never melted off the way it did in the lower, warmer valleys. Her hands and feet were always cold causing her to start wearing skins she'd fashioned into shoes and mittens early, meaning they would wear out early.

She had hoped warm weather would linger on the mountain tops longer, but it didn't. It never had. Sometimes she wondered what it would be like to live down in the valleys where life appeared to remain longer than on her mountain. Even the sun appeared to shine warmer in the valleys than on her mountain. Since her father died, she'd been forced to venture closer and closer to the valleys to obtain food. She would gather what she'd found and then rush back to the cabin as fast as possible. Her dad feared the valleys and so did she, but the valleys also drew her.

"What lies beyond the valleys?" she had asked her father after he'd returned from one of his trips.

"Hell on earth," was his answer.

"How is that possible?" she'd asked in her naive way of wanting to know answers her father wasn't able or willing to give her.

"It's the people, Striker. There are mighty evil people out there."

"All of them are evil?"

"There's a few good ones, but only a precious few."

"Tell me about people," she continued.

"Evil," he said the word again that he most often used. "You never want to come into contact with them."

"You come into contact with them," she pointed out.

"Only from necessity. I have no other choice. It's my job to provide for you as well as protect you from evil."

Everything her dad did appeared to be for her necessity or for her protection. Her dad never claimed he needed any of the things he brought back to the mountain, although he got more use from them than she did, except for the books. He insisted she sit outside in the sunlight and read whenever possible. He'd rather she read than help him work.

"It's a parent's job to labor for their child, and the child's job to benefit from the parent's labor," he would say as though it was his duty to take care of her. She also tried to take care of him the best she could – in her own small way she did care for him.

She loved finding a warm, sunny spot to read a book. The sun stimulated her body, while the books stimulated her mind. She read over and over the books that told about families. There were mothers and fathers and other children who laughed and played together. She had come a long way from reading about Dick and Jane and a dog named Spot books to reading encyclopedias, books called novels and how-to books. In those books she found things impossible to believe. Nothing remotely similar to things existing on her mountain. She often wondered if such things were only fairytales, like the books she had first read and wanted to believe were real, but knew they weren't.

"What is fiction," she'd once asked her dad.

"Lies," he told her. "It means what you're reading is nothing but a bunch of made up lies a person has come up with."

"Are the encyclopedias lies too?"

"They're supposed to have some truths in them. Just remember, they were written according to other people's opinions about the research they discovered."

"Why do people lie?" she had persisted.

"Many reasons, and none of them are good. Now hush with your questions and let me get back to work."

Striker often became more confused with her dad's answers than she'd been with her questions. Now, most all her answers came from other people's opinions and research.

The summer and fall weather had been too good and lingered too long without there being payback. Striker's dad always warned her about *too good* of a thing. He also warned her about having too much fun. "Never trust things that are too good to be true," her dad would tell her. "You can count on them coming back to slap you in the face. Same goes for having too much fun. You pay, Striker. You always end up paying for what you get."

Striker liked it when things were too good. She also liked having fun, which didn't happen often. Having too much fun was something she couldn't wrap her mind around. Now that her dad was gone, she remembered most everything he'd told her, and would make an attempt to look what he'd told her up in books to find further information. Not that she didn't believe him, she simply wanted knowledge to back up the truths.

She did find information on having too much fun. She'd concluded it wasn't the amount of fun that was a bad thing. It was the letdown after the fun ended. People became sad and depressed when they were no longer having fun. She compared the warm summer months to fun, and then the sad depressed time to winter.

"To everything there is a season," she mumbled as she dragged deadfall from the surrounding woods, knowing soon the snow would be so deep she wouldn't be able to see deadfall. Oftentimes the snow would become too deep for her to get far from the cabin. She'd have to shovel a path from the door to the wood pile. "A time for fun, a time for sadness. A time for warmth, a time for cold. A time for life, a time for death," she added, causing the dog to prick his ears to listen.

In the weeks since the dog had shown up, he'd started following her, taking every step she took as though he was afraid another man would show up. Striker feared the same thing. When one man came, surely there would be more to follow. That was why her dad had been so careful in never leaving any kind of trail to their cabin. He'd warned her about breaking twigs and scuffing up the ground when they walked. She hadn't been as diligent about abiding to his instruction since he was gone. That proved to be a mistake. The man had found her, and so had the dog. She suspected it had been the deer trail that he'd followed. She should have gone back and done her best to wipe out the drag trail. She hadn't. Lesson learned.

She also learned her dad was right. There really were bad men willing to hurt her. She compared them to the wolves that were always on a killing hunt. Time had finally taken away all the hurting places the man had left on her body, but not in her mind. Evil she had never witnessed before had become real. The only good thing about the horrible event had been the dog.

In the time since the dog had shown up, she'd become attached to it. Just knowing he was there, gave her comfort. Since her dad's death, she no longer felt completely alone. The dog could never compensate for her dad, but he was company. The only time the dog wasn't watching her, or lying outside her cabin door, was when he wandered off to catch his own food. He was the greatest rabbit catcher she could imagine. Sometimes he would even bring a half-eaten rabbit to the cabin door as though he was offering it to her.

"Eat it yourself," she would tell him, and he did. She also shared her food with him, but it wasn't enough to fill their bellies. It was only enough to keep them both alive.

As for the wolves, their howls were now sounding from distant mountains instead of coming close to her cabin as they had once done. Not one single wolf had dared to dig in the man's grave the way they had done her dad's.

She did her best not to think about the man, the way he had hurt her, leaving bruises on her skin and fear in her mind. She thought he had tried to mate with her, but she wasn't sure. She knew little about such an act in humans. Even the books her dad brought home had very little on such subjects. Such things were so far from her world she put them out of her mind as something that didn't apply to her. What was most important, a constant necessity, was survival in the harsh mountain wilderness. Still, her dad's warnings, and the man showing up, haunted her in nightmares as the days and weeks came and went. Not that she judged time by days and weeks, she judged time by the temperature, along with the behavior of animals and plants. There were all kinds of explanations about seasons in the books she read, but no book could ever teach her as much as living with nature did.

~~~~

After the beloved warmth left the mountains, winter didn't hesitate to lock everything in its deep-freezing grip. The winds howled all night long causing the cold to feel even colder. Stricker heard a loud noise and opened the door a crack to see what caused the noise. A tree limb had fallen only a few feet from the cabin. Easy firewood, Striker thought. She was wearing every article of clothing she had. Right now, she almost regretted burying the man in his clothes. It was foolish of her to waste the simplest of things.

At the time, she didn't want the man's torn clothes to be a constant reminder of him. She needed no reminder. He had engraved himself in her mind and no matter how she tried to forget about him, she couldn't.

Before she could close the door back, the dog shot past her inside the cabin. He was covered in so much snow she'd hadn't seen him lying next to the door.

"Poor thing," she said as she looked at the dog. "You're cold too, aren't you?"

She was suddenly mad at herself for assuming the dog would find a sheltered spot to keep him out of the storm, but he hadn't. He had kept his vigil by her door. She took several sticks of wood and fed them into her fire without being as conservative as usual. The storm had given her the gift of firewood without her having to trek up to her waist through the snow filled woods. She would splurge with fire and food this one time.

She filled a pot with melted snow, put in some deer meat along with remaining chunks of dried wolf meat. The deer meat was for her and the wolf meat was for the dog. She added a potato to make their meal go farther. She and the dog both needed something warm to eat to help with the unusual cold spell. When such cold arrived, her dad always called it a deep-freeze. This cold spell went beyond that description.

She'd tried to count the days winter would last. Seven months, from October through April, roughly two hundred and twenty days. She was still able to discredit a few days in October. Also, very little had come back to life by April. That meant she only had one hundred and forty-five days to gather enough food and firewood to get her through the bad days. She'd allotted a certain amount food for each day. If she ate more one day, she'd have to skimp on another day.

At least the dog had been able to catch rabbits, an occasional turkey, and a few quail to keep himself from starving. With this storm bringing snowdrifts almost to the top of her cabin, he would not be able to scavenge for himself.

"We'll be okay," she told the shivering dog. "Winters are always like this. I've survived them and so will you."

The dog looked up at her from where he'd huddled next to the stove and thumped his tail on the floor. She felt a touch of remorse for not allowing the dog inside the cabin before now, but he'd seem to prefer being outside, as she did. The cold had now become life threatening and the dog was intelligent enough to seek warmth regardless of the confinement. From now until the weather broke, she and the dog would eat very little and huddle in the front room with the bedroom doors closed. She'd keep the fire going enough to heat water and keep them from freezing to death. She'd read that a person could go between twenty and thirty days without food, but only four days without water. Considering the snow outside, she and the dog would be able to have water for a very long time.

Chapter 37

~~~~

Lady Biswell gently ran her finger over the picture of Reg McFarland and smiled. He'd been the kind of man Joe Whitson deserved having go after him. She didn't regret one thing Reg did to Joe Whitson. Her only regret was that she hadn't done more herself. If she had been the woman back then that she was now, she wouldn't have needed Reg McFarland or anyone else to take care of Joe Whitson. She would have done what Reg did herself.

Looking back, she realized how young and naïve she actually was during that time. Today, children twelve years of age knew more about life than she knew at eighteen. She realized she'd been sheltered too much by parents who loved her. She'd been spoiled and pampered without ever once being allowed to see the evil side of life. All she'd ever known were kind-hearted people.

She had been sixteen years old when Sam Braden came into her life. She was one of seven cheerleaders and Sam was a fresh-faced kid who had just graduated from the school of law enforcement. Being security at ball games was one of his first jobs. All of the cheerleaders had a crush on the handsome young man, but he paid them no attention. He kind of reminded her of those Buckingham Palace guards who made a point of not paying attention to anyone regardless of what they did. He totally ignored the cheerleader's adolescent attempts to attract him.

"Watch me," She had bragged to the other cheerleaders. "I can wrap him around my little finger if I want to."

Much to her surprise, that was exactly what she did. At the same time, he had wrapped himself around her heart.

She was seventeen when she married Sam. Her parents had claimed she was too young to get married, but they finally gave in when she said she would elope with him. They knew Sam was a good man, if not exactly good enough for their daughter. They concluded her and Sam marrying wouldn't mean they would lose their daughter.

"We'll have gained a son," her father told her. "We'll look after you both," he told her. And they did – as long as they were alive.

"You taught me how to stand up and fight like hell, Reg. Most important, you taught me never to give up on anything. My only regret in marrying you was that you assisted Joe in having a heart attack before I found out who had my daughter. But I can't really blame you for what you did to Joe. I would have done worse as soon as I was able."

Lady Biswell placed the picture of her third husband back in the trunk and took out the wedding picture of her and Sam. She ran her finger tip over Sam's face, pressed the picture to her chest, and began to cry. It had been a long time since she'd allowed herself to cry, even in private. She didn't want to be weak, needed to be strong – even when she wasn't.

"A person can get a long way by pretending, Sam. I've spent every day of my life since you were killed pretending you were still with me. I still do. You've help me get through each day when I might not be able to do so otherwise. All I have to do is close my eyes and you'll still be beside me, holding my hand.

"We make love almost every single night, Sam. It happens over and over just like it did back then. Remember our wedding night, Sam? Of course, you do. Neither of us could ever forget how much we were in love, how much we're still in love.

"I know you don't hold it against me for marrying again. They were different kinds of marriages than you and I had. They were marriages of convenience. Nothing more.

"Oh, you want to talk about your daughter. Oh, Sam. I'm so very sorry, but I can't do that right now. Her memory hurts me too much. She was all I had left of you. She was all I had left of me too. She was the only reason I remained alive. Without her, I would have joined you while they had me in that asylum. Surely, you understand why I didn't."

Chapter 38

~~~~~~

The one thing Alice hadn't expected was for Bentley Doss to show up knocking on the door of her little shack after such a long time had passed. His bitch dog, along with Reeve's male dog, were in one of the back lots almost healed from their wounds, but definitely not able to ever fight again. She just hoped all her care for the dogs did not go to waste by Buckworth making them into bait dogs. She took a deep breath and opened the door for him. She always kept her door locked and never opened it to anyone. The place was so far back in the sticks few people knew she stayed in the shack full time. This time she made an exception.

"Good day to you, Miss Alice," he said respectfully. "I hate to bother you like this, but I hope you'll understand I just couldn't help myself. Something has been bothering me for a long while and I had to get it off my chest."

Alice understood only too well, but she pretended otherwise. "What can I do for you, Mr. Doss?" she asked without inviting him in.

"I need to know about my dog."

"What dog?"

"The last one I brought here to fight."

"I don't keep track of all the dogs brought here to fight," Alice told him, which was true. She only remembered the ones that she buried or tried to save their lives.

"I was hoping you'd remember," he said, and then went on to tell her when it was.

"That was a long while ago. What do you want to know about her?" Alice decided not to claim lack of memory toward everything. The man did appear to be in genuine distress.

"Was she killed? I mean, did she linger? Did she suffer?"

"When a dog's body had been ripped to pieces, she suffers the same as you would."

"Did she linger?" he asked again.

"Don't you remember what happened?" Alice asked, although she knew the answer.

"I hate to admit it, but I don't remember a thing. I only had one drink, maybe two at the most. You see, I'm not a drinking man. Looks like I couldn't handle it. I - - - I, well, I feel guilty for not calling the fight in time to save her. I'd become right attached to that little bitch."

Alice might have felt sorry for him if he hadn't been one of the men who participated in dog fighting. She hated those men and yet here she was, associating with them at each fight. She readily admitted to herself that something terrible was wrong with her, otherwise she would - - - would do what? Turn them in to the law? No way. Not after what the law had done to her when she was innocent of the charges. Innocence made no difference. Her license to care for animals were taken away. The law had deliberately and knowingly ruined her practice and her life.

"It was obvious you weren't in control of yourself," is all she said.

"It's taken me a while to gather enough courage to talk to you. I was told I made a right pitiful fool of myself."

"I wouldn't go so far as to say that. I can say you didn't carry a tune too well."

"I really was singing songs?"

"You were making an attempt at it."

"That bad, huh?"

"Right bad."

"And my dog?"

"You didn't call the fight."

"My handler didn't either?"

"He told me to bury her," Again, Alice told him the truth, but not all of the truth. "He didn't think you'd want to spend the money to try to save her considering what condition she was in."

"What condition was she in?" Bentley Doss wanted to know.

"Ripped to shreds. It would take nothing short of a miracle to save her. Seeing what happened to your dog ought to make you give up dog fighting for the rest of your life." She knew she was preaching, but she didn't care. "Seeing those poor dogs after fights keeps me from sleeping at night. It's a shame and a disgrace. A nightmare I tell you. A real nightmare in flesh, blood, and guts."

Bentley Doss hung his head refusing to look her in the eyes. "Can't rightly argue with you. Like I already said, I hated to bother you, but I had to know. I reckon I'll be going now."

Alice watched him turn around and leave with his feet dragging and his head still hung. She'd told him the truth about his dog. It had taken a miracle to save that dog, but she'd done it.

Buckworth showed up a short time after Bentley Doss left. Alice was still in a bad mood making her hate Buckworth and the dog fighting he encouraged even more.

"I sold Norman James' truck," he told her. "If he's not come out of those mountains in all this time, he won't be coming back."

Alice agreed with him on that fact. Norman James had most likely become food for wild animals. As for his truck, Buckworth had already stripped everything of value from it. He'd even sold the rearview mirror along with other parts.

"Didn't know there was anything left to sell," she told him.

"Got my money back," he told her.

Several times over, she thought. "What about his relatives? Aren't they looking for him? Put out a missing person report or something?"

"Ask me, if he had relatives, they don't want him back."

Could be, Alice thought. Still yet, there might be somebody somewhere who would eventually start looking for him.

"Have you given up on finding the Kangal dog?" Alice asked.

"If James hasn't shown up by now, he never will," Buckworth told her with confidence. "I've always heard nothing goes into those high mountains and comes out alive. Appears to me both James and that dog have proved it to be true."

Alice didn't know if that was true, nor did she care one way or the other. Something told her that Norman James would never show up again.

"Bentley Doss came asking about his dog a while ago," she said.

Buckworth became alert. "What did you tell him?" he demanded as though Doss showing up was all her fault.

"I gave him a good going over for letting his dog to be torn up the way she was. I also told him his handler told me to bury his dog."

"And?" Buckworth demanded.

"He left."

"He left thinking his bitch is dead?"

"Reckon that was what he thought."

"Has she bred yet?" Buckworth had the nerve to ask.

Alice rolled her eyes. "You don't know much about dogs," she informed him.

"I know if they stay around me, they better earn their keep, or they'll become dead dogs."

She'd heard his ranting about 'pay your way or don't stay' often enough. She paid her way many times over, but her resolve to stay was getting harder with every day that passed. There had been times when she considered getting into Norman James' truck and driving away, never to be seen again. Instead, she watched the truck being sold off one piece at a time. If her absence could lead to Buckworth not fighting dogs again, she'd have done it long ago. She knew her being there mattered very little to Buckworth. Her presence only mattered to the injured dogs.

"Order more supplies," Buckworth informed her.

She gritted her teeth and turned her back him, so he couldn't see her face. "Why?"

"I've scheduled a mighty big fight," he said proudly.

"It's wintertime."

"So?"

"Vehicles leave tracks in the snow."

"People who travel back into this God forsaken piece of hell come for one reason and one reason only. For the fights."

"A plane could fly over and spot the tracks from the air and notify government officials since this is near government land. Even a kid with a drone and a camera could take a picture that would give this place away."

"Hunters," he insisted. "It's deer hunting season. If anybody did happen to see tracks, there's the explanation."

Alice didn't argue further. She had warned him and that was all she was inclined to do where Buckworth was concerned. What she wanted to do was find a way to stop the cruel practice of dog fighting, not only with Buckworth, but with all the dog fights happening in the entire world. Why didn't the men who got off on brutal, cruel fighting get in the pit and fight each other? See who would call the fight to keep them alive.

~~~~

Alice was filled with anger and rebellion as Buckworth readied things for the coming fight. Every instinct she'd developed through the years was warning her of impending danger. Somehow, she had to get away from the shack in the deep woods – and she had to take the dogs to a place where they could be set free. How she was going to manage such a feat was a puzzle.

If she turned the dogs loose, chances were they would remain near the shack because that was where they were being fed. If she walked away by foot, how could she take all the dogs with her? Even more problematic was where would she go with the dogs.

Alice went out back and walked from one lot to the next watching the dogs, wondering what she could do to stop the upcoming fights – to stop the death or mutilation of the dogs she was caring for as well as the dogs brought in to fight.

"What are you doing?" a voice said from behind her.

She jumped and whirled around. "Where did you come from? You nearly scared the life outta me."

"Sorry about that," said Blackburn with a slight grin. "I decided to go for a walk and ended up here."

"A walk in this snow?" she questioned, not believing a word he'd just told her.

"I walked in the tire tracks. Seems like a lot of vehicles for this bad of weather."

Alice shrugged as if to indicate it wasn't that unusual.

"Buckworth planning another fight?" he asked.

Alice saw no reason to lie to him. He'd shown up at most all the recent fights. He'd passed Buckworth's approval and would most likely be at the next fight.

"He's always planning the next fight. He has this idea that the next fight will make him rich. It's never happened. Do you know what the definition of a crazy person is? It's someone who keeps doing the same thing over and over again while expecting different results."

Blackburn nodded. "That's one of the definitions," he agreed. "Another definition could be a person who stays with the status quo when she knows it's time for her to leave."

Alice gave him a hard look. "Exactly what are you getting at?"

"I want to know why you're here when you hate dog fighting?"

"To keep the dogs alive," she told him.

He shook his head. "I don't believe that for a minute."

Anger flared in her eyes as she glowered at him.

"I believe you are simply afraid to leave because you have no place to go."

The truth in that statement almost defused her anger. "There is some truth in that remark," she admitted. "But I want you to know I'm always trying to keep the dogs alive."

"Makes you feel good to know you've saved a life, doesn't it?"

"If you really are – were a doctor, you'd understand such as that."

"I do understand it all too well. There's another reason I'm here. I believe you're a good person who doesn't deserve what you'll receive if this place were to be raided during a dog fight. Why stay here, Alice? Why not pack up and leave?"

Alice smiled at his softly spoken question. "I can't leave my dogs," she told him.

"The dogs would be taken care of properly."

"You mean put down?"

"No, I don't mean that at all. They would be taken to a no-kill animal shelter where good homes would be found for them."

"These are fighting dogs." She pointed out.

"Do they fight each other when they get together?"

"Some do, but most of them won't fight unless they are provoked and prodded until they have no choice other than fight.

"Let me ask you something, and I want you to think about it before you answer. If a vehicle showed up to take you safely away from here, would you leave?"

"Depends," she said without thinking about it.

"On what?"

"Who was driving the vehicle. Where I was being taken. What would happen to me, and if I could take two of the dogs with me."

"What if the vehicle was in your name and you were able drive off and be able to go wherever you chose, never to be heard from again. And yes, you would be able to take two of the dogs with you."

"I could be packed in less than ten minutes," she said with a touch of humor mixed with sincerity.

Blackburn nodded with approval. "There will be a car parked in the same place Norman James' truck was parked, but there is a condition attached."

She rolled her eyes. There was always a condition attached.

"You don't say a word to anyone. You stay here until time for the fight to start then slip the dogs into the car and get the hell away fast, understand?"

Alice wasn't sure if she understood what he was telling her or not. "Are you saying Buckworth will be busted tonight?"

"No. that's not what I'm saying. I don't know when or if Buckworth will be busted. What I am saying is that I believe you're too good of a woman to be subjected to something that is destroying your heart and soul. I've bought a vehicle and registered it in the name of Alice Danbert. Take it. Don't question your escape, and don't look back. Ever."

Blackburn handed her a set of keys, turned his back the same way he always did, and left her standing there with her mouth open and her hand gripping the keys. Was she to believe him? Was he actually telling the truth and a vehicle would be waiting for her? Was her dilemma being solved, or were her problems just beginning?

Chapter 39

~~~~

Striker opened her eyes to hear the sound of water dripping off the roof of her cabin. She reached out her hand to stroke the dog lying on the bed beside her. She knew he would be there, always was, but she needed the assurance.

She eased from under the moth-eaten hides they had slept under. Her fire had burned low giving off little warmth, but the room wasn't as cold as she expected. Could it mean Spring was finally arriving, or was this what her dad used to call a January thaw? Her dad had always used that snap of warmer January weather to restock their firewood supply.

She wasn't sure if it was January or March. It could even be April for all she knew. As usual, winter days had run into one another. She'd started out the winter by making marks on a stick, but, as usual, she'd stopped after a while. She crossed the room, picked up the stick, and started counting. She'd stopped marking after sixty marks. How many days had it been since her last mark? She didn't know the answer to that, didn't much care. One day ran into another when all she and the dog did was sleep. The light in the cabin was always dim or non-existent. She couldn't pass the time by reading without light, so there was nothing to do other than sleep.

The dog raised his head to watch her. Poor dog, he was skin and bones, as was she. Their supply of food was running mighty low. For a long time now, they had been staying in bed and only eating what she thought of as half-rations. She hadn't counted on having a dog to feed. He might have been able to hunt for his own food if she'd let him out of the cabin, but she couldn't make herself do it. The howling of the wolves had come closer to her cabin and she feared if she let the dog out, the wolves would kill him. Some nights the wolves howling sounded as though it was outside her cabin door, and other nights it sounded as though they were hunting down in the valley.

Striker opened her bedroom door to get firewood for the stove. When she realized the snow was going to be too deep to gather firewood, she'd filled her bedroom with wood. She needed to heat water to boil the remains of the deer meat with the remains of potatoes and dried herbs. As she opened the door, the dog lunged past her almost knocking her over. A moment later she realized the dog had something in his mouth, while shaking his head viciously. He turned and dropped the dead rat at her feet.

She let out a relieved sound. "Good boy. Good dog." He had saved them a little longer from starvation when she had been feeling hopeless and too tired to do anything other than crawl back in the bed. She sank to her knees and hugged the dog before she took the rat in one hand and gathered a few sticks of wood in the other hand. If there was one rat in the the wood pile, it was likely there would be more? Maybe she and the dog wouldn't starve to death after all.

The dog eagerly licked the rat's blood from his mouth. Every drop of rat blood was a speck of life-giving fluid. His instincts had been to eat the entire rat, but he'd controlled his instincts.

"We'll survive," she told the dog. "Both of us will." She knew if she died, the dog could survive by eating her. If she killed the dog, she could survive by eating the dog. Neither was an option. She was determined they both should live. Not only was the snow melting, the dog had provided food for them both.

Once they had both eaten the rat, they went back to bed. She had moved the bed next to the stove where they would stay warmer. She and the dog both drifted off to sleep. When she awoke, she still heard the dripping of water from her roof. She forced herself to get up and make her way to the door where she tried to push it open. Snow was drifted against the door until opening it was impossible.

"Dad," she mumbled. "We should have thought to make another door that opened inward."

She promised herself when summer came, and she'd regained her strength, she would at least make a small door that opened underneath the overhanging rock so the door would be more sheltered. She would be able to get outside when the snow drifts covered the cabin. When her dad was alive, he kept a path shoveled away from their door. Lack of food and warm clothing had kept her from attempting to shovel a path.

The dog perked his ears when she spoke, but he didn't offer to get up from the bed. Even the dog realized he needed to conserve his strength. She looked at the dog. "Next year," she promised him, "things will be better. With your help I'll grow a bigger garden, go to different mountains, go down into the valley to find more food. We'll fare better next winter. I can promise you we'll not starve again."

She returned to the bed, curling up against the dog. All they had to do was survive a while longer.

Chapter 40

~~~~

Alice had very little to pack. She owned nothing other than two changes of clothing, two pairs of shoes, one pair of work boots and a heavy winter jacket – plus a pistol and knife she always carried. All her things could be worn or stuffed in a grocery bag in a matter of seconds. Better still, her change of clothes and shoes could be left behind. Their absence might warn Buckworth she had run off. If they remained, he might think she had been forcefully taken away.

She wanted to take Doss's bitch and Reese's male dog with her, but she wasn't sure how to get them away from the shack without drawing suspicion. Buckworth was already there getting things set up for the night's fight.

"Got things ready?" his voice seemed extra loud as he spoke. It was all Alice could do to keep herself from jumping with nervousness.

"Everything is ready, but I need to ask you something."

"What?" he raised his voice with impatience.

"It's Doss and Reese's dogs. I'm afraid a handler or someone else will wander out back and see that they're still alive."

Buckworth frowned. She had a point.

"I was thinking about taking them way out into the woods where they can't be seen, put a muzzle on them so they can't bark, and leaving them there until after the fight is over and everyone is gone."

"Humph," he grunted. "Sometimes you come up with good ideas, but you're still not worth what I pay you."

"Do it or not?" she questioned, ignoring his attempt at insulting her.

"Do it and be quick about it. I want you here instead of wandering out back in the underbrush."

"No problem," she told him, and hoped she spoke the truth.

~~~~

Thirty minutes before the gate keepers and security guards were supposed to arrive, she put on her heavy winter coat and boots, made sure she had her pistol, knife, and the keys Blackburn had given her, She put muzzles on the dogs and clipped their leads onto their harnesses.

She almost squealed when she turned around and saw Buckworth watching her. Thank goodness she hadn't packed her few spare possessions.

"I'll be back shortly," she told him.

"Hurry and take them a long way into the woods. I'm glad I thought about hiding them. No need to take a chance on somebody seeing them. You'd be up shit creek if somebody recognized those dogs.

"You're right about that," she said. "The locals wouldn't want to bring their dogs here to fight ever again once they lost trust in me doing what I was told."

Buckworth was pleased with her taking responsibility.

It was all Alice could do not to look back to see if Buckworth was watching as she led the dogs into the woods. Anything she did out of the ordinary might trigger Buckworth's warning signals. She had done her best to appear as calm and undisturbed as usually. She'd had a lot of practice in such appearances. Inside, Alice was quaking and telling herself Buckworth didn't know anything about

Blackburn's plans. Problem was she didn't know his plans either.

If something went wrong, if the vehicle wasn't there, no one would know the difference since Buckworth had okayed her moving the dogs. If she was caught leaving in the vehicle with the dogs, then what? She needed to think of a good explanation and think of it now.

She gave the dogs some lead and let them pull her through the woods at a slow run. Every minute counted. Every second counted. She had to be long gone before Buckworth checked again to make sure everything was ready before the first person showed up. She was thankful, his dog handler was already there. She disliked and distrusted the Phillip man equally as much as he seemed to dislike and distrust her.

Calm down, she told herself. If there is no vehicle there, what does it matter? She'd simply tie the dogs to a tree and return to the shack exactly the way Buckworth expected her to. If the vehicle waited, it was a game changer. It was escape or be dumped in the bury hole along with all the dead dogs.

She gritted her teeth as beads of sweat broke out on her forehead and upper lip as she neared the place Blackburn said he would leave the vehicle. She saw nothing.

"Shit!" the man had lied to her.

What had she expected? Yet, she had hoped. She passed the place where Norman James' truck had been parked and led the dogs into concealing undergrowth to tie them up. She stopped in her tracks. Blinked once, twice before she dared take a full-throated breath of air. There right in front of her was a dull, oxidized gray Jeep Cherokee. Its color blended in so well with the undergrowth she'd almost not seen it. A more perfect vehicle couldn't have been chosen. Not only did it have four-wheel drive, it was the same color and make as half the vehicles in this part of the county.

She stood still listening and looking around in case there was the slightest noise or the tiniest of movement. She detected none. Still she waited, observing the actions of the two dogs. The male cocked his leg and happily relieved himself on a tree trunk. Doss's bitch was her usual calm self. They both looked at the vehicle, lifted their noses into the air and sniffed in question, but with no concern.

Alice moved to the vehicle, looked and listened again before she reached for the backdoor handle. It opened. She guided the dogs inside.

"Stay," she told them and they both sat down in the floorboard.

She hardly dared to breathe as she reached in her britches pocket for the keys Blackburn had given her. She inserted them into the ignition without closing the jeep door. The engine turned over in perfect running condition. She eased the door closed, making sure it shut almost noiselessly, put the gearshift into drive and moved forward. Before she realized she actually was escaping, she was out of the woods and driving on the snow-covered road in the same tracks Buckworth had driven in on.

~~~~

Alice Danbert drove all night long, only stopping once to fill up the tank with gas in the early morning light. Much to her irritation, she had to go inside to pay for the gas in advance, but that was okay. She didn't have a credit card or any other kind of identification. The old man who sat at the cash register paid little attention to her. She handed him thirty dollars, not sure how much the gas tank would hold.

She stuck the nozzle into the tank and let the gas run until the pump clicked off exactly on the thirty-dollar mark. She got back in the Jeep and drove away. The tank was a little over three quarters full, which was okay. When she needed gas again, she'd stop at a place where she could buy a bag of dog food, some water, plus bread and bologna for her.

As she drove, she realized exactly where she was going. When she was a small child, her mother had taken her way back into the hills of West Virginia. The man who lived there had begged her mother to stay with him, but her mother had laughed and told him she wasn't the staying kind.

He'd replied, "If you're bound and determined to run off, you'll do it no matter what I say, but won't you please leave our little girl with her daddy? You know she'll always be safe with me."

She was relieved her mother hadn't left her behind. Now she was going to find out if she really would be safe staying there with him.

Chapter 41

~~~~

Griff looked at the front page of the newspaper with lifted brows. He'd seen the man in the picture before. He was the one who had stopped by wanting to buy dogs when Kang was a pup. He had known there was something evil about the man the moment he'd set eyes on him.

"Just as I thought," Griff mumbled to himself. The man ran a dog fighting ring in the next county over. The man owned a small warehouse in town where he sold farm supplies and animal feed, while pretending to be one of the town's outstanding citizens.

He continued to read about how the man had tried to conceal his illegal operation by having it hidden in the rugged foothills next to the National Forest. He'd chosen a pretty good location except for one thing. Too many car tracks had been spotted by a plane and then reported to the proper authorities. The crudely built shack had been surrounded during the middle of a dog fight. Everyone was arrested on the spot, except for a few who escaped on foot. Didn't take long for them to be tracked down in the snow and arrested.

All the dogs had been taken to a local humane society where they would be cared for properly until they were ready to be put up for adoption. Dogs with injuries received immediate medical care.

The article went on to say several bait dogs were also taken to the shelter. They were thought to be dogs stolen from the surrounding area.

"What are you reading?" Griff tensed at the sound of Lady Biswell's voice. She was looking over his shoulder.

"Have you read this morning's newspaper?"

"No, why?"

"A dog fighting ring was busted."

"Good."

"It was less than thirty miles from here by way of road. Closer as the crow flies."

He now had Lady Biswell's attention. "And?" she questioned.

"I've seen the man in the picture before. He was the one who showed up a while back asking about your dogs."

Alice jerked the paper from Griff's hands and held the picture closer her face. She frowned.

"He was the man driving that black Suburban with the tinted windows. He was tall with a fat belly and an aggressive manner. He was overbearing to say the least. Just talking to him caused me to think of dog fighting," Griff said.

"Why didn't you tell me?"

"I did. You said he passed you on the road while you were walking Kang. The newspaper also reported a lot of local dogs were stolen to use as bait dogs."

Lady Biswell let out a horrified gasp and then sank down in a chair beside Griff. "Do you suppose - - - could it be possible?"

"Only one way to find out. We'll have to go to the proper authorities and ask."

Lady Biswell slapped the paper against her thigh. "Let's go, right this minute."

"I've not fed the dogs yet."

"We'll do it when we get back. I can't wait a moment longer."

Lady Biswell beat him to the truck, got behind the wheel, and was driving off before Griff slammed the passenger door shut.

"Slow down," he told her. "Five minutes won't make a difference."

"It makes a difference to me. It might also make a difference to Kang."

Griff slowly shook his head. "It's been a mighty long time. Most likely if he was stolen, he won't still be around."

"Exactly what are you saying?"

"Dogs don't last long with people such as that. They usually fight short-legged dogs like pit bulls, or pit bull crosses. Kang was a long-legged guardian dog. He'd most likely be used as a bait dog to teach the bulls to go for the belly."

Lady Biswell's face lost color. Griff thought she was going to faint while driving. "Shit, I'm sorry I said that. They most likely have never seen Kang. You said he pulled loose and ran off. It wasn't like somebody stole him."

"Somebody found him and took him. I'm sure of it. If not, he'd have come back to me."

Griff had to agree with her, but he didn't have to confirm her suspicion. At the same time, he didn't want her to get her hopes up just to be let down again. It was far better to accept the fact that the dog was long gone than for her to keep on hoping.

"You remember that man who called me up recently wanting ten thousand dollars in trade for my dog?" Lady Biswell said.

"I remember," Griff relunctly admitted.

"That's proof Kang was still alive."

"Be reasonable, even you thought the man was trying to rip you off."

"But what if he wasn't? What if he really did know something about Kang?"

"Knowing something about him and being able to get him back for you are two different things."

"Yes, but - - - "

"No buts. Let's not jump to conclusions or have false hopes until we find out more about this dog fighting ring. Most likely Kang was never there."

"He had to be somewhere," she said stubbornly. "Somebody somewhere knows what happened to him even if he isn't one of the dogs that was saved. Regardless, I have to find out what happened to him. I won't stop searching until I know the truth," she informed him.

He knew that to be a fact. Lady Biswell never gave up on anything. When she went after something, she went all out. "Say, where exactly are you going?"

"To the sheriff's department, obviously."

"It's not our sheriff's department that busted the ring. It was the next county over."

"I know that, but our sheriff's department can contact theirs. Our department knows how desperately I've been looking for my Kang. They'll be as anxious as I am to get to the bottom of this."

Griff couldn't argue the point with her on that. He didn't think a single week had passed she hadn't called the sheriff's department for news of her missing dog. If she hadn't been the richest, most influential woman in the county, they'd have threatened to lock her up in jail or a mental asylum.

Griff turned a little pale as she broke the speed limit by pressing the gas pedal all the way to the floor. Fortunately, it was before most people traveled to work. Even the law enforcement agencies were just waking up.

He drew in his first non-stressful breaths of oxygen when she screeched to a stop in from of the sheriff's department. She was out of the truck and through the department's door before Griff's legs were steady enough to walk.

"We were expecting you," Griff heard a tired sounding man say. "We were surprised it took you so long. The newspapers were delivered a good thirty minutes ago."

"I came as fast as I could drive," she informed him. "What do you know about my dog?"

"Nothing," the man told her gently. "We know about the same as you do about the dog fighting ring bust. We weren't a part of it and weren't informed about it. All we know is what we read in the paper."

"You can't be serious."

"I know you're disappointed, but I am serious. We know nothing more than you know."

"Then find out something."

"That's what the chief is trying to do. He's been on the phone for the past thirty minutes."

"Let me talk to the chief," she demanded.

"More than glad to let you do that. I'll take you back to his office." He made eye contact with Griff as he opened a door for them to enter the hallway that led to the chief's office.

"Wait here. He'll be in as soon as he gets off the phone." The young deputy eased out the door and shut it softly behind him. Griff took a seat, but Lady Biswell paced the floor from one side to the other.

"Do your best to remain calm," Griff dared suggest. "Sit down. Take it easy."

"I am taking it easy," she informed him. "I simply can't stop my mind from seeing my Kang with his guts ripped out."

"Kangal dogs are bred to fight mountain lions. They know how to keep their guts from being ripped out," Griff said in an attempt to calm her. It didn't seem to work.

Fortunately, for Griff, Chief Adkerson came into the room. The look on his face was not encouraging.

"Lady Biswell, Griff," he greeted them as he entered. "I've been on the phone for the last hour trying to find out more about this dog fighting ring bust. It seems a man named Ronald Buckworth had been running it. He and everyone who was attending the fight were arrested. How much do you know about dog fighting?" Chief Adkerson asked Lady Biswell.

"Virtually, nothing. What I want to know is do they have my dog?"

"That's what I've been trying to find out. After all this time, it's unlikely. However, anything is possible," he quickly added after seeing Lady Biswell's expression.

"I have to know one way or the other," she told him as tears sparkled in her eyes.

"I understand and I'm waiting for a call back," Chief Adkerson told her gently. "While we wait on the call, let me give you a little information on dog fighting. It's illegal in all fifty states plus Washington DC, Porto Rica, Gaum, and the Virgin Islands. In most states, it is considered a felony to attend a dog fight even if you're not fighting your own dog. Most dog fights are run by gangs and other unlawful groups or individuals. It's another form of illegal gambling. As much as half a million dollars has been confiscated during a single dog fighting raid.

"It is estimated that an average of around 16,000 or 18,000 thousand dogs are killed each year in organized dog fights in the United States alone. That does not include the underground dog fights such as street fights and backwoods fights like was just busted. This Buckworth man was one of the little guys, but still a criminal and a plague on society.

"I should let you know that Kangal dogs are almost never used in dog fighting. In the United States it's the pit bull dog and pit bull mixes that are most often used. There are also dog breeds such as the fila brasileiro, dogo argentino, the tosa inu, and the presa canario that are the choice fighting dogs. As I stated earlier, in the United States it is considered a federal offence to even attend such an event."

"Can I possibly take a look at the dogs that have been confiscated?"

"I'm not sure at this time," he told her. "I imagine there will some way people who have dogs gone missing will be able to see the dogs."

"Surely someone would know if a large male Kangal dog is in the group," Griff said.

"Yes, I should think finding that out would be easy enough. As soon as I get a return call, I'll make sure to ask. Since I'm not sure when I'll get that call, Griff, why don't you take Lady Biswell out to breakfast. You can stop by the office when you're finished to see if I've found out something more."

"Chief Adkerson, are you trying tactfully to get rid of me?" Lady Biswell asked.

"Yes, I do believe that's what I'm attempting to do," he grinned. "I know how much your missing dog means to you. I hope you realize we've done everything we know to help you find him."

"Yes," she said sadly. "I realize all you've done, and I thank you."

Griff stood up and put his arm around her shoulders. She instantly stiffened, and he dropped his arm. "Thank you, Chief Adkerson," Griff said as Adkerson made a point of opening the door for them to leave his office.

"Where do you want to eat?" Griff ask her.

"Surely you don't think I could eat a bite of food."

"I know, but we have to eat something."

"I thought you were a man who ate breakfast the moment he got out of bed."

"Cereal," he admitted. "A sausage and egg sandwich sounds good right now."

"Then I'll stop at a drive through window and get you one – on our way to the sheriff's office where the bust took place."

"Surely not," he mumbled.

"Does that mean you want to get one in this county?"

Griff let a breath of air escape his lips. He knew arguing with her would do no good. "Tell you what. Why don't you drop me off back home and I'll do the feeding, while you try to find out more about your dog."

"Good idea," she told him. "No need for my other dogs to go hungry. Having you with me won't speed anything up."

~~~~

Lady Biswell dropped Griff off at the house. drove back onto the road and stepped on the gas pedal. She hadn't gone far when she suddenly slowed down to a reasonable speed. There was no reason to risk having an accident or endangering someone else's safety on a chance she might find her beloved dog.

She remembered taking a similar chance on finding her daughter. Unfortunately, Joe Whitson had died from a sudden heart attack before he divulged the whereabouts of her daughter.

"His death saved you a lot of time and trauma," her attorney, Reg McFarland had told her. "I'm sure you realize he was planning on having you recommitted to the mental asylum."

Yes, she knew. He had been threatening to recommit her, but Reg had promised he'd make sure Joe's threats never fell on fertile ground, as Reg had put it. Reg already had her an appointment with the best mental health doctor in existence, according to Reg. She kept the appointment and was assured she was one of the sanest women he'd ever had in his office. She had laughed.

"That might not be saying much," she'd told him.

"You're the only one who can determine how sane you are and how sane you'll remain. I believe you are a strong woman. You now have to prove it to yourself."

He had assured her it was common for women to become overly stressed when losing both her parents and her husband so close together. To make matters worse, being pregnant was another stress factor on her body. In addition to all that, having her baby forcefully taken away from her and being declared incapable of raising a child was enough to make a mother appear insane.

Lady Biswell decided she both loved and hated the doctor. He made her feel strong and at the same time he also made her feel stupid.

"Learn," he told her. "Always go the extra mile to find out everything there is to know about everything."

"Exactly how am I supposed to do such as that?"

"Education and research. Become a snoop. Question everything and find the right and wrong answers. Then make sure you know which answer is wrong and which is right."

She had taken the doctor's advice to heart. She had started by moving back into the house she had shared with Joe Whitson. She had a right to everything he owned because their divorce had not gone through before his death. Joe had told her he had no living relatives, at least none he knew about and added with a laugh. "My daddy was a rounder. He was a traveling salesman, and you know how they are."

No, she didn't know how traveling salesmen were, but she was getting a good idea how her husband was. She realized he had no intention of ever telling her where her baby was, even if he actually knew. Joe was such a habitual liar even he didn't know when he accidently told the truth.

She had confronted him. He confronted her back with his fists. He found he liked beating on her almost as much as he liked lying to people in order to cheat them out of their money. She took great pleasure in having his body cremated. When she had been given his ashes, she was repulsed.

"Toss them into the trash heap," Reg had told her.

She was so inclined, but at the same time human ashes deserved something slightly better. "Where are his parents buried," she'd asked Reg.

"Don't have the slightest idea, but we can find out if that's what you want."

"That's what I want," she'd told Reg.

~~~~

Reg McFarland stood by her side every step of the way, guiding her as to her rights as a widow. When she discovered Joe Whitson had a half-sister still alive, she made a point of having Reg check her out. The half-sister and Joe had never gotten along. According to Reg, they hated each other with a passion. That knowledge alone caused Lady Biswell to feel kindly toward the half-sister.

When Reg told her Joe's half-sister had three children, a dead husband, and was barely keeping soul and body together, she made a decision. She had Reg send the sister money each month. She insisted Reg tell the half-sister the money was coming from an insurance policy Joe had taken out and named her as a benefactor.

After serving as her attorney for two years, Reg McFarland made her an offer she couldn't refuse, when she'd gone to his office to consult about her dead husband's tax evasion.

"I've just got back from having my yearly physical," he told her. "The doctor informed me I am in the advanced stage of cancer and that I only have a limited time to live."

"I'm sorry to hear that," she'd told him, and she truly was. She'd not only come to respect the hardnosed attorney, there was also something she liked about him.

"I want to tell you something, and after I finish telling you, I want you not to refuse my request, but to think about what I've said for a very short time, like ten minutes. Can you agree to that?"

"Of course, I can agree."

"Good. I hoped you would say that."

Reg McFarland had gotten married to his high school sweetheart. She had gotten a job as a waitress to help put him through law school. As soon as he graduated and got a job, she'd stopped working and they'd started a family. She'd gone into premature labor at eight months. She had suffered a brain aneurism and died in the hospital bed. An emergency c-section had been performed but the baby boy hadn't survived. Reg never married again, never got over losing his son, along with the only woman he'd ever loved. He blamed himself for her death as well as the death of his baby son. Lady Bisswell learned he'd had the baby placed in his wife's arms in her coffin. Every Sunday since her death, he went to their grave and placed two white daisies at the base of the headstone. White daisies were his wife's favorite flower.

"I have my burial plot beside theirs," he told her. "I want you to promise you'll see that I'm buried there."

"I will," she told him with all sincerity.

"Plus," he added, "I want you to marry me tomorrow."

"Pardon me?" she questioned. Surely, she hadn't heard him correctly.

"I'll repeat that I want you to marry me tomorrow."

"Why?" she blurted out.

"Because I'm an old, dying, no account ass hole who never did anything good for another person. I want to do something good for somebody, and you're the one I've chosen."

"I see," she said calmly. "You've been diagnosed with brain cancer."

Those words brought a slight grin from Reg. "Prostate cancer. It has already spread to my bones and organs. The doctor wanted to do surgery immediately, but I told him no. To be honest, I want to find out if there's any truth in the possibly I'll be reunited with my wife and baby in the hereafter."

She opened her mouth to refuse, and then closed it. She'd promised to wait ten minutes before she gave him an answer.

~~~~

She stopped thinking about her past life when she stopped her truck in front of the sheriff's office. This time without squalling tires. Actually, she got pleasure out of scaring Griff. He was such an uptight fuddy-duddy.

She walked in and went straight to the receptionist sitting at a desk. "I had a dog stolen from me and I'm hoping he might be in the group the dog fighters had."

The woman gave her a slight smile that was as tired as the woman's face. "Join the crowd," she said and pointed to a dozen people sitting in chairs waiting."

"They all had their dogs stolen?"

"That's only part of them. There's been more." She took a sheet of paper from her desk and fastened it on a clipboard. "Fill this out and then return it to me when you're finished. Make sure you add your phone number. If the feds have a dog matching your description, they'll call you."

"That's it?" Lady Biswell said with obvious irritation.

"That's it, and it's all I can do."

"I want to see the dogs. See if mine is among them."

"The dogs aren't located here. They were taken to a shelter."

"My dog is a Kangal not a pit bull. He would be recognizable instantly."

"I'm sure it would be, but I have nothing to do with the dogs. I only take the information you fill out on that questionnaire and turn it over to the feds. Like I just told you, if they have a Kangal dog fitting your description, they'll call you."

Lady Biswell was so irritated she almost slammed the clipboard down on the desk, but she didn't. If there was the slightest chance of finding her dog, she'd take it.

Chapter 42

~~~~

Striker hadn't been mistaken. There really was water dripping off the roof of the cabin, and it wasn't a January thaw. It was the arrival of spring. Warmer air was rising up from the valley and melting away the snow covering the high mountains. Finally, she was able to open the door more than the crack she used to get snow to melt.

"We'll go outside soon," she told the dog as she closed the door back and put her arms around the dog's neck. He nosed her right back with mutual affection.

Being able to go outside wouldn't help their hunger a great deal unless the dog could catch a rabbit or some other game. Nothing green would be growing in this cold. She wouldn't even be able to find cattail roots in the frozen mud down in the lower valley until it warmed up enough for her to put out shoots. If the sap in the trees had started to rise, she would be able to strip bark from Birch and Sassafras trees to boil a nutritious tea for her to drink. She wasn't sure if the dog would be willing to drink such a bitter brew. She could also tap Sugar Maple trees the way her dad had shown her and gather wonderful tasting liquid. So far, the dog ate and drank half of whatever she consumed.

The dog was bone-thin with his ribs showing. Striker knew she had to be just as thin and bony if she ever took off all the ragged clothes and animal-hides she'd shrouded herself in. The most her body was ever exposed was when she had to squat to relieve herself. Food had become so scarce that need didn't occur often for her or the dog. She and the dog both used a corner of her dad's bedroom when they could no longer go outside. There was little odor since it froze almost as soon as it hit the ground.

Striker took off the rabbit fur gloves she had worn thin and dropped them in the pot of boiling water hair and all. After it boiled a while, she would drink the broth and give the cooked skin to the dog. Their supply of deer jerky was long gone as was the supply of rats the dog had been able to catch. Even the supply of wood stored in her bedroom was down to a few small sticks.

Soon, the hide she wore for clothes would have to go for boiled broth and dog food unless they were able to get outside and find something to eat. Even the wolves had left the mountains for lower land where the wildlife had migrated. For several nights in a row she had heard their high-pitched howling rising up from the low lands. One night, she had even heard the sound of gun shots echoing of the mountains. It was a sound she had heard several times before.

"The wolves are in the livestock," her dad had explained the first time she had heard shots.

"What is livestock?" she'd asked.

Her dad had gone through the books until he found pictures of cattle, sheep, goats, and horses. "These are known as livestock," he told her. He then found pictures of chickens, ducks, and geese. "These are known as fowl. When food gets scarce in these mountains, predators are forced to head for the low country and people. The noise you hear are gunshots. People are trying to kill those predators in order to save the lives of their livestock and fowl."

Striker had done her best to get an idea about people, livestock, fowl, and predators and what was right and wrong concerning such things. She found she couldn't come to any conclusion. Her dad sensed her confusion.

"You've known me to kill animals for food, haven't you?"

She'd nodded her head.

"You've known animals to kill other animals for food, haven't you?"

Again, she nodded.

"What it comes down to, Striker, is survival of the fittest. It's nature's way of keeping the only the strongest alive and reproducing."

She thought she understood what her dad had been trying to tell her. What she now understood, was if she was going to be one of those to survive, she would have to come up with a better way provide more food and better shelter.

Right at the moment, there was little she could do.

Chapter 43

~~~~

Lady Biswell had already called Chief Adkerson twice before he had received a call about the dogs that were confiscated.

"According to the information I received, there was no Kangal in the group," Chief Adkerson told her.

"How do you know?" Lady Biswell did her best not to sound too impatient, but she was. Surely it didn't take weeks to find out information as simple as asking about a very distinctive dog.

"I'm sorry I can't be of more help to you. I know how desperate you've been, but I only know what I was told," he informed her. It was obvious he was getting tired of her calling him. "I assume what I was told to be true. Otherwise, they would be as anxious as you are to return your dog. Even you pointed out that Kangal dogs aren't known as fighting dogs. Plus, that breed of dog would be easily spotted. If I'm told no Kangal dog was in the group, I have to assume that information to be correct."

"Why won't they allow me to at least look at the dogs? I can see no harm in that since they want to find good homes for them."

"You've got a point. I was also told most of the dogs except a few of the most vicious pit bulls were returned to the owners they were stolen from. They are holding onto those vicious pit bulls as a matter of precaution."

"I only want to look so I can be assured my dog isn't one of those that remains. Surely, that's not too much to ask."

Chief Adkerson agreed. "Unfortunately, the feds don't listen to anything I have to say or suggest. Sorry," he added. "If I hear anything else, I'll let you know, but I have to say this. Your dog has been missing for several years now. You've even offered a two-thousand-dollar reward for his return. If he were still alive, someone would have gotten in touch with you by now. If you don't mind me saying, it would be a lot easier on your peace of mind if you accept the inevitable."

"Thank you for your advice, but my gut instinct tells me my dog is still alive. I appreciate your help. And, if you hear anything further, please call me immediately."

"I will," he assured her.

Lady Biswell felt the old familiar depression setting in. Never, since the day she got out of the asylum had she allowed depression to control her. When she felt it coming on, she became more determined to fight harder.

She renewed her ads along with Kang's picture in as many newspapers as she could get in contact with. She offered a thousand dollars for any information the informer could prove to be true. She doubled the two thousand to four thousand for information leading to his return.

She started calling the sheriff's office every three days since the raid had taken place, asking if there was information on the dogs and when she would be able to see them.

She was told the paper she filled out describing her missing dog didn't match any of the dogs they had confiscated. Yet she wasn't about to give up. There was no doubt in her mind Kang had been stolen by the horrible man named Buckworth.

It was over a month later that she got a call about the dog fighting ring's dogs.

"I'm trying to get in touch with a Nedra Biswell." The deep voice of a man said.

"This is she," Lady Biswell told him. "Who am I speaking with?"

"I'm one of the federal agents who busted the dog fighting ring in your area. I have your missing dog report in front of me. I've been told you are an extremely persistent lady," he sounded somewhat amused.

"I'm determined to find my dog if that's what you're referring to."

"Can you describe what he looks like?"

"If you have my missing dog report, you should already know," she said.

Lady Biswell gave him a detailed description of Kang anyway.

"Your description fits a dog I was somewhat familiar with," the man told her.

"Is he still alive? Do you have him?" she tried to keep the desperation she felt from sounding in her voice.

"He was alive the last time I saw him. And, no he was not one of the dogs we rescued."

Her hope took a tumble. "Where did you last see him?"

"He was receiving medical treatment for wounds that occurred during a fight."

Lady Biswell sucked in a breath of air. His words caused a stab of pain to shoot through her. Kang, her precious dog had been used for fighting. He'd been injured and needed medical treatment. Her teeth gritted and her fists balled up.

"I was told the dog recovered enough to escape his enclosure and was never seen again."

"He's still alive," Lady Biswell almost shouted into the phone.

"As far as I know he is. Sorry I can't be of more help. I've told you all I know."

"When was this? How long ago since he escaped?"

"I'm not sure of the exact date he escaped, but it was early Fall. I'm thinking September, but don't hold me to it."

Lady Biswell clutched the phone in her hands long after the man hung up. Her Kang was still alive. She knew he was. But why hadn't he returned home? Why hadn't someone seen him and made an effort to collect the reward money?

Chapter 44

~~~~

Striker cried tears of joy when she finally pushed the door against the snow drift until it opened. There were still several feet of snow piled up, but the warm air had finally arrived and the sun had come out of the winter sky shinning warm enough to melt away most of the snow.

Kang shot past her, bouncing and rolling in the snow.

"Where did all that energy come from?" she asked the happy dog. She certainly didn't have the energy to bounce about especially after struggling to push the door open. Now, if she could only find some sort of food in the snow.

She no longer had leather moccasins on her feet. Instead, she had wrapped her feet in the ragged remains of her father's overalls. She had boiled the moccasins, and she and the dog had eaten them several days before. She was now cutting off strips from the bear skin and boiling them in the snow water. She'd stuck her last stick of firewood in the stove that morning. No longer had she a choice other than forcing the door to open enough for her to get out.

The heavy winter snows had caused a lot of deadfall to break off the trees. She could see several small branches sticking out of the snow and made her way to them. She clutched a limb and dragged it through the snow into the house. She got her dad's axe and started chopping the limb into pieces small enough to fit in the stove. She couldn't help noticing how slowly she chopped and how long it took. Every time she had a stick short enough to fit in the stove's firebox, she crammed it in thankful there were still enough fire coals to catch. She had a tub full of ashes she'd taken from the stove during the winter. She'd need to drag them to the garden.

"Ashes are fertilizer for the garden," her dad always told her. "Never waste a spoonful if you can help it."

She needed all the fertilizer she could get if she intended to grow a better garden. She never wanted to starve again. If only she had the strength to stomp or shovel a path to a sunny, sheltered spot in the woods, she might be able to find young hemlock plants that had put out buds. She and her dad ate every bud they could find each spring.

After she put wood in the stove, she took the handsaw and made her way to a birch tree. She picked off all the buds she could reach and sawed off a few small limbs. She ate the buds and dragged the limbs back to the cabin where she could strip off the bark to boil into a tea. She would then use the limbs for firewood.

Once the bark had boiled, she added snow to cool it enough for her to sip slowly. If she drank it fast, she feared it wouldn't settle on her stomach. The liquid was too precious for any of it to come back up

Much to her amazement, the dog returned with a rabbit in his mouth. Striker cried again. The dog had eaten the head off the rabbit, but the body was intact. She took out her knife and gave the dog the guts, feet, and skin. She put the rest of the rabbit in water to boil. She remembered what her dad had told her about parasites. She felt a little guilty about not boiling the discarded remains for the dog, but he had been terribly hungry. As soon as all the plants and herbs had returned to life, she would find wormwood for her and the dog to eat. Walnut hulls also killed parasites but it would be many months before any would be available.

The dog's portion of the rabbit had been gulped down in the blink of an eye. Once the rabbit had boiled thoroughly, she stripped the meat from the bones, sucked the marrow out of the bones before she gave them to the dog. While she ate sparingly, the dog ran out into the snow again.

Hours had passed, and the sun had gone down before the dog returned with a half-grown raccoon in his mouth. Striker had grown worried sick that the dog would not return. She hurriedly closed the cabin door she had left open. The dog had eaten the head again.

Striker took the hide, guts, and feet and dumped them into a different pot of boiling water from the pot she had her bark and rabbit in. She knew to ration the food in case the dog wasn't as lucky during the next few days. Once the dog's food had boiled for about ten minutes, she added snow to cool it. She allowed the dog to eat only half of the broth and remains. She would save the rest until tomorrow and perhaps even the next day. She only drank a little of the raccoon broth before she fell asleep. What she drank of the birch broth, and eaten of the rabbit meat, had been enough for her.

She and the dog both fell asleep easier that night. She had gathered enough deadfall to keep them warm. Plus, the food had helped ease the hunger cramps in their bellies. For the first time in what seemed like forever, she hadn't feared she and the dog might not wake up.

The dog continued to find game most every day. She stripped bark and dragged in deadfall as she watched the snow become less with every day that passed. Finally, the snow melted enough until she could make her way to the cave where her potatoes were buried. When she dug down, they were all still there along with several heads of cabbage and a few carrots and turnips.

Striker laughed until she sank down to the cold, hard ground and let the tears run freely. She didn't stop laughing and crying until the dog licked her in the face.

~~~~

When the spring finally returned to the mountain, it was there to stay. Groundhogs and snakes started coming of their burrows as though they'd never holed up for the winter. Birds returned to start building nests before the leaf buds had opened up. Crows cawed and fought for their favorite trees. Geese honked as they flew overhead during the night. Even the distant sound of wolves howling no longer had a haunting sound.

She found two nests of turkey eggs and didn't feel one bit guilty about taking every single egg home for her and the dog eat. She knew the turkeys would keep on laying until they were able to sit on the eggs. Neither she nor the dog were able to get enough to fill them up no matter how much they ate. It was as though winter's starvation had left a huge emptiness inside them that would never be filled again. But with each day that passed, the dog was a little less bony and so was she.

There was no way having food to eat now made her forget how hungry she'd been a short time before. She wasn't going to let that happen again. Just as soon as the ground thawed, she started shoveling up the garden and adding more space to it. She didn't have a great variety of seed, so she simply had to do a better job of growing what she had.

She was thankful she had buried her seeds with her potatoes or they would have been eaten long before now and she really would have been in bad shape. Needing things and remembering her dad going off the mountain with furs to trade for things made her think of the money she'd found on the man. She'd checked in her books to make sure it was real money. It was – and a lot of it. There was over a thousand dollars. Her dad would have been rich if he'd had that much money. He often talked about money and taught her about its value. He also taught her about people and their greed for money. He told her there were people who would do just about anything for money.

"It's just paper," she said as she thought about it. "Only pieces of paper. "No matter how many pieces of paper there are, it doesn't help me one bit."

But it could buy seeds if her dad was still alive. Maybe, just maybe, before she planted the garden, she'd find a way to slip off the mountain the same as her dad had done. One thing was for sure, she'd need clothes to wear. She didn't even have any skins left to cover her up. All that was left were the remains of her father's shirt and overalls. She'd even boiled the thin strips of hide she'd used to fasten the rips back together. She was all but naked. It didn't matter. The dog didn't care and neither did she. Still, clothes came in mighty handy when she ran through briars and brambles. It kept them from scratching her skin.

Today she had started again at first light shoveling over the dirt in her garden. When she took a break to drink some broth, she had been sweating so badly it caused her to discover how awful she smelled. She thought about going to the creek to wash, but what happened with the man had turned her against going near the creek. Instead, she decided to fill the stove with deadfall and fill every pot and bucket she had with water. It would take warm water and a lot of scrubbing to get all the dirt and smell off that had accumulated on her body and in her long braid of hair

She chided herself for spending more time than she should have washing herself, but she'd forgotten how good it was to feel clean. While she was re-braiding her freshly washed hair, the dog came inside with the remains of a rabbit, his contribution to their daily meal. He sat down with the rabbit between his paws and watched her.

"You've caught enough rabbit to put a little weight on both of us. See how fat I've gotten?" she told the dog as she rubbed her hands over her body. My ribs don't show nearly as much as they did. I think I might have grown a little taller too, but it's hard to tell."

She was afraid the supply of rabbits and groundhogs would run out soon, causing the dog to travel farther and farther away from the cabin. Having the dog meant she no longer had to use the traps to catch food. She'd forgotten to take the traps up once the snow got deep. She'd have to do that soon. Her dad would be displeased because she had not been able to grease his traps to keep them from rusting, but fat of any kind had been a hard thing to come by.

Chapter 45

~~~~

"**W**hat do you think you're doing?" Griff asked in complete surprise when he caught Lady Biswell dressed in rough clothes, hiking boots, and filling up a large backpack with supplies she had stored in the kennel office. It was five o'clock in the morning. Daylight hadn't even arrived.

She took a deep determined breath, refusing to make eye contact with him. She dreaded the encounter she was sure to have with him, but it couldn't be helped. There was no way she would be able to leave without letting Griff know where she was going.

"I'm going on a hike," she told him lightly.

"With a sleeping bag, rifle, and enough food to last a week?"

"How do you know what I've got in my backpack?"

"I've got eyes."

"Indeed, you have, and you use them to spy on me."

"I'm not spying. I'm observant – as my boss lady pays me to be."

"True," she told him as if her hiking trip was a frivolous thing. "I might be gone over night."

"Where do you plan on taking this hike?"

"I'm going into the mountains."

"Why?" he tried to keep his voice sounding curious rather than demanding. Going into those mountains would be a stupid thing to do.

"I had a dream last night."

"About hiking?" he asked, although he thought he knew the answer.

"Right."

He had no intention of letting her get away with only half a truth. She had become more restless and determined to find a long-gone dog. Griff knew as well as she did that Kang, her beloved dog, was still haunting her.

"It's time to give it up," Griff told her firmly. "It's been two years. You're never going to get that dog back."

"I've no intention of getting over anything. Kang is still alive and I'm going to find him."

"By heading into the mountains after all this time– alone?"

"I like hiking alone," she told him firmly.

He shook his head. "It's too dangerous," he added just as firmly.

"I told you, I had - - - "

"A dream," he finished the sentence for her. "Exactly what did you dream?"

She lifted her eyes from her backpack to glare at him. "I dreamed if I'd go into the mountains, I'd find Kang."

"Surely you can't believe that's possible after all this time. He'd have found his way back home if he'd been running loose in the mountains."

"Don't you think I've thought of that already? All I know is I had such a convincing dream, I'm willing to take a chance on finding out if I can find him or not. There's no use arguing with me on this. I've already set my mind to it."

"Fine." Yes, he absolutely knew it was useless to argue when she'd *set her mind* to something. No stubborner person had ever drawn in a breath of air. "Then I'll have to go with you."

Her back straightened and her chin lifted up. "You'll do no such thing. Your job is to look after my dogs."

"That's a fact, but you still can't go into those mountains alone. Don't you realize how remote and dangerous those rugged mountains are? You could get lost and never find your way out. Not only that, there's all kinds of wild animals in those mountains. Haven't you read the newspapers lately. There's been an increased number of mountain lion sightings. Not to mention wolves and poisonous snakes. A hiker got attacked and killed by a mountain lion not long ago. It was on television. You had to have seen it."

"I realize that, but nothing is going to stop me. I've got both a rifle and a pistol."

Griff knew her statement to be true. He also knew nothing he said would stop her from doing what she'd already determined to do. "Give me an hour and I'll call my nephew and have him fill in for me here, so I can go with you."

"I'll not have you leaving my dogs with a stranger. You're the only person I trust them with."

"Then my nephew will have to go with you," he told her. At least she'd be safer with his nephew than going alone.

"No. I'm going alone."

"It's either me or my nephew, because you're not leaving here without one of us."

"Just who do you think you are to be telling me what I'll do or not do?" she demanded in a huff.

"I'm a man who cares about you. One who has no intention of losing my job because my boss takes off and never returns. In case you haven't noticed, I happen to like it here." He took out his cell phone and dialed a number while Lady Biswell fumed.

"My nephew says he'll be here in two hours. Let me see what you've got in your back pack."

"Two hours. I plan on leaving now."

"You'll do no such thing."

"Don't tell me what I can and can't do."

Griff grinned. "I wouldn't dare tell you what you can do or can't, but I do plan on keeping you alive if I have to hogtie you and sit on you."

"Just you try it," she snapped.

"Don't tempt me. Now, let's see what you've packed. How long do you plan on hiking?" he asked a bit cynical.

"Until I find Kang."

He shook his head as he opened her backpack. "Lady Biswell, it's been a long time - - -" he began.

"Don't you dare *it's been a long time* me. I know what you're going to say without you even opening your big mouth. Do you think I've not gone over the time he's been gone? Which really isn't that long. It has only been months, not years. They had him, but he escaped."

"Don't you think he'd have found his way home by now?"

"He ran to the mountains because he was afraid those horrible men would capture him again."

"How do you know that?"

"He told me."

"In your dreams," he couldn't help but roll his eyes upward in mockery.

"Don't get smart with me Griff Jenkins."

"You do realize you're going on a wild goose chase, don't you?"

"Maybe I am, and maybe I'm not, but I'll never rest unless I do this."

"I know," he surprised her by saying. "I only wish I could go with you on this crazy hike of yours."

Oddly enough, she found she wished he could too. She had always felt safer knowing Griff was nearby. It wasn't she couldn't take care of herself. She was sure she could handle a gun better than he could, and she could certainly think circles around him. It was just that he - - - well - - - he simply made her feel safe.

"I keep thinking about him having to fight to stay alive. The man who called said he'd been injured during a fight."

"He must have won the fight," Griff said before he could stop himself. He knew a little about dog fighting. He didn't like what he knew. "At least he was smart enough to escape."

"And smart enough to head for high ground," Lady Biswell added. "He was afraid he'd be caught again if he came back home."

"What makes you think you'll be able to find him? There's thousands upon thousands of acres in that national forest."

"I'm not going to find him," she said confidently. "He'll find me."

~~~~

It took a little over two hours for Burk Jenkins to show up. He was young, fit, and all the things Griff wished he still was. It just didn't seem fair that reckless youth had all the stamina, while age had finally acquired wisdom, but without the stamina to use what they had learned. Griff wanted to tell the young man how lucky he was along with how frivolous he was to waste even one day of his youth on things that didn't matter.

"I'm here," Burk said with a broad grin and a sparkle of anticipation in his eyes. "I'm ready to tackle those mountains. Been wantin' to do it ever since I can remember. Just been waiting for an excuse to get at it."

"Don't think it'll be exactly a Sunday picnic," Griff warned him. "You'll have to pick your trail carefully. There's some rough going in those mountains. I've heard there's some old animal trails leading into the high country if you can find one."

"Don't worry, old Unk, I'll look after you." Burk never missed an opportunity to needle his uncle. Burk had worshiped him when he was growing up, and still did in his own way.

"It's not me you'll need to look after," Griff told him with a slight grin, although he wasn't exactly feeling amused. Burk might not be as cocky when he learned he'd be looking after Lady Biswell.

"You're not the one going with me?" A little of Burk's enthusiasm faded.

"Nope. You've been given a great honor today. This trip will be a test of your strength and endurance. In more ways than one," he added in an undertone.

Burk's enthusiasm faded slightly. "Why am I getting a feeling that I should turn around and go back home."

"Probably because you should, but you won't. It's going to be your job to keep a stubborn, hard-headed woman alive until she wears herself out."

"Oh, shit. Not - - -"

"Yep, Lady Biswell."

"I'm outta here."

"No, you're not," Griff was quick to tell him. "If you help her find that dog, there's a two-thousand-dollar reward, plus payment for time spent."

"But you're talking about Lady Biswell – an old woman. She won't make it far."

"In that case your job will be easy. Besides, if you don't go, I'll have to. If I go, you'll have to replace me here. Had you rather take a hike or shovel dog shit out of the breeding lots?"

"Now that you put it that way."

"Right. Here she comes. What kind of supplies have you got with you?"

"The usual. Sleeping bag. Jerky. Dehydrated stuff that won't spoil. First-aid kit. Water bottles and purifier. Flashlight. Hatchet. Knife. Two space blankets. Extra pair of socks. You know, the usual."

"Not sure about the jerky. There's bears in those mountains."

"It's sealed and hiking approved. Won't give off smells."

Griff still wasn't sure about the jerky, but he wasn't up to arguing.

"You're not packing a tent?"

"Tents are heavy. Didn't think I'd be gone long enough to need one. Checked the weather forecast. It's good for the next week. Got a lightweight tarp, though."

"I've got the same things, minus the jerky, plus my rifle and pistol," Lady Biswell told them. "I assure you both I've prepared for this, did my research. I also have a map and a compass. I read that clapping one's hands and barking like a dog scares bears away, plus I bought a can of bear spray."

Griff didn't comment on that. Computer advice and reality were worlds apart. "Do you have matches and flares to send up if you should need help?"

"Matches in waterproof container," Burk told him with a grin and shake of his head. "I'm an experienced hiker, Uncle Griff," Burk added with a touch of humor. "I've also packed my cell phone."

"You might be, but Lady Biswell isn't," Griff pointed out. "Cell phone batteries die, plus there's places where you can't get reception down in the gullies."

"I assure you, I'll hold my own with anybody, regardless."

Griff wasn't so sure about that, but he knew better than to express his opinion.

"Good luck to the both of you".

"We'll use smoke signals if our flares don't work and our batteries go dead," Lady Biswell smarted off.

Griff said nothing back. She and Burk would make a good match.

Chapter 46

~~~~

"I got me a dog, Dad," Striker said as she stood over her dad's grave. "See him right over yonder. He watches over me and brings in meat for me to cook, kinda like you used to do. I know you sent him to me Dad, and I thank you. I've been mighty lonely without you, as you already know. I've not forgotten about you. I try to remember everything you taught me. I've added a heap more to what I've learned about surviving on this mountain. It's been hard without you, Dad. Mighty hard, but I've made it so far and will continue to survive. I know I will. Don't look like I've got a choice."

She didn't tell her dad how afraid she was. Didn't think there was any need. Not only was she afraid of her own survival, she was afraid her father's spirit might leave her. She needed to talk to him. Needed him to guide her through life, however long it might be.

"Dad, I hope you can forgive me for making you a promise I've not been able to keep. I don't know how to find Aunt Nellie. From what I've read in the books you brought, there's more people down in the flatlands than I can count.

Striker drew in a deep breath of the still chilly air and turned away from her dad's grave. As for the sunken in grave beside her dad's, she intended to dig right over the top of it as though it had never been there. She was going to forget about that horrible man the best she could. One thing was for sure, she wasn't going to be caught unaware again. At least she had the dog to protect her if she was ever stalked.

The outdoor air was a lot better to breathe than the stale air inside the cabin. She'd scraped and carried every bit of her and the dog's refuse out of her bedroom and piled it up a little way from the garden. If it had been anything other than human and dog waste, she'd have put it on her garden. Her dad had warned her often enough not to do such as that.

"No animal will eat their own manure, and there's a mighty good reason not to. Parasites, Striker."

Her dad always had parasites on his mind. He talked about them over and over as though parasites were the most dangerous things in the world. He had instilled things in her mind that she would never forget, even if she wanted to. And yet there were other things she needed to know. Things he'd never said a word about.

"Those parasites can destroy a man in a hurry. I've seen it done many a time. Under-developed countries grow their food in human waste. They have water runoff from barnyards that goes straight into their drinking water. Then they wonder why they have the trots all the time. Nastiness, Striker, that's what it is. Most adults you see over there in those foreign places are nothing but little dried up shells of people. That's because parasites are eating them up from the inside out."

Striker knew her dad was talking about the time he was in the war. But let her ask one question about it and he'd shut up like a turtle going into its shell. If he talked at all about his life before the mountain, it would be in his own time and on his own subject.

"Thought we were gonna starve to death during the last part of winter, but we didn't," she told her dad.

Got right weak, though. Both of us did. I still hain't got over it right good. Remember telling me how folks got rickets? I'm kinda worried on that count, Dad. You said folks, especially children, got spindly legs and pot bellies. As you can see, I reckon I've got a touch of rickets. I've been eating all the Hemlock new growth I can find, but it's not helping much. I've not be able to find any rose hips. Reckon the animals scarfed up them way back in the fall. Don't have any dried apples left either, but I'll be all right Dad. You ought not to worry."

Striker stopped talking and wiped the sweat off her face with the back of her hand. She didn't want her dad to worry about her, but she was kind of worried about herself. She got tired easier that she could remember, but that was expected considering it was still early spring and the food supply wasn't yet plentiful. She would have to take her bow and arrows down into the valley in hopes of spotting a small deer. She'd have done it before now, but she knew she didn't have the strength to drag anything up the mountain. Besides, her dad had instilled the fear of the valley in her almost as strong as the fear of parasites.

She simply couldn't get enough to eat, although she felt like she was eating all the time. Her potatoes and cabbage were getting fewer and fewer to plant, and she couldn't let that happen. It was better to feel hungry now than to starve during the winter.

She kept craving something, but she wasn't sure what it was. She wanted something with a tart taste to it. She figured it wouldn't hurt to leave her garden shoveling for a few minutes. It was early April. She still had time to shovel up the garden even if she did slack up for an hour. She headed out to find a greenbrier patch. She hated greenbrier. She was always getting tangled up in them, but their little reddish, forked shoots had a tart taste to them. If she could find enough, they might help ease her craving. She found several very small ones and ate every single one she could reach, but it only made her want more.

Greenbriars had a vicious way of entwining themselves from the ground to high in the trees and ripping flesh if she tried to pull them down. Their thorns were more than Striker wanted to tackle especially in her near naked state. Hopefully, by the time winter came again, she'd be able to gather enough hides to make clothes. So far, the dog had eaten every single hide from his kills.

"It'll have to be enough," she mumbled as she looked into the tree for the forked shoots, unless she wanted to go farther into the woods in search of more greenbriers. What she really wanted to do was lay down in a sunny warm spot and take a nap, but she didn't dare. She had to work every minute of every day if she wanted to survive another winter like the last one she'd just experienced.

Chapter 47

~~~~

Lady Biswell's legs ached so badly she wanted to scream. Her pride kept her silent. She wasn't about to complain about the speed Burk set. It was obvious he'd slowed down greatly to accommodate her.

"Need to rest yet?" Burk asked.

"I'm okay. I want to go all the way to the top of that bald as soon as possible."

"I've never hiked in that direction before. I've heard it's mighty rough hiking. I've heard stories about hunters going in that direction and never showing up again. That bald is supposed to be an Indian burial ground. It's sacred, you know. When folks trespass on sacred land, bad things happen to them."

"That's where I want to go," she told him. "I've been cursed all my life. One more won't make much difference."

"Looks to me like you've been mighty lucky in life," he couldn't resist saying.

"Looks can be deceiving," she was quick to say.

Burk wanted to ask her more questions about her being cursed, but he knew better. Uncle Griff said she refused to talk about her past and got mad when he asked. It was easy for Burk to tell she was winded. He thought it admirable that she refused to stop to rest, but not wise. If a hiker became overly exhausted, it took longer to regain their strength. He'd heard his uncle talk about the amount of pride Lady Biswell had. He figured she would fall flat on her face before she'd complain.

"I need to stop and adjust the socks in my boots. Don't want to get a blister this early on," he told her even though his socks were perfectly fine.

He sat down on a log and started taking off his boots one at a time. Lady Biswell hesitated, and then sat down on another log. Sweat had gathered on her face and dampened her hair. He was sure sweat was soaking her clothes as well. Having sweat soaked clothes was a no, no when it came to hiking during freezing temperatures. When sweat evaporated, the body cooled down. The one thing he didn't want was having to carry her off the mountain.

He gave her a good twenty minutes of rest before he started out at a much slower pace.

In midafternoon, he took two protein bars out of his pocket and handed her one. "We'll stop and eat these before we go on. I've got my pockets full of protein bars we'll need to eat before tonight. These are the extras I didn't pack in the odor proof containers. Hand me back your wrapper. I'll keep them in this plastic bag until we make camp. Once we get a fire started tonight, we'll burn them."

"Aren't you being extra cautious?"

"Not in the least. Actually, I've cheated on good advice by having these bars in my pocket instead of in an approved container. In my way of thinking, our body needs to stock up on as much energy as possible when we first start out."

Lady Biswell suspected he was trying to scare her. Bears didn't usually come down this low, and then her common sense told her different. If bears and wild animals didn't come down this low, why did farmers need guard dogs to protect the stock?

"Have you hiked these mountains a lot?" she asked.

"Some, but not a lot. This mountain is too close home. My buddies and I usually make a long trip of hiking. When we're short on time, we've taken quick trips in these mountains, but never to the bald. We've made a point of respecting sacred ground. There's some right good rock cliffs we've planned to climb but haven't gotten around to it."

"Will we be required to climb rock cliffs?"

He grinned. "Nope. We'll find a way around them. It takes some good safety equipment to go rock climbing. We're just hiking."

"I'm going after my dog," Lady Biswell told him.

"That's what Uncle Griff said. He also said if we found him, I'd get the reward money," he added hopefully.

"Which had you rather have, the reward money if we find Kang, or to be paid an hourly wage?"

"What's wrong with both?" he grinned.

"You think both would be fair?"

"I do. I should be paid for giving up my time to take you into these mountains and making sure you stay alive and uninjured. You've been offering a reward for whoever aids in finding your dog. If I aid you in finding him, I believe the reward could apply."

She chuckled slightly. "I like your way of thinking, and I agree. How long do you think it will take us to reach the bald?"

"Two, three days if we can keep up this pace. Longer if it rains or something unforeseen comes up."

~~~~

That night Lady Biswell lay on the hard ground in her sleeping bag. Burk had insisted she lay her tarp on the ground, put her sleeping bag on the tarp, and then fold the tarp over her sleeping bag to keep the ground moisture, and the dew, from getting her sleeping bag damp

To put it mildly, she was miserable. Even Burk's snoring kept her awake. He had cautioned her not to move her sleeping bag away from the fire or him.

"Mountain lions always go for a woman first," he'd warned her. "There's just something about the smell of a female that's irresistible."

She had refused to have her bedroom anywhere near her last two husband's bedrooms. They snored louder than Burk, but that wasn't why she refused to sleep in the same room with them. She simply wasn't attracted to them in a sexual way. Fortunately, they were both too old to care.

Reg McFarland was the least demanding of her husbands, but he required more of her time. He hadn't died as soon as the doctors thought. He had lived for fifteen years while she waited on him hand and foot. The doctors credited it to her tender care, but she credited it to his stubbornness.

The one thing the doctors were right about was that his mind started misfiring shortly after she married him. He couldn't remember things, couldn't practice law, couldn't help her find who had her daughter. The one thing he did prove was that she wasn't mentally insane.

She had been placed in the asylum due to stress caused by the loss of her family. Losing her parents and her husband so close together had put her in a period of deep mourning she was slow to snap out of. Once she was placed in the asylum, she had been given medicine to keep her in a near unresponsive state.

"Makes patients easier to handle," Reg had informed her, and the judge had agreed. Reg had then sued the asylum and staff, not for money, but for better patient care. All his law suit accomplished was for the small asylum to be closed down, making it more difficult to trace who had her baby. She never gave up and neither did Reg, until his mind left him.

She had tried to obtain her records from the asylum, but all her records had mysteriously disappeared. As for the staff, not a one of them admitted caring for her or even knowing her while she was a patient. They didn't deny her being there either. They all claimed a lack of memory. There were so many patients coming and going during that time, how could they be expected to remember them all.

Reg had wanted to know how many women had babies while admitted to the asylum. The numbers were staggering. Almost half the women were pregnant when they arrived or got pregnant while they were there. Joe Whitson handled many of the adoptions for the women who did not have relatives whom wanted their babies.

Reg discovered most of Joe Whitson's clients wanted a baby so badly they never questioned where or whom he was getting babies from. They were more than willing to pay his exorbitant fees for finally being able to adopt a baby. As for the asylum, the less hassle and red tape they could avoid, the better.

"I find myself caught up in a dilemma," Reg told her. "I've never cared about what was wrong or right, nor even what was best. All I cared about was winning my cases. How I won those cases didn't matter," he told her needlessly. "Of course, you already know that. Anyway, my dear, I'm going to put some of my burden on you."

"I won't go into detail as to how I managed it, but I've had most of the asylum files read and have received reports on the babies that were adopted, most of the babies that were adopted, were done so illegally. If the files come to light, the lives of many babies will be disrupted."

"And?" she had questioned when he stopped talking.

"And I'm not sure I want that to happen."

"Why not?"

"Think about it. Those babies are now in loving homes. They're being taken care of by parents who love them. A lot of them don't even know they've been adopted. What right does anybody have to disrupt their happiness, their families?"

"I want my baby back," she told him. "She was stolen from me without my permission."

"I know, but will she be happier with you or where she's at?"

"You know where she's at, don't you?" she'd shouted.

"No, but I'm getting closer. Look at it this way. Most of the women in the asylum needed to be there. A lot of those women got pregnant after they were committed. Who the babies' fathers are is anybody's guess. Some fathers were most likely other inmates."

"My husband was the father of my baby, and I never signed over my right to her. I never signed any adoption papers. I never signed my name one single time while I was there."

"Didn't you sign a release form when you got out?"

"No. Joe handled all that."

"Interesting," Reg had said.

She found it a lot more than interesting.

Oddly enough, a few days later, the building where the asylum used to be caught on fire and all the files burned with the building.

"Interesting," Reg had said again.

She found it worth her time to go through Reg's files when he wasn't around, which wasn't often.

"It's no use," Reg told her one night after she had given his medicine.

"You know you have to take your medicine," she told him.

"I'm not talking about my medication. I am talking about you going through my files."

She didn't deny what she was doing. "I'll not stop until I find my daughter. You know where she's at, don't you?"

"I do. I've known for a while now."

Hell truly had no such fury as she had right then. She might have beaten him to death with his bottle of medicine, if she hadn't realized he was the only person left who could tell her where her daughter was.

"Then I suggest you tell me all you know," she said in a voice that was deadly cold.

"Yes," he agreed. "It is time you know everything."

A piercing squall followed by another brought Lady Biswell straight up. "Burk," she yelled.

"I heard it," he said as he hurriedly got out of his sleeping bag. "Bobcats, if I'm not mistaken. Most likely fighting over breeding rights." He grabbed more deadfall and tossed it on the fire, hoping he was right about the breeding part. Bobcats could be vicious if they took the notion. They might also be hungry.

Lady Biswell grabbed the pistol that lay beside her leg in the sleeping bag and fired a shot into the air.

"What the hell?" Burk said in surprise.

"Think I scared them off?"

"Don't know about them, but you scared the shit outta me."

Chapter 48

~~~~

Striker had trouble sleeping, which she was doing more often lately. She couldn't find a comfortable position to lay in. She even went out into the pine woods and cut short pine boughs to make her bed a little more comfortable. It helped only a little.

She didn't know what was wrong and started to fear she had not cooked her food properly. Could it be possible she had gotten those parasites her dad always talked about? Parasites along with rickets could be her problem. Those, plus not sleeping, could be the reason she was always feeling tired. She knew for a fact that her stomach was always tore up. Her guts tumbled and rolled a lot lately even though she was eating better than usual. At least her bones were not poking through her skin the way they had been.

The dog had brought in another possum yesterday. Possums always had a lot of fat on them. Her dad told her a no fat diet wasn't good for a body. She and the dog had made light work of eating it up. The dog took more food than she did. He didn't like the herbal teas she was always drinking.

The dog followed her outside as he usually did. She didn't go far away from the cabin at night when nature called for her to relieve herself. Although she always took her bow and arrow with her, she wasn't able to see very far. The dog always remained alert and seemed to be standing watch over her. She felt a lot safer with the dog, especially since she had heard wolves howling a time or two lately.

She tensed when she heard the sound of a gunshot echoing off the mountains and feeding itself back down into the valley. The sound had come from a long way off, but it was still unsettling to her. Her dad always became antsy when he heard gun shots, and so should she. The dog had cocked his ears forward, listened, and then appeared unconcerned.

"Hunters," she told the dog as she looked up at the moon shining through the limbs of the trees. The winds had to be blowing just right to carry the sound from down below up the mountain. It happened often when the weather was clear. Nothing to worry about, she tried to assure herself. Hunters had never come this far into the mountains – and then reality hit her. One had. He was buried in a grave next to her father.

"What are we going to do?" she whispered to the dog. "What if the hunters come?"

She and the dog went back to the cabin, but she still wasn't able to fall asleep until it was nearly dawn. It took a lot of determination to get up, drink a cup of Sassafras tea, take her dad's shovel and head back to the garden to continue digging up the ground. It would be time to plant the potatoes and cabbage soon.

Chapter 49

~~~~

Lady Biswell awoke as the darkness turned a pale gray. It had taken her a while to fall asleep after being scared by the bobcats. A few of them had come to the farm after her chickens before she'd gotten the Kangal dogs. Nothing bothered her chickens after that. She did have problems with mice and rats. It kept Griff busy setting traps. She wouldn't let him put out poison in case her dogs got some of it. She couldn't keep barn cats either. Kangal dogs were known for their hatred of cats, any kind of cats.

The fire had burned down while she and Burk were both asleep. She got a stick of wood and stirred in the ashes to find there were still a few live fire coals. She picked up a hand full of dry leaves to stick on the coals. When they flamed up, she broke small branches and fed them to the flames. She then put larger deadfall on the fire until it was burning good. Once she had gotten the fire going, she slipped off into the woods to relieve herself in a sheltered spot.

By the time she got back, Burk was sitting up rubbing his eyes much like a little boy would do.

"So, you finally woke up, did you? I was beginning to think you were going to sleep all day."

"It's only five o'clock," he told her.

"I know. I overslept."

"You didn't oversleep," he told her with a slight grin. "Admit it, the ground was so hard you couldn't stand to lay on it any longer."

"You could be right about that."

"I can guarantee you one thing, you'll sleep better each night we spend on this mountain. It'll be an exhausted sleep."

"You do know how to inspire your hiking partner."

"Just telling you the truth. How about cooking us up a breakfast of bacon, eggs, pancakes, and hash brown. I'm kind of hungry."

"Be glad to, as soon you pull those ingredients out of your backpack."

"What? You didn't bring them? What kind of a hiking partner are you?"

"One who brought trail mix and dried fruit."

"Me too," he admitted. "But I was hoping you cheated."

"At least I can make us a hot cup of sling coffee."

"Sounds good." He yawned. "Don't use it all up today. We'll need it worse as the days wear on to help us get started each morning. What's the chance you might shoot a rabbit with that pistol of yours."

"Slim. Might get one with the rifle if I could see one."

"You know, there's not been a single rabbit while we've been hiking. Those two bobcats we heard last night must keep them cleared out. How's your feet?"

"They're good."

"For real, or are you just saying that?"

"For real, I think."

"Good. Make sure you doctor them up again before we take off. Blisters on your feet is a bad thing. Not only will it slow us down, if they become infected it'll be difficult to get you off this mountain – alive," he added to make his point sink in.

~~~~

It was the third day of hiking and Lady Biswell felt every muscle and bone in her body aching. She'd never imagined they would be struggling to get through such rough and rocky terrain, not to mention how cold and miserable the nights were. The temperature, the very air itself, was different than down in the valley. She didn't know which was worse the cold weather, the rhododendron hells they had to crawl through on their bellies, or the rock cliffs they had to climb over, or the struggle to find a way around them. All of it had been more of an endurance test of her determination than she'd ever imagined. She now knew why hikers and hunters avoided climbing on this side of the mountain.

"When will we reach the bald," she asked Burk. She'd done her best not to complain, but her feet hurt from the blisters, and her backpack had doubled in weight. She was certain she had aged five years in the last three days.

"Maybe tomorrow," he told her. "If I can find a way to get us over this rock cliff. If not, it will take longer, because we'll have to find a way around it. Seems to me like there ought to be a path somewhere on this side of the mountain."

He stopped, turned around and looked at her.

"We can turn around and go back if you want."

He had no hope whatsoever of getting that two thousand dollars. Reaching the bald would only be reaching the bald. Her dog was long gone. He just hated to see her disappointment – and his empty pocket – when the dog didn't miraculously show up.

"How long will it take if you can't find a path?"

"Another day, maybe two depending. Exactly what made you pick this mountain to climb?" Burk asked her for the first time.

"This mountain came to me in a dream." She didn't bother explaining how her dog had told her to climb the mountain. Once you were in a mental asylum, you were hesitant to tell anyone much about yourself. "Once crazy, always crazy," people tended to think.

"Kind of wished you'd dreamed about an easier mountain to climb."

"Me too," she admitted. "This is a lot more difficult than I expected."

Burk noticed she'd been favoring her right foot a little. "Set down and take off your shoes," he told her.

"Oh, no. There's no reason to do that. My feet are fine."

"Do it or I'll not take another step."

"Really - - -" she objected.

"Do it."

She slowly sank down on a rock and took off her hiking shoes.

"Socks too," he told her.

She eased her socks off her feet.

"Just as I thought. You've got blisters the size of my thumb nail. Why didn't you tell me before now?"

"I didn't want to slow down."

"That's the worse excuse you can come up with when you're hiking. Blisters always slow you down. I'll get the first aid kit. You can put some cream on those blisters and cover them with band aids while I try to find a path over this rock cliff."

He gave her the cream and band aids from his first aid kit and left his backpack at her feet.

"I won't be long," he told her as he disappeared.

She pampered her feet the best she could and then sprinkled baby powder on her feet and in her socks before she put her shoes back on. The blisters really weren't as big as his thumbnail.

They were only half that size. She should have stopped sooner for the band aids, but she didn't want him to think she was a wimp.

He wasn't gone long before he showed back up.

"Found it," he said with pride. "It's not much of a path and it hasn't been used recently, but it'll get us on top of these rocks."

"Once we're on top of those rocks?" she had to question as he strapped his backpack on.

"According to the maps we've got, it will be a rather easy climb from the top to the bald."

"Easy. I'm beginning to really like that word."

"Are you okay? Want to rest a while longer?"

"What I want is to find my dog and get him back home where I can sleep in a comfortable bed."

"I'm not trying to doubt your word or anything like that, but can you tell me why a dog would be on this mountain?"

She hesitated for a few moments. "I've just got this feeling," she said, knowing it sounded as feeble to him as it did to her.

"I hope you're right. I have to keep the image of twenty hundred-dollar bills in my vision to keep me marching onward and upward."

"I thought you were this great outdoors man who did this sort of thing for fun."

"It stopped being fun about five miles back and turned into hard work."

"I couldn't agree with you more. Hope there's no more laurel hells in the path you found."

"Sorry to disappoint you, but it looks like there very well might be."

Lady Biswell took a deep breath and tried to convince herself she was up to a few more days of hiking torture and disappointment. She had been certain her Kang would have found her long before now. What was she going to do if they reached the bald and there was no Kang to be found?

The answer was the same as with all the other disappointments in her life. She would continue on, and only cry at night when no one could see her.

Chapter 50

~~~~

Striker had her slingshot around her neck and her bow and arrow in her hand. When she got to the garden, she saw several crows searching through the ground she had shoveled up. She stood behind a tree trunk, took the slingshot from around her neck and picked out a rock. Her aim was true. All the crows flew away but one. She rushed forward and grabbed it in case it was only addled.

"Got it," she told the dog, and headed back to the cabin. She'd pick the feathers off and gut the scrawny bird. "I do declare," she mumbled. "Corn. There're a few grains of whole corn in its craw. I'll save them to plant in case they'll come up." She put the corn in a jar and set the jar where it would be safe.

She laughed out loud at her good luck as she put the puny bit of skin and bones in the stew pot to have for supper. She let the dog have his usual remains to eat right then. Most likely he'd catch something to go with the crow before night fall.

She picked up her slingshot in a thoughtful way. For some reason, she was craving a gray squirrel to add to the crow. It wouldn't take long to make their way to the big oak tree that grew above the cliff. There wouldn't be any acorns this time of year, but there was a good chance the squirrels would be searching in leaves and rock crevices where acorns had fallen and not yet been found. Even she might be able to find a few acorns lodged in the rock cliffs, but it was too dangerous for anything other than a squirrel or snake to crawl over those sheer walls.

Her dad had always forbidden her to play near rock cliffs when she was little, but he often took her there to shoot squirrels with her slingshot. Using a bow and arrow on squirrels was a waste of an arrow.

~~~~

Striker got to put in some resting time when she went squirrel hunting. That resting time might have been what she was craving more than the taste of squirrel meat, but food was something she would never pass up. At least her hunger and cravings were slowing down a little. She found herself a concealed spot in a clump of weeds near the trunk of the big oak tree where she could watch the rock cliff. She laid her bow and arrows a few feet away and took her slingshot from around her neck. She'd gathered several good rocks and placed them in a pile near her leg where they were easy to reach.

Kang was beside her when all of a sudden, his ears perked up and he became alert. A rabbit shot out of the laurel hell and headed back toward the cabin. Kang's long legs jumped clean over the top of her in full pursuit of the rabbit. She knew he wouldn't stop chasing it until it was in his jaws. Oh well, there were times when Kang had trouble staying still when they were squirrel hunting. He was always watching and listening and sniffing the wind. Most likely that was why he was good at bringing in game for them to eat. If their luck held, they would have both squirrel and rabbit to add to the stringy bit of crow.

She grinned as she remembered hearing her dad say, "Looks like I'll have to eat crow," when things went wrong for him, and he knew he'd have to do them over.

Crow really could be a hard thing to swallow unless you were extremely hungry.

She had almost fallen asleep when the sound of a squirrel's chattering got her attention. She put her best rock in the pouch of the slingshot and waited. A grunting sound came from the laurel hell to the side of the rock cliff. Much to her horror a man's head stuck through rhododendron leaves.

Her breath caught in her throat. For a moment she couldn't move a muscle the shock was so great. The memory of the man on top of her, hurting her, returned full force. Fear mixed with blinding fury took over.

She pulled back the slingshot as far as the rubber would allow and let fly.

The man's hand flew to his head an instant before he hit the ground. She grabbed her bow and arrow and let fly. Much to her amazement, she missed him. The arrow sunk into the rhododendron branch in front of the man's face.

Something started screaming to high heaven, and she didn't think it was coming from the man. She saw the screaming person right behind the man who was still lying on the ground. She grabbed another arrow and loaded it in her bow, while wishing she'd brought her crossbow. It had a lot more power and might be just a hair more accurate. She wouldn't have missed the man if she had used it. She steadied her aim. She didn't intend to miss the second one.

Just as she was ready to let fly of the arrow, a tan streak shot in front of her, headed straight for the man. She lowered her bow slightly, afraid if she shot, she would hit her dog. Something inside her cringed. It was one thing to shoot the man, but it was going to be something else watching her dog rip him to shreds the way he'd done the other man.

"Kang!" she heard someone shout out as the dog leaped into the air, passed over the man, and landed on whom had been screaming.

There was laughter and crying and what sounded like the whines of a happy dog. What was going on? Why wasn't her dog defending her? What was she supposed to do now?

There were hunters. Two hunters and she'd only gotten one with a rock. She had no idea if the rock had done its job or if she'd only hit him a glancing blow. Come to that, she didn't even know what it would take to kill a man. The slingshot sure couldn't kill a ground hog and a man was a lot bigger than that.

"Run for the cave." That's what her dad always said for her to do if men showed up. It wouldn't be as easy to find the cave as the cabin. To make matters worse, she'd just filled the stove full of deadfall. There would be heat waves coming from the cabin if not smoke.

~~~~

"Kang! Kang! It's really you. You're for real. For real! You're alive." Lady Biswell was sobbing over and over again as the dog licked her in the face, knocked her to the ground, and then licked her some more.

Somehow, she managed to set up and when she did, Kang started growling and made a move toward Burk.

"No! Stop!" Lady Biswell shouted in total surprise at Kang's actions. Never before had she seen him want to attack anybody.

Kang stopped instantly, but a rumble continued in his chest.

"Oh, my goodness, Burk. Are you all right? Are you alive?"

Lady Biswell crawled on her hands and knees to where Burk was laying half hidden in the rhododendron leaves. She quickly placed her hand on the side of his neck to check if he still had a pulse. He did. A trickle of blood was running from his forehead into one of his eyes. He was out cold but still breathing.

Lady Biswell crawled backward, grabbed him by the feet and pulled him down the path a way and out of the rhododendron. She dropped her backpack and got her emergency kit out. She took out a gauze pad, drenched it in water and rubbed it on his face. She then poured the small bottle of alcohol on the wound. When she did that, the stinging made him groan, but he didn't come around. She put a clean gauze pad on his head along with three strips of tape. The dog sat by her side and watched.

"Wake up," she told him as she slapped at his jaws. "Open your eyes, Burk. We've got to get out of here, and I sure can't carry you. I can't even drag you in all these rocks."

Lady Biswell was shaking like a windblown leaf. She wasn't exactly sure what she'd seen. It looked for the world like a young naked woman, but not exactly. There were strips of something furry looking hanging from her shoulders, and she had what appeared to be a bow and arrow in her hands. She'd even heard the twang as she shot an arrow at Burk. The arrow was still sticking in a laurel branch. Whatever it was had been ready to shoot an arrow at her an instant before Kang leaped on her. Kang had most likely saved her life.

Could it possibly have been an Indian? Were there wild Indians living in these mountains? She'd never heard of such thing. Could it have been an adolescent bigfoot? It didn't appear to be as tall as she was, but she hadn't gotten a good enough look at it. Was it some kind of animal? But it had looked more human than animal. Whatever it was, it was dangerous. It had almost killed Burk. If it hadn't been for Kang, it would have shot her. Where had the thing gone? Was it hiding somewhere waiting to finish the job?

She stuffed the emergency kit in her backpack, slung it on her back, and grabbed Burk by the feet again. She pulled with all her strength, moving him only a few feet until he lodged against a large rock at the beginning of another laurel hell. It had been difficult enough for each of them to crawl through it. Getting herself and an unconscious Burk back through that laurel hell would be almost impossible.

"You've got to wake up," she told Burk. "For the Lord's sake, you can't die on me now. Not after we've come this far together. Not after we've found Kang. We've got to get out of here."

Suddenly, Kang took off running back the way he had come.

"No, Kang come. Come!" she shouted but it did no good. She tried to run after him, but only took a few steps. She was too afraid of that . . . that Indian to go further. Besides, Kang was gone, and she didn't know what direction he had disappeared. She grabbed hold of Burk's shoulders and shook him soundly. She thought he flinched, but she wasn't sure.

She dropped her backpack again and took out the water bottled and squirted water all over his face and head. It seemed to help a little. He moved his hand slightly and groaned.

~~~~

Striker tried to hide exactly as her father had instructed her to do. She went to the very back of the cold, damp cave and huddled down behind a large rock making herself as small as she possibly could. She laid her arrows next to her where they could be easily reached and inserted one in the bow – and waited.

If only she had her crossbow with her. She hadn't taken time to get a single thing out of the cabin, not even the crow she was cooking or her crossbow. And her books. What would the hunters do with her books? Would they take her dad's tools? What about the few cooking utensils? She didn't have much, but it was barely enough to keep her alive. There was no way she'd ever be able to replace a thing.

And the dog? What had happened to him? Why hadn't he attacked those hunters? It appeared he'd been glad to see the screaming one. The one who had kept saying Kang, Kang, it's really you. You're for real. For real. You're alive."

She wondered how long she would have to stay hidden before they left. But what good would their leaving do. They would know where she lived and tell others about her. They, she thought. Perhaps there was only one left. It was possible she'd killed one of them. She thought about that for a while. Could it be she really killed another person? Was he someone's dad? Would that someone miss him as much as she missed her dad?

And the other one, the one with the high-pitched screaming voice, the one Kang was so glad to see, was that a man too? Could it possibly have been a woman like she'd read about in books?

A slight noise sounded in the cave and a tan streak broke through the dim light. The dog had come back to her. He hadn't deserted her after all. She opened her arms and hugged him in desperation. His entire body was wiggling with happiness. He licked her in the face and whined. He ran toward the cave opening, and then turned around and ran back to her. He did that several times as though he was trying to get her to follow him, but she wasn't about to do that. Finally, the dog bounded out of the cave and didn't rush back.

~~~~

Burk's eyes fluttered and then opened. "What happened?" he mumbled. "My head hurts."

"I found my dog," she told him. "But he ran off. I hope he comes back."

"I don't feel so good," he told her.

"Oh, thank goodness you're still alive," Lady Biswell said. "Are you okay? I thought you were going to die on me."

"Why does my head hurt?"

"I think you were hit by an arrow. There was one sticking in a branch."

"An arrow?" he questioned as his hand went to the knot on his head.

"That's right. I think an Indian girl shot you. A naked Indian girl, almost."

"Uh, could you say that again?"

"I think a naked Indian girl shot you with a bow and arrow," she repeated.

"You're shitting me," he told her. "Did I fall down that cliff?"

"I am telling you the truth."

"Can't be," he mumbled as he tried to sit up. "Can't do it." He laid back down. "I think I'm going to puke."

"You've got to stand up. We've got to get out of here. She might come back and finish us off."

"Things are spinning and I'm seeing two of you."

"Oh, shit. Sounds like a concussion. Let me look at your eyes," she found her flashlight and shined it into his eyes. "Oh, double shit. Your pupils are uneven. What in the world are we going to do now?"

"Call for rescue. Maybe a helicopter can lower a bucket for me."

"I already tried. Both your and my cell phones have dead batteries."

"I turned my off. Try it again."

"Already did. It showed no bars and then died."

"Send up smoke signals," he mumbled.

"Don't think it didn't cross my mind. Most likely we'd draw more Indians."

"I'd laugh at that, but my head hurts too much."

"I'm not joking. I wish Kang would come back. I don't know why he ran off," she said.

"Kang?"

"My dog."

She got the bottle from her backpack, opened it and shook out two pills. She put the bottle back, lifted his head, stuck the pills in his mouth and held the water bottle for him to drink.

"Do you know how to make one of those sled things, so I can drag you out. You're too heavy for me to carry you. I've tried dragging you, but it didn't work too well. I had to walk backward, and your head kept hitting roots and rocks."

"So that's why my head hurts. It's called a travois."

"Know how to make one?"

"Cut two saplings. Tie them together with the rope and fasten the tarps on the rope so I won't fall through." He groaned. "I can't talk right now. It makes my head hurt too much."

"Rest," she told him. "I'll think."

She was deep in thought as what to do about getting them off the mountain – and with her dog – when Kang came bounding back to her. He was bouncing about and trying to lick her in the face. He didn't seem the least concerned about their situation. She wondered if he could have been with the Indian girl all this time? There was no way she could have stolen him. The dog fighting man had done that. They'd kept him for a year and a half before he escaped. According to the man who called her, it had been over seven months since he escaped.

"Stay," she mumbled to the dog as she hugged him close. He sat down at her feet and whined. She hurriedly cut a length of rope and fashioned a collar and lead out of it. She then tied the rope to a sapling. She had no intention of allowing Kang to run off again.

Kang growled and pulled against the rope.

"Hush," she told him gently. Stay. I've got to figure out what to do next."

Kang sat down, but it was obvious to Lady Biswell that he didn't like being tied up. Surely, he hadn't forgotten all the times she'd had him on a lead.

~~~~

The longer Striker huddled in the cave, the more anger started replacing her fear. How dare hunters come to her mountain. If there were any kind of animals here, they belonged to her. She needed them to stay alive. Let those hunters stay down in the valleys where they belonged. What was really puzzling to her was why the dog was happy to see one of them? The dog must have known and liked one of the hunters.

She couldn't stay huddled there forever, and she certainly couldn't allow hunters to find her cabin and destroy everything she owned. That would be a death sentence for her. It was obvious she had to fight for what belonged to her. Slowly, she eased to the mouth of the cave with her bow and arrow ready to shoot.

Nothing. She didn't see a thing, not even her dog. She did hear what sounded like somebody chopping wood. Thankfully, it wasn't coming from her cabin. She listened for a long time, but the chopping didn't stop. What could the hunters be doing? Should she go back in the cave and wait, or should she be brave enough to find out what was going on?

She shuddered as she remembered how the man had attacked her. She certainly didn't want it to happen again, and it could if she hid in the cave and did nothing. All those times her dad had told her to hide in the cave was when he expected to return and save her. He wasn't here to save her now. If there was any saving to be done, she'd have to do it herself.

She eased from the cave to where some bindweed vines grew. She gathered hemlock twigs and pine boughs and tied them around her waist and chest with the bindweed vines to camouflage herself the best she could. She rubbed dirt on her arms and face until the white of her skin wasn't as easily seen. She then slipped through the woods, staying in the underbrush as much as possible.

She didn't go toward her cabin to get her crossbow. If they hadn't found the cabin, she certainly didn't want to lead them to it. The slingshot, bow and arrows, and the knife fastened around her waist would have to be weapons enough.

From the sound of the chopping, they were still near the same rock cliff they were at earlier, which was good. She would be able to lie on her belly and look over the rock cliff without them seeing her. If it was the same hunters she'd heard two nights before, they had a gun. If only she'd learned to shoot the guns the man left behind, she'd have a better chance of taking them out, but it was too late to think about that now.

She crawled through the underbrush like a cat stalking a mouse until she reached the rock overhang on the cliff. Just as she thought, she could see the wooded area below. She saw the man she'd shot lying on the ground with a sleeping bag similar to the one the man who attacked her had. Her dog was tied to a sapling, while the other person was chopping at another sapling with a hatchet. The sapling fell on the ground.

Her dog cocked his ears, lifted his nose up and whined. He had gotten wind of her and started chewing on the rope he was tied with.

"Stop that, Kang." The hunter said. "It's okay. You've been tied before. I don't want you running away again. We've got to go home, Kang. We've got to get out of this place. I don't have time to chase you." The hunter kneeled down in front of the dog and hugged him. The dog started licking the hunter in the face, bumping the cap off the hunter's head.

Striker squinted her eyes to get a better look. The hunter had long hair to go along with the high-pitched voice. Woman, striker thought. Could this be a woman instead of a man? She'd never seen a woman before, except in books. She looked closer, trying to see the features of the hunter's face. There was no beard or mustache. The man she'd hit with the rock had a pitiful excuse of both. So did the hunter, the dog killed. Her dad had a full-face beard, long, thick, and black.

This hunter had a face as free of hair as hers was. Even the hunter's body looked like hers except the hunter's breasts were larger and hung lower. Yes, striker decided, this had to be a woman, the first she'd ever seen, and she was whispering soothing words to the dog. The dog was obviously unafraid of the woman, even happy to have her arms around him.

The man she had shot with the rock made a moaning sound and said something. The woman rushed to him.

"You woke up. How do you feel?" the woman asked.

"Not so good," the man said. "This headache won't ease up. What was all the noise about?"

"I'm cutting down saplings to make a travois, so I can drag you off this mountain. We've got to get out of here before that Indian comes back. She might have gone to get the rest of her tribe. We won't have a chance of staying alive then."

The woman sounded scared. What was she talking about? There were no Indians anywhere on this mountain. According to the books she read, Indians were on reservations or mixed in with other people.

"Have you seen the girl again? Has she come back?"

"Not that I've seen. I'm sure she'll kill us both if she does. You're lucky that arrow didn't killed you."

"I know. I was hit before I got a chance to see her."

Striker tensed. Were they talking about her? Had to be. She'd been the only other person on this mountain. It certainly wasn't an Indian girl who shot the arrow at him. It was her.

"You still got your dog?" the man questioned the woman.

"Yes, thank goodness."

"Will I get the reward money?" he asked.

"If we get off this mountain alive, you'll certainly get the award money."

"We'll get away from here just as soon as my head stops hurting and I'm able to walk."

"I'll continue to make the travois."

"Good luck," he said, and closed his eyes.

"Head hurting? Need more aspirins?"

"Yes. Give me three."

She took the bottle from the back pack and shook out two more aspirins. She carefully lifted his head and put the pills in his mouth. She then held the water bottle to his mouth and let him drink.

The woman looked to be a lot older than the man. Could he possibly be her son? The woman was being extremely gentle with him, and she was also trying to make a sled out of saplings with the intention of pulling him off the mountain.

She hadn't killed him, but she had wounded him until he couldn't walk. She almost felt guilty about doing that. This man hadn't tried to attack her, but it didn't mean he wouldn't have.

"Are you hungry?" the woman asked the man.

"No. I'm hurting too much to eat anything."

"Okay, but you'll need to eat something. You'll have to keep up your strength if we're to get away from here."

"I know."

"I'll feed Kang, and then fix us something later."

"Okay," he said, and closed his eyes.

The woman took a bag out of her backpack, stuck her hand in it and let the dog eat out of her hand.

"I never gave up on finding you," the woman said. "You are my baby. I never gave up on finding my baby girl either. I found you the same as I found her. I don't give up, Kang. I never give up on anything."

Striker frowned. She wasn't sure exactly what the woman was talking about. She was talking about the dog, that was obvious. She was also talking about finding her baby girl. Did she have a daughter to go with her son?

Striker was surprised when she realized the woman was crying. She buried her face in the dog's neck and sobbed so hard her shoulders were shaking. She felt sorry for the woman, but there was one thing for certain. That woman wasn't going to take her dog away. But there was no big hurry for her to cut him loose. She wanted to watch the woman for a while longer. She wondered if her own mother looked anything like this woman?

What would it feel like to have a mother lift her head and give her water to drink? What would it feel like to have a mother's hands rubbing over her the way this woman was rubbing the dog? An overwhelming pain shot through Striker. She'd had a mother once, but she couldn't remember her. She had no doubt her dad had loved her and cared for her the best he could. But he wasn't the doting kind. He never held her in his lap or held water to her mouth that she could remember. He always told her she had to do things for herself. She had to grow up strong and tough.

Striker felt a tear slide down her cheek. It made her mad at herself. Her dad would be disappointed in her. She hadn't been strong or tough lately. She'd cried lately, and that made her mad at herself.

"I'll do better, Dad," she thought, as another tear slid down her other cheek.

The woman finished feeding the dog and poured a little water in her hand for the dog to drink. He lapped at it a little but seemed disinterested in water. They had all the water they could ever want to drink. Food was different. Striker had never seen the little brown cubes the woman was feeding the dog, but the dog seemed to like them a lot.

The woman turned her hand over and then wiped it on her pants leg. She picked up the hatchet and looked about for another sapling. She picked out one the same size as the one she'd cut down and started chopping. The dog seemed satisfied to lay down and watch her. Every so often he'd lift his nose and look toward the rock cliff. He knew she was there.

Striker found she couldn't stop watching the woman chop at the sapling. She spent her entire life wondering what a woman looked like, and finally there was one right in front of her.

Striker shook her head as she watched. The woman obviously hadn't had a dad teach her to chop with a hatchet. She was beating at the tree instead of hitting the trunk at an angle while she twisted the blade slightly to make a large chip of wood fly off. The woman looked wimpy and had too much soft flesh. The man the dog had killed had too much soft flesh too. She wondered about the man laying underneath the sleeping bag. She couldn't tell about him.

The woman obviously became impatient with her progress and hit the tree hard at the wrong angle. The hatchet ricocheted off the trunk and came back to hit the woman in the fleshy part of her thigh. She screamed almost as loud as she screamed when Striker had the bow and arrow pointed at her and the man.

Blood started gushing from her leg a moment before she fell to the ground. The woman grabbed hold of her leg with both hands trying to stop the flow of blood. It didn't seem to help much.

Take off your belt and twist it tight above the cut, Striker thought, but the woman didn't do it. She continued squeezing her leg with both hands.

The dog seemed to know the woman was hurt bad. He started whining and lunging to get to her. When he saw the rope wasn't going to turn him lose, he started biting on the rope. It took only a minute for him to bite the rope in two. He ran to the woman, whining and licking her in the face. It did no good. He turned away from the woman and ran straight up the path to Striker. He nosed her in the face, turned and ran a few feet toward the woman. When the woman didn't get up, Kang ran back to Striker and took her arm in his mouth and pulled.

It was obvious he was trying to get her to help the woman who was bleeding out fast. Okay, Striker thought. Without the woman's help, the man wouldn't make it off the mountain. Without her help, the woman would bleed to death. Striker's problem would be solved. At least, better solved for a little while. She would have her dog back, plus clothes, plus all the supplies they were carrying in their backpacks. She would even have shoes to wear when the weather got bad.

All she had to do was lay still and not get up, but she couldn't do it. She stood, and the dog twirled around in circles with joy before he ran down the path through the Laurel hell. Striker slithered through the Laurel hell right behind him.

The woman screamed when she looked up and saw Striker.

"I won't hurt you," Striker told her. "The dog made me come help you."

"Go away. Don't touch me," the woman yelled at her.

"If I go away, you'll bleed to death."

The woman looked from Striker to her leg. She was sitting in a pool of blood.

"You tried to kill us," the woman said.

"I thought you were men who would hurt me."

"We came to find my dog. We knew nothing about you."

"I know that now. Do you want me to save you, or had you rather die?"

"I don't want to bleed to death."

"Are you wearing a belt?"

"Yes."

Striker was glad. She didn't want to use the leather strip that held her scabbard. "Take it off and give it to me."

"I can't turn loose of my leg."

Striker placed her dirt covered hands on the woman's leg above the cut and squeezed. The woman quickly unfastened her belt and handed it to Striker. It took only a few seconds for Striker to have the belt fastened around the woman's leg. She twisted the belt until the bleeding slowed down to a trickle.

"Can you hold this tight until I go get some things to stop the bleeding?"

"I've got a first aid kit in my backpack."

Striker ran to the backpack, took out the first aid kit, and opened it. She dropped it on the ground and took off running. She had to hurry. She couldn't allow the blood supply to the lower part of the woman's leg to be cut off for long.

Striker came back with a box of alum, a curved needle and fishing line. When the woman saw the needle and fishing line, she started screaming again.

"It's okay," Striker said as she sat the box of alum down and transferred the needle and fishing line to her left hand. "This won't hurt. . . much."

Striker swung her right hand with a pine knot in it at the woman's chin. It was a good firm hit. Just right to accomplish what she wanted. She counted on the woman having what her dad called a glass chin. The punch knocked her out cold. The punch would have been less risky on breaking the chin if she had used only her fist, but she didn't want to take a chance on breaking a bone in her hand when she needed both hands to sew up the gash.

Striker wasted no time in tightening the belt around the woman's leg again. The minute or so the belt was loose had allowed blood flow to the woman's lower leg. She poured half the box of alum in the wound and began putting stiches in the woman's thigh, drawing the sides of the skin together tightly.

Her dad always said deep cuts needed stitches on the inside, but he didn't have the kind of sutures doctors used that dissolved by themselves. "Sew up the wound deep and tight," her dad instructed her when he'd cut himself. She'd sewn up her dad's right arm and took the stitches out a week and a half later. He hadn't needed to be knocked cold to keep from feeling the pain. He got staggering drunk instead. The liquid in her dad's jug was long gone.

Fifteen minutes later the woman started coming around.

"You hit me," she complained.

"Had too. You wouldn't have let me sew up your cut otherwise. You're still bleeding a little, but you'll most likely live. I put a lot of the alcohol and antibiotic stuff from your first aid kit on it before I bandaged it for you."

"Are you an Indian?"

"No."

"Who are you?"

"Nobody."

"Why are you naked."

"It's warm. I'll wear clothes come winter."

"Where's your husband, or man, or whoever you live with."

"Died."

"You're all alone?"

Striker didn't answer. There were two of them and only one of her, but they were both injured – not to mention being as weak and timid as a baby bird.

"My chin hurts almost as much as my leg does. Are you sure you know what you're doing?"

"You're alive," was all Striker said.

"I have extra clothes in my backpack. Put them on."

"I don't want your clothes."

"For goodness sakes. Put them on. It's not fitting to be naked when a man's around."

Striker remembered she was naked when the man had attacked her. The woman had a point. She went to the backpack again and got out the clothes. She went behind a bush, slipped the off what remained of the hemlock, pine, and furs and put the woman's clothes on. They were too big, but it didn't matter. She rolled up the pants legs and long sleeves a turn. Striker wasn't sure if she liked wearing clothes again or not.

"Is there water nearby?" The woman asked.

"Yes."

"Then fill up the water bottles, built a fire, put water in the pot along with one of the bags of dried vegetables, and cook us something to eat."

Striker got the empty water bottles and the pot. The dog followed at her heels.

"Make sure you wash the dirt off your arms and face," the woman called out as Striker walked away.

She'd already washed her hands before she sewed up the woman's leg. That woman was almost as bossy as her dad. Striker took time to go to her cabin and put wood in the fire. She scooted the pot of crow all the way on the back part of the stove to save for later. It appeared those two had a lot of little bags of dried stuff.

When Striker got back, the man was awake. "Who the hell are you?" he questioned.

"The wild Indian who shot you," she told him. His eyes widened. The woman chuckled. She had managed to scoot from the sapling she'd been cutting to lay near the man. There was no way she could walk on that leg. It would cause too much pain. The woman looked up at Striker and sucked in her breath.

"You washed you face," she mumbled in disbelief.

"So?"

"You look . . . you're not an Indian." The woman still seemed a little taken back.

"Nope." Striker walked away to gather leaves and twigs to get a fire started. She'd seen some precious matches in the backpack. She'd use one of them and tell those people she would keep half in return for keeping them alive. The dog stayed right by side her.

"How long has Kang been with you?" the woman asked when Striker returned and bent down to get the fire started.

"Since . . . a long time." She had started to say since the man arrived.

"Since when?" the woman persisted.

"Since Fall. I don't have calendars."

"When did your husband die?" The nosy woman kept on asking her questions.

She must not have hit the woman hard enough on the chin to keep her jaws from flapping. She thought of her dad. He'd been dead for years. As for the man the dog had killed, it was probably best not to talk about him."

"Too long," Striker said.

"How far along are you?"

"Far along what?"

"Pregnant? You're obviously going to have a baby before long. You've got a good-sized belly for such a thin girl."

Striker was stunned by what the woman had just said. She was so stunned she couldn't think of words to say. Could it be possible her belly wasn't caused by rickets? No way.

"I got rickets," Striker finally said. "Winter was hard on me."

The woman kind of chuckled. "You're trying to be funny. How old are you? Do you live near here?"

"Your tongue is flapping at both ends with questions," Striker shot back at her. "I've not asked you questions. I've only kept you alive." Which she was almost regretting doing. She hadn't spoken a word to another person in years. It was too much talking and listening all at once. She wanted to run away and let them have at it. Why she didn't, she had no idea.

"I wasn't cut that bad," she insisted. "I wasn't about to bleed to death."

Striker sat the pot of water on a rock in the middle of the fire she'd started and dumped an entire bag of dry stuff in the water to boil.

"I'm going," she said.

"No, no. Please don't leave us here alone. Burk has a concussion and I can't walk. What will we do if those wolves we heard howling the last two nights come after us. Surely your folks will let you stay with us tonight. What is your name?"

Striker didn't answer for a while as she thought. If they knew she lived close, they would tell someone, and they'd come find her.

"I'm April." She thought this month might be April. "I live on the far side of yonder mountain. My folks are trappers. They trade furs for supplies." It wasn't a total lie.

"How old are you?" the woman wanted to know. "You look young, and yet . . ." The woman didn't finish her sentence.

"Old as the mountains and young as the Spring." Striker wished the woman would shut up with the questions. She'd never learned how not to answer someone. Her dad claimed all questions deserved an answer.

"What are your names?" Striker decided to ask a few questions herself.

"This is Burk Jenkins. His uncle works for me. I hired Burk to help me find Kang, my dog. I was told he escaped from bad people last fall. I'm known as Lady Biswell because my husband claimed to have some kind of royalty in his blood line. If I may speak frankly, all he had in his blood was an excessive amount of alcohol. What is your last name, April?"

She could not think of a last name. Her dad never told her a last name? If so, she didn't remember it at the moment. Her name had simply been Striker. She barely remembered her dad's first name. To her he was Dad.

Burk had opened his eyes and was looking from Lady Biswell to Striker. Perhaps, when his concussion settled down, this would be nothing more than a bad hallucination. A wild Indian couldn't possibly have shot him in the head with an arrow. The same wild Indian couldn't have sewn up

Lady Biswell's leg to stop her from bleeding to death. He couldn't have been looking at a pregnant, naked, wild Indian before Lady Biswell made her put on her spare clothes. Surely Lady Biswell wasn't obviously insisting the wild Indian stay with them, so she could ask more questions of her.

"I must have gotten hold of some bad weed," Burk mumbled. "Gotta ease up on that stuff."

Chapter 51

~~~~

Lady Biswell was certain reality for her no longer existed. It was obvious blood loss and the hit on the chin were causing her to see things that couldn't possibly be real. People looked like other people all the time. Resemblances didn't mean a thing. If only this girl would tell something about herself, it could put Lady Biswell's vivid imagination to rest. How could she get this girl of questionable existence to talk about herself?

"Please, you have to eat a share our food. After all, you're the one who cooked it," Lady Biswell insisted when Striker started to leave them.

Striker really did want to taste the wonderful smelling food. Did she give in and eat or did her stubborn streak prevail? "Eat it while you've got it," she heard her dad's voice tell her.

"There's two tin cups in my backpack and one in Burks. We have spoons and forks. We ran out of water, but we have purifiers."

Striker dipped out a cup full of the vegetable soup for Lady Biswell and the man named Burk before she got herself some. It was the most delicious food she had ever eaten. A lot better than the crow that was in her pot on the back of her stove.

She ate half the cup and called for the dog to come to her. He got up from where he lay between her and Lady Biswell to lay his head in Striker's lap. Striker held the cup for him to eat the rest, which he did.

Lady Biswell lifted her brows in puzzlement. Never before had she seen Kang eat vegetables. "You don't like the food?" Lady Biswell asked.

"It's delicious," Striker told her.

"Then why did you feed it to Kang?"

"Dog and I share our food with each other. He eats half a rabbit, I eat half a rabbit. He doesn't like boiled tea much"

"Did you share his dried dog food?" Lady Biswell questioned.

"What's dry dog food? The stuff you fed him earlier?"

"That's right. I brought it with us. It's his favorite and one hundred percent nutritionally complete. Are you familiar with nutritionally complete?"

"I'll look it up in the encyclopedia," Striker told her.

"You have encyclopedias?" Lady Biswell would never have guessed it, although the girl did speak good enough English. "Where did you get them?"

"My dad always bought books for me. He said my mother wanted me well educated."

"Where did you go to school at?"

"My father educated me."

"So, you were home schooled," Lady Biswell wasn't surprised.

"Dad taught me at home, yes."

"Did you mother teach you as well?"

Striker didn't want to tell this woman anything more about herself. "Do you have seeds to grow the vegetables in that soup?" Striker asked.

"Griff and I buy our seeds at the garden center. We plant a large garden every spring."

"Can I buy seeds from you? I have money."

"If you'll come home with me, I'll give you all the seeds you want."

"You live down in the valley?"

"Yes, I do. You said you live on the other side of this mountain."

"On the other side of yonder mountain," Striker was quick to tell her. "I never go down into the valley. It isn't safe. Bring the seeds to me."

"It would be a very long walk back up this mountain. I don't think I could do it on this leg."

"Meet me halfway."

"You can go home with me. I assure you it is safe. I have a farm with cattle and more dogs. Do you live on a farm?"

Striker had read about farms. Her dad had talked about having a goat when she was a little. "You have a goat?"

"No. Like I said, I raise registered cattle."

"Dad had a goat when I was little. I drank the milk."

"What is your dad's name?"

"Harlan," Striker answered this time before she could stop herself.

Lady Biswell gasped. Her face turned pale. The horrible vegetable ration churned in her stomach and she gagged as it threatened to come up.

"Are you sick?" Striker asked.

"Harlan Mason," Lady Biswell blurted out. "Your father is Harlan Mason?"

Mason. Yes, she did believe that was his name and hers, although she'd never heard her dad use their last name, it was familiar. She had read that name in her dad's bible. This must have been the woman her dad traded with when he left the mountain. Otherwise she wouldn't know her dad's name.

"You know my dad?" Striker asked.

"Yes," Lady Biswell answered as her hands clutched together in her lap. I knew your dad very well a long time ago."

If this woman and her dad knew each other very well a long time ago, then she was surely a good person. Was the man she'd shot with a rock a good person too?

"Is this Burk a good man?" Striker blurted out.

"He's a very nice young man," Lady Biswell said. "Why did you shoot him?"

"I thought he was going to hurt me."

"Have you been hurt before by a man?" she asked gently.

"Once," she admitted, and instantly regretted her hasty answer. She knew it was best not to talk about the man Kang had killed.

"Was he the father of your baby?"

Again, Striker was stunned by the mention of a baby. She knew nothing at all about people having babies. She needed to go home and check her encyclopedias.

"You're obviously going to have a baby. That's why your stomach is so large."

"Rickets," she told Lady Biswell again. "I got rickets. Dad said vitamin C cures rickets. I haven't eaten enough yet. I need rose hips."

"Is your dad the father of your baby?"

"He's only my dad. He has no other baby." Striker was puzzled by what the woman was saying. Her words weren't making sense at all, plus they were making her feel very uncomfortable.

"I'm ready to get off this mountain," Burk suddenly spoke. "Concussion or no concussion. Cut leg or no cut leg."

Lady Biswell and Striker both looked at Burk. They had momentarily forgotten about him. Kang growled at the sound of his voice.

"That dog hates me," Burk added.

"He doesn't like men."

Striker agreed.

"Describe your dad." Color was returning to Lady Biswell's face and something similar to hope had taken its place.

"He was tall and broad, and very strong."

"Did he have dark brown hair and green eyes?"

"And a thick beard. Gray was starting to show in his hair and his beard, but he didn't know it," Striker added as though it might make a difference in his description.

"Do you look like him?" Lady Biswell was holding her breath, waiting for her answer.

"My dad always said I'm the spitting image of my mother. My hair and eyes are the same color as hers."

Lady Biswell licked her dry lips. "Is your mother dead?"

Striker nodded but didn't answer.

"Are you fifteen or sixteen years old?"

"Fifteen."

"You'll be sixteen in July, right?"

Again, Striker nodded. How did she know?

"Was your mother's name Abby?"

"You knew my mother?" Striker questioned.

Lady Biswell put her hands over her face and started crying as though her very heart was breaking.

Striker didn't know what had happened to make the woman cry so hard. Burk was listening intently as he looked from Lady Biswell to the girl.

When Lady Biswell finally got her crying under control, she motioned for Striker to sit down beside her, which she did.

"Tell me about my mother," Striker said. "Dad would never tell me about her."

"Okay. There are things I think you should know. It's a long story so bear with me until I tell you all of it. Okay?"

"Okay," Striker agreed.

"When I was your age, I fell in love with a policeman," Lady Striker began. She told Striker her story up to the point where her third husband started losing his mental ability.

"Reg told me he knew where my daughter was. At the same time, he couldn't remember me, much less my daughter's name or who had her."

Chapter 52

~~~~

Nedra spent months going through every single file Reg McFarland had. She found nothing that told her about her daughter. She knew the information had to be somewhere. Reg knew nothing at all about her or her daughter until she got him to represent her in the divorce. It was possible he found the information in Joe Whitson's files. All attorneys kept files. They also destroyed files that could incriminate them in any wrongdoing.

She couldn't get help from the asylum files since the place burned down including their files. As Joe Whitson's widow, she was entitled to his files along with everything he possessed. It was going through Joe's files that she got to thinking about his half-sister and the money she was sending her each month. She had an urge to meet this half-sister and see exactly what her monthly checks were going toward.

His sister's name was Viola Crawford. She was still living in the family homeplace.

When Nedra stopped Reg's Cadillac in front of the old farm house, two boys rushed out the door to see who had arrived, followed by a woman in a faded blue dress and a stained bibbed apron. The woman looked like she had come out of Nedra's grandmother's time. Her hair was in a twist at the back of her neck and her face had a sweet, welcoming smile.

As Nedra got out of the car, a little girl ran out of the house to clutch Viola's legs. The little girl was beautiful, but thin and frail looking.

"You must be Joe's widow," Viola said before Nedra spoke. "I wondered if you would ever show up. "I'm Viola Crawford. These two boys of mine are, Jimmy and Robert. This sweet girl is my daughter, Abby.

"It's nice to finally meet you. I never knew Joe had a half-sister until after he died."

"I'm not surprised. My brother didn't talk about his family often. To be honest, I think he was ashamed of us. Oh, dear. I shouldn't have said that. It's not Christian. Please forgive me. Do come inside. I was making cookies for the children. They have been extremely helpful lately. Boys, finish stacking up that firewood for me. I'll call you when I get the cookies baked."

The boys rushed off to do as their mother told them.

Nedra followed Viola inside. The place was scrubbed clean. The furnishings had obviously been in the house for years. The wear was evident. Viola certainly hadn't spent any of her monthly check money on upgrading their living quarters.

Viola took her into the kitchen and indicated she should sit down at a scarred pine table. There had to be years of scrapes and stains on the wood. Like the rest of the house she'd seen, it was scrubbed spotless.

"Do you drink tea? I don't have any coffee since my husband died. I never acquired a taste for it, although I did love the smell of it perking on a cold winter morning. Coffee perking and cornbread baking bring back wonderful memories for me," Viola told her.

"I agree with you. I still remember my mother fixing breakfast of a morning and cooking supper at night. Every time I smell coffee perking or cornbread baking, I want to laugh and cry at the same time."

"Joe said your parents and first husband died within a few months of each other," Viola said as she got a pitcher out of the refrigerator and poured a glass.

Little Abby looked up at her mother hopefully. "No, dear," Viola told the child. "You know you're not allowed to drink tea. It has sugar in it. Would you like a glass of milk?"

The little girl gave her mother a half nod."

"Abby is a diabetic. The doctors won't allow her to eat sweets."

Nedra looked at the little girl and thought of her own daughter. She would be slightly bigger than this little girl.

"How old are you Abby?" Nedra asked.

"Seven," the little girl said, which surprised Nedra. "I'm little."

Viola gave her daughter a loving smile as she placed the glass of milk in front of her. "What Abby means, is that she's small for her age.

"Momma gives me a shot twice a day," the little girl said proudly. It hurts but I never cry. Momma say I'm tough as ten penny nails."

"That you are. You are momma's special girl, aren't you?"

The little girl nodded with obvious pride.

"Tell me, Nedra, what brings you to visit us after all these years?"

"Nothing special. I was going through Joe's things and was reminded he had a sister I'd never met. I thought maybe I should meet you and your family."

"Did Joe talk about me?"

"No. He wasn't much to talk about his life. His job was his world."

"I'm not surprised. Joe was always ambitious, even as a child. He was ashamed of his background. He wanted to be important, a rich man. Was he ever happy?" Viola asked.

"Honestly, I don't think he ever was."

"I can't believe he died of a heart attack. He was never sick a day in his life that I knew about."

"I was told healthy men had heart attacks too."

"My husband died in a farming accident. The tractor rolled over on him."

"My first husband was a policeman. He was shot and killed."

Viola said nothing about Nedra being married for the third time, and Nedra was thankful."

~~~~

Lady Biswell sat there with the empty tin cup in her hands, staring at it as though it held some sort of fascination.

"No matter how hard I tried, I couldn't find my daughter. I cried myself to sleep almost every night. I searched through all the files, papers, and even scrap sheets of paper, and scribbled notes I could find from both Joe and Reg. I could find no indication of where my daughter was. I asked Reg numerous times a day about her, hoping he'd just have a few minutes of clarity and tell me what he knew. He never did.

"I had no family other than the sweet Viola and her children. I decided to make them my family, and Viola welcomed me with open arms. I discovered that little Abby's health care took just about all of the money I gave them each month. I, on the other hand, was a wealthy woman. I had more money than a person could hope for, and yet I had nothing.

"Odd, how people spend their lives striving for money only to discover it's nothing but paper. Viola, on the other hand, had unconditional love for her children, and them for her. They even had enough love left over for me to receive some."

"I helped Viola with her expenses as much as I could. I even insisted on paying for her sons' college educations. Little Abby didn't want to go to college. All she wanted to do was stay home with her mother. She was such a beautiful child who turned into a beautiful young woman.

"Abby was nineteen years old when she fell in love with a man several years older than her. Viola was against her getting married. She tried to convince Abby that her poor health would play a factor in her marriage. "A man needs a healthy wife," Viola had gently told her.

"Abby came to me in tears. She said she was deeply in love and wanted to be a wife even when her life expectancy was less than average.

"Viola and I discussed Abby's health and the idea of her getting married. We decided to pay a visit to the doctor and see what he had to say about Abby's health and her getting married. He saw no reason for Abby not to get married, but he warned she should never get pregnant.

"When we got back to Viola's house, Abby had left a letter on the scared pine table. She wrote she had eloped with the love of her life and hoped Viola would accept their marriage.

"Abby later told us the man she married was the restless sort with demons that haunted him. He'd gotten religion as a teenager, but at the age of eighteen he joined the army and was sent to fight in the war.

"Abby said he'd seen the worst in people that ever existed. She said he woke up almost every night screaming because of the flashbacks he was reliving.

"A few months after Abby got married, Viola discovered she had lung cancer. She'd never smoked a day in her life, and yet she was going to die. She hadn't gone to the doctor until it had already metastasized and gotten into her bones. The doctor told her she had three months or less to live.

"Abby and her husband traveled about a lot. He couldn't find a place where he could settle down. He couldn't keep a job more than a few weeks at a time. Abby never complained about him, and only visited Viola a time or two when they were in desperate need of money.

"When Abby found out about Viola's cancer, she and her husband moved in with Viola. Abby was eight and a half months pregnant. Never once had she written Viola that she was pregnant. Abby also admitted that she'd never once been to see a doctor. Her husband didn't believe in doctors any more than he believed in wars."

Tears were streaming down Lady Biswell's face, but she kept on talking.

"Abby's husband had gone into town, when she went into labor. Viola called me. We rushed Abby to the hospital. Viola and I sat in the waiting room holding hand and praying while Abby was delivering her baby. She'd ignored the doctor's warnings, gone through her entire pregnancy without ever seeing a doctor. She hadn't even taken her diabetes medicine since the day she got married. Not once had Abby complained about feeling sick. Her life, her joy was centered on her baby and her husband. She didn't believe God would ever let anything happen to her."

Lady Biswell breathed hard and was silent for a minute or two before she started talking again.

"Abby died giving birth to her healthy baby daughter. She was named Abbigail after her mother. Her father went wild with grief. After Abby's funeral, he disappeared, leaving the baby behind. Viola was too sick to care for herself much less a baby. Reg McFarland had died by that time. I was living alone. I moved Viola and the baby in with me. I hired a full-time nurse to take care of Viola. I devoted myself to the baby. I told myself she was the daughter I never got to raise. God had surely sent her to me to make up for my own little girl. Her dad showed up twice to see his baby, but every time he looked at her, she brought back Abby's death. He'd start crying and shaking all over before he ran out of the house. It would be months before he'd come back again. The last time he came, Viola and I begged him to sign over papers to allow me to adopt the baby. He refused.

"Viola got worse, and her sons were notified she only had hours to live. I was sitting on her bed with the baby in my arms. Viola started talking about Abby.

"I'd always wanted a little girl," Viola said. I had two boys as easy as pie, but I never got pregnant again. I don't know why, but I reckon God had his reason."

"Her words puzzled me. She had Abby. I thought her mind had left her, but she continued. She said right before her husband died, Joe told her he'd found a baby girl who needed adopting if we could come up with five thousand dollars. It took every penny we could scrape together, but we did it and adopted Abby. When we found out about her diabetes and weaknesses, we consulted a doctor. He said to find out as much as we could about Abby. We went to Joe. He said all he knew was that Abby's mother was in an asylum when Abby was born. The doctor thought all the medicine the mother was given caused Abby's condition.

"I was stunned. I asked Viola why she hadn't told me this before. She said she didn't think it was important. I then asked her if Joe ever told her who the mother was. She said he never did. She even said she and the doctor tried to find out from the asylum who the mother was, but it did no good. It would have cost more money than Viola ever dreamed of having to hire lawyers. Joe refused to help in any way. He claimed anything he might know was confidential. So, Viola just gave up. It didn't matter. Knowing about Abby's mother wouldn't change a thing.

"I went into a kind of shock when I realized I had been with my little girl for all those years and didn't even know it. None of us realized Abby was my daughter or that little Abbigail was my granddaughter.

"I left little Abbigail with the nurse while I went to Viola's funeral. When I came back, the baby was gone. The nurse said her father came and took her away. I had the law go after him. I hired private investigators to go after him.

Every time they got word of his whereabouts, he'd be gone by the time they arrived.

"I thought I would go out of my mind. I'd lost my daughter and then I'd lost my little granddaughter. Her father had managed to take her, and they disappeared off the face of the earth. There was never again a trace of them, never."

Lady Biswell sat there silently staring into the dying ashes of the fire for a long time.

"Abby's husband's name was Harlan Mason," she said.

Striker's mouth dropped open, closed again, then opened. "You're Aunt Nellie?" she said.

"That's what your mother and her brothers called me."

"I promised Dad I'd find you, but you found me. You kept my promise."

Chapter 53

~~~~

By morning, Lady Biswell had a fever and was barely able to sit up. When Striker checked her leg, it was red and swollen. Her face was flushed, her lips chapped, and her eyes had a glazed look to them

"We've got to get her to a hospital," Burk told Striker. If not, she might die. That leg is infected.

"I'll be okay," Lady Biswell insisted.

"Not if we're out here when the rain hits. Look up. The sky is clouding over sooner than the weatherman forecasted."

Striker looked at the sky. She knew signs of the weather a lot better than he did. She lived with them. It would rain in two days' time and then a cold Spring spell would hit. "Can you walk?" she asked Burk.

"I think so. I'm not as dizzy-headed as I was, but I don't think Lady Biswell can walk all the way off this mountain on her leg."

Striker gathered herbs her dad had used when he got cut and made a poultice for Lady Biswell's leg in hope it would draw some of the infection out.

"She's going to die," Burk told Striker when Lady Biswell couldn't overhear him. "That infection is sure to kill her. She needs to be in a hospital."

"Where is the hospital?" Striker wanted to know.

"If we can get her home, Uncle Griff will drive her there."

"Point out in what direction her home is?"

"How? All I see is trees."

"On top of the rock cliff you can see in the distance. Too bad you can't make it to the bald. You can see forever up there. Can you walk?"

"We'll find out," he said as he stood up. He wasn't nearly as dizzy as he had been yesterday, but he was far from being his normal self.

He crawled through the rhododendron hell back up the path where the girl had shot him in the head. The girl slithered through like a rabbit. He stood on the rock cliff, took the compass out of his pocket and pointed in the direction of home.

"Did you shoot the gun three nights back?" Striker wanted to know.

"Lady Biswell did."

"Then you're pointing in a different direction. You took the long way to get here. You should have gone the way the crow flies."

"You know of an easier route off the mountain?" he questioned. "According to the map, we came the easiest way. Coming straight up would have been too steep a climb."

Striker knew nothing about maps or how to get off the mountain. All she knew was the quickest way from where they stood to Lady Biswell's home was a straight line.

"I'll make the travois," she said. "I'll pull her off the mountain. You'll have to walk or stay here."

"I'll walk, he told her."

Striker chopped the other sapling down and cut them to size. She only wanted a foot or so of the pole touching the ground. The more contact with the ground the easier the saplings would get stuck on rocks and roots. The hard part would be having the saplings rest on her shoulders as she carried Lady Biswell's weight. The woman was thin as a willow reed, but even an empty travois would feel heavy after a while.

She used the ropes to fasten the saplings together and crisscrossed the ropes to keep Lady Biswell from falling through. She covered the ropes with the tarps and cut a few hemlock and pine boughs to absorb the bounce when the travois hit a rough place. She spread out both backpacks for Lady Biswell to lay on.

Burk watched her work with disapproval. He could do a much better job if only he were able.

Lady Biswell objected the entire time Striker worked on the travois. "There is no way my pregnant granddaughter is going to pull me off this mountain. I'm perfectly capable of walking." She tried to stand only to discovered she wasn't capable.

Striker considered taking them to her cabin and hoping time would heal her Aunt Nellie but decided against it when she looked at Lady Biswell's leg again. The woman was so skinny the blade must have chipped the bone. Striker hadn't thought about that when she hurriedly sewed her leg up. She wondered if she should cut the stitches loose and hope the bone chip might work its way out. If she did cut the wound open, it would most likely start bleeding again. She didn't think Aunt Nellie would be willing to be knocked cold a second time.

Striker had considered the sled her dad had made before she started on the travois. It would have been a lot quicker to use it than to take time to make a travois, but it would also take a lot more strength to pull it. The runners were made from logs and came into a lot more contact with the ground. The travois would be a lot easier for her to pull.

While working on the travois, Striker had thought about what Lady Biswell had told her. Why hadn't her father been willing to tell her more about her mother. Why hadn't he told her about her grandmother. But then her dad had thought her grandmother had died. He thought Lady Biswell was her Aunt Nellie and nothing more. Her dad had told her to find her Aunt Nellie and would have probably told her more if he'd been able to talk longer. Her father had mentioned the war, so what Lady Biswell told her must be true. Not that she doubted the poor woman. She had no reason to lie. Plus, the dog liked her. As for Burk, he was a man and she wasn't about to trust one of those ever again.

Time hadn't permitted her to go back to her cabin and check in the encyclopedias about being pregnant. The man had hurt her body all over, but she didn't know enough about human mating to know if mating was what he had done to her. She simply didn't have time to think on such as that right now. She'd get the injured woman home and think about such as that once she was back in her cabin.

She was afraid to go down into the flat land, but her dad had gone down there many times and it hadn't taken him three days to go down and come back. "Is it safe to go into the flatland?" She asked Lady Biswell as she loaded her onto the travois.

"It's safe," Lady Biswell said through clenched teeth as she did her best to scoot her body with her good leg. The pain in her leg had become almost unbearable overnight. Nothing would feel better than to stick a knife in the wound to let the pressure out. She knew the girl had no idea what she was doing when she sewed up her leg with fishing line, but she hadn't been able to stop her.

Lady Biswell was still in as much of fix now as she had been when her leg was bleeding. She knew she had to get to the hospital or she would die. At the least, she would lose her leg from gangrene if the infection continued. Not only was she in a fix, her granddaughter and Burk were in one too. If her granddaughter tried to pull her down the mountain, she was taking a chance on going into labor. She doubted Burk was in condition to help either one of them. He hadn't been the rugged mountain man he perceived himself. She had considered the possibility of Burk going down the mountain and sending a rescue team for her, but Burk might not make it alone. Her granddaughter could go with Burk, but then she would be left alone and she most likely wouldn't survive until help arrived. The infection in her leg was increasing fast. Red streaks were starting up her leg and she knew what that meant – blood poisoning.

"Is there no one close by to help us," Lady Biswell asked Striker.

"No," Striker told her firmly.

"What about your family."

"Dad's dead."

"I thought you lived with someone over yon mountain."

"I live alone," Striker decided to tell her the truth.

"Where?"

"On the mountain."

"How long?"

"Three winters."

"You've been alone on this mountain since you were twelve?" Lady Biswell had to be hearing her wrong.

"I'll tie you on," Striker told her. "Prepare yourself for a bumpy ride."

"At least I found Kang plus my granddaughter," Lady Biswell said as Striker squatted down and placed each sapling pole on her shoulders. She'd put the skins she'd worn as clothing on her shoulders to protect her skin from the poles. She knew what the poles would do to flesh and bone before much time passed.

Striker set her sight on a straight line and started walking at a fast pace. She had pulled Lady Biswell straight down the mountain for a good mile when darkness came. All three of them were glad to stop for the night. Lady Biswell was in so much pain she didn't think she would survive another bump. Burk was staggering from tree trunk to tree trunk. Striker's shoulders ached like they were getting ready to crack off. The only one not affected was the dog. He stayed beside Striker and growled every time Burk got close her.

Once they had stopped, she wasn't sure she could move her arms enough to make a fire and cook some more of the soup. Her shoulders were rubbed raw and her hands were blistered from gripping the poles.

"I've got trail mix in my backpack," Burk told her. "Lady Biswell is lying on top of it. Don't let that dog bite me when I pull it out."

"Come here," Striker said, and the dog came to her. Her shoulders and arms hurt too much to put her arm around him.

Burk pulled out the trail mix along with the flares."

"Praise the lord," he burst out with glee. "I'd forgotten about these. What time does Griff do the feeding?" he asked Lady Biswell.

She did her best to understand what Burk was asking her, but he seemed to be talking from a long distance away.

"I know he feeds the dogs before he checks on the cattle," Burk said. "He'll not be able to see the flare very well if it's not dark. It's dark now, so I'll set one off. I'll set another one off before daylight in the morning."

Burk set up the flare and struck a match to it. It made a whizzing sound as a giant flame shot into the air and up through the trees. Striker cringed.

"That thing can set the woods on fire," she told Burk as she watched it. We'd really be in a fix if that happened. We couldn't outrun the flames."

The girl had a point. He'd have to be more careful if he shot off another one. Besides, he wasn't sure Uncle Griff or anyone else would see the flare.

Burk took aspirins and poked two in Lady Biswell's mouth before they drank water and then ate their trail mix. Striker ignored the pain in her hands and arms long enough to eat the trail mix and feed the dog some more of the brown pellets. She drank water from the bottles she'd filled up earlier and poured some in her hand for the dog. She suspected the dog had already found a stream. He was continuously running far ahead of them. Animals could smell water and so could she, but not nearly as well as animals did.

All three of them fell right to sleep from exhaustion.

Striker was the first to wake up. The sky wasn't even gray. It was broad daylight. Burk was still asleep and so was Lady Biswell. She didn't know where the dog had gotten to. She got a handful of the trail mix and ate it. She would need all the strength she could get, but she didn't want to take time to build a fire and cook food. She took hold of Burk's shoulder and shook him firmly. He groaned and opened his eyes slowly.

"No," he mumbled. "I don't want to wake up."

"It's late," Striker told him. "It's daylight already. We'd best be going."

She checked on Lady Biswell who was still sleeping. She'd groaned on and off all night long. Striker handed Burk the bag of trail mix. "Eat that while we walk," she told him as she lifted the poles on her shoulders. She didn't think Lady Biswell was awake enough to eat.

"It's too late to shoot off a flare," Burk said. "I don't think Uncle Griff saw it last night."

"How much farther?" Lady Biswell asked as she came awake.

Striker looked at Burk for an answer. She had no idea where they were. All she knew was she was trying to go down the mountain in a straight line the same way a crow would fly.

"My brain feels a little confused," Burk admitted. "So, I'm thinking if it took us three days to hike up the mountain, we ought to be able to go down twice as fast. Plus, we meandered around the mountain to keep us from having to climb straight up. She's taking us straight down the steep part. I'm hoping we can make it in a day and a half if we can keep up the pace."

If that were true, Striker thought, they traveled half a day yesterday. They should make it the rest of the way today if she could stand to pull the travois all day long.

Just when Striker decided the lay of the land wasn't too rough, they came upon a rock cliff. She'd have to find a way to go around it for there was no possibility of climbing down it.

"This rock cliff takes up half the mountain," Burk said. "It'll take hours to find our way around it."

Striker saw a gap in the rocks. "We can go that way," she said.

Burk took a look. "Holy shit," he mumbled as he held onto a tree trunk and looked down the narrow gap. "We can't go that way."

"Got a better choice?" Striker ask him.

Burk looked around and didn't answer. This was a gully cut out by years of rain water smack dap in the middle of a rock cliff that encompassed half the mountain. There was no way a person could walk up that gap and he questioned their ability to go down it.

"It's slick. We'll slide easily," Striker told Burk.

"How will we ever stop sliding?"

"By using our feet. There're dips in the rocks. We'll use those to slow us down."

"You don't have shoes on. It'll rip the skin right off your bones."

He was right about that, but what choice did she have.

"Take Lady Biswell's shoes off and put them on. She doesn't need them."

Burk was right about that. Striker lay the travois down where it would brace itself against a rock until she could get the shoes off Lady Biswell and put them on her own feet.

"You want to go first?"

"No," he was quick to answer her. If I go first and that travois gets away from you, it'll knock me clean off this mountain."

~~~~

Five days, Griff thought. Lady Biswell and Burk had been gone five of the seven days Burk thought it would take to reach the top of the mountain and then get back. That was if all went well. He was sure they both packed enough supplies to last longer than that. The thing that concerned him was the weather. A thunder storm was coming sooner than earlier forecasted. Griff feared it would be a frog strangler of the worst kind. Following behind the rain would be a cold front. It wouldn't do a young buck like Burk any harm to get soaking wet, but Lady Biswell was a different matter. She wasn't exactly a spring chicken, and neither was he. Griff knew it would be hard on him to hike for five days and then get soaking wet. It was a lot colder on that mountain than down here in the valley. If Lady Biswell got wet and then chilled when she was exhausted, and her resistance lowered, it could very easily give her pneumonia. They had taken tarps and Burk would know how to make a shelter out of them, but that was no guarantee they could stay warm or safe.

There were also wild animals to worry about. Mountain lions, bears and wolves were still roaming in those mountains regardless of what the wildlife people tried to claim. There were also coyotes, but they were little cowards and offered little danger to adults. Burk might be good at hiking, but he wasn't an experienced hunter. At least Lady Biswell could shoot a gun. He knew that for a fact.

It was useless for him to worry, but he did. He couldn't help himself. He really had grown mighty fond of that cantankerous woman. Evidently her four dead husbands felt the same way. There was one thing for sure and certain. He didn't want to become her fifth dead husband, but he did like having her as his boss lady.

As for Burk, that boy was as tough as a pine knot. Always had been or he wouldn't have asked him to go with Lady Biswell. Plain fact was that as Lady Biswell's kennel and farm manager, he should have been a more forceful man. He should have put his foot down on her crazy idea of climbing that mountain in an effort to find a dog that had disappeared a long time ago.

"Stupid. Plain stupid," Griff said out loud.

But then, if a man had ever been born who could do anything with that woman, he didn't know who he was.

~~~~

Pain caused Lady Biswell to come out of her blessed stupor back into reality. She lay on the makeshift Travois and tried her best not to scream with every bump that jarred her leg. It was all she could do not to yell out to stop pulling her downhill at such a fast pace. She'd rather die on the spot than go through more of the bone shattering pain she was enduring. Then she opened her eyes and saw Burk staggering behind the travois and thought about her skinny, pregnant granddaughter who was pulling the travois. She felt ashamed of herself and held in her screams as well as her pleadings. They had to be suffering too. Besides, this was all her fault. None of this would have happened if she hadn't insisted on searching for her dog. But then, this was surely meant to be. She wouldn't have found her dog or her missing granddaughter if she hadn't been overly determined. She might have simply died an old woman without ever knowing where Harlan Mason had taken that precious little baby all those years ago. One thing was for certain, no private detective would have found them living on that mountain, and neither would she if it hadn't been for her missing dog. Life, she thought, oh how life had a way of kicking you in the teeth just to see what you'd do next. The quirks of life could be downright amusing at times.

Lady Biswell might have burst into fits of laughter if she hadn't been in so much pain. Life had always kicked her in the teeth. Yet, people looked at her and thought she was the luckiest person alive instead of being the unluckiest. She appeared to have everything a person could possibly want, when actually she had very little that mattered. She had lost everyone she'd ever loved. She's lost her parents, her husband, and her baby. She hadn't known Abby was her very own daughter until after Abby had died. And now, when she'd found her granddaughter, she was the one who was going to die. The saddest part was the poor girl needed her and she wasn't going to be there for her.

The poor girl knew nothing about life. Harlan Mason might have taught her to read and hunt game, and stay alive in the wild, but he certainly hadn't taught her about the necessary things a girl needed to know. The poor little thing thought she had rickets instead of being pregnant. Most likely she too would die when the baby was born. Lady Biswell started praying that she would stay alive long enough to help this granddaughter of hers.

"Not yet, Lord. I can't die yet. I'm the only one who can help her. Don't let me die yet." she was praying out loud over and over again.

~~~~

By the time the travois had rammed Striker to the bottom of the gap, sweat was running down her face and stinging her eyes. The clothes Lady Biswell insisted she put on were wringing wet and ripped in a dozen places. She longed to take them off, but she couldn't stop pulling long enough to do it. Not that she would strip them off while there was a man watching her.

She didn't want to be in this situation, and she wouldn't be if she hadn't wanted to eat squirrel. All this was her fault. She was the one who shot the man in the head with a rock. It was justice that she had to pay for addling him.

But then, if things had happened differently, she wouldn't know what she knew now.

"Dad," she said silently to herself. "Is this your way of punishing me for not leaving the mountain to find Aunt Nellie? Did you decide to send her to find me? If so, why didn't you make it a lot easier on all of us? I'm not sure if I can keep going, Dad. There's nothing about me that doesn't hurt. From the top of my head to the bottom of my feet is one great big ache."

And then she remembered all those days and nights she and Kang stayed inside the cabin starving to death. She hadn't died then, and she wouldn't die now. All she had to do was keep putting one foot in front of the other – and keep the travois from knocking her over when they went down a steep bank too fast.

"Are you going to stop for lunch? I could use a rest after sliding down that brutal gap of solid granite," Burk told her.

"No," Striker answered. "If I stop, I'll never get started again."

"I'm exhausted," Burk told her. "I need aspirins and maybe a smoke."

"And I need to grow wings and fly out of here, but I'm not going to do that either."

"I can't go on like this," Burk whined.

"Stay here then," Lady Biswell surprised them both by saying. "I'll send Griff back after you."

Burk was silent as he thought about it. "If she can keep going, so can I," but he wasn't sure about that.

Hours later they had left the steep ground of the mountain and reached the flat land in the valley. The travois became much heavier to pull, and Striker became much weaker. Her body was trembling from the top of her head all the way down to Lady Biswell's shoes.

"I can't go on," Striker mumbled as the poles fell from her shoulders and she sank to the ground.

"Finally," Burk mumbled. His knees buckled, and he sank down beside Striker.

Lady Biswell's fever had increased to the point where her pain was nothing more than a vague memory somewhere beyond her reach, and she was thankful.

~~~~

Griff was walking across the back yard when he came to a sudden stop and stood looking at the mountain. He was certain something bad had happened. He could feel it in his very soul. Unexpectedly, something hit him in the back of his legs, and he was almost fell face first. He staggered and caught his balance.

Much to his amazement Kang was there tugging at his arm.

"Where on earth did you come from? Where is Lady Biswell? Did you run off and leave her?"

Relief washed over Griff. They were back, and Kang had run ahead of them. Kang! Lady Biswell had been right about the dog. But why was the dog acting so strangely? He wouldn't stop whining and pulling at his arm. His teeth ripped the sleeve off his shirt. The dog had never done that before. The dog didn't like him, but he wasn't trying to bite him.

"Something's wrong, boy. You want me to follow you?"

Kang turned loose of his arm and ran a few feet ahead, stopped, and looked back at Griff. Kang continued on when he saw Griff was following him.

Griff followed the dog beyond the farm, across the long swampy valley to the foot of the far mountain when the dog ran far ahead and started barking. Griff ran at a trot toward the sound of barking.

What he found was beyond his belief.

"Oh, gracious me! What in the world has happened Lady Biswell, Burk, can you talk to me?" Griff jerked out his cell phone and dialed 911.

"I've got an emergency here," Griff told the dispatcher. "This is Griff Jenkins out at the Biswell farm. I have three unconscious people – Lady Biswell, Burk Jenkins, and I have no idea who the girl is. Send an ambulance as fast as possible. I repeat, I have three injured and unconscious people."

Chapter 54

~~~~

Griff sat in the waiting room of the hospital telling Chief Adkerson what had happened.

"Lady Biswell went in search of her dog. She found him too. I shut him up in the kennel while the medics loaded them in the ambulance." He didn't tell the Chief that Kang came within a hair of biting him when he pulled him away from the girl.

"You say you don't know her?"

"Never seen her before in my life. Have you talked to Burk yet?"

"No. I'm waiting on the doctor to give me an okay first. Which shouldn't be much longer. Seems Burk was in better condition than the other two."

Griff looked up as the doctor came into the room. "What's the news, doc?"

"Burk has a mild concussion along with several scrapes and bruises, but he's going to be just fine. We're going to keep him overnight to be on the cautious side."

"What about Lady Biswell and the girl?"

"Their doctors are still with them."

"Would I be able to talk to Burk now?" Chief Adkerson asked.

"I think so. I gave him some extra strength Tylenol to ease his pain, but it shouldn't affect his coherence."

"Thank you," Chief Adkerson said as he got up and left the waiting room.

"Tell Burk I'll be in shortly," Griff told him, and turned to the doctor." "Could you find something out about Lady Biswell and the girl for me?"

"I'll try. Wait here for a few minutes."

Griff watched the doctor leave the waiting room and sat back down. No matter how hard he racked his mind, he couldn't figure out how the pregnant girl got to be with them. He thought the girl was dressed in Lady Biswell's clothes. She was even wearing Lady Biswell's tennis shoes. What was more puzzling, was the bow slung over her left arm, the quiver of arrows on her back, and the knife fastened around her waist.

It was evident why Lady Biswell wouldn't need her shoes, and why she was strapped onto the travois. From what he saw through her ripped, bloody pants, that right thigh of hers was not in good condition.

Lady Biswell had started mumbling as the medics loaded her on the stretcher, but none of her mumbling made sense.

The doctor returned a few minutes later. Griff stood to up to receive the news.

"Lady Biswell is in surgery. According to the surgical nurse, x-ray showed that her thigh bone had been chipped and the chip was moving about causing extreme pain. Someone had sewn the gash up with fishing line, which probably kept her from bleeding to death. Naturally, the unsterile materials caused an infection. There were also muscles and ligaments that were cut. The surgeon is working on those at this time. He fears there might be some nerve damage for a while, causing some numbness to surround the injured area, but nothing permanent.

As for the young girl, she went into labor and is in the delivery room. I haven't gotten much information about her. According to the nurse, it was evident she was the one pulling the travois instead of the young man. The nurse said her hands and shoulders were rubbed raw."

~~~~

Striker was waking up to the sound of a baby crying.

"She appears healthy," a voice said.

"How premature is she?"

"A few weeks. Her finger nails don't show her to be premature. Her length is good, but she is very thin."

"So is the mother. I doubt she would weigh ninety-five pounds and she was pregnant."

"Her muscles are well defined, and she had to be strong to pull the woman's weight on those sticks."

The sound of several voices, the feeling of being enclosed, and the bright lights shining caused Striker to panic. She had no idea what had happened after her world started spinning around and everything went black.

"Easy, easy. Take it easy. Your baby is just fine. She's a beautiful little girl. She surprised us all by weighing in at four pounds eleven ounces."

Striker felt a needle jab into her arm and a few moments later she seemed to be floating on a white cloud. She was no longer panicking. Nothing had her afraid, but she was still puzzled.

"Where am I?" her mouth slowly formed the question that was in her mind.

"You are in the hospital and you just had a baby."

Hospital, she thought of the word. She'd heard it before, plus she'd read the word before. She wasn't exactly sure where or when. To be honest, she didn't care because she felt safe and terribly good. Things weren't clear. She felt as though she was floating through some kind of strange dream. She tried to wake up but couldn't do it.

"Here. Hold your baby." Someone said, as a little naked, crying thing was placed on her chest. Her hands slowly lifted to keep it from falling off. There were bandages on her hands.

"Baby," she mumbled. Was this a real human baby? It didn't look like the babies she'd seen in books. A vague image of babies wrapped in blankets in the arms of smiling mothers drifted into her mind.

"What are you going to name your baby?" someone asked.

"My baby?" Striker mumbled.

"Yes, it's yours. You just had a baby girl," the voice continued. "Didn't expect it to happen this soon, did you?"

Striker tried to shake her head. "No." she mumbled as memory creeped in. The woman who cut her leg had said she was going to have a baby. "Rickets," Striker mumbled.

Several people laughed. "I hope that is not what you're going to your baby," a woman said.

"Will she need incubation?" someone asked.

"As long as her weight doesn't go below four and a half pounds, she probably won't. How is her breathing?"

"Good so far. She's pink now."

"Look, momma, she's trying to suck her fist. She's hungry. Want to try feeding her? You plan on breast feeding, don't you?"

Someone lifted the baby off her chest and wrapped it in a blanket and then laid it beside Striker. The oddest feeling came over her as she looked at the baby. She didn't want it taken away from her. She would fight to keep it.

~~~~

"Where is Abbigail?" Lady Biswell asked the morning after her surgery.

"The girl who was with you?" the nurse attending her said.

"Yes. She's my granddaughter."

"She's still in the delivery room. She's been in labor for several hours now. She was far enough along until the doctor thought it would be better to let her labor continue than try to stop it. The doctor had to give her medicine to keep her calm."

"Is she going to be all right?"

"According to her doctor she is. The doctor determined she had fainted from overexertion. That same overexertion put her into labor. There's no wonder after pulling you off that mountain in that homemade travois."

"Can you take me to her?" Lady Biswell said.

"You're just waking up from surgery."

"I know, but my granddaughter is going to be afraid. She won't know what's happening. She's never been in a hospital before. She'd never been around people before either."

The nurse gave her a strange look. "Why not?"

"She and her father were hermits."

"Hermits?"

"They lived alone on a mountain top."

"Okay," the nurse said. "I did hear such talk, but I didn't believe it."

"Believe it. Please take me to her, or she'll panic."

The nurse pushed a button and ordered a wheelchair be brought to Lady Biswell's room. She helped Lady Biswell into the chair and pushed her to the delivery room. As the nurse pushed the door open, she heard Striker yelling, "Don't you touch my baby."

Lady Biswell saw Striker sitting up in bed with a baby wrapped in pink blanket clutched in her arms. The nurse was staring at her as though she didn't know what to do.

"It's okay," Lady Biswell told the nurse. "Just back off from her bed a little. She's afraid."

"I'm leaving this place," Striker raised her voice as she glared at the nurse. "She tried to take my baby from me."

"Once the medication wore off, she went crazy," the nurse told Lady Biswell. "I've called for the doctor. He should be here with a security aide any moment."

"Take it easy," Lady Biswell told Striker. "She's not going to take your baby. I heard you had a baby girl."

"I'm leaving here," Striker told her.

"Okay," Lady Biswell said. "We'll leave together, okay?"

Striker looked at the wheelchair Lady Biswell was in and then at the bandage on her leg. "You've not got the infection any longer?"

"The doctor took the bone chip out of my leg and pumped me full of antibiotics while you were in labor. We've both been here overnight, and you finally had your baby a couple of hours ago. My fever has gone down a lot and I'm not out of my head any longer."

"I want to go home."

"So do I," Lady Biswell assured Striker.

The doctor and a security aide came rushing through the door. Striker almost jumped out of bed when she saw the two men.

"It's okay," Lady Biswell was quick to tell the doctor and security aide. "She was upset. She thought the nurse was taking her baby away from her."

"What made her think that?" the doctor asked.

"I was only going to check the baby's vitals. When I reached for the baby, she woke up. I thought she was going to attack me."

Lady Biswell wheeled her chair next to the bed Striker was huddled in. "Would everyone please leave us alone for a few minutes."

"Are you sure?" the doctor asked.

"Of course, I'm sure."

When they had left the room Striker said, "I'm leaving here right now."

"Take it easy," Lady Biswell told her again. "I'm going to call Griff to come get us and drive us home. He is taking Burk home right now."

"You were right," Striker said. "It was a baby."

"Who is the father?" Lady Biswell couldn't stop herself from asking in a low whisper.

"The man who attacked me," Striker told her.

"Did you know him?"

"No."

"Where is he?"

"Gone," was all the answer Striker intended to give.

"Can I see your baby?"

Striker lowered the blanket from the sleeping baby's face but kept her arms around her.

"Oh, my goodness. She looks exactly like you did the day you were born." Tears came to Lady Biswell's eyes. "This is almost more than my poor heart can take.

Lady Biswell closed her eyes for a few moments.

"Listen, dear," she said when she opened them again. "I need to tell you something and I hope you understand. When we leave here, we'll go to my house. You won't be able to go back on the mountain for a long while."

"Why not," Striker frowned.

"For two reasons. First of all is that your baby would not be safe. A young baby's cry will draw wild animals. And second is that you won't be able to walk a lot for a long time."

"When my dad was dying, he told me to go find my Aunt Nellie. He said I was too little to live on the mountain alone."

"But you did live for three years, didn't you?"

"It wasn't easy. I was always hungry. The dog was hungry. I'm hungry now. I don't want my baby to be hungry."

"I'll have some food brought to you."

"I don't want my baby to ever be hungry, especially during the winters."

"You and your baby will never be hungry at my house. You'll never be cold either."

"And the dog?"

"I raised Kang. He always got fed twice a day. Griff and I eat three meals a day."

"The dog is at your house now?"

"Yes, he's there now."

"Okay. Let's go now. Dad will be happy that you found me," she said.

"He could never be as happy as I am that I found you."

Chapter 55

Much to Lady Biswell's distress, Striker named her baby girl Rickets, but the name put on her great granddaughter's birth certificate was Riki Samantha Braden, after her great grandfather, the only man Lady Biswell ever loved.

Abbigail Mason was written down as the mother's name even when Striker insisted her name be put down as Striker.

"The birth certificate requires your lawfully given name," Lady Biswell explained. Striker accepted that, but she didn't like it. She had always been Striker, never an Abbigail.

The space where the father's name should be was left blank.

Lady Biswell was both surprised and thrilled at how easily her Abbigail, who insisted on being called Striker, adapted to living in the house and on the farm. Having Kang there seemed to ease Striker's original fears.

It took two solid years before Striker would allow Griff to get near her or Riki. Slowly and surely Griff won her over. Lady Biswell thought Striker watching Griff while he took care of the dogs and the other animals on the farm helped convince Striker that Griff wasn't a bad man.

It took longer than two years for Striker to tell what happened to the baby's father. "Kang killed him when he attacked me," Striker told Lady Biswell right out of the blue one day. "I buried him."

"What was his name?" Lady Biswell asked.

"I don't know." And that was all Striker ever told her about her baby's father.

Lady Biswell had a vague hope that someday her precious granddaughter would find a man she loved as much as she, Nedra Braden, had loved her Sam Braden, but Striker hadn't so far. Harlan Mason had instilled in his little daughter such a powerful fear of men Striker could never wipe it from her mind. The man who attacked her sealed that fear.

Yet, Lady Biswell still had hopes for her beautiful granddaughter to find happiness with a man she would learn to love. Lady Biswell knew only too well what it was like to live without that special kind of love.

On a beautiful spring day, Striker put Riki in a snuggly strapped to her chest and hiked the mountain with her. Striker had her knife fastened around her waist, her bow in her hand, the arrows in the quiver on her back, and Kang trotting by her side.

The cabin was still there. The brittle bones of the crow still in the pot. The potatoes in the cave had sprouted and then shriveled up to almost nothing. Weeds had grown in her garden spot. She walked over to her father's grave. The rocks she'd stacked high on it had sunk to almost ground level. The grave beside his had a dip in the dirt. Oddly enough, she no longer felt hatred or fear toward the man who had attacked her. He had paid with his life and at the same time given her the greatest gift she had ever known.

"I never found Aunt Nellie, Dad. Can you believe she found me? I like living on the farm. I've not been hungry or cold since I left this mountain. I've brought your granddaughter to see you, Dad. I found the short path you always took. It was easy once I figured out where to look. I'll bring her back to the mountain for a visit when she gets older. I want her to learn everything about life. There will be no secrets kept from my little girl. Oh, by the way, I named her Rickets."